'A spellbinding epic that captures the resilience and spirit of Jiyoung Han's unforgettably drawn characters. I'll be thinking about this powerful debut for many years to come'
Jung Yun, author of *Shelter* and *O Beautiful*

'This novel is a testimony of, and a testament to, the indestructible spirit of women. It forces you to hear and see, to bear witness, to make sure nothing like comfort women ever happens again. Terrific writing. Enchanting in every way!'
Chikodili Emelumadu, author of *Dazzling*

'A rich, sweeping novel that brings together magical realism and the brutalities of the Pacific War. An incredible multi-generational story with unforgettable characters. Make time for it'
Emma Nanami Strenner, author of *My Other Heart*

'A powerful and deeply evocative portrait of occupied Korea that bears witness to the courage of women in the face of unbearable brutality. Unflinching and unforgettable, it's both the story of one family's survival and an epic history'
Amélie Skoda, author of *Bethnal Green*

AF073391

Praise for *Honey in the Wound*

'Han brilliantly immerses readers in her birth country's history and offers a testament to women's strength in the face of brutality. It's a knockout'
Publishers Weekly

'Han has incorporated extensive research into a revelatory work of harrowing fiction . . . exposes a diabolical world of pain and validates the hidden powers of "powerless" women'
Kirkus

'Riveting and poignant, Han's debut explores how memory transforms into secrets, dreams, and testimonies that bond people across distance and time . . . [*Honey in the Wound*] powerfully bridges the individual with the collective: Young-Ja's story is not just a personal testimony, but a tribute to all those who suffered under colonialism'
Booklist

'Jiyoung Han's sprawling, magical family novel follows generations of supernaturally gifted Korean women as they grapple with the legacy of the Japanese occupation. With stunning, lyrical prose, Han follows these powerful women from ancient forests to modern-day Seoul. *Honey in the Wound* is a spellbinding debut about survival, family, magic, and the meaning of home'
LitHub, 'Most Anticipated Books of 2026'

'*Honey in the Wound* is unspeakable history given the power of myth and fable. Every word is truer than truth'
Anton Hur, award-winning translator and author of
Toward Eternity

'*Honey in the Wound* is a spellbinding debut, both a lyrical fable and unflinching testimony. Jiyoung Han deftly weaves magical realism into a devastating account of the Japanese Imperial Army's brutality in the early 20th century, granting her characters – and voices like them silenced throughout history – power and agency. The resulting work leaves one shaken. Absolutely unforgettable'
Karissa Chen, author of *Homeseeking*

'A fierce and mythic family saga, *Honey in the Wound* moves with the urgency of anti-colonial resistance and the grace of folklore. Even as history bears down, its most magical moments rise from the sorrow, fury, and enduring love of ordinary lives. Refusing to let the ghosts of the Japanese empire fall silent, the novel honours the truth still burning in the wound'
Silvia Park, author of *Luminous*

'With heartbreaking passion, *Honey in the Wound* refuses to turn away from the dark underbelly of history, putting words to those who are forgotten and who survive despite. Jiyoung Han's prose is lush and fiercely inventive, wresting immense beauty and hope from great despair. This is a startling and unforgettable debut'
Janika Oza, author of *A History of Burning*

'In Han's courageous debut, magic is a form of resistance which, like hope, bolsters the human spirit. Within seemingly ordinary people, there are extraordinary powers. This isn't just a story, it's a record of the brutality of invasion, occupation and war'
Eve J. Chung, author of *Daughters of Shandong*

HONEY IN THE WOUND

ABOUT THE AUTHOR

JIYOUNG HAN was born in Seoul, South Korea, and grew up in the American Midwest. She has lived and worked in four continents but now calls San Francisco home. When not writing, she conducts research in climate change and human decision-making.

HONEY IN THE WOUND

JIYOUNG HAN

MANILLA
PRESS

First published in the US in 2026 by Avid Reader Press
An imprint of Simon & Schuster, LLC
1230 Avenue of the Americas, New York, NY 10020
First published in the UK in 2026 by
MANILLA PRESS
An imprint of Bonnier Books UK
5th Floor, HYLO, 105 Bunhill Row,
London, EC1Y 8LZ

Copyright © Jiyoung Han, 2026

Interior design © Lexy East, 2026

All rights reserved.
No part of this publication may be reproduced, stored or transmitted in
any form or by any means, electronic, mechanical, photocopying or otherwise,
without the prior written permission of the publisher.

The right of Jiyoung Han to be identified as Author of this work
has been asserted by her in accordance with the Copyright, Designs and
Patents Act, 1988.

This is a work of fiction. Names, places, events and incidents are either the products
of the author's imagination or used fictitiously. Any resemblance to actual persons,
living or dead, or actual events is purely coincidental.

A CIP catalogue record for this book is available from the British Library.

Hardback ISBN: 978-1-78658-731-2
Trade Paperback ISBN: 978-1-78658-732-9

Also available as an ebook and an audiobook

1 3 5 7 9 10 8 6 4 2

Design and Typeset by IDSUK (Data Connection) Ltd
Printed and bound in Great Britain by CPI (UK) Ltd, Croydon CR0 4YY

Every reasonable effort has been made to trace copyright holders of
material reproduced in this book, but if any have been inadvertently
overlooked the publishers would be glad to hear from them.

The authorised representative in the EEA is Bonnier Books UK (Ireland) Limited.
Registered office address: Block B, The Crescent Building
Northwood, Santry Dublin 9, D09 C6X8 Ireland
compliance@bonnierbooks.ie
www.bonnierbooks.co.uk

For those whose histories have been buried.
For those who have faced a second death.

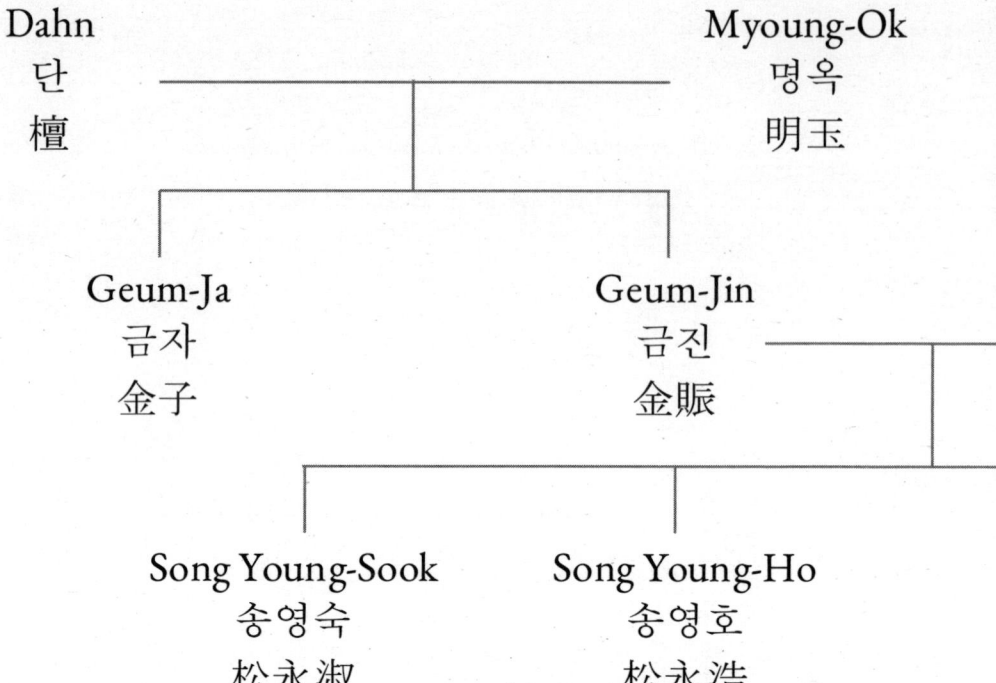

Song-sajang
송사장
松

Song Jung-Soon
송정순
松貞順

Song Young-Ja
송영자
松永子

Song Joon (Jun / Shun)
송준
松(本) 俊

Matsumoto Rinako
松本 凛那子

Manchukuo

Baek Yong-Woo
백용우
白龍優

Feng-nüshi
鳳 女士

Meiyu
美玉

Tayiji
太子

PART 1
GEUM-JIN
금진
金賑

CHAPTER ONE

Unnamed mountain in the Empire of Korea, 1902

The twins departed this world with a cry, much in the way they came into it. At birth they cried, lungs chilled by the night air of their first breath. At death they cried, hearts chilled by the bayonets that tore through their kin.

Geum-Ja came first. Impatient to escape the womb, she writhed past her brother and pressed against the cervix before her budding eyes could perceive the light of her destination. She kicked her mother's intestines twice every afternoon to announce her readiness until one day she kicked herself out into the world. Geum-Jin was less eager to leave the warmth of his origin. He lingered in the space left to him by his sister, but was coaxed to emerge and relieve his screaming mother.

Myoung-Ok held the glistening newborns against her naked chest, sprawled on the floor of her hut. They were already as large as urns and she worried that her weakened body could not nourish two. The last hunting season had been sparse. The straw shoes that her fingers had reddened to weave were not selling in the village—few had money to spare after the middling harvest. Foraging in the mountain had always been enough for her, but would it be enough to give her children a good life?

Myoung-Ok was not accustomed to such thoughts of the distant future and was unsettled by the stab of foreboding. She clutched her babies and wept, despair and joy spilling from her eyes. Despair and joy seeped from her pores, tracing paths of sweat down her tanned skin. Despair and joy flowed from her breasts, swirling out with her milk.

Geum-Ja took to the right breast, drinking in the salt of her mother's despair. Geum-Jin took to the left breast, drinking in the tang of his mother's joy. Their mewling, hungry mouths drew out the burden of feeling from Myoung-Ok's body and she calmed. Drunk with their first emotions, the babies were claimed by slumber, their mother's tenderness glistening on their lips.

Myoung-Ok came to know what she would name her children only after feeling their weight press into her arms: geum, or gold, in hopes they might prosper in a way she never had herself. The sudden provenance of this wish surprised her, as she had always been more concerned with the gold of a fallen gingko nut than with the gold of a coin.

Myoung-Ok was a child of the earth: when she was born, she slipped out of the womb and cratered into the rice paddy below, squirming in the mud before her mother could set down her sickle. Myoung-Ok's spirit was so drawn to the ground that the taller she grew, the lower she crouched to work the land. Her gaze drifted to insects flitting at her feet, or acorns hiding under fallen leaves. Her ears inclined to the dirt, listening to the sounds of roots expanding and animals burrowing into their dens. She was so preoccupied with the life underfoot that most people in her village pitied her as deaf and dimwitted, unable to fathom any other reason for her indifference to them.

Myoung-Ok shrugged off this condescension because she in turn believed people were petty and stupid. As many assumed her deaf, they did not cloak their words with grace while she crawled about. Myoung-Ok was thus witness to the judgment and duplicity laced into the daily squabbles of village life. She far preferred the warmth of the earth's embrace, allowing it to consume the salt in her tears and the iron in her blood to push life out from its depths in tribute. When she was a child, some swore they saw a trail of mountain garlic sprout in her wake as she ran crying from a scolding. Foot-shaped clover patches still grew near the stream where Myoung-Ok once cut her heel on a sharp stone. Her downcast eyes could tell which herbs tasted the sweetest, but those same eyes seldom looked to the stars—the heavens never attracted the earthbound Myoung-Ok's esteem. Perhaps it was for this snub that she was given no gift for foresight: despite their mother's aspirational faith in geum, gold was not the metal to foretell the twins' fate.

Iron severed the viscera connecting mother, daughter, son. Dahn wiped his butcher's knife with a cloth. He was a large man, as tall as the roof of his hut and as broad as an ox. He had never encountered another person who stood taller than his chest, and was more likely to recognize the hair whorl atop a head than a face. But his heft made him no less gentle—he dipped the cloth in heated water and cleansed the weeping Myoung-Ok of her sweat and blood. He would wet, wipe, and wring, wet, wipe, and wring until the bowl was murky with human fluid. Dahn pressed his whiskered lips to his bride's damp hair and stroked his babies with his broad hands. When Myoung-Ok informed him of their names and her worries, he nodded and fed her the seaweed soup whose ingredients he had sold extra furs in town to acquire. He rose once the soup warmed Myoung-Ok's body and the sun hazed in through the door.

Dahn ascended into the mountain forest with his bow and arrows slung around his thick shoulder. Despite his enormous build, he softened his footfall so no beast could hear him approaching. Neither fallen branch nor leaf betrayed his location. Deer and boars had rarely ventured near his hut since new tiger tracks emerged in the nearby terrain a few moons ago, but Dahn knew he could not miss his prey today. The new urgency of fatherhood pushed him higher into the mountain forest beyond his usual hunting grounds.

Dahn scanned the forest floor for tracks or half-eaten leaves, though his thoughts lingered on his wife back home. The day he met Myoung-Ok, she had been rustling out of sight behind a tree when Dahn nocked an arrow and waited for what he assumed was a beast to rear its head. In the shock of seeing instead a young woman alone so high up the mountain, he stumbled and let go of the bowstring. The arrow struck the tree not a palm's breadth from Myoung-Ok's face. She did not acknowledge her brush with the fatal point and continued to gather mushrooms in her skirt, pawing at a damp bed of dirt. Dahn approached to fetch his arrow and examine her for injuries. When he stood before her, Myoung-Ok paused her harvest and stared at his feet. She whispered something Dahn was too tall to hear and placed some mushrooms before him without once glancing up. She then bunched up her skirt and fled downhill, ears glowing red. Having caught nothing that day, Dahn bit into the pillowy flesh of the mushrooms the strange maiden had left.

The day after he had nearly killed the girl, Dahn set out west. He hoped to find rabbits whose fur he could sell to the hatmaker. He had not walked far when he crossed a spiky chestnut shell on the ground. Dahn thought this peculiar, as there were no chestnut trees in this stretch of the forest, but his hunt for movement in the underbrush remained unbroken by his curiosity. When he stepped over the second and third chestnuts, however, he suspected they had taken passage on the coat of a roaming beast. He quickened his pace in anticipation until he faced a buck that he felled with two shots. He sold its tongue for a rich man's feast, its antlers and testicles to a traveling medicine seller, its meat and skin to the butcher.

Two days after he had nearly killed the girl, Dahn set out east. In his scramble up a rock formation, he pressed his hands onto something wet. He had crushed a ripe bokbunja berry between his fingers and its dark-red juice dripped down to his wrist. He did not need to look around to know there were no bokbunja brambles nearby. He wiped his sticky hand on his bearskin vest and proceeded to climb. When he rose up another boulder, he saw more bokbunja ahead. As with the chestnuts, Dahn followed the berries until the rocks plateaued into a cluster of bushes housing two large roosting pheasants.

He pierced both necks with a single arrow, then traded their meat and feathers for some beef and rice wine.

Three days after he had nearly killed the girl, Dahn woke with eyelids heavy from wine and a belly fuller than it had been in months. He considered resting for the day but remembered he did not know what penury the next season might bring. He set out south and wondered if he might see another trail of displaced fruits. It was not long until he stepped on a single red bean, its gleaming sisters marking a path up to the mountain spring. Dahn readied his bow as he climbed up to the water but lowered it when he saw Myoung-Ok washing her hair with berry-stained fingers, her discarded clothes and a pile of red beans lying on a nearby boulder. He was startled by his own arousal and moved to turn away when she repeated what she said to him the day he nearly killed her: "I feel your footsteps in my chest."

She beckoned him to her with a glance, as she had with her trails of nuts and berries. Dahn disrobed and joined her in the spring. The friction of their skin washed away the dirt on their bodies and warmed the water until the frogs jumped out in alarm. Her long black hair swirled on his back and his fingers tensed on her hips as they both shook with release.

A crow called out in the distance, bringing Dahn back to the need to provide for his newborns. In the last year, he had gone farther out from his edge of the mountain in search of game. The last time he went into the village to sell his furs, he overheard another hunter speculate that tigers were driving away the boars. Market stalls buzzed about a farmer whose calf was lost to an unknown predator in the night. Dahn reminded himself to check on the traps around his hut when he returned home, though he suspected the tigers were too clever to fall into them. Every week he encountered rotting animal carcasses sprouting thick clouds of flies. Angry claw marks appeared on old pines that could not defend themselves. Despite ample signs of their presence, the tigers had yet to allow Dahn even a fleeting glimpse of a swaying tail. But the heavens were not so cruel as to make all creatures so elusive. Before the sun lifted off the horizon, Dahn spotted a boar sniffing around thirty paces ahead. In a single motion, he shrugged the bow from his shoulder and let fly an arrow into the creature's eye and brain. He lowered his head over the fallen beast and thanked the mountain for its gift before swinging his catch over his shoulder and journeying into town.

As the smiling jangseung totems in the village outskirts came into view, Dahn raised his chin and let his coarse hair fall over his eyes. He fixed his gaze above the heads of morning marketgoers to avoid the gawking and whispers floating around his elbows, something he had forced himself to do since he was a young boy whose extraordinary size attracted fear or derision. He had learned not to care what they said and let the crowd scurry out of his path. Dahn spoke to no one and no one dared speak to Dahn. Once he reached the butcher, he dropped the boar on the ground and held out his hand until the sufficient weight of coins fell into his palm. No further effort was needed. No one would cheat the mountain giant who was rumored to have crushed the skull of a charging bear with just his hands, the bear whose skin he wore every day as a warning to other bears, and perhaps to humans as well. With the butcher's coins jangling in his money bag, Dahn walked to purchase rice from the old grain seller who was either too ancient or too blind to cower in his presence.

"You better save up what rice you can, young man. Officials took most of it two nights ago to send off to Japan and there's only barley left for us," said the old woman, slapping a sack of grains. "Their soldiers will be in your mountains soon too. I hear they want to hunt down tigers for their emperor."

CHAPTER TWO

Unnamed mountain in Chōsen, Empire of Japan, 1915

Myoung-Ok kept her twins within her field of perception at all times. This was no challenge when they could only crawl around with bugs in her herb garden. But as the seasons passed, the twins' braids grew long and their legs began carrying them from her sight. Myoung-Ok would thus put her ears to the soil to listen for roots groaning as Geum-Ja climbed her favorite trees, or for the staccato of Geum-Jin's delighted hops when he chased a dragonfly. To ensure she could always hear them, she occupied the twins with earthbound pursuits—finding pinecones that generated seedlings when planted, digging for insects that signaled soil fertility. Myoung-Ok cultivated her children's love for the earth so that the earth would love them in return. Every day the soil crooned under the twins' eager attention, relaying to Myoung-Ok what their tender hands achieved through her lessons of the natural world. The pleasure of watching her children learn helped her to forget about the knots of foreign boot prints creeping up the mountain.

Dahn, too, noticed these boot prints, but observed with cautious relief their tendency to stay shallow in the foothills, still some distance from his family's mountain refuge. Whenever he saw concern groove into Myoung-Ok's brow, he stroked it away with a callused thumb and left a kiss in its place. He would then turn to whittle bamboo into arrows and weave bowstrings from sinews and hides. He did not wish to be caught lacking should he need to direct his strength toward a manner of beast different from those he was accustomed to having in his sights.

When the twins were old enough to walk in silence, Dahn carved small bows from a mulberry tree and taught them to hunt. The children watched to mimic their father's soft tread. They saw from his gaze where to aim their arrows. They heard from his exhalations when they should release their bowstrings. They shifted with the loving corrections to their stances and allowed their chins to be redirected toward new targets in the distance. Geum-Ja and Geum-Jin conveyed their appreciation of their father's attention by excelling at their tasks.

The twins were equal in their prowess—as with nearly all their taught skills—until the moment the arrow struck its mark. Geum-Ja always shot out first to inspect her work while Geum-Jin followed, wiping away a tear at the loss of life. Dahn pretended not to notice this difference as long as his son's remorse did not lead to hesitation. Hesitation could mean hunger. Hesitation could mean death. After bowing their heads in gratitude to the mountain, Geum-Ja liked to skip ahead, carrying whatever she could of their haul. Geum-Jin preferred to hold fast to Dahn's thick pointer finger and assure himself of his father's presence.

When not trailing after one of their parents, the twins taught themselves how to play. They had never once met other children and so invented their own games. In the game they called "new noise," Geum-Ja would close her eyes and guess which bird or insect sound was her brother's imitation. No other person would have been able to distinguish Geum-Jin's shrike call from the real thing, but she could discern which had the signature breath of her twin and which were the true cries of the forest. In "find the treasure," one twin would hide a straw shoe for the other to find. Geum-Ja loved to hide: she savored her precious time alone to discover new crevices of the mountain. Geum-Jin preferred to seek, eager to show his sister there was nothing she could hide from him, for they were one.

Geum-Ja's favorite game was "flying." She would climb into the trees and jump from branch to branch, yelling after Geum-Jin to follow her. This was the singular game where he was not his sister's match. So rare was this imbalance between the twins that Geum-Ja did not notice her brother was not by her side the first time she climbed to the top of a tree and poked her head through the forest canopy. She gazed around at neighboring mountains she had never seen before, dumbstruck at the immensity of the world beyond her home. Her roaming eyes halted at the village walls and rice paddies in the distance. She had heard her mother and father speak of the village before, but seeing evidence of life outside of her own stoked a blend of curiosity and drive that words alone had never done. She reached for her brother's hand to acknowledge this fascinating discovery and realized then that he was not there to share in her revelation. She descended to a crying Geum-Jin who feared she had left him behind. She hugged and reassured him she could never leave him, for they were one.

Even as she reached her first monthly blood, Geum-Ja could not forget what lay beyond the foothills. When she asked Myoung-Ok about the village, her mother clucked and told her that life was better in the mountains.

"People bring the burden of expectation," she said. "Being trapped in that expectation is suffocating, even for the richest yangban in the village."

Geum-Ja did not understand her mother's words but made no mistake of her tone. When Dahn headed to the village to trade his furs, Geum-Ja climbed onto his jige carrier to accompany him. He grabbed his daughter and placed her down by her brother, patting her on the head. Geum-Ja did not understand her father's reason but made no mistake of his intent. She did not move from where Dahn had planted her and stared in his wake long after he was out of sight. Concern creased into Myoung-Ok's face as she heard a new timbre of sigh escape her daughter.

Myoung-Ok endeavored to push thoughts of the village from Geum-Ja's mind. She listened to the ants' chatter to discern where honey leaked from a new hive and taught the twins how to extract honeycombs without upsetting the bees. She took them to swim in the mountain spring and fed them wild strawberries until their teeth and lips burst with red juice. She led them to a small grove where thousands of fireflies danced at dusk, their light an eerie flame licking at the trees. In these moments nothing existed for Myoung-Ok but the golden laughter of youth that had never known a day of anguish. When a distant yowl broke through the peals of the twins' delight, Myoung-Ok sat up from the grass and reached for her children.

"It's an animal. Sounds like it's in pain," said Geum-Ja.

"We should help it," said Geum-Jin.

The twins raised their eyebrows with such eagerness that Myoung-Ok laughed.

"All right, let's go help it. But you must listen to me if I say we need to go."

With a twin's hand in each of hers, Myoung-Ok descended the mountain trail toward the raspy yowling ringing through the tree branches. They came to a clearing where the noise emerged from a pit in the ground. All three peered over the edge to meet the eyes of a tiger, larger than a cub but not yet grown into full ferocity. It paused its cries to look up at Myoung-Ok and the twins, tilting its head to examine the new presence. Geum-Ja and Geum-Jin had never seen a tiger before and pulled at Myoung-Ok's sleeves in excitement. Before she could think of a way to help it without becoming its prey, she heard voices grow louder at an unfamiliar cadence. She signaled to her children to be quiet as she tried to identify who was approaching. Myoung-Ok could not understand their strange words, but when she counted at least six separate speakers, all men, she pulled her children into a bush beyond the clearing, willing it to protect them. The compliant branches wrapped around the trio in a thick tapestry of wood and leaves. Crouching low, she placed her hands over the children's mouths to stifle any noises.

"Don't make a peep. And keep still," she whispered.

Through slivered gaps in the leaves they saw men in fitted tan uniforms surround the pit. The tiger's howls began anew. The men spoke in rapid, excited inflections. One man placed a small white stick in his mouth and lit its end on fire. Smoke pushed out of his nostrils like an angry boar in the cold of winter. A mustachioed man across from him squatted and spat into the hole below. The group's laughter intensified when the smoking man picked up a rock and threw it with great force into the pit. The resulting crack was followed by a screech unlike any sound Myoung-Ok had ever heard. She tightened her grasp over her children's mouths. The mustachioed spitter picked up his own rock and declared something that made the others whoop. He wound his arm theatrically and hurled the rock, trying to outdo his companion. The screeching crescendoed until another man removed a black tool from his belt, curled his finger into it, and pointed it to the ground. A terrifying, alien thunder boomed from the clearing. All nearby birds fled into the sky as the screeching muted into a whimper. The man flicked at the black tool and released another clap of thunder.

Geum-Jin's hot tears dripped down the fingers Myoung-Ok had clasped over his mouth. She held tight, pushing back the scream gated behind his teeth. Geum-Ja had not moved, her eyes fixed ahead. The tenor of the men's voices changed as they barked out commands. Two others dressed in hanbok came out into the clearing and lowered themselves into the pit without a word. The men in tan uniforms tossed one end of a rope down and pulled the tiger out, its body void of the muscular tension that once made it so formidable. The men kicked and nudged at the carcass to inspect its dirt-covered paws and cracked, bloody head. The two in hanbok crawled out of the pit and scurried to bind the tiger's paws to the poles they had brought. They lifted the poles to rest horizontally on their shoulders, the tiger hanging upside-down by its bound feet. Its pink tongue fell limp out of its open mouth. The wound on its chest bled in rivulets around its neck, a delicate red noose that dripped onto the ground. The uniformed men bantered as they trudged in procession back downhill.

Some time after the men's voices had faded, Myoung-Ok released her children. Saliva glistened on the teeth marks the twins had left on her fingers. They walked back to their hut in silence, glancing over their shoulders every few steps to check that those cruel, foreign words did not follow them home.

The twins were no longer permitted to play outside of Myoung-Ok's earshot. Myoung-Ok and Dahn did not have to enforce this ban, however, as Geum-Jin shadowed Myoung-Ok everywhere she went, locking her in an unending flow of conversation as if silence might invite memories of the uniformed men. In contrast, no words had left Geum-Ja's lips since the return home. She would sometimes climb to the top of the tallest tree next to their hut and sit for hours. When not aloft, she paced by the tiger trap behind the hut and stared out beyond the bushes, ears tuned in to the rustling chorus of forest life. Myoung-Ok and Dahn gave their daughter the space to make peace with her thoughts—so long as she did it within the boundary of their protection.

Geum-Jin struggled with this change in his sister. She refused to play their usual games and did not respond when he called her name. She would eat neither the fruits Geum-Jin foraged nor much else Myoung-Ok prepared. Untethered from his twin, Geum-Jin tried to calm the thump of disquiet in his chest. But slumber became elusive.

In the dark of night, under the sounds of his father's snoring and his mother's even breathing, Geum-Jin lay awake knowing that Geum-Ja, unstirring, was also not at rest. He eventually dozed off in silence, not wanting to feel the pain of offering a word that would not be returned. When he awoke again not long after he had shut his eyes, his sister was no longer lying beside him. Startled, he sat up and went in search of her. Geum-Ja was standing outside amid the soft trill of crickets, facing the forest with her back to the hut.

"What are you doing? Come back inside," he murmured as he approached, his voice drenched with sleep.

"I can't. They're so loud," she whispered back, not breaking her distant gaze.

Hearing his sister's voice for the first time in days, Geum-Jin's eyes welled with relief.

"What? The crickets?" He ventured closer, hoping to keep her talking.

"They're crying."

"Who's crying? What are you talking about?"

Geum-Ja turned to her brother with an expression he had never seen her face hold before. The ice in her eyes snapped him awake.

"You don't hear them. In the forest," she said.

"Stop teasing me."

"They're afraid of what's coming."

Geum-Jin stepped away from the new unfamiliarity of his twin's face, which, until this moment, had always been a reflection of his. "Come back inside. It's the middle of the night."

Geum-Ja looked at the ground. She said nothing and turned to the forest again.

"You're scaring me," he said, voice wavering.

She did not move. Geum-Jin stretched out his hand, wanting to touch her shoulder. He hesitated and retracted his arm, backing away toward the hut. He paused at the threshold, looking at his sister's figure in the moonlight, and felt the emptiness of longing for the first time in his life. He did not understand where his twin had gone, but she was no longer within his reach.

"Geum-Ja, please come back to sleep," he whispered a final time. She continued to face away from him as he lay down inside, head at the door. He kept vigil over his sister until he could no longer fight off the call of slumber.

The following dawn, Myoung-Ok and Dahn rose to an empty hut, their son curled up half outside the door. They searched all around their home, the latrine, the surrounding trees. When they did not see their daughter, Myoung-Ok put her ears to the soil. She could hear the dirt compressing under Dahn's heavy pacing feet and the slight tremors of Geum-Jin's agitated sleep. Sweat glittered across her temple as she strained to make out hints of Geum-Ja over the sound of her own accelerating heartbeat. But the earth was not responding to her daughter and she knew that Geum-Ja was no longer in the mountain forest. Myoung-Ok called after Dahn to scoop up their drowsy son and ran down to the village for the first time in over a decade.

The farmers starting their morning in the rice paddies were startled to see a woman emerge from the forest with a giant and a child. Their curiosity grew into shock when they recognized who it was. No villager had seen Myoung-Ok since she had led the giant back to her parents' small choga house and informed them that she would be living with him henceforth. Myoung-Ok's father was too drunk to either reject or accept his daughter's announcement. Myoung-Ok's mother eyed the boar that Dahn tossed at her feet as an offering, relieved to have one less mouth to feed. This story danced on the villagers' tongues for months after Myoung-Ok rode on Dahn's back into the mountain. Some reckoned that a boar was more than enough in exchange for a dull girl with no marriage prospects. Others swore they had not heard Myoung-Ok utter a single word before that day. Some even imagined that the giant would simply eat her in a mountain cave and she would never be heard from again.

Myoung-Ok marched past the farmers whose unburied memories stunned them into silence. The men left the fields to follow her in procession until they reached a small crowd gathering at a stretch of the village walls. Myoung-Ok pushed away a screen of whispering men and women to see a straw shoe and a girl's hemp jeogori shirt pressed into the mud by what appeared to be large animal tracks.

Myoung-Ok dropped to the ground and released a bitter wail that rattled the earth. The crowd startled as their footing shook and squawking crows launched into the sky. Dahn shoved stumbling bystanders out of his way and took his wife into his arms alongside Geum-Jin. His enormous chest absorbed the echo of her shrieks. The villagers turned away in pity, walking back to their homes and fields with their own grim conclusions.

An older farmer approached Myoung-Ok and Dahn as the crowd scattered to their day's labor. With an eye flickering over Geum-Jin's uncomprehending face, he said, "You're lucky it was only your daughter and not your son. Go home and make sure the tigers don't get him too."

For many mornings thereafter, Myoung-Ok rose before the sun and looked out toward the forest, her dry sobs ringing with the roosters' cries in the village below.

CHAPTER THREE

Unnamed mountain in Chōsen, Empire of Japan, 1917

After Geum-Ja's disappearance, the villagers dug traps around their homes to protect their families from tigers. While these covered pits may have warded off nocturnal prowlers, they did little to defend against other beasts with designs on the village children. Government officials had begun to sweep through the fields to abduct farmers' sons, cut off their braids, and force them into school to learn Japanese. In the early days, many farmers did not pretend to understand what it meant for the Empire of Japan to seize control of their country; their general lot in the secluded village had not much changed whether paying taxes to a Joseon yangban or a foreign official. But as the months passed, their backs ached from their sons' absence in the fields. Their stomachs atrophied from diminishing crop shares. When the boys of the village came home with angry switch marks that teachers left on their calves, there was no recourse for parents but the hope that the children might now study their way to a better fate.

Despite these hardships, life persisted. On summer evenings, villagers returned home from their labor and called in their children for supper as they always had. Most children played coy on the first call, claiming they heard nothing but the cry of the cicadas. On the second call, the more acquiescent youth turned homeward. On the third call, even the most rebellious bid their friends farewell for the evening, ending the chorus of names as families tucked into their meals. The beautiful Soon-Hee was always the first to return home after hearing her name. She would race past her brothers to help with dinner and receive praise for being a dutiful young girl.

"Soon-Hee, come here," her mother cried, stoking the fire under the gamasot to keep dinner warm. Soon-Hee often reported back stories of friends that her mother mined for gossip about the other families in the area. A few days ago, Soon-Hee had mentioned a friend's complaints about having to bury heavy jangdok pots at home. Soon-Hee's mother surmised that this family was likely hoarding extra rice in the jangdok and hiding it from their Japanese landlords. Kimjang season was still far off, and no one would bother with burying prepared foods in jangdok during the late summer. She chuckled as she wondered what new rumors she might glean tonight. But there was still no pattering of feet outside their choga house.

"Soon-Hee, if you don't come here right now, you'll be in big trouble! What has gotten into you today?" she yelled, getting up from the food and heading out to find her daughter.

"Soon-Hee, where are you?"

When she stepped out into the road by her home, several children ran past her in heed of their own dinner calls. None were Soon-Hee, nor was her daughter among the little ones coming toward her. Panic shot through her as she quickened her walking pace toward the field where children sometimes played. It had not been long since the crazy mountain woman had carelessly lost her own child and made an embarrassing scene in front of all the villagers. She started to run, swiveling her head left and right in a desperate bid to catch a glimpse of her child. She slowed at the sight of Soon-Hee near the edge of the mountain forest, skipping toward her with a clump of wildflowers in hand. Relief neutralized the panic as quickly as it had risen, which in turn slipped into annoyance. The woman ran up to her daughter, grabbed her arm, and spanked her across her bottom.

"Didn't I tell you not to go by the mountain? There are tigers there that eat little girls like you!"

"I was just playing with a friend," Soon-Hee wailed between gasps for breath. "I didn't realize we were out so far—"

"Who was it, huh? That skinny little Choi brat? I knew she was a bad influence; don't play with her anymore."

"No, not her," cried Soon-Hee, tears leaving a streak of clean skin on her dirt-covered face.

"Well, who was it?"

"It was a girl with yellow eyes." Soon-Hee sniffled.

"What?"

"A girl with yellow eyes. She gave me these flowers and said she was gonna show me where they grew on the mountain."

Her mother smacked Soon-Hee across her bottom once again for telling lies and pulled the sobbing girl home as the cicadas drowned out their cries.

Geum-Jin rose before the sun to set about his work. He softened his steps so as not to disturb his ailing parents, though their sleep had been heavy as of late. Myoung-Ok would tire herself from weeping so much the hut floor was covered in grass that kept dying under the weight of their feet. As soon as the grass yellowed, she would shed new tears and force more sprouts to appear. The hut was beginning to smell of rotting plants. The thatched roof also had not been replaced since the last monsoon season, when Dahn still had full use of his arms. Insects and mold-ridden straw fell from the roof while they slept, but Geum-Jin knew better than to tend to something his father took pride in doing himself.

Nearly a year after Geum-Ja had disappeared, Dahn returned from a hunt with his bearskin vest soaked in blood. Myoung-Ok dropped the plants she had been gathering and ran to her collapsed husband. Geum-Jin did not understand what beast could have hurt his father so. Based on Dahn's grunts, Myoung-Ok knew to put a knife to flame and sink its hot blade into the gurgling wound on his shoulder. In a single flick she dug out the pieces of Japanese iron embedded within.

Dahn faded into a deep sleep. His enormous body emanated a fever that broiled the air inside the hut. Streams of sweat flooded the soft ground. Geum-Jin shuttled urns of water from the spring while Myoung-Ok ground medicinal herbs into paste mixed with the healing balm of honey and applied it to her husband's throbbing shoulder. A putrid yellow fluid trickled out from under the plaster after two days. Dahn's breathing turned erratic.

At sunrise, Myoung-Ok ascended to the spring to bathe and instructed her son to look after his father. She would go to the village apothecary and buy medicine, for there was not much else they could do on their own. Geum-Jin nodded, shedding tears in silence. He wiped away Dahn's sweat and fed him what small spoonfuls of barley gruel he could, ignoring the noxious smells oozing from his father's body. At sunset, Myoung-Ok entered the hut with her hair shorn to her ears and a paper packet in her hand. She patted Geum-Jin's head and trailed her fingers down his braid. She unwrapped a small, acrid brown ball from the packet and placed it into her husband's discolored mouth. Dahn woke up three days later, holding on to life for the cost of his right arm and his wife's beautiful black hair.

With Dahn unable to move his arm or use his bow, the responsibility of hunting fell on Geum-Jin. The first time he went out to hunt on his own, Myoung-Ok ran after him and forced him to take off his fur skin.

"I won't have my only son also mistaken for a beast."

Geum-Jin whittled his own arrows, tracked prey, and learned to broker a fair price for his offerings at the market. While he could not deny a certain pride at growing into his duties, he did not enjoy his descents into the village where girls running about with long black braids reminded him of what his family had lost. But he knew he must put his parents' needs before his own comfort and endeavored to secure provisions for them every day. He threw himself into his labors, as eager to be of use as to keep distracted from the fear that Geum-Ja's loss was his fault. He could not bring himself to tell his parents about the last night he had seen his sister—had he simply begged her to stay or dragged her inside the hut rather than returning to sleep, she might never have been taken by the tigers at all.

The drumbeat of self-blame grew louder in the night, and Geum-Jin struggled to sleep. The slightest tremor in the hut was enough to rouse him: his father's dream-soaked grunts, his mother's tears, the body aches he bore from his daily work. Once awake, he would lie in the dark for hours, the night song of mountain insects haunting him with memories of the games his other half so adored.

On yet another restless night, Geum-Jin stirred with the urge to relieve himself. He slipped out of the hut with practiced ease, his father's snoring steady behind him. Although the moon shone bright over the passing clouds, he did not need light to find his way to the latrine. He faltered nonetheless a few paces from the herb garden, where a figure stood watching him. He froze and stared back, afraid of what it would do if he moved.

"Are you a ghost?" he whispered.

The figure glided forward and embraced him. Geum-Jin nearly lost his balance from the force of his sister's arms, grown furry and thick. The soft, tan face he had always known blurred as he blinked away his tears.

"How are you here? We thought you—"

"Come with me."

Geum-Jin stepped back out of his twin's grasp. "What are you talking about? Uhmuhni and Ahbuhji will be so relieved to see you—"

"No, it'll be better if they don't know I'm here." Geum-Ja's eyes flashed yellow.

Geum-Jin wondered if he were dreaming, for his true twin would never suggest deceiving their parents in a time of need. "But . . . you're home."

"My home is now beyond these mountains, on terrain untouched by people. This land will soon be lost. We have to leave." Her long black hair cascaded into stripes along her back.

Geum-Jin stared. Was this truly his twin? She spoke with that voice he knew better than his own, but her words felt strange. Doubt tugged down the corners of his mouth. "Uhmuhni and Ahbuhji aren't well. They haven't been since you disappeared. They can't leave this place. Please, come back. I know things will get better if you just come back."

"No, our parents can't leave. They belong to this mountain, and the mountain will care for them in its own way. But you and I are different. We can still go somewhere human destruction can't follow us."

Geum-Jin stepped away from the creature before him. Her eyes shifted from yellow to black with each breath, tufts of hair growing and receding from her broad face. His head started to shake of its own accord.

"No," he said. "I can't do what you did." Tears no longer clouded his eyes. Heat seeped into his ears. "I won't do what you did."

"It'll be harder to find game here," she said, voice louder. "The forest is shrinking to meet the demands of men. Beasts that roamed these lands are fleeing north. But the tigers can protect us." Geum-Ja walked forward and embraced her brother again. "Come with me."

"Please, stay with me," he replied into the fur of her shoulder.

Geum-Ja tensed at her brother's plea, her yellow eyes glowing wet under hooded black lids. She grabbed his wrists with fingers that flashed into claws. Letting her tears fall into his palms, she said, "Rub this into our parents' feet while they sleep, and their souls will not run from their bodies. But don't tell anyone I was here or the medicine won't work."

She slipped into the darkness, where three pairs of yellow eyes blinked at Geum-Jin before disappearing.

Geum-Jin returned to the hut and dabbed his parents' toes with the balm in his hands. He lay back in his covers and stared at the rotting ceiling, wondering whether he had dreamt up a being that both was and was not his sister.

The next day, Myoung-Ok and Dahn rose, feeling better than they had in months. Outside the hut, they discovered a freshly slain deer and a pile of ginseng roots, large pawprints trailing away into the forest.

CHAPTER FOUR

Unnamed mountain in Chōsen, Empire of Japan, 1918

The inability to move his right arm did not stop Dahn from returning to his usual tasks. He threw knives at fleeing hares, chopped firewood, and mixed clay to patch up his home. Although his left arm had never been weaker than his right, it lacked its finesse. With his left arm, his prey eluded his blades, his ax missed its mark, his hut fell into disrepair. This new ineptitude pushed Dahn into bouts of moroseness. He vacillated from frustrated exertion to refusals to do anything at all. Moments of inactivity at least did not generate visual reminders of his clumsiness; with nothing to test his immobile right side, he could continue existing in his former glory in peace. But Dahn was changing.

The first time Myoung-Ok leaned in to correct the angle of a log that Dahn failed to hit with his ax, he flew into a rage and threw the log downhill. Although Myoung-Ok had never thought such an eruption possible, she jumped on her husband and wrapped her arms around his neck. She clung tightly, squeezing her legs around his tree-trunk body until his breathing steadied.

"Come back to me, my love," she whispered into his ear, and ushered him back to the present. "Let me feel your footsteps in my chest."

Myoung-Ok had since spent every morning foraging for roots to brew into teas that could quell the fire in Dahn's blood. She would lie with him while Geum-Jin was out hunting, caressing his temple and nuzzling her face into his musk. Some days, she felt his desire firm against her body and gave in to his familiar hunger. In the evenings, she fed Dahn ground jujube mixed with honey to guide him to slumber.

Despite Myoung-Ok's efforts, Dahn's outbursts worsened. At first, they merely rose in frequency but could still be soothed by his wife's firm, earthy hands. As these spells persisted, however, they began to last until recognition drained from Dahn's eyes, leaving a void that was not of this world. Myoung-Ok was grateful that Geum-Jin was mostly gone during the day, for she feared what it would do to Dahn to know his son had witnessed his transformations. To know his son had seen the bruises under her sleeves. At night, when she thought everyone else was asleep, Myoung-Ok wept quietly until a new mat of grass grew on the floor where her head lay.

Although she fixated on Dahn, Myoung-Ok did not fail to notice that Geum-Jin kept the firewood stocked, her herb garden tended, and the yard full of pelts to take to the market. Her child was now the first to rise before the sun and the last to lie down in the dark of night. On one of the rare times he returned home before sunset, she observed that hair had started to grow on his lip. When Geum-Jin dropped a bag of barley at her feet, Myoung-Ok took his callused hands into her own.

"Geum-Jin-ah, I'm sorry."

"It wasn't too heavy." He smiled and tapped at the bag with his foot. "I'm the one who should be sorry I can't do more—"

"You're our only precious child, yet you carry all our—"

Groaning came from inside the hut. Myoung-Ok touched her son's tanned face and walked back to care for Dahn before she could finish voicing her thoughts.

The spring market echoed with vendors calling for customers to browse their wares. Men and women in white hanbok crowded about to see what their neighbors had to offer. Geum-Jin pushed through the market surge and set his jige carrier down to lay out his pelts for the shoemaker. Last week, the older man had requested more deerskin to fill orders from a wealthy Japanese couple who had come into possession of nearby farmland. The shoemaker was not keen on the prospect of selling even his scraps to these foreign land thieves, but he knew refusing their business would only place his family in danger. He had heard that in the next town over, a man and his wife were dragged off to a city prison because the couple had accidentally brushed a Japanese official's arm on the street. In another rumor, an official had forced an elderly woman to eat a cockroach that flitted out during a home inspection. He had no desire to test the veracity of such claims with his own life.

The shoemaker had come to enjoy buying from Geum-Jin. Although he was curious to know where the giant hunter had gone, he never inquired, as he much preferred his substitute's friendly verbal manners. He would never have been able to gather the nerve to request anything from the giant, let alone get a fair price for it.

He handed Geum-Jin his coins and smiled. "Young man, the tailor down the road might be open to buying some of your pelts. He was telling me he needed some fur linings."

Geum-Jin bowed in thanks for the tip. As he put the jige straps back on his shoulders, four serious-looking men approached the shoemaker.

One man wore round spectacles and a Western-style black suit. A shorter, jittery man also donned black, though with a leather bag slung over his shoulder. The remaining two were expressionless soldiers in tan uniforms. Geum-Jin tensed his grip around his jige straps, remembering the first time he saw men dressed in that tan fabric. He tried to remain calm, hoping he would not draw their attention. Nearby marketgoers eyed the four strangers and hurried away to a safer distance. The nervous man with the leather bag looked to his superior before turning to the shoemaker.

"The village administration will be assessing the quality of all market vendors. You will cooperate or your business will be reported for insubordination," he announced, using many words Geum-Jin did not understand. The shoemaker gave a slight nod and gestured toward his workshop. The man started walking inside but paused when his bespectacled superior glanced at Geum-Jin and said something curt in Japanese. The man with the leather bag turned to Geum-Jin and translated: "You, boy. How old are you? Why aren't you in school?"

Geum-Jin regretted not having departed as soon as the officials came. He took a few steps back. "I don't live in this village. I was just about to leave so I can get out of your way."

The official in glasses narrowed his eyes at his aide's translation. As Geum-Jin strode away from the group, the official clicked his tongue, sending the two soldiers rushing to grab his jige and arms. The other vendors and marketgoers scattered out of the way as Geum-Jin flailed in an attempt to break loose of the soldiers' grasp. His pelts fell on the ground, becoming sullied by the dust kicked up in struggle. Passersby stopped, whispering and watching the scene unfurl.

"*Futeisenjin*," hissed the bespectacled official, spitting at Geum-Jin's feet. He barked something at the aide, who passed him a knife from his bag. The official pulled Geum-Jin's braid and ran the point of the blade against it. The close gleam of the knife made Geum-Jin think of his father: hesitation could mean death. He screamed and put all the strength he could draw from the sinews of his body into headbutting the official's face. His jeogori sleeves and jige straps ripped as he jerked free of the soldiers in their moment of shock. The crowd gasped and the official fell to the ground, dropping his knife and cracked round spectacles. All stood stunned as Geum-Jin darted down the market street. The official clutched his bleeding nose and shouted at the soldiers to run after the boy.

Geum-Jin wove around the marketgoers, not daring to look back at his pursuers. When he burst out of the throng of white hanbok in the main market strip, he sprinted to the village gate toward the mountains. He could not think, he did not know if he was breathing, he could not see what propelled his feet forward. He only knew he could not lead the soldiers to his home and veered westward to a forest far away. A loud pistol shot rang behind him in the open field. Once he dashed into the tree line, he zigzagged in his ascent. Jagged bark hit his cheeks as a bullet clipped a nearby tree. His chest burned and he felt he could not run for much longer. When another shot rained splinters on his head, he ducked, though the force of his momentum tripped him into the ground. The pounding footsteps of the soldiers grew louder as Geum-Jin tried to drag himself off the forest floor. When he looked up, his senses left his body. A snarling tiger pushed its hot breath over his face and Geum-Jin thought he might finally perish.

The soldiers yelled upon sighting the tiger and aimed their pistols at the deadlier target. The tiger growled and leapt over Geum-Jin, lunging at the armed men. The soldiers released more panicked shots, none hitting their mark. The tiger, unfazed, roared and swiped a giant paw at one of its attackers. The man's pistol fell from his grasp as he jumped back to dodge the tiger's claws. When the tiger crouched to pounce again, the unarmed soldier clutched a handful of dirt and tossed it into the beast's face. The tiger thrashed and roared as the soldiers fled back down the mountain.

Geum-Jin stared in disbelief, splayed out on the ground and unable to control his fearful shaking. Twigs and leaves snapped under his trembling legs and the tiger turned toward the noise. Geum-Jin swept the ground with his hands and gripped a fallen tree branch, raising it to place something between him and the predator. The tiger growled, saliva glistening on its bared fangs. Geum-Jin swung his arm back, preparing to strike.

"Brother, calm yourself. She means no harm."

A second tiger stalked toward him, her eyes on his. Geum-Jin drank in rapid gulps of air and tightened his hold on the branch. Although the familiar voice dulled the crest of his panic, his fallen body would not stop shaking.

"Shh, you're safe." The tiger pushed her broad head into her brother's chest until his tremors stilled.

Geum-Jin lowered the tree branch and stroked the soft fur of her neck. Had he died? Was this a dream? His mind raced with questions, but he could not yet seem to find his voice.

Met with her twin's silence, Geum-Ja continued to speak, a low rumble in her beastly throat. "This land can no longer fend off man. Most of the tigers have gone north. We, too, will leave to join our kin. Come with us."

"I haven't changed my answer since you last asked." Geum-Jin's tongue lashed with a harshness he had not intended. He dug his fingers into the dirt and glanced at the other tiger pacing behind his sister. He looked away when its yellow feline eyes met his.

Geum-Ja sat, growling softly as her tail flicked back and forth. "Those soldiers know what you look like. Do you think you'll be able to go back to that market ever again? How will you survive with no money?"

Geum-Jin knew she was right, but he was angry that she dared to lecture him. "You left us," he spat. "You have no right to doubt me. I'll find a way. I'll hunt in other forests, I'll find another village—"

The other tiger stopped its pacing and growled at this outburst. Geum-Ja slinked over to nuzzle the tiger's tense neck with her head. When her companion calmed, she turned to her brother once again.

"Every day they cut down more trees to feed their industry, to lay their claim on the land," said Geum-Ja. "This mountain won't be able to support you for much longer."

Geum-Jin turned his face to the ground and closed his eyes. He did not wish to hear any more.

"I stopped by the hut to pay final respects to our parents. They won't be of this world much longer. The iron in Ahbuhji's shoulder is poisoning him to madness. There will be nothing left for you here."

Geum-Jin jerked his head toward the beast before him. "How could you say that—"

"Death will free them from their pain," she growled. "You cannot."

He could not accept this creature as his sister. The true Geum-Ja would never utter such a curse. He stared in disbelief as she continued her wretched speech.

"There is no medicine that can help our parents. The kindest thing you can do for them is to let them die in peace."

Geum-Jin held his head and buried his face in his knees. Geum-Ja set her large paw on his feet. "This forest leaves us tigers nothing. With the power of iron, humans no longer revere the earth or fear us. The soldiers make sport of killing our young. If you must stay here, don't let them make sport of killing yours."

He placed his hand on his sister's muzzle and pressed his forehead against the fur of her broad chest.

"I'm sorry I left you that day," he said. "I wish I'd made you come inside. Then maybe Uhmuhni would be herself again and Ahbuhji would still be strong. It's my fault we lost you."

"You never lost me, brother. For we are one."

Geum-Ja put her maw to her rear. With a sharp lurch of her jaw she ripped off her tail, her pained roar echoing in the forest. Blood dripped from the fur of her muzzle as she laid the torn piece of herself at her brother's feet.

"I leave a part of me with you, should you wish to find me again."

Geum-Ja and the other tiger slinked away into the trees. Geum-Jin picked up the bloody tail and the soldier's abandoned pistol from where it lay gleaming in the dirt. He climbed homeward, his racing heartbeat pounding in his ears.

The ominous words of his sister-creature reverberated in Geum-Jin's thoughts. To see her whole brought him some relief from his guilt, though it did not quell his fury that she would invite death to the family with her careless tongue. She was also not incorrect: he did not know what he would do now that he could not return to the village. His pulse thumped with the warning that the forest would ebb away and expose his family to danger. Frustrated tears leaked from his reddened eyes. How would he explain to his parents what happened? He did not wish to imagine what his reactive father would do once he learned that the pelts and jige had been lost in the market. And although his mother had never once expressed disappointment toward him, he dreaded the idea that she might for the first time today. Geum-Jin was so preoccupied with his worries on the ascent home that he did not notice his mother's screams until the collapsed roof of their hut came into sight, its rotted straw and wood surrendered to their decaying weight in a jumbled heap.

"Uhmuhni! Ahbuhji!" he called out as he ran to his remaining family.

Spittle flew from Dahn's roar as he swung his ax in erratic bursts. When the ax lodged into a tree, he pulled on it in a manic rage until he fell backward from the force of it coming loose. On the ground, he grabbed the nearest rock and hurled it into the tree. Myoung-Ok yelled at him to stop, trying to get closer so she could calm him as she had always been able to before. Dahn picked up another large rock and threw it at his wife. It hit her in the stomach and she, too, fell back.

"Uhmuhni!" Geum-Jin shouted as he ran to her.

Dahn jerked his head at the noise. His empty eyes fell on the Japanese pistol in his son's hand. He released an animalistic cry, picked himself up, and charged at the boy. Geum-Jin tumbled to the ground, air forced out of his lungs by the full weight of his enormous father.

Dahn's first punch cracked Geum-Jin's nose. Geum-Jin stared up at his father, his shock immobilizing him against any instinct for self-preservation. Somewhere distant, his mother screamed. Dahn's second punch made Geum-Jin's vision turn red. The third punch drowned out all sounds but his own pulse exploding in his head. Then Geum-Jin's world turned black.

Myoung-Ok threw herself onto Dahn's left shoulder and tried to pry him off their son. She shouted for him to stop, but he flung her away before striking Geum-Jin once more. Blood splattered on his fist and on the leaves of the forest floor. When she saw the red pulp of her child's face, Myoung-Ok drew on all of her resolve to do what she had known she must since the first day the light left Dahn's eyes. She hastened to find a hunting knife near the debris of the hut and ran until its point slid into Dahn's neck. Dahn turned to her—eyes still empty—and fell on his side.

Myoung-Ok released an earth-shaking howl and threw herself on her husband as he rolled onto his back. As his heavy breathing faltered, Myoung-Ok's prone body rose and fell with every labored inhale and exhale. Green sprouts spread on Dahn's chest where his wife's weeping head lay, spilling tiny leaves down his shoulders and onto the forest floor. Guttural sounds neither beast nor human, perhaps from the earth itself, rang through the forest as Dahn bled out.

When the giant lungs beneath her eventually stilled, Myoung-Ok bellowed for the earth to grieve. The ground quivered in time with her rasping sobs, sinking Dahn's slack form into the soil glazed red with his blood. As tears left her body they took with them her breath, her grief, her flesh, disintegrating her essence into leaves that cascaded onto the ground. Myoung-Ok let out one final wail as her body crumbled into a pall of grave dirt and grass, engulfing her lost love in a final embrace as she, too, surrendered to the earth.

When Geum-Jin woke, he did not know how long he had been unconscious. Excruciating pain throbbed in his head and he could not fully open his eyes. Congealing blood slid into the lines of his grimace as he sat up. He looked around and called for his parents. The collapsed hut roof sat rotting in the yard, but in the place where his father had fallen was a large grassy mound. Geum-Jin dragged himself to the edge of the raised earth. He knelt and bowed until his head touched the soil, watering the growing grass with tears in farewell to his buried parents.

CHAPTER FIVE

Cheongju, Chōsen, Empire of Japan, 1920

Without the tigers' culling presence, the remaining beasts of the mountain ran free and bold. Deer picked at the sprouting crops every morning. Packs of wild boars charged into the fields, trampling the tilled soil and destroying the pigpens that jailed their sisters. Liberated sows and oxen absconded into the forest, happy to shed the domesticity that chained them to their human masters. Then came the pests. Black clouds of insects that eclipsed the sun descended on the village. Their buzzing horde consumed stalks of barley and rice before their grains could ripen. They bore holes through the wood of grain storage, devouring caches of corn and sorghum. Desperation gnawed at the empty stomachs of the villagers. What little food the farmers managed to produce was confiscated and shipped overseas to cater to the rising needs of the Japanese Empire. They were left with meager government rations, if that, and resorted to pouring more water into their flavorless gruels to make them last longer.

When recruiters appeared in the village promising jobs for virtuous and hardworking young women, the hungry villagers shipped their daughters off to distant factories to support Japanese manufacturing. Some families were awarded bags of grain for their sacrifice. Others were not quite so lucky. All were promised money that their children would send home after settling into their work. Weeks and months passed; no family received a single coin, or even a letter to confirm their daughters' safe passage. Everything had been taken from them, down to the very flesh between their backs and their bellies.

Hungry and humiliated, the country broiled with protest. Farmers, students, scholars, workers, poets: all linked arms to push against the emperor of Japan. They demanded liberation from the yoke of tyranny and taxation, to be able to determine their own livelihoods, to live free of discrimination, to preserve the dignity of their heritage. Millions in white hanbok marched through the streets, waving their flags in the faces of the Japanese officials who had robbed them of their land and coerced them into servitude. Chants of "Mahnseh! Mahnseh!" echoed from city to city, growing so loud that Japan could not ignore the call across the East Sea. It acted swiftly; armed forces marched in droves to stain Joseon red with the blood of her children. Teachers were strung up and dunked into water until they could breathe no longer. Fingernails were ripped from the hands of young girls. The elderly were locked in freezing cells until frostbite claimed their toes and noses. The loudest of the baekuiminjok were executed in public to the wails of their brethren until the swell of resistance waned, its revolutionaries dispersing to China, where they could plot and bide their time in refuge.

As his country mourned its gallant sons and daughters, Geum-Jin sat alone and unmoving on the mountain. In one night he had lost everything—his family, his home, his purpose. He did not know where to turn or how to endure. So he sat. He neither ate nor drank, allowing rain or snow to trickle into his mouth only as it fell from the sky. His nose, untouched since his father's fist broke its bones, sat crooked on his brown, gaunt face. His braid coiled on the forest floor as his hair grew. Grass and brush sprouted to his elbows. At first, he was resigned to paralysis by the weight of his anguish. But as his heartbeat slowed in his immobile, wantless state, so, too, did his thoughts, until they ceased to ricochet in his skull. Once so quick to tears, Geum-Jin found that he could not shed any more. To any passing traveler, he may have appeared a weatherworn bodhisattva statue obscured by overgrown grass.

The seasons flowed by with humidity, monsoons, and snow. None were able to wake Geum-Jin from his torpor. He remained frozen until one day, after a long snowfall, his stomach growled so loudly it summoned his eyes to look upon the light of day once again. He felt hunger. He felt the bite of the winter wind. He felt the urge to move, his joints cracking when he shifted his weight and stretched out his legs. Thousands of prickling stings shot through his limbs as his blood circulated once more. He stood up, shedding accumulated snow from his head and shoulders, and walked to the mountain spring. He broke the shallow ice on the edge of the water to drink and plunge his head within. The frigid bite of the water pained him at first, but its shock was insufficient to distract him from the weight of deep sorrow that had rooted into his veins. He wondered if this heavier body was what he would have to carry for the remainder of his life.

After unraveling his braid and rinsing his hair, he tied it into a topknot and returned to the remains of his family's home. He dug around the wreckage to find hunting knives, his bow, and his father's still-full coin purse. Along with the soldier's pistol and Geum-Ja's tail, he packed what he could salvage of his former life into a cloth bundle and donned his father's large bearskin that fell to his knees. He paid one final bow to his parents' snow-dusted grave and set out north in the direction of his twin. He would not remain here if there was a chance he could find family.

On his journey through the mountains, he began to hunt once again. He caught a few hares and found that his body had not forgotten the movements of deboning or skinning. But his arms were now weak. With each eager bite of gamey flesh, Geum-Jin willed the hare to bestow its vigor into his body. After a fortnight, Geum-Jin had several new pelts to trade and aid him on his trek north. His wandering took him down a mountain slope toward snow-laden fields and straw-thatched roofs. A bustling town lay ahead, much larger than the village of his childhood.

Geum-Jin walked through the streets, scanning for signs of tailors, shoemakers, and other shops that might value his pelts. He lowered his gaze and drifted to the edges of the road when uniformed soldiers passed, wondering if his old village had also thus thickened with military presence. His skin prickled with an animal alertness so focused on dodging the soldiers that he did not at first notice the suspicious looks the townspeople cast in his direction. When Geum-Jin stopped an older man to ask where he could trade his pelts, the man recoiled and waved him away. He walked from shop to shop, seeing if anyone had interest in his furs. Shopkeepers turned him out, frowning at his dirty bearskin and worn, rural-looking clothes. Some even mistook him for a beggar and yelled that they had nothing to give him before he could protest. One tailor to whom Geum-Jin did manage to show his pelts offered him only a third of the going price. Geum-Jin declined the sale.

As he gathered his furs, the most enchanting sound Geum-Jin had ever heard rang out from behind him. It spoke human words, yet could not be a human voice, for it was clearer than the delicate chirp of a songbird and more beautiful than the sound of any instrument that could have been crafted by men.

Geum-Jin turned to face a woman with pinned-up hair wearing a dark-gray Western-style coat. Her face was plain and otherwise unremarkable except for a large web of splotchy raised flesh striating her left jaw and cheek. She addressed the tailor in that inimitable voice.

"I'd like to take a look at your newest winter stock."

The tailor scampered to his wealthy-looking customer. He bowed and pulled out reams of fabric, laying out jackets and skirts of all different colors. The woman with the burn scar fingered a pale-blue cloth. "How much did this fabric sell for last?" she asked.

"The lady has excellent taste! This is one of our finest offerings," said the tailor, naming a steep figure the last customer had paid. Geum-Jin balked at the cost, wondering how people could afford to pay so much for so little.

The woman smiled. "Quite extravagant indeed. And how much do you think this fabric is actually worth?"

The tailor's obsequious smile drooped as a red flush traveled from his neck onto his face. He cleared his throat and whispered a number that was significantly lower than the first, unable to offer anything but fact to her silvery tones.

Geum-Jin, too, wanted to tell her everything, anything, if she would just look at him and direct that heavenly voice to his ears. For the first time since the start of his sorrows, he felt the ripple of something within him that was not grief. A new restless sensation he could not quite place.

The woman clapped her hands in delight. "Well, what a very fair price. I can't argue with your generous offer. I'd love to order a fur-lined winter hat then, with this exquisite fabric."

The tailor looked as if he would burst.

"Now then, to be able to make a quality hat, you will also need quality furs. How much are his pelts worth, do you think?" she asked, gesturing toward Geum-Jin. The acknowledgment sent a jolt through Geum-Jin's body that made the hair on his arms stand straight. The tailor bit his lip before he mumbled a price three times higher than what he had previously quoted Geum-Jin.

"How lucky it is that someone is here to provide the pelt I'd need for the hat," the woman said, flashing her teeth.

When the tailor gave Geum-Jin his money, he asked both of them to leave his shop at once, promising that he would send for the lady's servant when her order was ready. They walked back out into the market street, where an older attendant was waiting for the woman with the burn scar. Geum-Jin bowed and thanked the woman for her help in making the sale.

"You must be a visitor. Welcome to Cheongju. Don't let these old men cheat you out of your money."

She nodded in farewell and walked with her attendant down the street. Vendors otherwise eager to draw the attention of customers avoided the eyes of these two women, hoping they would not have to contend with the voice so sweet it charmed their tongues to reluctant truth.

Geum-Jin watched the women walk away before inspecting the coins in his hand. Dirt was packed under his fingernails and crusted in the lines of his palm, even speckled across the loose threads of his fraying jeogori sleeve. He began to see the wisdom of investing in more presentable clothing. After finding a different tailor from whom to purchase new shirts and pants, he walked to the end of town to an inn that would accept him as a guest. There he asked the old proprietor if she knew the woman with the burn scar.

"Oh, that's Song Jung-Soon-ssi. Her family is famous in Cheongju. Aigo, it's a shame about her face. Song-sajang will never be able to marry her off, the poor girl."

Jung-Soon was the second child of Song-sajang, a lean, cunning man who inherited his family's silver mine and cultivated an appetite for business. He divined from an early age that the mine's ore would be finite, and so diversified his ventures with lumber and construction. By the time he was a young man, his company had built many of the newest, more modern buildings in Cheongju. When a new government edict gave the Japanese preferential access to Joseon's forests, Song-sajang's lumber company was the only one whose land holdings were left unseized in the entire region. Song-sajang never seemed to have to apply for new permits or pay special taxes, even as his rivals folded under the hostile bureaucracy choking out the locals for Japanese industry. No one knew what he had done to defend his business against foreign encroachment, though the people of Cheongju liked to make a game of speculating: perhaps some powerful yakuza oyabun was indebted to him, or he had tricked a dokkaebi into rewarding him with great fortune and power.

Song-sajang had no particular love for the Japanese but thought that their modern industrialization would be good for the country. In the time he had spent abroad in his youth, he had seen what advanced roads, bridges, and technology could do to improve lives. He prided himself as a pioneer of progress, bringing the benefits of foreign influence to Cheongju without bending to its will. He was enthralled by his own machinations to build and profit, and developed an aversion to anything that could distract him from his pursuit. It was only at the unrelenting insistence of his parents that he took on a wife and sired heirs. His parents selected for him an obedient wife, but nothing could be done to make him love the children she bore him. His only son showed no signs of intelligence, while his youngest was a daughter: irrelevant. Song-sajang thought about sending his son abroad to England to see if hairy Westerners might make him less of a stupid oaf. His daughter he did not think about at all.

When Jung-Soon was five years old, she was found injured inside a burning shed. Her brother had locked her in and run away as a joke, not realizing the oil lamp within had fallen and spread its flame when he slammed the door in his sister's face. The groundskeeper saw the smoke before he heard her screaming and ran to extinguish the fire. By the time she was pulled out, she had suffered deep burns on the left side of her face and body. After the accident, adults fixated on her physical appearance. Her mother often told Jung-Soon that she would never be able to achieve a favorable marriage with such a deformity. On the rare occasion Song-sajang noticed his daughter's presence, he would tell her to cover her unseemly face with her jangot headdress. Every day, servants and townspeople expressed their pity for her disfigurement, even if they meant it without her parents' contempt. For years Jung-Soon shrank into her jangot, wielding its silk as a shield against the barbs of others' judgment.

Because people so readily offered their candor to a quiet, ugly child, Jung-Soon did not discover her voice could compel the truth until she was old enough to go into town with her attendant. When vendors first started giving her lower prices than other customers, she believed it came from a place of pity and refused to give them her business. But when the apothecary looked shocked to reveal his scar cream was an ineffectual mix of ground acorns, or when the potter admitted that a vase was cracked before he had sold it to her, she surmised that her voice was not one so easily ignored. Jung-Soon found excuses to go to the market each day to test her gift. With each indication that she could draw out truths beyond those regarding her lack of beauty, her confidence grew, as did her propensity to leave for her outings with her jangot discarded in her room.

At first, people feared Jung-Soon, suspecting the daughter might be as ruthless as the father. But when they saw that she did not abuse her abilities to humiliate, and that she understood how small lies preserved harmony, they learned to keep a respectful but still distant rapport with the girl. The boldest among them even courted her patronage as a signal to others of their trustworthiness. And so Jung-Soon's voice became Cheongju's most well-known secret that no one dared speak about lest they reveal how they personally came to know it. The Song family may have been the last to remain unaware of Jung-Soon's gift, however, for they had never tried to hide their cruel truths from her.

Geum-Jin rose in the early mornings to hunt in the nearby forest and returned to the inn to prepare his pelts. The proprietor offered him space in the yard to skin and stretch out furs provided Geum-Jin let her take one of her choosing. When he finished his morning's work, he went to town to sell, hoping to catch sight of Jung-Soon. He learned from the more talkative shopkeepers that Jung-Soon liked to frequent the book trader when she came to the market. And so Geum-Jin plucked a bouquet of camellias from a tree near his inn and kept watch near the book trader's shop, ears searching for that beguiling voice.

When the chime of that heavenly sound finally hit his ears, Geum-Jin pushed through the market crowd and offered the camellias to Jung-Soon. Surprised by the gesture, Jung-Soon laughed, telling him she already had all the flowers she could want, and that they might make another woman happier. Geum-Jin did not know what to say, but was overjoyed to have caused the electrifying chord of her laughter. When she walked away with her attendant, Geum-Jin resolved to try again.

The next time he saw her with her attendant in the market, he gifted her expensive dried persimmons he had saved up to purchase. Jung-Soon laughed again and told him that she had never known hunger, and that they might make another woman happier. Geum-Jin savored the echoes of her laugh and was not discouraged by her rejection. She nodded and smiled at him as she departed.

Jung-Soon brought her attendant to the book trader again the following day, claiming she had forgotten something. Geum-Jin was surprised to see her again so soon, but was prepared to gift her with a beautiful white rabbit pelt. Jung-Soon did not laugh this time. She smiled and told him that there was greater strength in preserving life than in destroying it, and that the pelt might make another woman happier. Geum-Jin bowed as she left, pondering what he could do to make this woman happy.

The next time Jung-Soon came to look at the book trader's collection, Geum-Jin approached her empty-handed, declaring that he would gift her with choice. He had paid a young boy to lie to Jung-Soon's attendant so she would run back to the Song manor on an urgent call. Jung-Soon smiled and said that she had never been out in town without her attendant before. She accepted Geum-Jin's invitation to stroll to the outskirts of Cheongju, where the snow had not been trodden to gray by busy marketgoers. Geum-Jin asked if he could hold her hand. Jung-Soon nodded and let her cold fingers slide into the warmth of his palm.

"Do you know how old I am?" she asked, suspecting she was at least a decade his senior.

"No, but that doesn't matter."

She laughed, raising her eyebrows at his answer. She then asked him what she had been curious to know since he offered her the camellias. "Why are you wooing me?"

"I love your voice and how you use it. I want to hear it every day until the day I die."

There was no hesitation in Geum-Jin's declaration, no struggle to choose the right words to mask his intentions. Jung-Soon had rarely encountered such unguarded frankness beyond the remarks people liked to make about her scars. She stopped walking down the snow-laden path and faced her companion.

"You won't like my voice if I ask you questions you don't want to answer. I can force you to show parts of yourself you wish to conceal." Jung-Soon scanned his flushed face for an apprehension she hoped not to find.

"There's nothing I want to hide from you. Your voice makes it easier to tolerate the truth." Geum-Jin stepped closer, the steam of his breath warming her nose.

"It's not always good to hear the truth," she said with a sad smile, looking away as Geum-Jin drew nearer. "People's truths can be cruel."

"Nothing would be crueler than never hearing your voice again," he whispered in her ear.

Jung-Soon blushed and met Geum-Jin's eyes. There, she saw herself reflected in his truth.

Jung-Soon entered her father's study and announced that she would be leaving home to marry a poor hunter of uncertain origin. He did not look up from the papers at his desk until she declared that Song-sajang would be giving her enough money to build a house outside of town in the mountains. He set his pen down and considered the gall of his daughter for the first time.

"Absolutely not. Only a blind fool would marry you, and I open my purse for no fool. Now, get out, I'll be hosting guests soon."

"As you wish."

Jung-Soon bowed and exited the study.

Later that evening, Song-sajang sat in the parlor with his Japanese guests from the railway company. They puffed on American cigars and drank sake while discussing a rail line expansion through Cheongju. It would bring more commerce to the town while increasing the government's capacity to transport goods to the southern ports of Busan. Song-sajang would provide the lumber and labor to help the company break ground, being paid handsomely for the trouble.

Jung-Soon entered the parlor holding a bottle of Western spirits. She wore a deep-blue fitted modern dress that made her skin glow.

"Otō-sama." Jung-Soon's beautiful voice turned the head of every man in the room who expected a face to match. Although they were disappointed by what they saw, they were intrigued by her unusual scar and by the revelation that Song apparently had a daughter. Jung-Soon continued to speak aloud in unaccented Japanese as she toured the room offering whisky to the guests.

"It's such an honor to meet the men my father has been toiling so hard for," she said, floating from man to man. "Forgive a daughter her pride, gentlemen, but my father has been working day and night to ensure the success of your investment. He's personally seen to every last detail of this project, from the budget calculations to the lumber selection."

Song-sajang kept his eyes locked on his daughter as she glided about the room serving whisky. He did not act on his instinct to make her leave, for his guests seemed pleased by the new drink and womanly presence. She continued her lyrical soliloquy on his business acumen even in the slowing Japanese economy, sympathizing with the gentlemen who were dealing with unusually high costs of labor and materials in such a difficult time. The men savored the tinkling of her voice as much as they did their whisky, chuckling at this woman's impressive grasp of their circumstances.

"Have you planted your secret daughter with this speech to make yourself look good?" said one of the guests. As the men laughed, Song-sajang's lips curled into an acknowledging smirk that belied his increasing vexation at Jung-Soon's unexplained presence.

Jung-Soon turned to her father, all coquettish smiles. "Otō-sama, can you remind me how you plan on dividing your contracted budget between materials and labor?"

She then announced to the rest of the room that she was taking on a modest home construction project inspired by her industrious father, and wanted to take the opportunity to learn from the rare gathering of experts. Song-sajang wanted to tell her that was enough and to leave, but found himself unable to form the words. He then focused on articulating the budget numbers he wanted his guests to hear but could not move his lips. Instead, he felt a deep urge to reveal that he would skimp on wages and use poor-quality lumber to pocket the difference in the contract. He turned red and crushed the cigar in his hand, giving in to his loosened tongue.

"It's too complicated to get into fine details now," he said, clenching his hands into fists, "but I'm cutting into qual—"

"Of course," Jung-Soon interrupted, watching her father squirm. "You said you wouldn't have to explain such complex details to me if you built the home yourself. Perhaps I am being troublesome now. You were right, Otō-sama, I've taken on too much and it would be much more convenient for you to handle the planning and costs of my new home, no?"

The guests chuckled knowingly at Jung-Soon's concession, for construction was not a domain for women. Some thought that she was truly Song's daughter if she had the pluck to try to manage such a job in the first place. No one seemed to notice just how strained Song-sajang's neck had become, or the searing glare he shot his daughter.

"Yes, I will take care of it," he said, all venom through gritted teeth. "You should run along now; you've entertained our guests long enough."

Jung-Soon smiled at the men, bowed, and left the parlor.

CHAPTER SIX

Cheongju, Chōsen, Empire of Japan, 1931

"Young-Ho-ya, it's time to feed the chickens!"

Young-Sook brought out a basket of dried corn, tossing her braid over her shoulder so as not to have it fall into the grains. Young-Ho's narrow, close-set eyes peered out from behind the garden plants. He hurried over, clutching leafy green stalks in each fist.

"I told you, not that corn. The chickens don't like it. They want mugwort today." He held out his hands and presented his elder sister with his harvest.

"Did you ask Ahbuhji if you could take that from the garden?"

"I'm the one who planted these with him. I can do what I want. Babies, come get your breakfast!"

The chickens gathered around Young-Ho's short legs. They clucked at his knees, stretching their necks to get at the leaves bundled in his hands. He laughed, eyes curving into puffy, downturned crescents as he lowered the mugwort to the birds he had raised since they hatched in his palms. He squatted low to the ground to examine each chicken as they ate, looking over their feathers to make sure their shine had not dulled. Young-Ho's tantrums had abated since he was given sole responsibility for the brood—he was at his most serene when his careful attentiveness bore fruit, and the chickens flourished in his custody. They laid their happy eggs every morning and trailed him around the yard, clucking back while he chattered away. Young-Sook smiled at her ten-year-old brother's crouched, focused form, keeping watch for anything that could make him stray from his peace.

Young-Sook put away the basket of corn and skipped toward her mother and her sister, Young-Ja. Jung-Soon sat peeling garlic on the wooden walkway wrapping around their home. Discarded skins sat in a papery nest as stray wisps floated into the yard. Young-Ja sat beside her with her hands deep in a clay bowl, squelching the buchu chives from their garden into a piquant swirl of gochugaru, ginger, and garlic. She pinched a few blades of the marinade-steeped buchu and raised them to her mother's lips. A smile spilled across Jung-Soon's face as she tasted the leaves and pretended to nibble at her daughter's red-tinged fingers.

"You always know exactly how to raise my spirits," Jung-Soon said, tapping her youngest child on the nose. "The perfect taste of spring happiness."

Young-Ja grinned and revealed a gummy gap where a new tooth was starting to crest. She called to her older sister—buchu fingers extended—eager to see her joy spread to yet another.

Young-Ja was often found by her mother's side preparing food for the family. Since the first time she popped a berry into her brother's mouth and watched delight bloom on his face, she took pleasure from feeding others. It began with small, foraged gifts like fruits—sometimes even an extra sweet from the market she yielded to her siblings. When found fruits were not enough, she taught herself to transform them—drying, preserving, juicing—and presented these embellishments to everyone with pride. Once Jung-Soon permitted Young-Ja to use a knife and tend to the fire, she watched over the gamasot every day and developed a fine intuition for cooking that far exceeded her parents' knowledge. Her child hands grew deft, sensing the exact weight of salt to sprinkle in, or the right combination of oil and heat to draw out the flavor of garden vegetables—all to thrill her family's palates. Her fingertips imbued her food with an exuberance that nourished her family every day. Young-Ja in turn grew plump on the satisfaction she alone could render.

"Can we go to the market again today?" Young-Sook asked, an errant gochugaru flake on her shining lips. "I want to see the cows and buy more candies—Young-Ho already ate all the sweets from yesterday."

"Promise you'll be back in time for dinner. I'm making something special tonight," said Young-Ja.

Jung-Soon smiled at her daughters. "No, my sweets, there will be no market for us today. We have guests coming in the afternoon. Don't forget to make extra buchu kimchi for them, too, Young-Ja. They could all use a bit of your happiness today."

Young-Ja scrunched her nose in a proud smile as she continued her hand-mixing. Jung-Soon set down her knife and wiped her hands on a damp cloth before reaching over to Young-Sook and pulling her into her arms. She kissed her giggling eldest on the forehead and suggested that she practice her calligraphy with the new paper and ink they had bought in town. Young-Sook kicked off her shoes and went inside to set up her writing tools. Jung-Soon drank in the scene of her three children busy with their own endeavors, free of the shame and confinement she had once known. She was proud of the little domain she had built with Geum-Jin to shield their family from the country's ongoing turmoil. Her children would have their entire lives to confront a world that sought to subjugate them; Jung-Soon wished at least to preserve a sense of dignity in their youth.

Geum-Jin taught the children everything he had learned of the natural world, bearing the knowledge passed down to him by his own parents. Once, after instructing Young-Sook not to fear the noble spider, he was delighted to find all three of his children urging spiders to spin homes near theirs so that summer bugs would stop pestering them in their sleep. When Young-Ho found eggs in an abandoned quail's nest, he requested his father's help to incubate them, later recruiting his sisters to set the hatched birds free into the forest. And little Young-Ja liked to squat with her father and siblings in the family garden, chattering about whose vegetables might grow the best despite knowing it would be hers every time.

Jung-Soon, in turn, taught the children what she had schemed to learn of the human world at their age, hiding in the wardrobe during her brother's private lessons and reading pilfered books by candlelight. The money her father complained about having wasted on her brother had paid out in her stolen mastery of literature, history, and mathematics, all of which she now passed on openly to her children in daily tailored lessons. Young-Sook was quick to absorb all subjects but showed a particular passion for brushwork. Young-Ho struggled with his sums but loved to discuss the meanings of the fables they studied. Young-Ja showed no strong preference and seemed content to engage in any activity by her mother's side. The desire to protect this life—the fruits of the attentive parenting she had never received—made Jung-Soon all the more eager to see her guests that afternoon.

At the market the day prior, Jung-Soon handed the rice cake shop granny a few branches of forsythia to hang over the entrance of her store. To passersby and customers, the yellow blossoms were a welcoming sign of spring freshness. To a select few of Cheongju's working women, they signaled an invitation to tea in Jung-Soon's mountain home in one day's time. No one paid much mind to the odd pairs of women who walked up the forest trail outside of town. If they did, the women would appear to be gossiping wives out to forage for herbs in the woods. But their conversations were not the casual prattle one might overhear at the market. These women's tongues bore a more defiant intent.

Teatime was inspired when Jung-Soon first returned to the Cheongju central market after Young-Ja's birth nearly a decade ago. For each of the three years she welcomed her children into the world, Jung-Soon had not left her new mountainside home. Geum-Jin insisted on handling all supply runs into town, sparing his nursing wife any need to make the two-hour journey herself. Geum-Jin thus strove to keep Jung-Soon wanting for nothing. So when she declared her wish to enjoy time to herself for a long-overdue trip into town, he just as eagerly took all three children into his arms and sent her off without a worry.

Jung-Soon descended the mountain at a rapid clip, buoyed by thoughts of Cheongju's vibrant market. Although she wished to visit all her favorite vendors, she would stop by the book trader first to browse at her leisure, unburdened by the weight of any other purchase. But Jung-Soon's tread slowed as she crossed the threshold into town. Strokes of kanji and hiragana swept across storefronts that were no longer manned by familiar faces. The rhythmic cadence of Japanese drowned out the passing whispers of Korean, while no street was left free of a stony face in uniform. The book trader she had long relied on to learn about the world now offered only a modest collection of government-approved Japanese-language books. Her chest tightened at the many townspeople shuffling through the market with downcast eyes, seemingly wary of being perceived. Jung-Soon scanned the street for something that could help her regain her bearings. A young soldier shifted his weight from foot to foot at the market's main entrance.

"Excuse me, sir, I'm terribly sorry for the intrusion, but I seem to have lost my way. Could you please tell me how to get to the railway station?" Jung-Soon asked, layering her voice with honey.

The young man softened at Jung-Soon's unaccented Japanese, making himself amenable to what looked to be a finely dressed, wealthy woman. Likely the wife of some official visiting from Japan. He politely set his eyes on hers, trying not to look at the burn scar splotched across her face.

"I only just got here last night, so I don't know these streets well myself. But I think if you turn right at the next intersection and keep walking, you should be able to see it down the road. I can accompany you, if you'd like."

"Oh, thank you kindly, but no, I couldn't trouble you so." Jung-Soon flashed an innocent smile at the soldier. "You said you arrived last night? What brings you to town?"

The soldier smiled back, glad to break the boredom of his post. "A large group of us were sent here to seize the textile factory. They needed men to help arrest all the workers."

"Arrest all of them?" Jung-Soon willed steadiness into her voice, forcing a tone of casual curiosity. "What have they done?"

"The official line is criminal dissent. But it's mostly to scare the Chōsenjin in this town into submission."

"That's . . . quite the undertaking. What will you do with the arrested workers?"

"Some we'll execute as an example, some we'll send to labor overseas. We'll strike tomorrow morning."

"Ah. Well, you must be quite busy then, so I'll be on my way. Thank you for your assistance." Jung-Soon bowed and slipped back into the crowd before the soldier could realize his tongue had not loosened of his own volition.

Jung-Soon rushed down the street with no destination in mind, only the instinct to flee. The urgency of what she had learned caught at her throat. What could she do? Was it her place to get involved? Where could she go with this knowledge? If a single soldier she had randomly selected on the street revealed such a hand, what would the many others reveal? Part of her wished to flee town and gather her babies to her chest in the refuge of the mountain forest, far from the concerns of this world. But her gait slowed as she wrested command of her breathing. Jung-Soon knew she could not leave until she passed on what she had learned.

To her right was a small shop where an old woman hunched over to steam a new batch of rice cakes, somehow not yet run out of business despite the rice shortages under Japanese rule. Jung-Soon stepped into the shop and asked the woman for the price of her treats. When she leaned over to pay and take the warm tteok into her hands, she whispered into the old granny's ear. "If you know anyone who works at the textile factory, please tell them not to go into work tomorrow. Something terrible will happen if they do."

Jung-Soon left grimaces in her wake as she stooped down to whisper into the gnarled ears of the other working women across the market. As each purchase of goods added to her load, she passed on her heavy words. She made her rounds of the stalls and shops until she could carry no more. Arms straining, she hastened home to her family's embrace, wondering if her words had taken root.

When Jung-Soon returned to the market the following week, she received an additional scoop of millet from the grain seller, an extra stretch of hemp fabric from the tailor, the freshest cuts from the butcher. The rice cake shop granny refused her money and sent her along with a steaming batch of songpyeon rice cakes, one for each of the fathers, brothers, and sons Jung-Soon's warning had spared. She tried to decline these gifts—business was hard enough in those days—but the vendors would not take back what they had given. They asked her to pay instead with whatever else of value her singular voice could extract.

Jung-Soon took to chatting up unsuspecting soldiers throughout Cheongju, though never the same one twice lest they recognize her distinct burn scar or her designs. While the market women expanded their web of whispers to disperse Jung-Soon's warnings, they were not content to sit idle, waiting for the next tip. Like so many across the country worn down by the subjugation of foreign rule, these women did what they could to engage in their own acts of resistance. With Jung-Soon's help, they gave decoy tips to soldiers who were sniffing around too close to a dissident group. They reallocated food to families that had been forced to surrender their harvest. They sewed writings on Korean liberation into the lining of podaegi baby wraps—the authorities would never suspect old ladies carrying their grandchildren to be distributors of anti-Japanese literature. When it became too risky to conduct such affairs in town, Jung-Soon led the women into her mountain forest for tea. For years they schemed to help their neighbors and protect their families, evading the notice of the police. For years they supported one another through a thousand such little acts, quashing the fears that would have paralyzed them in isolation.

While they took very seriously their duties to their community, the women also looked forward to their congregations simply for the pleasure of one another's company. Their camaraderie brought out in them certain qualities they had not always recognized within themselves—the women were delighted to discover their own daring. The oldest among them, the rice cake shop granny, once mixed dog droppings into her specialty red bean rice cakes and sent them to the Cheongju police chief as tribute.

"If I'm honest, I was so nervous at being caught I shed a layer of skin just wringing my hands," she said. "But then that son of a bitch came to my shop and demanded that I prepare the same rice cakes for him again. So I make sure to deliver the exact recipe every Monday morning to the station."

Jung-Soon laughed so hard at this story that she tumbled back into a screen door and broke its thin wooden panes. Their capacity to experience joy, no matter how fleeting, was a sign of the inextinguishable spirit of their people. Something they swore would never be taken from them.

CHAPTER SEVEN

Cheongju, Chōsen, Empire of Japan, 1931

The day after the forsythia hung, the women assembled in Jung-Soon's home to discuss the latest spike in police home raids.

"It's just like what happened after the student protests in Gwangju a few years ago," said the vegetable farmer. "Soldiers are barging into homes without any warning. They're hitting multiple houses a night."

"They nabbed the fishmonger just the other day. The one who owns multiple boats," said the tofu vendor. "You remember Pak Chul-Soo."

"Oh no, poor Mrs. Pak. She has a fifth child on the way... We'll have to send her some extra barley, maybe help look after her youngest."

"Jung-Soon-ssi, can't you just go ask and figure out who's next?" the seamstress pleaded. "Some of my neighbors have stopped leaving their homes to avoid getting noticed. I heard they're taking old ladies and kids too. Even if they have no idea what they've done."

The rice cake shop granny waved her hand to dismiss the thought. "You know we can't just send Jung-Soon-ssi everywhere. Someone who recognizes her will get suspicious, and then where will we be?"

"I'm afraid I may not be so useful at the moment anyway." Jung-Soon sighed. "The last few men I spoke with had no idea which homes would be next. These low-level soldiers are going out the minute they get their orders and it's unclear who's making the list of families to target. They don't know enough in advance to pass anything on to me in casual conversation."

"So maybe we need to get you in front of someone who does know," said the seamstress.

"No," the rice cake shop granny interrupted. "She'd draw too much attention if she forced any real secrets from them. We have to stick to small talk. Things they can't pin back to her."

Cheongju had grown restless with fear. Not only did these raids damage people's homes and dwindling valuables, but loved ones also vanished without a trace. Families spiraled not knowing where their kin had been taken, for the local jail had filled up with accused dissidents long ago. Anxious mothers and fathers seeking answers were pushed out of the police station every day under threat of disappearing themselves should they dare question the authorities. A fugue of sobs and whispers served as the score for the Cheongju market. Those lamenting their losses wailed as they dragged their feet through the streets over the steady beat of speculation about prisons in the north, or enslavement in factories. Some accounts assumed the worst, reporting that people were being shot and tossed into shallow graves in the mountains.

While the women pondered what they could do, Geum-Jin tended to his garden and looked after the children. He was happy to care for the home while Jung-Soon worked with the women of Cheongju, so long as they were careful not to put themselves in any real danger. Although he preferred to keep his family as far from the Japanese as possible, he could not help but admire his wife's dedication to the welfare of her people. So Geum-Jin stepped in where he could, in bids to minimize the risk to Jung-Soon and ease her burdens. He went in her stead to shuttle messages to neighboring towns or to guide political refugees through the mountain forest. He whispered sweet reassurances to slacken the grooves of worry on her face. With his vigilance, he would do everything he could to protect his loves. To protect the happiness he feared could be dashed as quickly as it had been before.

Geum-Jin's greatest joy rose from his children and watching them grow into their best qualities. Young-Sook had her mother's voice and poise, and Young-Ho, her determination. In Young-Ja he saw something of himself, his compulsion to give everything he had to his loves. This was both a blessing and a curse: a tension that played out in her fixation with food. He recognized that Young-Ja could not help but put all of herself into what she served, and that the family fed on a youthful happiness she was fortunate to be able to generate every day. Geum-Jin knew that a time would come when they would taste her woe or her anger—all he could do was prepare to weather those moments by her side. He wondered then how evident his childhood truths had been to his own parents and felt a pang in his chest knowing they would never get to see his beautiful babies.

Geum-Jin kept the memory of Myoung-Ok and Dahn alive through his children's grasp of mountain life. Every time he taught them to identify a plant, he thought back to when his mother had taught him and his sister the same. In weaving rope or whittling, he demonstrated for his children the careful techniques of his father. To lull the children to sleep at night, he recounted stories his mother had told him. Of wily kumiho, a nine-tailed fox that could shapeshift into a woman to lure foolish men into traps. Of grateful magpies that saved a scholar in the clutches of a giant snake. Of farmers who acquired rare treasures when they outwitted the impish dokkaebi. He imagined his parents as the stories' heroes and wove what he remembered of their traits into his narration. He sometimes worked Geum-Ja into his characters as well, hoping his sister had found a happiness in the wild equal to that which he found in his family.

Young-Ho or Young-Ja typically drove the story choice for the evening, with the generous Young-Sook yielding to her siblings. Some nights, they requested their favorites. Other nights, they wanted to hear something new. But each time, they requested that their father tell a long story in an effort to delay their sleep.

"There lived a young girl who had loooong hair and a loooooong skirt. She met a boy with a looooong nose and they walked by a looooooong river—"

"Not that kind of long!" Young-Ho giggled as Young-Ja sat up in protest for Geum-Jin to take them seriously. Geum-Jin retold the story of a tiger that kept trying to trick a brother and sister to let him into their home so he could eat them. The brother and sister were too clever to fall for the tiger's chicanery and ran away into the woods. The tiger chased them until they had no choice but to flee into the sky and turn into the moon and sun. By the end of the tale, Young-Sook and Young-Ho had fallen asleep, but Young-Ja remained awake, staring up at Geum-Jin's crooked nose. He brushed away the hair stuck to her round face and told her to close her eyes.

"I don't want to sleep," Young-Ja whispered. "What if a tiger comes for me in the night and I can't see him?"

Geum-Jin held his youngest to his chest. "Don't worry, my baby, it's just a story," he explained. "There are no tigers coming. Most of them left Joseon a long time ago."

"Why did they go away?"

Unease bubbled in Geum-Jin as he recalled his twin's parting words from so many years prior. He suspected that tigers had been hunted to extinction in the country now, but he did not say this aloud.

"The tigers were all scared away by brave fathers who protect their daughters," he said to the yawning girl in his arms. "And I'll always protect you from danger."

Young-Ja laid her head on her father's shoulder, her breath smoothing into a steady beat.

"Young-Ja-ya, why don't—"

"Aya!" Young-Ja dropped her knife into the pile of onion slices. The line of cleaved skin on her finger bloomed red. "You startled me!" She held her bleeding finger with a scrunched expression, the acid of the onion stinging her newly split flesh.

Young-Sook picked up the water gourd by the door and glided into the kitchen. "Remember what Ahbuhji taught us. Hold your finger tight." She tipped water from the gourd over the cut, the trickle darkening into a puddle on the dirt floor.

Young-Ja watched, relaxing the muscles in her face.

"Now, blow on it," Young-Sook ordered as she gathered a jar of honey and some cloth from the corner of the kitchen.

Young-Ja obeyed and tried not to mind the prickling of her breath on the cut. She loved being tended to by her older sister and tried not to evince too much pleasure lest Young-Sook think her care excessive and halt her attentions.

"Sorry I made you slip," Young-Sook said, taking Young-Ja's hand into hers. She hummed softly as she applied a thin layer of honey on the cut, just as she had been taught by her father, and he by his mother. "Could you go with Uhmuhni to the market instead of me? Young-Ho's lost his bowl and he's having another tantrum. I can stay with him."

"Feed him some of the gangjeong I made yesterday, they usually calm him down." Young-Ja watched her sister wrap a clean strip of cloth around her sticky, reddened finger.

"We tried," said Young-Sook in sing-song as she tied the cloth tight. She pulled the dressed finger to her lips and gave it a gentle peck to signal that all was done, her humming vibrating on Young-Ja's skin. "Uhmuhni's with him now but he's not happy. I'll finish up here and keep him busy. You go to the market, and don't forget to bring back plenty of sweets!"

Young-Ja looked up to her smiling older sister and wished to be like her one day, knowing exactly what to say and do in every situation. And despite being the youngest sibling, now at nine years of age, Young-Ja aspired to be more like her older sister toward Young-Ho as well, having been encouraged to relay extra patience for her brother's needs. If she was to go to the market in Young-Sook's stead, she would bring back as much candy as they desired.

Jung-Soon and Young-Ja left once Young-Ho had calmed, though Young-Sook held her brother and sang his favorite melody to put him at full ease. To keep Young-Ho distracted from his lost bowl, Geum-Jin suggested they take a walk around the woods and forage for the season's edible plants. Young-Ho perked up at the prospect and ran to dress himself.

When Geum-Jin slid open the door to step outside, two police officers in black stood waiting in the yard. Geum-Jin pushed his children behind him as he nodded a silent greeting to the unexpected visitors. They did not return the courtesy.

"Seen any young men in the woods around here? Some students burgled a landowner's home and we're on the lookout."

Geum-Jin mustered his stilted Japanese to explain that he had not seen anyone. "No, people don't come to mountain often. Too high."

The men sneered at his awkward speech. "Liar," they said.

A sheen of cold sweat dotted Geum-Jin's neck.

Young-Ho tugged at his father's pants, wondering why they were not yet on their way. Before Geum-Jin could stop him, he peeked his head out from behind the door and stared at the police. Young-Sook ran to pull him back and revealed her presence as well.

"That's it, everyone step out right now where we can see you," the police demanded, eyeing Young-Ho with a special curiosity. Although Geum-Jin held his arm out in front of Young-Sook, she grabbed Young-Ho's hand and stepped out onto the walkway.

"That's all, no student here," said Geum-Jin.

"That's a funny looking one," said one of the officers, pointing his baton at Young-Ho. "What's wrong with his face?"

Geum-Jin stiffened. "Please leave if no more business."

The police smirked at his imperfect Japanese. "But we do have business."

They pushed Geum-Jin to the side and barged into the house, tracking mud onto the clean floors. Young-Ho fell back and started to bawl as the men rummaged through their belongings, wrenching drawers out of chests and toppling over vases that shattered on the floor. The police yelled at Geum-Jin to shut up his brat—Geum-Jin placed himself between the police and his children and gestured at Young-Sook to take her brother outside. He turned to the men, trying to steer their attention away from the destruction of his home.

"Please, what are you looking for?" he said, mustering as much clarity as he could in this foreign tongue. "I give anything you want, just tell me what are you looking for."

The police ignored his pleas and continued their rampage. When they got to a stack of Jung-Soon's books, they paused to flip through them, thinking they might have found some reason to arrest the Chōsenjin and his dirty little children. But most were Japanese-language books on commerce and agriculture, nothing that even they could argue looked incendiary. They slammed the books on the ground and moved on to the large wardrobe in the corner.

The men flung open the doors and pulled out the wardrobe's contents. Clothes, blankets, and other items were tossed out in clumps. Among the discarded items were Geum-Ja's tail and the soldier's pistol Geum-Jin had wrapped in cloth and hidden away long ago. Worried the police might inspect the cloth bundle and discover this contraband, Geum-Jin kicked it under a pile of clothes. He then picked up the tiger tail and offered it to the intruders.

"No money here. Only this." He thrust the tail at the men kicking around the blankets on the floor. "Take, please. No other money."

The police stopped their ransacking to inspect the tail.

"Hm, this isn't a bad find. Tigers haven't been seen around here in a while," said one of the men as he stretched out the length of the tail.

"It'd probably fetch a decent price at the market," said his companion. "No one has to know we got it on the job."

The police looked at each other as if to confirm they would find nothing else interesting in the house. They took the tail and stepped outside, leaving a shaken Geum-Jin with a final word: "You're lucky we're not in the mood to listen to crying brats today."

Once the police disappeared into the mountain forest, Geum-Jin ran to embrace his son and daughter. Young-Ho wailed into his father's left side while Young-Sook held on to his right in silence. Geum-Jin did not release his children from his grasp until they let go first, suggesting to their father they restore order to their home before their mother returned.

Geum-Jin and the children had finished tidying up by the time Jung-Soon came back from the market with Young-Ja. Young-Ho ran outside and buried his face in his mother's stomach as soon as he heard her approach. Jung-Soon and Geum-Jin exchanged looks as a trembling Young-Sook recounted what the police had done. Geum-Jin brewed root tea to help calm his family while Jung-Soon comforted her children with the sweetest reassurances her voice could muster. Once the children fell asleep, Jung-Soon and Geum-Jin stepped into the dark outside to deliberate on what could be done. He showed her the old pistol he had saved.

"I'm going to start carrying this on me. We should also think about leaving the house for a while. Maybe the police will lose interest if they can't find us."

Unwelcome visitors boded ill. It was not likely their home was found by chance—they were high enough in the mountain that outsiders would not know the location unless told, and no one would bother to make the taxing ascent without reason. Access to their home was designed to be by intent only—this enabled Geum-Jin and Jung-Soon to shield their children from the daily indignities of the Occupation. Their only visitors were Jung-Soon's teatime guests, and they did not think it likely that something could have failed in that chain of subterfuge. Political resistance benefited from employing the invisibility of poor, older women—power never expected its downfall at the hands of those it deemed insignificant. The Cheongju police likewise seemed too arrogant and lazy to stalk old women into the mountain.

Jung-Soon did not want to think that outright betrayal was an option, though with the right pressures, she conceded, a desperate mother might be coerced to do the unthinkable. Her mind raced through all the women she had hosted in her home over the years. Each had been courageous enough to risk everything in her own right, but no one was without vulnerabilities. Every person had attachments and families that could be used against her. But pointing fingers would do little good now. Whatever, whoever it was, Jung-Soon could not afford to dwell on the cause of this exposure: she needed to act swiftly to protect her family's peace. And so she resolved to visit her father for the first time in over a decade.

Jung-Soon had not called on her family since the day she left to wed Geum-Jin. Once she tasted a life free of their disdain and unsavory wealth, she no longer wished to be associated with them or their close dealings with the Japanese. Nothing had tempted her to knock on the door of the Song manor since her departure and the lack of regard was reciprocated. This direct threat to her children, however, made it so that she could not ignore the possibility that her father could wield his influence to stave off the raids.

But she did not get to visit Song-sajang as planned, for six armed Japanese men appeared at their door the next morning.

CHAPTER EIGHT

Cheongju, Chōsen, Empire of Japan, 1931

Morning sunlight pooled in the yard. Its glow reflected off the boots stomping in the dirt, the rifles rattling in tense hands. No clouds cast shadows on the chickens dispersing or on the children running to hide behind their father in the garden. The light shed its warmth on all standing beneath it.

The two policemen from the day prior had returned, joined by four armed soldiers in tan uniforms. This parade seemed excessive; Geum-Jin wondered why such a show of force was warranted for an unassuming family in the woods. Tyranny thrived on spectacle, but there was no neighborhood audience in the mountain for whom to perform their intimidation. No one else to spook into obedience lest they be the next target.

Sweat dripped down Geum-Jin's temple, collecting at the bottom of his chin. He stood in front of his children with his arms stretched out, trying to occupy as much space as he could to shield his babies.

One of the police shouted at everyone to line up and receive their visitors. Young-Sook and Young-Ja each clasped one of their brother's hands behind their father. Jung-Soon emerged from the house, stray hairs loose around her face from a rushed bun she had been pinning in preparation for town. Ice slid down her spine at the strange Japanese voice. Despite the fear spreading in her chest, she did not allow it to enter her voice when she demanded to know why the men had come. A stocky, mustachioed soldier smirked.

"I'd heard rumors of a rebel leader in the mountains, but all I see here are an ugly dog and her feral little runts."

He pointed his bayonet at Jung-Soon and told her to stand by the others while they searched the house. She glided out slowly so as not to betray her panic and stood with Geum-Jin to flank her children. Two soldiers kept guns pointed at their captives while the remaining men entered the house and demolished all they could reach. Crashes erupted from within, punctuated by the intermittent crunch of breaking wood. The family stared in silence, holding hands to assure one another of their presence. When they were finished, the four men kicked down the sliding wood door and filed back into the sun. The mustachioed soldier demanded to know what Jung-Soon was hiding.

"We have nothing to hide. We're just a poor family that bothers no one."

"This is the first time I've heard the Song family called poor," said one of the policemen. The group chuckled at Jung-Soon's grimace.

"Some dirty little Chōsen peasants have been permitted to get rich, but it's made them arrogant," said the mustachioed soldier. "Weeds that grow too tall need to be cut down."

"I wouldn't know anything about that," said Jung-Soon. "As you can see, we have nothing of value to you."

"We can find value in many things." The lead soldier's gaze fell on Young-Sook. He reached out to grab her braid, his eyes slithering down the eleven-year-old's body.

"Don't you dare touch her," Jung-Soon snarled, pulling Young-Sook toward her.

The soldier stepped forward and slapped Jung-Soon across the face. "You're mouthy for a Chōsen bitch, aren't you?"

The children whimpered as red fanned out on their mother's cheek, her hair escaping completely from her bun. Young-Sook buried Young-Ho's face into her chest and covered his ears with her hands. Geum-Jin lunged for his wife but was restrained by the two police officers. In the scuffle, the pistol tucked into the waist of his pants clattered to the ground. As Geum-Jin tried to push away from the tangle of police limbs, the soldier who had slapped Jung-Soon picked up the fallen weapon. He examined the pistol, brushing the dirt off the barrel and weighing it in his hand.

"What a fun little relic you have here. I don't think the military issues these anymore."

He touched the barrel of the gun to Geum-Jin's temple and pulled the trigger. Jung-Soon shrieked and fell to her knees. Young-Sook and Young-Ja started to cry.

The trigger caught and did not shoot. The soldier tapped the gun against his palm and pulled on the trigger to another impotent click.

"Aren't you lucky?" He sneered as he threw the defective old pistol on the ground. The other men laughed. Stunned, Geum-Jin stopped thrashing.

The lead soldier ordered the men to beat Geum-Jin. The police dragged him away from his family into the center of the yard, where two soldiers took turns pounding their fists into his face. Jung-Soon screamed for them to stop but the nearest soldier cupped his hand over her mouth to stifle her pleas. He folded her into him, neutralizing her flailing with the weight of his body. Young-Sook and Young-Ja embraced each other over Young-Ho in an attempt to shield his eyes.

The soldiers' faces were expressionless as they followed their orders, blood streaking across their hands with each wet thud of knuckles on cheekbone and nose. When Geum-Jin's head hung slack, the soldiers' fists and knees flew into his stomach until he coughed up globules of blood. Strength left his legs and he slumped to the ground motionless, held up only by the police behind him. The children wailed. Urine trickled down Young-Ho's legs, soaking through his pants and into his sisters' skirts as they clutched him tight.

The mustachioed soldier signaled to the man restraining Jung-Soon to bring her to him. She jerked about in resistance but was greeted with another vicious slap and shoved to the ground.

"You know what's worse than a Chōsen bitch? A Chōsen bitch that needs to be humbled." The soldier stood above her, pointing the bayonet of his rifle at Jung-Soon's throat.

"Strip."

Jung-Soon rose to her feet, wiping the dirt from her hands. She met the soldier's eyes and spat on his face. Surprised by her boldness, he dragged the back of his hand across his cheek to wipe away the slug of her saliva. He then jerked his arm back as if to strike her once again but turned to the crying children instead. In a forceful swoop, he pried Young-Ho from his sisters and kicked him to the ground. The boy's head struck the dirt with a dull thump. Young-Ho howled, pained confusion contorting his face. The soldier pointed his bayonet at him.

"Stop! Please, stop!" Jung-Soon shouted, regret for her impulsive act rising through with bile in her throat. "I'll do what you say."

Young-Ho's gasping bawls went unchecked as Jung-Soon unbuttoned her blouse and let it slide from her shoulders.

With the haze of violence fogging his vision, Geum-Jin groaned as blood drooled out of his mouth. Blurred shapes melted into sounds before his eyes came into focus on the burn scars of his wife's bare shoulder and the unbuckling of a belt. Rage hammered through his pulse as he screamed and tried to lunge out of the policemen's arms. He was no longer a body but misfortune itself, set to annihilate any wretch in his path.

As he broke free, a roaring flash of orange leapt out of the trees and made a shuddering landfall in the yard. The mustachioed soldier did not have a chance to react before he was knocked onto his back and the jaw of a large, tailless tiger ripped into his throat.

When the armed men grasped the reality of the beastly apparition, they started to shoot. The tailless creature pounced away from their bullets as she hunted for more flesh. Amid the tiger's lunges at the men in uniform, Geum-Jin and Jung-Soon rushed toward their children, screaming at them to run. One of the soldiers—having just dodged a lethal swipe of the tiger's claws—grabbed hold of Young-Sook and bolted downhill, hoping to escape the beast and retain a prize.

Jung-Soon charged after her abducted daughter but was halted by a bayonet skewering into her soft stomach. The sound of her eldest's name dissolved in her throat as she gasped for a breath that choked on a gurgle of blood.

Unearthly bellows surged from Geun-Jin's wretched mouth as he threw himself on the soldier who had impaled his wife. For Geum-Jin, there was no longer any sound, any sight, any sensation but the imminent demise of the man squirming beneath him, spit flying from his red, struggling face. He grabbed a large rock from the ground and bashed it into the soldier's head. Still, the soldier stirred. He swung the rock again until the bone gave away with a crack. He raised the rock once more in an arc of pure momentum, though it did not find the soldier's skull. Instead, the rock tumbled from Geum-Jin's grip when a bullet ripped through his temple and spurted a trail of blood in its exit. His slack body thumped on the soil, vacant of all its propulsive anger.

A deafening roar rattled the bones of the sunbathed soldiers, children, and corpses, curbing all movement within the vibrations of its rage. In the same breath, the tiger sank her fangs into the arm of the soldier who had fired his rifle. The soldier had not yet cried out in pain when the tiger wrenched back with such power she tore his arm free of its socket.

Jung-Soon, body and blood spilled into the ground, rasped at her remaining children. "Run! Go, now! As far as you can!"

Young-Ja, frozen, clutched her wailing brother's hand before the prone shell of her mother, words liquefying into garbled noise. Young-Ho's howls crescendoed amid bursts of gunshots. *Breathe*, she wished to tell him, *this isn't really happening*. But her words would not surface. Her brother's shrill anguish hung unbroken in their sunny yard, drowning out her mother's fading pleas to run.

"Please . . . go." Jung-Soon struggled to lift her lips from the soil. Young-Ja felt as if she were sinking into the earth, beneath the echoes of her brother's screams, beneath her mother's ebbing scratches in the dirt. Only Young-Ho's hand anchored her to the frenzy of the yard until a bullet that missed the tiger tore through the boy's heart, silencing him mid-gasp. As his corpse slumped to the ground, Young-Ja dropped with him. Father, mother, brother, she would join in the earth. She shut her eyes and curled into her fallen kin. What she could not see, she did not have to accept.

The dirt at Young-Ja's nose yielded under the heavy thud of a paw. She opened her eyes to the tiger looming overhead, breath wet and hot, pupils so contracted her yellow eyes seemed ablaze. Viscera dripped from her teeth and reddened muzzle. She tensed her tremendous frame into a crouch, fur and tail stub raised electric before lunging at Young-Ja with a grotesque roar. The earth, the air, the sky, all shook with the tiger's sorrow, the sound jolting through its remaining witnesses. *Leave this place*, she seemed to cry, *only death awaits us here*. Young-Ja faced the beast, awash in the roar. There, in the yellow abyss of the tiger's eyes, she at last met with horror and began to run.

Young-Ja fled into the woods. Thunderous shots continued to reverberate in her chattering teeth. She held no thoughts but to run. She did not notice that the roars subsided, overtaken by blasts of gunfire. Her legs continued to carry her deep into the woods and up the mountain, going beyond the periphery of what was permitted to her before. She ran up the peaks and down their other sides. She ran through water, on stone, across sand. She ran as her feet bled. She ran as the air escaped her lungs. She ran until her tears evaporated and she was no longer a girl, no longer a body in pain, merely forward momentum shot from a years-taut sling. She ran until darkness overtook her and gunshots stopped ringing in her ears. Until she was alone.

PART II
SONG YOUNG-JA
송영자
松永子

CHAPTER NINE

Cheonan, Chōsen, Empire of Japan, 1931

A tigress slinks to the pond. She crouches at its edge and breaks the surface of the water with the tips of her whiskers and long pink tongue. Her yellow eyes are not downcast as she drinks but aimed straight ahead, staring through pupils that enlarge as the sun sets. A large rope as thick as a tree trunk descends from the heavens, crashing into the water. The tigress creeps forward to examine the apparition. She steps into the pond to sniff the rope before leaping onto it. Her claws catch on the woven strands and she begins to climb, ascending into the sky until she is but a pinprick, barely perceivable from the ground. From her pinprick flickers a light, one of many scattered throughout the night sky.

"*Okita.*"

"*Daijōbu, shinpai shinaide.*"

There were no more stars when Young-Ja woke, but wooden rafters that buttressed a low ceiling. Two pairs of watery brown eyes peered down at her through age-worn faces whose wrinkled contours obscured their gender. They spoke to her softly in the language she was not taught, their words filtered through a haze that veiled her ears and eyes.

"*Mizu wo nomu?*"

"*Kanojo wo nemuraseta hou ga ii.*"

A soft hand wiped away the sweat on Young-Ja's forehead.

"*Soudane. Jya, oyasuminasai.*"

She closed her eyes again and sank into the pain radiating through her body, from the ache in her back down to the burning stings on her legs and feet. In the darkness beneath her eyelids her mind pulsated louder than her wounds, looping blood spray and screams until she could not distinguish where and whether she was. She wished for darkness, for nothingness, for the release of silence.

Retired textile merchant Uchida Masaharu and his wife, Seiko, left for Chōsen three days before the Kantō earthquake claimed the lives of everyone they knew. Believing their timely departure to be a blessing from God, they disembarked on the peninsula toward the cheap land they acquired in the small town of Cheonan. The area was not known for its agriculture, but with three families working their rice paddies, the Uchidas would never have to labor again in their old age. They were determined to put their losses behind them and savor their remaining years in relative ease. Both—though especially Seiko—believed there was honor in benevolence, and although Chōsenjin were mostly uneducated and unrefined, the couple made an effort to show charity to their tenant farmers. They exacted less of the harvest for rent than their younger neighbors, and would even gift the farmers' children little sweets Seiko picked up at the market. Masaharu thought that attending to the children was going too far, but he allowed his lonely wife her indulgence.

Masaharu and Seiko had issues conceiving and were unable to bring life into the world. The Uchida family were quick to place blame on Seiko, believing her weak constitution and narrow hips to be the cause of Masaharu's misfortune. Seiko bore the humiliation in silence for she did not think she could leave—no other man would accept what a low-level merchant discarded as barren. But even as Masaharu bedded the mistresses his family arranged for him, no children came, and the Uchida couple were left childless into their old age. By then Masaharu and Seiko had long become accustomed to each other in all the banalities of familiarity. While love never took root between them, time forged their proximity into habit until one could not imagine life without the other.

For nearly eight years, Masaharu and Seiko took their daily morning stroll in Cheonan, following the creek on their property line at the foot of the mountain. When they spotted a corpse half sunk into the creek, Masaharu tried to steer his gasping wife away from the sight. Upon closer inspection they saw that the corpse was a girl with shallow breath and grave injuries—Seiko implored her husband to do something. The girl was not so little that the elderly couple could carry her back to their home on their own, so they called for one of their tenant farmers to pluck her out of the creek and take her inside.

The girl slept four nights, running a fever and fighting off infections from the gashes on her feet and legs. Seiko bathed her and sat by her side, whispering to the girl as she floated in and out of consciousness in paroxysms of mumbles and screams. She named her Kiyoko—pure child—for her round, naive face. When Kiyoko woke, she trembled and cried, refusing to speak or eat. Seiko continued to tend to her nonetheless, viewing her as a stray kitten that could be tamed with steady enticements of food, shelter, and patience. Kiyoko at least would not run for the time being. Wet scabs were still clotting on the bottoms of her tender feet and confined her to a modest radius of space beyond her futon.

After a month of tearful bedrest, Kiyoko shuffled into the kitchen where Seiko was preparing breakfast. Seiko ran to brace the girl at her elbows and steady her still frail balance.

"Is there anything you want?" she asked Kiyoko. "Tell me what you need."

The girl looked up, eyes brimming wet with uncertainty. Seiko tried to usher her toward a chair in the corner when the girl said something in a soft, hesitant voice. She bent down to hear what the child was muttering and caught a single word.

"... cha ..."

"Tea? You want tea?" Seiko repeated the word back to the girl, who nodded and gave Seiko the first sign of understanding she had been trying to coax out for the last month. Encouraged by the interaction, Seiko assembled all the necessary materials—a pot, several boxes of tea leaves, cups. When she filled the pot with water and set it on the fire, Kiyoko tugged at her sleeve and gently pushed her away. She gestured from Seiko to the chair and the old woman understood that the girl meant to prepare the tea herself. Delighted by her initiative, Seiko sat and watched the serious child sniff at the tea leaves to make her choice of brew. Her movements were deliberate and learned. There was a knowing confidence to how long she waited for the boiling water to simmer down before steeping the tea, then again before serving it.

Seiko received the cup into her cold hands. She smiled at Kiyoko and lifted the tea to her lips, its woody aroma richer than any she had been able to induce from the leaves before. As the liquid heated her tongue and flowed down her throat, grief spilled into her and displaced the breath from her lungs. She wept. She cried for the children she did not have, she cried for the love she never found, she cried for the family she lost to the maw of the shaking earth in her homeland. She cried for little Kiyoko, her pitiful state, her aloneness. In receiving this tea, Seiko unknowingly drank from the well of the girl's unspeakable sorrow and shed it as her own. The old woman's life, unfulfilled, stood as a ready vessel for the burdens of another life lived too quickly, of another life so fractured it could no longer sustain itself. Unable to take another sip, Seiko set the cup down and took Kiyoko into her arms. She breathed in the warm scent of the child's head and let her tears soak into her long black hair. The child, too, unfurled in the safety of the embrace, her wet sorrow staining Seiko's kimono.

When the old woman calmed, she walked to Masaharu reading a newspaper in the drawing room and declared that Kiyoko would be staying with them as their child. He grunted in assent.

Young-Ja's knuckles reddened from kneading the yeot taffy she made of fermented rice and barley malt. She pulled at the warm batter, continually stretching and folding to keep it from hardening. This toil burned the muscles in her forearms and fingers, but the rhythmic physicality helped to quiet her racing mind. When the yeot had been sufficiently worked, she rolled it into narrow cylinders over the walnuts she had harvested and chopped earlier that morning. Her mind flickered to Young-Ho and the time he lost a loose tooth to one of the sticky yeot candies their mother had brought home from the market. He had cried, clutching the wet yeot piece that held his tooth, his mouth a large oval of blood and foamy sugar. Young-Sook ran over to hug him and praise his courage with a voice nearly as assuring as their mother's. Young-Ja let the memory leave through her fingertips as quickly as it had come, trying not to dwell on the unachievable desire to share this fresh batch of sweets with her lost siblings.

With her yeot candies in a basket, Young-Ja followed Mr. and Mrs. Gil to the market. The Gils were mild-mannered tenant farmers on what was now Uchida land—their family had tended to the rice paddies there for generations on behalf of an absent landlord before the Japanese came and stripped the former Joseon yangban of their property. Since the morning Mr. Gil was ordered to carry Young-Ja into the Uchida home three years ago, they took pity on the girl. As they watched the Uchidas dress her in kimono, give her a Japanese name, and speak to her in their tongue, the Gils made a habit of calling on her so that she might have opportunities to hear her own language. Young-Ja was reserved at first, devoid of the playfulness they would have expected of a child her age. But over time, she eased around them, eventually taking interest in accompanying them to the market where they sold their rice. The Gils let Young-Ja roam around the nearby stalls while they tended to their sales, watching her brighten as she perused the market's offerings. Young-Ja came by their choga house a few days later with a small package of yeot she had made to thank them for taking her to the market. Stunned by the exquisite taste of the candies, they encouraged her to make more and sell it, imploring the Uchidas to let them chaperone the child whenever she wanted to go into town.

Young-Ja's yeot had become famous across the Cheonan central market in the last three years. Everyone came to the Gils' rice stand to look for the yeot girl who sometimes made an appearance with new flavors of candy at a good price. People clamored for the taste, lauding her as an angel who had descended from above with a sample of a heavenly banquet. Very few seemed to notice that these confections were the cause of their intense pangs of nostalgia. The first woman to try Young-Ja's new ginger yeot became so awash with thoughts of her mother that she closed up her busy restaurant and traveled two days on foot to visit her. An old scholar wept when a yeot piece melted on his tongue, lost in the acute longing to see his childhood home in Daegu—everyone who saw him believed he was simply compelled to tears by the delicious flavor. The yeot moved children to stop squabbling with their siblings and even the stoniest of men to express their gratitude to their families in unusual fits of inspiration.

With walnuts in season for the fall, Young-Ja looked forward to selling her new yeot creation. She had grown to enjoy the praise lavished on her by her customers. Anticipation of this flattery drove her to experiment with new flavors that could rouse delight and keep the townspeople coming back for more. This demand for something only she could provide made Young-Ja feel needed. There was safety in being needed, a safety in serving. With each piece of yeot that sold she assured herself she would not so easily lose the footing she had found in Cheonan.

Several people had already started to gather near the Gils' stand hoping for Young-Ja's appearance. Among them was a striking man in a dark, Western-style suit. Mrs. Gil blushed as she showed him their rice, offering to sell it at a fair price. The man smiled, revealing straight white teeth. The tan complexion around his large brown eyes was smooth, and his thick black hair was swept back in a stylish cut. Young-Ja had never seen anyone who looked like him before. He regarded the Gils' rice for a moment before turning to the pile of yeot in Young-Ja's basket. He curled his lips and bent down to address the twelve-year-old girl.

"How are you today, little lady? I've heard about your sweets and would like to try some." He rubbed a few coins together between his fingers and flashed his teeth.

Young-Ja lowered her gaze from the bold stranger's and handed him a few pieces of yeot wrapped in paper.

"Nothing to say?" He continued to examine her face with a knowing smile.

Young-Ja looked away and squeaked out a no, accepting his coins in her hand. He popped a candy into his mouth and contemplated her in silence a little while longer before walking away, turning curious heads in his wake.

A flurry of gossip possessed the vendors as they tried to uncover the identity of the dapper newcomer. After a day of widespread inquiry, people knew of him as Baek Yong-Woo, a merchant who had become rich through his connections in China and Japan. Those drawn to scandal even ventured to say Baek Yong-Woo was visiting Joseon now to oversee his opium poppy farms and their shipments to Manchuria. Whatever his reason for coming to Cheonan, the ladies of the market paid extra mind to combing their hair and straightening out their skirts should he decide to stop by their stalls.

Every time Baek Yong-Woo came to the market, he would check to see if he could acquire more of the famous Cheonan yeot. He would linger and try to talk to the young vendor, asking her whether she had help making it, where she had learned her recipes, what inspired her craft. The market women noticed this interest and would also cluster around the Gils' rice stand in bids to catch the man's eye. And while Young-Ja did not need help to sell all her sweets before the day's end, Baek Yong-Woo's easy smiles and winks guaranteed an audience that was just as eager to consume all her offerings within the morning.

When Young-Ja returned home from the market, she placed her earnings into Masaharu Ojii-san's money box and set about her chores. She tied back the sleeves of her kimono and took the laundry out to the creek to wash. On her way back to the house, she saw Ojii-san watching her through the window. She smiled and bowed, eager to show him that she was hard at work hanging laundry in the yard. After picking out some greens from the garden to dress up for dinner, she returned inside to tidy up and cook. Heartened by the quick yeot sales that day, Young-Ja was relieved to be in the proper state of mind for meal preparation. Neither Ojii-san nor Obaa-san would be troubled with any unwelcome heaviness shed into her cooking that night. They might even enjoy their meal so much that they would request the same dishes again.

At dinner, Young-Ja spoke to her grandparents about her day at the market. She made an effort to animate her speech and add flourishes that made the stories more interesting, knowing that this little performance would amuse the kind couple who had taken her in when she thought all was lost. Seiko Obaa-san praised her improving Japanese while Masaharu Ojii-san corrected her grammatical mistakes. When it was time for bed, Young-Ja brewed the root tea her father taught her to make and served it with a smile to the old couple before she retired into her own room.

Young-Ja took a deep breath as she changed into her sleeping garments, grateful for another day without incident. No one had wept as soon as her tea touched their lips. No one had recoiled from the taste of food she had accidentally steeped in thoughts of her family's violent demise. No truly bad spells had occurred in over a year—at age twelve, she had become much more careful to contain herself, or to stay clear of the kitchen when she could not. Above all, she had learned to keep busy enough so her mind simply could not make space for despair. Young-Ja was starting to allow herself the belief that she was, in fact, not a burden to the Uchidas. That as long as she masked her sorrow and stopped it from disturbing others, Ojii-san and Obaa-san would not throw her out. She would not have to be alone again.

Despite all the cheer Young-Ja could muster for her grandparents during waking hours, she still dreaded the night. Without the rest of the world to keep her centered on the immediate present, her mind would drift to that final day. Young-Sook was letting Young-Ho braid her hair while her father tended to the bellflowers in the garden. Her mother was humming inside the house getting dressed for town. If the images ever shifted from that sunny morning to the devastation of the soldiers' arrival, Young-Ja would cry out and shake her head as if the movement could prevent the terrible thoughts from dropping anchor in her mind.

Young-Ja did not understand why her family had been taken from her, one by one. Why she had run and ended up the only one to survive. Would it have been better to stay and let the tiger or the soldiers kill her? To die alongside her loved ones? That day had been so inexplicably monstrous she wondered at times if it had happened at all, if it were all just a nightmare of a family that had never existed. Perhaps she had fabricated memories of her mother's courage, her father's tenderness, her sister's patience, her brother's affection. It was less painful to think she had imagined her family than to know she had lost them. To know she had fled as they lay dying at her feet. With each night that passed, the contours of their faces started to blur in her mind. Young-Ja would squeeze her eyes shut trying to remember her father's crooked nose, the spiderweb of her mother's scar. Some nights she could not summon her siblings' faces or voices in her mind and she would cry herself to exhausted sleep.

That night, her howling thoughts had started to fade into slumber when the door opened and someone entered her room. Obaa-san would sometimes hear her crying and check on her, but this was not Obaa-san's soft tread.

Ojii-san sat down beside her. He ran his fingertips down her hair and crept under the covers. A firmness pressed against Young-Ja's back as his bony fingers gripped her shoulder. She tried to get up and ask what he was doing. He placed his hand over her mouth.

"Shh, be quiet," he whispered.

Young-Ja froze as Ojii-san stirred, grunting softly and tapping the back of her sleeping garment until his motions came to a halt. He laid in silence for some time and crept out as quickly as he had crept in.

Young-Ja did not sleep. When sunlight misted into her room she rose to put away the covers. A wet stain marked where the old man had lain. She bunched up the bedding and rushed toward the creek to launder away the evidence. While walking she felt an unfamiliar sensation between her legs and crouched by the creek to discover a red-brown paste smeared on her thighs. Startled, she plunged her body into the creek with her arms full of the soiled bedding. When she emerged drenched from the cold water, Young-Ja could not tell where the creek started and her tears ended. When Seiko stepped out to see what was causing the early morning splashing, she saw Kiyoko crying and wiping between her legs—she knew to run inside and retrieve a cotton cloth for her beloved child to wrap around her maturing body.

That night, Young-Ja laid in her covers terrified that Ojii-san would return. She held her blanket tight and kept her eyes open until she could no longer fight off her fatigue. He did not appear. In the following days, Masaharu Ojii-san behaved as his usual self—reticent yet gentle, and mostly uninterested in her until all three in the household sat down for their dinner conversation. When Young-Ja finally started to think that she had perhaps imagined the dreadful nighttime visit, Ojii-san showed up in her bedroom again.

Seiko was always the first to fall asleep and the first to wake. Her sleep had become shallow in her old age—she learned that it was best to keep still in the night so as not to chase away her slumber with a restless body. The newfound sense of purpose that came with Kiyoko's arrival had helped Seiko find peace through more of her nights, but the falling autumn temperatures were stoking a chill in her bones that brought back the disruptions to her rest. When she first noticed Masaharu's midnight absence from bed, she did not think much of it. After it persisted over several nights, however, her curiosity overrode her instinct to keep still and she followed him out of the bedroom. Her breath caught when she saw him slip into Kiyoko's room. She stood, facing the door in the dark, knowing what she must do.

When Kiyoko came into the kitchen to start breakfast, Seiko was already tending to the fire.

"Don't worry about breakfast, little one. I'll be serving you today."

Seiko grilled some mackerel she had picked up at the market—Kiyoko's favorite—and served it with freshly made rice and miso soup. The two ate in the kitchen, sharing gentle smiles in between bites. Kiyoko started to wash the dishes after they finished eating but Seiko stopped her, explaining that they could clean up together after coming back from the market. Holding hands, the pair walked to the tailor and bought a new coat for the girl. Kiyoko tried to stop Seiko from her extravagant purchase, but the old woman insisted that its warm wool would be useful for the coming winter. Kiyoko smiled and donned her new navy-blue coat with its shiny black buttons.

They strolled around the market after leaving the tailor. Seiko was not partial to sweets, but anytime a sugary treat caught Kiyoko's eye, she pulled out a few coins to gift her a sample. Once they finished a lap around the stalls, Seiko walked Kiyoko to a small office at the edge of the main market strip. Inside was a man looking for young girls to work at factories—with Japan engaged in numerous war efforts against China and the Soviet Union, the need for manufacturing labor was high. The recruiter glanced at Kiyoko's short figure.

"Not what we're looking for. Too young, too inexperienced."

"She's a quick learner," said Seiko, "and she works very hard."

"No, too runty. Give her at least another year."

As Seiko continued to argue, Kiyoko lowered her head, her chin tucked into her chest as tears streamed down her pink cheeks.

Unable to convince the man, Seiko stepped out of the office and reached for Kiyoko's hand. The girl had her hands tucked into her new coat and made no show to take them out. Seiko knelt down and cupped her palms on Kiyoko's drooped shoulders. She sighed and moved to explain herself when a clean-cut young man in a black suit approached. By his familiar greeting, he seemed to know Kiyoko already, but he addressed the older woman in polite, unaccented Japanese.

"Madam, if you're looking to put the girl to work, I could take her. My business is in need of someone who can cook and clean."

Seiko stood to regard the man's genial, monied appearance. She searched his eyes for deceit and found none; whether due to its true absence or the limits of her perception, she would never know, though she would spend the remainder of her life convincing herself of the former. She pulled Kiyoko into a tight embrace and pressed her nose into the child's warm scalp a final time. She then nodded at the man before hurrying away without another word.

"Obaa-san," Kiyoko cried out. "Don't go! I'm sorry, I'll work harder! I'll be a good girl!"

Seiko's chest tightened at her beautiful child's wails, grateful that the man held the girl in place. She did not know how to live without Masaharu after so many decades, but she would not let Kiyoko come to harm under their roof. She did not know what else to do, so she continued home, knowing she would not be able to keep walking if she looked back.

CHAPTER TEN

Railway from Chōsen to Manchukuo, Empire of Japan, 1934

The train shook as it clacked forward. Young-Ja sat with her feet up on the seat, her hands clasped at her shins, forehead against her knees. Nausea tickled her throat. She blinked away her tears and tried not to look at the blur of passing landscape through the window. Her mind dashed through all the things she should have done not to upset Obaa-san. If she had worked harder to complete her chores or prepare food untainted by her distress, if she had brought in more money from her yeot sales. If she had barricaded her door at night, or fought Ojii-san off like she wanted to. Then Obaa-san would not have blamed her and thrown her away. She would not be alone again.

Baek Yong-Woo presented Young-Ja with a yakgwa cookie and some water from his canteen. She did not budge. She had not spoken a word since she came into his charge, and barely seemed to register where she was going. He did not know what compelled the old Japanese woman to give her up, or how the girl had come to be under her care in the first place, but he recalled the woman's reluctant shaking as she released Young-Ja from her embrace, the pleading in her eyes.

"You know, I also grew up without my parents," said Yong-Woo. "But I learned how to make money and take care of myself. Life works out." He paused, waiting for the girl to react. She did not, so he continued.

"You're quite the gifted young woman. We're going to a place where your talents will help many people in Joseon."

Young-Ja lifted her head and examined the man sitting across from her. He bit into the yakgwa she had not taken and flashed his straight teeth. She fidgeted with the hem of her coat and let her eyes lose focus on the grainy wood of the train floor. Yong-Woo continued to talk at her. He asked whether she could read, how much Chinese she knew, how much time it took for her to pick up Japanese. He asked if she had ever left Cheonan before. After some more failed attempts to wrest conversation from the girl, Yong-Woo admitted defeat and opened a newspaper. The two sat in silence for some time until Young-Ja whispered something Yong-Woo's ear could not quite catch. He set aside the paper and leaned forward—he smelled like fresh pine needles—and Young-Ja repeated her whisper.

"I need to pee."

Yong-Woo chuckled. "Is that why you look so miserable? It's not good to hold it in for so long." He gestured to the end of the car. "There's a toilet in the lavatory compartment there."

Young-Ja stood up—faltering for a second to catch her balance on the moving train—and walked to the back of the car. She opened the door to a cramped room with a toilet in the corner: a small wooden bench with a hole in the middle.

Young-Ja had never seen a toilet quite like this before and wondered why it was raised so high from the ground. She gathered up the skirt of her kimono, tucked the fabric into the obi, and stepped up onto the seat to squat over the hole. As she relieved herself, a sudden rush of water ran inside the seat. She yelped at the unexpected cascade, losing her balance and slipping her left foot into the hole. The water soaked into her sock and wooden sandal as she stared down in disbelief. She cried out, not understanding what she had done wrong.

A knock at the door made Young-Ja jump down from the toilet. She folded down her skirt from her obi, shame staining her cheeks.

"Are you all right?" It was Baek Yong-Woo's rich tenor.

Young-Ja let out a defeated squeak.

He tried again: "Would you like some help?"

The girl opened the door, cheeks and neck flushed red. Yong-Woo appraised the scene with a gentle smile. He helped her take off her wet sock and poured clean water over it from his canteen. He wiped her feet with a handkerchief he pulled from his jacket.

"Next time, you just need to sit on the seat. Some modern toilets flush water to wash away the impurities, that's all."

Young-Ja listened as she clutched Yong-Woo's sleeve, balancing on one foot while the other dried. Her breath steadied and she leaned into him, trusting he would support her weight.

Young-Ja exited the train into Gyeongseong Station and stood paralyzed. She did not know buildings could be so large, that man could construct domes so high and ornate. The platform was the busiest place she had ever seen, filled with bellowing machines and swelling waves of people shooting off in all directions. Her eyes bounced between the travelers bustling about in an array of different attire. Men in Western suits and hats checked their pocket watches. Others in hanbok wove through the thick crowd. Attendants carried bags behind women in colorful kimono. The only common theme Young-Ja could see from the busy tableau was that everyone was determined to be in a hurry.

Baek Yong-Woo whistled and cocked his head, beckoning her to follow. She ran to his side and clung to his jacket—she needed to hold something if they were to enter the fray of the crowd. Unlike the familiar herds of white hanbok in the Cheongju or Cheonan markets, this swarm felt inscrutable, a kinetic energy of complex adult concerns and desires Young-Ja could not parse. Her eyes darted around until they caught a line of tan uniforms marching toward them, rifles in hand. Young-Ja gasped and jumped behind Yong-Woo, gripping his jacket so tight he stumbled to a halt.

"Hey, careful, I almost tripped." Yong-Woo tried to turn and address the girl, but she held fast, her face buried into his back. He glanced at the passing soldiers and stood still, waiting until they disappeared into the crowd to address his companion.

"It's okay, they're gone."

Young-Ja did not budge.

"Listen, you've done nothing wrong. They're not going to do anything to you." Yong-Woo patted her shoulder and gently released her hold on his jacket. He squeezed her hand and bent down to meet her eyes.

"Just stick with me and you'll be fine." He smiled as Young-Ja gave a slight nod.

Young-Ja kept her eyes on the ground as Yong-Woo led her by the hand through the station. She was content to stare at shoes the rest of the trip if it meant she could avoid meeting the gaze of soldiers. But as they traversed deeper into the crowded space, Yong-Woo pulled her in brisk zigzags, bumping around the rush of travelers looking for their next train. When Young-Ja finally looked up so as not to collide into anyone, she froze. She faced two tall men deep in conversation. They had pale skin; light, sunken eyes; and tufts of sorghum-colored hair growing under their large noses. Young-Ja did not know people could look like this. She stared at the alien sight, not realizing she had come to a pause and was no longer holding Yong-Woo's hand. When a loud train whistle jerked her out of her gawking, she panicked, looking around for her companion in the horde. Yong-Woo tapped her on the back and explained that those two men were Europeans, that she could gape at more of them where they were going. Young-Ja blushed at having been caught in her indiscretion and took his hand again to board the next northbound train.

"Looks like you're quite interested in people," said Yong-Woo after they found their seats. He had been watching the girl's obvious awe with amusement and was glad to see her recover from whatever the sight of soldiers had brought on earlier.

"I didn't know there were so many types," admitted Young-Ja.

"They may all look different, yes, but people are more alike than you think." Yong-Woo looked around. He motioned at Young-Ja to sit next to him and directed her attention to the back of the train car. "For example, see that old woman in the blue kimono? Now look at the young man in the hanbok there, a few seats down from her. Look carefully and tell me what you think makes them similar."

Young-Ja considered for a moment before looking up at Yong-Woo with doubt etched in her brow.

"They're not similar at all," she said.

"Keep looking."

Young-Ja assessed the old woman and the young man. The graying woman appeared impassive, patiently waiting for the train to depart. Her kimono was a simple dark blue, but of a fine material. Japanese, of course, but likely rich. The young man was smoothing down his jeogori and watching the person walking past him in the aisle. His appearance looked clean enough, but his hanbok seemed too large, as if it were not made for him.

Young-Ja shared these observations with Yong-Woo. He praised her perceptiveness but did not yet seem satisfied with her answer. He encouraged her to imagine what they might be thinking based on their actions.

"How could I know what they're thinking?"

"Just try it."

The old woman was sitting by the aisle, knuckles white from clutching a handkerchief. She raised the cloth to wipe the sweat on her forehead, though it was autumn and the temperature was not high enough to induce perspiration. The old woman also kept looking down at her feet and shutting her eyes for long periods of time.

"That's better," said Yong-Woo, grading her additional details. "But how would you describe her emotional state?"

"She looks . . . nervous?" Young-Ja ventured with hesitation.

Yong-Woo smiled and hummed in assent. "And what about him?"

The young man swiveled his head, looking at the passengers walking by him in the aisle. Stray hairs that had come loose from his topknot flitted around in his constant shifting. He pushed himself as close to the window as possible and threw short glances outside. He tapped at the windowsill and could not seem to keep still.

"He looks nervous too."

"Very good, little lady. They're both nervous because it's their first time traveling on their own."

Young-Ja gasped, impressed with Yong-Woo's deduction.

"How can you tell that just by looking at them?"

"I overheard the man ask for directions earlier, and watched that woman be dropped off at the train station by her son."

Young-Ja wrinkled her nose and threw him an incredulous look.

"That's cheating—you said to find their similarities by looking at them. You overheard them so you already knew the answer."

"Hearing is a part of seeing, little lady." Yong-Woo smiled and shrugged. "With practice you can learn how to read people too. In the meantime, I recommend that you watch people's hands. You can always tell a lot by the hands."

Young-Ja spent the ride to Pyongyang scrutinizing the other passengers, a welcome distraction from her woes. She crafted elaborate stories about their character in her head, surprised how easily the conjectures came with each additional detail her eyes picked up. She had never thought to assume a narrative of others' emotions, to extrapolate their inner lives. How much had she missed in the past when all she focused on was herself, on how she might better please others with what she served? Would she have been able to pick up Masaharu Ojii-san's intentions by paying more attention? If she could look into the eyes of the soldiers from that morning, would she be able to understand their reasons for what they did?

"Your eyes will fall out of your head if you stare so hard."

Yong-Woo and his evergreen grin looked down at the girl. "You should be more subtle with your gaze. Most people don't like to feel watched by people they don't know, and often, even the people they do."

Young-Ja stared at her hands in her lap, hesitant to look up again lest she make another mistake.

"Public life's a performance," he continued. "If you want to be able to read people, you must make them think their actions are private. People will be quicker to reveal their true selves if they think no one's watching."

After arriving in Pyongyang, the traveling pair made another transfer and rode through the stark mountains of northern Joseon before crossing the border into Manchukuo. A few years prior, only some months after the Uchidas adopted Young-Ja, the Japanese military had sought to vilify zealous Chinese dissidents by setting off a small explosion on the railroad near Mukden. Crying foul at the unruly local terrorists they blamed for destroying law and order, the Japanese fabricated an excuse to invade northeast China. There, they established Manchukuo, touted to be a harmonious, modern state of industry and racial unity where Japanese, Koreans, Chinese, Manchus, and Mongols could live under the benevolent rule of an adolescent Chinese emperor. Behind the thin smokescreen of this throne, however, Japan exerted its military control over mainland Asia as the self-ordained superior of all Eastern peoples. Throngs of loyal subjects were shipped to Manchukuo to lock in this control.

The train Young-Ja rode was filled with university-educated Japanese who had learned Chinese in school—this alone qualified them for prestigious posts in the new government despite many of them having spent the last decade ruminating on classical poetry or Qing dynasty ceramics. Japanese of humbler backgrounds were still eager to resettle in Manchukuo, having been promised large swaths of farmland or better-paying industry jobs. Koreans had little choice: many were forced to the north to provide cheap labor to the growing number of factories and mines. They rode in the third-class or cargo cars in the back of the train where they would not inconvenience Japanese passengers.

Engrossed in her observations, Young-Ja lost track of how many hours they traveled, waiting in stations, transferring trains, bouncing on rickety seats. Her eyelids fluttered as fatigue set in. Her vision focused on a man in a deep-maroon changshan whose eyes grazed hers before turning to the window. She did not think much of it at first, but when he stole another glance at her, she started to take notice of him. He wore round glasses and had short, combed-back hair. He was relatively thin but his broad shoulders made him appear larger than he likely was. While he looked at ease staring out the window at the passing mountains, the glimpses he cast at Young-Ja seemed laced with urgency. She grew concerned and nudged Yong-Woo, looking down at her feet while asking why he thought the man in the changshan was staring at her. Yong-Woo patted her hand.

"People might just stare back at the strange person who was staring at them first," he said. "He probably doesn't mean any harm. Rest your eyes for a bit—we have about an hour left before we transfer a final time in Mukden."

Yong-Woo folded his jacket and placed it on the long seat. "Put your head down here and relax," he said. "I need to go to the toilet—"

Young-Ja grabbed his sleeve.

"Don't worry, little lady." Yong-Woo chuckled. "I'll be right back."

Young-Ja watched Yong-Woo stroll past the man in the changshan and through the door to the next car. The man was no longer looking at her, but out the window. Her need to believe in Yong-Woo's kindness allowed her to trust that no harm would come if she set her head on his makeshift pillow and let the vibrations of the train rock her to sleep.

A large jolt in the train stirred Young-Ja awake. Baek Yong-Woo had not yet returned. She was unsure how long she had been sleeping, but not much had changed in the landscape—they were still deep in the mountains. Had something happened to him? She sat up and noticed that the man in the changshan was not in his seat. Perhaps he had confronted Yong-Woo about her staring. Or had Yong-Woo abandoned her as well? Her chest tightened and she rose to search for the only person left to her in the world.

The next car over was much statelier than where she sat. Instead of open seating, shiny doors carved from dark wood gated private compartments. Young-Ja leaned into an empty compartment to examine the luxurious carpet and plush upholstery. At the creak of an opening door she jumped out, fearing she might be rebuked for trespassing. The man in the maroon changshan had just exited the toilet by the door. He walked back toward their original car without sparing Young-Ja a single glance. The anxiety brewing in her chest started to boil over—if Yong-Woo was not in the toilet, where could he have gone? She started to pace and considered knocking on one of the closed compartments to ask if anyone had seen her companion.

"What are you doing here? I told you to stay at our seat."

Yong-Woo emerged from the same toilet that the man in the changshan had just vacated. He smoothed back his lightly tousled hair and raised an eyebrow at her. His cheeks were flushed and there was a severity in his voice that Young-Ja had not heard before. She returned to her seat with him in silence. The man in the changshan was nowhere to be seen.

The sun hazed red as it set on the distant horizon. Baek Yong-Woo promised that this was the final leg of the trip, but Young-Ja was too captivated by the expansive plains to the west to mind. Some minor mountains sat in the distance, but she had never been able to see so far across such a flat landscape. She wondered how people came to discover this place, and how they managed to build a railroad for such long distances. Her siblings' faces flickered in her mind as she imagined what their reactions might have been. Young-Ho might have been scared to walk through the station and board the train, but with his sisters by his side, he would have quickly become entranced by the passing scenery. When the train started to slow, she wished they had not arrived so she could stay immersed in her daydreams of the open earth steeped in fading sunlight.

The other passengers murmured as the train chugged to a halt. They were still far from the city and had no business pausing on this empty patch of land—had there been a mechanical failure? One man stuck his head out the window and immediately pulled himself back in, yelling that men on horseback were boarding the train. Bandits.

The car erupted in panic as people scrambled to hide their valuables. One person ran into the toilet and slammed the door. Yong-Woo grimaced but stayed calm. He patted Young-Ja's shoulder and assured her that all would be fine.

"Just keep still and quiet until they leave," he advised. "These small-time bandits usually don't want to hurt people. They're probably poor farmers struggling to make money; they'll just want to take some valuables and run home to feed their families."

The door burst open and several men armed with pistols and spears barged into the car. Passengers huddled in their seats to distance themselves from the aisle and the heavy scent of sweat now permeating the air. The bandits had tied cloths over their noses and mouths to hide their faces, though their clothes were a mishmash of different styles and colors. They yelled something in Chinese, then in Japanese.

"Money and jewelry, now! No moving! No talking!"

The men pulled out sacks to collect goods as they stalked down the aisle, reaching into pockets and grabbing what they could from the shrinking passengers. A bandit wearing a dusty, fur-lined vest over a gray changshan stopped next to Yong-Woo and barked an order at him while waving around his pistol. Yong-Woo put his hands up and responded in calm, lilting Chinese. Young-Ja held her breath to avoid the bandit's sour odor and endeavored to be still. She could not stop her terror from shaking her body, however, and hoped that the bandit would not notice. She watched his hand reach into Yong-Woo's jacket pocket and dig for his wallet. The woman in the seat ahead of them shrieked at another rogue taking her purse, but Young-Ja's eyes never left the bandit's hand lest it hurt the only sympathetic person left to her. She swore she saw a flicker of paper in that hand, as if the bandit had placed something into Yong-Woo's pocket that was not there before. When the man stepped away with the wallet, Young-Ja released her breath and looked at Yong-Woo for a sign of what to do next. He continued to stare straight ahead with his hands raised.

As soon as the bandits filed into the next car, passengers started to cry out, turning to one another with their sundry grievances.

"My God, they took Mother's necklace!"

"Shh, stay calm, what if those criminals come back?"

"How did this happen? Where's the security on this train?"

"Weren't there soldiers at the last station? Why aren't they here?"

After some time, the train started moving again—Young-Ja looked out the window to the west and saw the men fleeing on horseback into the plains. Unlike the affronted Japanese civilians in their car, Yong-Woo did not seem concerned about having been robbed and maintained his calm, easy demeanor.

After the sun disappeared into the horizon, the train finally rolled into Xinjing, the capital of Manchukuo and Young-Ja's new home for the next seven years.

CHAPTER ELEVEN

Xinjing, Manchukuo, Empire of Japan, 1934

Changchun—"long spring"—was a modest stopover between its larger, more glamorous sisters, Mukden and Harbin. When the Japanese looked to establish the capital of their new Manchurian conquest, they rejected Mukden for its sprawling Chinese palaces and Harbin for its Russian urban planning. Instead, they opted for humble Changchun, flat and amenable to expansion in whatever image its new master desired. Japanese forces marched into the Chinese city and rechristened it Xinjing—"new capital"—paying local officials handsomely to facilitate the transition. These hanjian traitors found collaboration so profitable that they were able to acquire land across the sea in Japan, securing their escape should the countrymen they betrayed ever discover the extent of their duplicity. And so the Japanese erected large modern buildings from which to administer government and military affairs on continental Asia. While the invaders were not known for their sense of humor, they liked to embellish their new structures with the Chinese roofing style as if in a cheeky nod to the ruse of nominal Sino rule: Chinese hats were worn here, but the head of the beast was Japanese.

Each place Young-Ja had passed through since leaving Cheonan was larger and stranger than the last. She had seen, heard, and smelled more in the last few days of her journey than she had in all her life. Now she rode in an automobile whose engine growled as it propelled them around cyclists and rickshaws weaving through traffic. The moon hung low in the sky. Electric lampposts cast a distorting yellow light on people teeming about parked vehicles and horses. Night shadows hollowed out the stern passing faces whose overlapping shouts and calls made Young-Ja clutch Baek Yong-Woo's jacket. She shut her weary eyes to the congestion of the large city: towering buildings, unremitting lights, crowds swarming in the night with the vim of midday.

The car slowed as it turned into a dark alley away from the chaos of the main streets. It stopped at a large wooden door where a woman with a tight gray bun stood leaning on a cane. She was tall—nearly as tall as Baek Yong-Woo—and wore a loose, dark-green qipao with a high collar. The harsh light of the lamp rendered her cheekbones severe and imposing. The woman volleyed with Yong-Woo in rapid Chinese though her eyes bored into Young-Ja as she descended from the car and walked into the building.

A dimly lit room warm with the smell of herbs lay within. "Wait here," said Yong-Woo, leaving with the old woman through another door and shutting it behind them before Young-Ja could protest.

She looked around nervously, wondering if the room had darkened in the absence of Yong-Woo's brightness. Sounds of revelry—footsteps, chatter, clatter—came muffled from beyond the walls and ceiling.

When the door opened again, it was not Yong-Woo but a young girl with braided pigtails, perhaps the same age as Young-Ja. She was holding a large wicker basket at her hip and seemed surprised to see anyone in the room.

"Nǐ shì shéi?"

Young-Ja gave her a blank look.

"What are you doing here?" she asked in Japanese after eyeing the hem of Young-Ja's kimono under her coat. Young-Ja knew neither the answer nor how to engage; in that beat of hesitation, the other girl switched into Korean.

"You Joseon?" The girl had a heavy accent but spoke with such confidence that Young-Ja could understand her meaning. "Come with Bailong? Saw him."

Young-Ja scrunched her brow in confusion at the name, but the other girl took encouragement from eliciting a reaction and continued in Korean.

"Bailong—Baek. Yong. Woo. Chinese name." She tapped her chest with her free hand and said, "Meiyu." She raised her eyebrows in such affable expectation that Young-Ja found herself whispering back her own name.

Meiyu had a small nose and large eyes that sloped downward at the outer tips, giving her the winsome face of a sleepy puppy. She chattered away in patchwork sentences, explaining that she worked in the teahouse kitchen and was learning Korean. Young-Ja was struck by the girl's unassuming cordiality. Meiyu continued to monologue, speculating that they would work together. She grabbed Young-Ja's hand and pulled her toward the door when the old woman with the cane stepped back in and barked something in Chinese. Meiyu startled into a bow and slipped away without another word.

"You may address me as Feng-nüshi. I am the master of this teahouse." The old woman switched to Korean without pause.

"Where's Mr. Baek?" Young-Ja asked, looking at the door.

"He's no longer your concern."

"Where—"

Feng-nüshi banged the stone floor with the brass tip of her cane. Its handle was a bird's head whose beak glinted sharply even in the feeble light.

"Don't talk back if you don't want to be thrown out into the street."

Power rumbled under the calm veneer of the old woman's voice. Young-Ja, too tired and shocked to resist, lowered her head in submission. Feng-nüshi gestured at her to follow. They entered a busy kitchen occupied by women in the same Chinese work clothes as Meiyu: gray tunics and trousers with maroon pankou fasteners at the neckline. Not a single woman broke focus from her labor as Feng-nüshi approached, their hands and feet gliding across the steaming clamor of the kitchen with coordinated purpose. The crawl of stolen glances nonetheless tickled at Young-Ja's neck until everything came to an abrupt halt. Young-Ja stumbled to keep from running into the unmoving Feng-nüshi ahead.

A young woman in a gray uniform quivered as she looked up at her mistress. A plated custard dessert sat on the table, a depression on its smooth surface swooping into a peak from something that had disturbed its otherwise perfect form. Feng-nüshi said something in Chinese, voice staid and low. The trembling girl wiped her saliva-slicked finger on her uniform and shook her head. Noises in the kitchen died down as other staff paused their tasks, attention sucked to the unfolding scene.

Feng-nüshi said something again and the young woman reluctantly held out her hands. Before Young-Ja could blink, Feng-nüshi grabbed the girl's right wrist, pinned it to the table, and slammed the point of her cane handle through the girl's finger.

The girl screamed. The top of her pointer finger had been severed, the segment of nail, flesh, and bone bouncing not too far from the bloody stump. Feng-nüshi released her wrist and pried the cane out of the wooden tabletop. The girl collapsed to the floor, clutching her bleeding hand with gasping sobs. Feng-nüshi swung the cane to flick the blood off its handle and banged its tip on the ground. Three women rushed in to wipe the surface clean and dispose of anything that did not belong. The sobbing girl was taken out of the kitchen. The other workers returned to their tasks, an unspoken, viscous tension hanging in the air.

"Everything has a price. Never take anything you're not ready to pay for," Feng-nüshi said in Korean.

Young-Ja reddened as they exited the kitchen into a long, empty corridor. No longer impeded by tables and working women, Feng-nüshi quickened her steps and turned at the corner, disappearing from sight. The clack of her cane was the only indication that she had not evaporated away. Young-Ja's chest thumped with fear as she broke out into a half run. She did not wish to dawdle and give Feng-nüshi another occasion to express her displeasure.

The glint of the cane ahead led her down a set of stairs into darkness. Stacks of broken furniture leaned against the cellar wall. Feng-nüshi unlocked a door and flipped the light switch to reveal a small, windowless room piled with more broken furniture. An old tatami mat and chamber pot sat in the corner. Feng-nüshi gestured for Young-Ja to step inside. She pointed her cane to a gray bundle by the door.

"That is your new uniform. You will change out of your clothes now."

Young-Ja stared, unmoving. The old woman banged her cane on the ground, forcing a gasp from the girl.

"I do not like repeating myself."

Wet heat blurred Young-Ja's vision as she shed her coat and kimono, slipping into the gray tunic. The old woman swept up the discarded clothing with her cane.

"You'll work for your keep in the morning. Laziness will be punished."

The door shut, plunging the room into black with a click of the lock, the brisk staccato of the cane fading as it retreated.

Young-Ja fell to her knees and cried out, pounding on the door that would not open no matter how many times she turned the knob.

"Mr. Baek!" she shouted as she hit her fists against the door. "Mr. Baek!"

How stupid she had been. To think that Baek Yong-Woo would not abandon her too. Of course he had left her, she had done nothing of value for him yet. She had given him even less reason than Seiko Obaa-san to keep her around.

"Obaa-san!" she yelled through tears and snot, slamming her palms on the door. "Please, someone!"

She was alone again, as alone as the day her fear sent her fleeing from home, running from the monsters that had swallowed her family. Alone again, now in an unknown land far from her own. Young-Ja knelt by the door crying out until her voice went hoarse. She crawled—tired hands throbbing—feeling her way to the tatami in the black room.

The darkness brought its usual nightmares. Curled up, Young-Ja could not fight off the final sounds of her slain father, mother, siblings. Her delirium pressed her to the cold floor, pushing the air from her lungs and the strength from her legs until exhausted sleep silenced the roaring beasts in her head.

Brass thumped against wood in two loud raps.

"Lazy girl. Wake up," came the voice from the other side of the door.

Young-Ja blinked away the remnants of last night's agony from her puffy eyes. Her stomach dropped at the dampness between her legs. She flipped on the light and scanned her surroundings for any cloth that could soak the blood on her gray work trousers and the old tatami mat. Only broken furniture sat with her in the room. Would dirtying this uniform be enough of an offense to lose a finger?

Feng-nüshi unlocked the door and eyed the bloodstains on the girl and the mat. Young-Ja dared not breathe, waiting for the cane to fall as the old woman muttered something about filth.

"Pick up the mat."

Young-Ja scrambled to obey and followed the woman up the stairs. She could at least roll up the tatami to conceal its stain, but she could do nothing to hide the dark track of blood on her trousers as she walked in front of the kitchen staff.

Feng-nüshi struck the ground twice with the tip of her cane and announced something to the gathering workers in Chinese. The other women froze and listened, eyes darting from the stain on Young-Ja's pants to the bloom of red heat splotched across her skin. Young-Ja wanted to crumble into the grout of the stone tiles beneath her feet. But the agitating gazes slid away at the conclusion of the old woman's speech, all hurrying away to resume their activities.

Feng-nüshi led Young-Ja to the walled patio outside the kitchen. Tablecloths, linens, blankets, and uniforms lay in mounds of sweat and musk next to a large tub of water.

"I don't tolerate filth. You will wash everything here, starting with what you've soiled." She hit the tub with her cane before disappearing inside.

Young-Ja exhaled, trying to relieve the pressure building behind her eyes. Mortified, she looked over her shoulders for any observers before taking off her trousers and plunging them into the water. Tendrils of murky blood dissipated in a haze. She scrubbed at the blood smear until the thin skin on her knuckles rubbed off. With her trousers hung to dry, she turned to the tatami, hoping the straw weavings would not bear permanent evidence of her poor hygiene. Blood trickled down her legs as she crouched. She hurried to rinse herself clean before further sullying the mat, hot tears welling at her lashes.

A throat cleared behind Young-Ja. When she turned, Meiyu shoved a thick, long linen cloth into her hands. Rapid questions spilled from Young-Ja about where they were, why they were there, but the braided pigtails retreated behind the door before she could express her thanks. Young-Ja wrapped the cloth around her pelvis and scrubbed the tatami mat clean before turning to sort the laundry pile.

Back aching, Young-Ja looked up at the wall enclosing her inside the patio. Its smooth stone cast a long shadow into the yard, looming much taller than anything the girl could hope to scale. Even if she could slip away from the reach of Feng-nüshi's cane, what could she do next in her indecent state? She had no money, she did not speak the language of this land, she had nowhere to go. No one in those busy streets on the other side of the wall would recognize her or care what became of her. However demeaning a prison this teahouse may be, it was her sole path to survival. For now, survival meant avoiding the humiliation of perception. Survival meant keeping her pruning fingers intact. Young-Ja toiled through the wet heft of laundry until the clack of Feng-nüshi's cane announced that she was to return inside. She reached for the pants still damp on the line, but Feng-nüshi snapped at her to leave them.

Dizzying heat flushed back into Young-Ja's face as she shrank under the kitchen women's stares. She folded into herself and kept her eyes on the ground, clutching the linen around her hips as she followed Feng-nüshi to the storage room: another cramped, windowless space with a single buzzing electric light. The shelves inside were lined from floor to ceiling with jars of spices, teas, and preserves. A low table and a massive pile of yuja citrons sat in the center of the room, releasing a fresh, sweet aroma.

"Have you made cheong before?" Feng-nüshi asked, looking down at Young-Ja.

She nodded without thinking, trying not to mind the sharp beak of the cane now so close to her soft torso.

"Then fill these empty jars with yuja cheong." Feng-nüshi tapped one of the many large empty jars stacked by the wall.

"No." Young-Ja was in no state to handle food now. "No, not now, I'm not—I can't," she said, looking up at the old woman with urgency. Young-Ja did not want to know how many fingers she would lose if she contaminated this batch of cheong with the disgrace and fear that burned on her skin. She panicked, imagining the revulsion on Feng-nüshi's face from consuming anything she made now. Feng-nüshi would no doubt throw her out then.

"Please, I'll do anything else you want me to do, just—"

"If you have not personally filled these jars with cheong by the time I return, you'll sleep tonight with fewer fingers than you woke up with this morning," said Feng-nüshi.

Young-Ja contemplated the jars for a moment before holding out her shaking hands.

"Please. Give me something else to do. Anything." Young-Ja averted her eyes. She could not bring herself to watch the fate of her outstretched hands.

Feng-nüshi raised her eyebrows but did not raise her cane.

"I won't stop at your fingers," the old woman said, voice unfazed. "I'll take them from the others in the kitchen, one for each empty jar you leave."

Young-Ja froze at the threat and lowered her hands to her side in surrender. "It won't taste good," she said lamely.

"Work quickly. Though at least here your sullied appearance won't be an eyesore." Feng-nüshi disappeared again behind the shut door.

Shame and panic radiated hot through every limb even as Young-Ja sat alone, shielded from the needling stares outside. She grabbed one of the yuja fruits and began washing it with the tears of her humiliation. She sliced the yuja into thin slivers and blinked away the errant juice spritzing out from her knife. The bright fragrance of the yuja peels seemed to mock her. She whispered to herself that she had nothing to be ashamed of as she stacked the fruit slices in the jars between layers of honey, hoping to barricade her anguish within her and keep it from spilling into the cheong. But her ears burned hot each time she pulled up the slipping linen around her hips. Her eyes blurred with tears each time she pictured herself out on the streets of a foreign land. When she sealed the final jar of cheong, enveloping thousands of yuja slices to preserve in honey and lonely shame, Feng-nüshi reappeared to march her to the next task by the metronome of her cane.

Those prickling eyes Young-Ja felt boring into her that first morning did not return to graze her skin any day thereafter. No woman met Young-Ja's eyes as she washed hundreds of bowls, pots, and cups to spotless perfection. She counted each passing day with trepidation, wondering when someone would finally taste her cheong and expose her as a problem. She had given up daydreams that Yong-Woo might return to save her, though she still looked up occasionally, searching for Meiyu's smile. But there was no warmth, no familiarity to be gleaned from the gray backs turned to her. Only Feng-nüshi loomed, ever-present, doling out punishments at each misstep.

When Young-Ja cracked an earthenware pot and destroyed a batch of long-fermenting spirits, she was locked in the storage room to make quince cheong for hours. When she spilled an expensive pot of black tea and evaded the cutting arc of the cane's beak, she was screamed at to make ginger cheong until she stopped shaking from terror. When she fell ill and overslept one morning, she was made to scrub every surface of the kitchen through the night, not allowed to rest until she produced dozens of jars of pear cheong through the weary flutters of her eyelids. Each blunder pushed Young-Ja into isolation, where she filled countless jars with fruit preserves stewed in her fear, guilt, or shame.

As the months passed, Young-Ja was surprised to find herself with a roof still over her head; she had yet to confront any accusations of poisoning. She was starting to wonder if no one was meant to consume her cheong after all, if Feng-nüshi had merely devised cheong-making as punishment for her clumsiness in the teahouse kitchen. The food preparation that had once brought her such pleasure, such pride—an unfathomably distant lifetime ago—now only brought resentment and fear. Young-Ja could only let out a hollow laugh at the thought that her cooking might bring joy to anyone anymore. As her desire to serve dissipated, so too did her desire to eat. She did not dare sample the residue of honey left on her aching fingers, lest she lose them. Her nose deadened to the fresh scent of the fruits she preserved. When she swallowed her daily bowl of millet porridge, she did it not to sate her hunger but to stop the gurgling of her empty stomach from drawing Feng-nüshi's punitive attention.

Young-Ja often cried herself to sleep in her windowless room, though even her tear ducts were at times too fatigued from the day's labor to service her sorrow. But no matter how much she trembled under Feng-nüshi's glare, she resolved not to let her tears leave her room. If she allowed herself to crumble in front of the others, she did not trust she could pick up the pieces and make herself whole again. If only she could talk to the other kitchen workers—they clearly shared her fear of Feng-nüshi. But they at least had each other, a common language to cope with whatever miserable circumstance bound them to servitude in this hell. Young-Ja had no one. She would wilt in this vile cycle of washing, slicing, and despairing until she was cast out or collapsed into her grave.

CHAPTER TWELVE

Xinjing, Manchukuo, Empire of Japan, 1935

Since the bandits' message found his pocket on the train several months ago, Baek Yong-Woo had set out to work, conspiring to obtain the Manchukuoan government's spring construction plans and train shipment schedules. His outlaw associates liked to melt back into the vices of city life for the winter but depended on intelligence from their allies with public lives to plan their raids for the new year. Yong-Woo's network of government moles and teahouse spies had kept the bandits well fed with treasure-bearing intel for several seasons. In return, the smokescreen of these marauders' apolitical thievery enabled Yong-Woo and his rebel fighters to sabotage key points of Japanese infrastructure throughout Manchukuo—supply shipments, mines, factories—without exposing their agenda.

But Yong-Woo's information brokerage was beginning to hit its limitations. A rush of Japanese officers had been shipped out to beat back the swell of guerilla resistance and bolster security around the main arteries of industry otherwise bleeding out to raids. Unable to outmaneuver their leaks, Japan had thrown bodies at the problem. Despite early tip-offs to major weapons shipments or weak points in factory security, the doubling of patrolling soldiers was making it harder for Yong-Woo and his associates to act on their intel. And so a jolt of inspired hope struck when he chanced upon the guileless yeot seller in Joseon who did not quite seem to understand the influence she wielded over others. He had since devised a tactic that could turn his Manchukuo missions in his favor, but it required the patience of a few months to mature. He was on his way to confirm the success of his idea that evening.

Fenghuang Teahouse was closed at the late hour, but its doors were always open to Baek Yong-Woo. Since emerging as the only man to outdrink Feng-nüshi one boisterous night five years ago, Yong-Woo acted as her exclusive tea merchant, using the guise of tea plantation visits to travel and engage in anti-Japanese resistance activities across Asia. Feng-nüshi thus procured news from abroad alongside the finest teas at a great discount. Yong-Woo, in turn, bought himself a professional cover and surveillance over the Xinjing teahouse's most interesting clientele. This arrangement suited both to greater satisfaction than either had anticipated.

Feng-nüshi greeted Yong-Woo's late-night arrival with a nod and ushered him into the empty kitchen. Five small dipping bowls had been laid out on a table. A piece of paper sat in front of each bowl, each bearing their own Chinese characters.

"It is as you claimed," she said as Yong-Woo sat at the table. "I've managed to get a few types from her. Judge them for yourself."

Yong-Woo dipped a clean spoon into the gold quince cheong labeled "Guilt" on the far right. As the aromatic syrup glided on his tongue he saw Young-Ja's helpless face looking up at him from the train bathroom, her foot soaked in flush water. He felt her lean on him and grasp his sleeve without a friend left in the world. Guilt surged from his stomach to his neck, choking him of his breath. He questioned his judgment in leaving the child to rot in a foreign place where she could not defend herself. All so he could commandeer her in a war she likely did not understand. His eyes widened, unfocused, as he spiraled into his mind's self-flagellation. In that heavy place he sat silent, unable to move.

Feng-nüshi tapped the beak of her cane handle near a cup of water to redirect Yong-Woo to the physical world. He grabbed the cup and gulped down its contents, trying to wash himself of the remorse caught in his throat. He shook his head clear and looked up at Feng-nüshi. She pushed the next gleaming bowl toward him. "Focus."

Yong-Woo slid a spoon into the second cheong. "Shame." A citrusy, sweet preserve with translucent yuja rinds floating in honey. Its zest plunged him into a deep memory, one he had tried to forget for nearly two decades. The handsome smile of a young man greeted him, his rising cheeks lifting a small, dark freckle under his left eye. Yong-Woo was close enough to see individual eyelashes, to feel the warmth of his breath, to smell the skin of his boyish face. Heat balled in his stomach. His groin tensed as his lips jolted from that moist, long-awaited contact. But the perfect smile so long seared into his daydreams had distorted into a frown. A look of disgust. He was pushed to the ground and that beauty turned away from him forever.

The spoon fell from Yong-Woo's hand into a clatter on the floor. Several moments of dizzying panting had passed before he realized he was running his fingers through his hair, grasping at his scalp. He gulped more water, but the phantom shame lingered with the citrus aftertaste.

"Potent, no?" Feng-nüshi mused as she refilled his empty glass.

More so than the water, this remark pulled Yong-Woo back to his present. He wondered what kind of shame someone like Feng-nüshi carried, or how she had managed to induce such an intense variant of it in a child who could not have seen many years past ten. But he knew better than to pose such questions aloud. He supposed that to feel shame was to be human, to have confronted the pain of one's inevitable smallness. He sat, ruminating in the heat that burned his ears and coiled in his stomach. Perhaps he deserved to stew in his smallness a little while longer for having forced this on an innocent youth. He believed, however, that his quest for liberation would ultimately absolve him of any intermediary sins.

The tapping of Feng-nüshi's cane goaded Yong-Woo on, reminding him that this was not the time for introspection. He nonetheless hesitated to sample the other cheong. Wary of what else might possess him, he questioned whether he needed to try the others at all when the first two had so spectacularly delivered on their promise. But he would need to know what sensations they could induce if he were to deploy them in his work.

With a deep breath he dipped into the plum cheong labeled "Sorrow." Fat tears blurred a vision of his parents' wasting bodies as they took their final cholera-ridden breaths. Yong-Woo had stood alone in this vast world since he was a boy, with no tethers left to pull him toward any home. No warmth of a familiar hand to soothe his aches. Feng-nüshi forced two glasses of water down his throat between childlike sobs of "Uhmuhni! Ah-buhji!" before Yong-Woo was able to reach for the next spoon.

With the ginger cheong labeled "Fear," he nearly fell out of his seat, recalling how he had hidden in a wooden crate sixteen years ago and watched a soldier slit his neighbor's throat. Yong-Woo could still hear the clatter of Joseon's taegeuk flag falling from her slack hands as her knees hit the ground. Trapped in memory, he did not hear the sound of his own screams splitting Feng-nüshi's kitchen. When water proved ineffective, Feng-nüshi struck him across the face to bring him back to his task.

With the pear cheong labeled "Sleep," a weight fell on Yong-Woo's eyelids and whisked him to slumber. Feng-nüshi banged her cane a finger's width from his nose to wake him again. Straining to push the heaviness from his eyes, he looked up at the old woman in a daze. She gave a curt, knowing nod and pushed the glass of water toward him with the beak handle of her cane. She, too, had sampled the five cheong and now confirmed their very visible effects in the man before her. No further discussion was needed.

The cheong were ready for use.

"Young-Ja-ssi."

The familiar scent of pine needles beckoned Young-Ja from sleep. She propped herself up from the tatami and tried to discern whether Yong-Woo was yet another apparition come to torment her. She had become so practiced in stifling hopes of his return that she did not accept the man before her was real. In a single stride he crouched down beside the girl with a smile that could not possibly have left her on her own all those months ago. Young-Ja wrapped her work-sore arms around his neck and pushed her face into his chest, her tears darkening the lapel of his suit.

"Come with me." His voice left a soft tickle in her ear.

Young-Ja was allowed her first hot bath in Manchukuo. She was given soap, an ample towel, and new clothing to wear. Cleansed of her lonely grime, she walked with Yong-Woo through the expansive main floor of the teahouse for which she had been toiling all this time. The dark lacquer of the tables gleamed empty, but even in the dimmed lighting she stood in awe of the windows' elaborate woodworking patterns. Her breath caught at the glowing beauty of the red lanterns hanging from the immensely high ceiling. Yong-Woo slowed to yield to her curiosity, allowing her to indulge in the surrounding magnificence at her own pace.

As Yong-Woo made his way up the stairs and down an empty corridor of closed doors, he inquired after Young-Ja's time at the teahouse. The girl's answers were short and unrevealing. She recited a list of duties that were to be expected in a kitchen, but made no mention of Feng-nüshi or the many agonies she had been devised to suffer in the past few months. This refusal to complain further endeared the girl to him. That she was tougher than she appeared would be to both of their advantage.

Yong-Woo opened a door at the end of the hallway and informed Young-Ja that she could sleep somewhere new for the night: a well-furnished room with a wood canopy bed. Clean sets of the gray work uniform were stacked on an unbroken chair. Yong-Woo picked up a briefcase by the door, vials of fruit preserves tinkling within.

"You've been working hard, little lady, so get some rest tonight."

"Are you going to stay here?" Young-Ja whispered.

"I have some business to take care of elsewhere, but this will continue to be your home."

The girl grabbed his sleeve. He crouched down to meet her eyes and smiled.

"I know Feng-nüshi may appear unkind, but she'll protect you while I'm gone." He was sorry to leave this round-faced girl in such distress, but he needed to test her work in the field. They needed her to keep producing. The less she knew, the less she was coddled, the easier it would be to extract what they needed from her.

"Be a good girl and work hard. I'll be back for you."

Baek Yong-Woo walked out with his clinking briefcase, leaving Young-Ja in the dark of her new ornate cage.

CHAPTER THIRTEEN

Xinjing, Manchukuo, Empire of Japan, 1935

Fukui-jichō had chosen a righteous path all his life—he excelled in school, abstained from vices, and became a respected civil engineer in Tokyo. Although he gravitated to the arts, he buried his urge to compose poetry and devoted his waking life to supporting his family. Things became difficult to maintain, however, when his father and unwed elder sister fell ill with consumption. Arranging for their care at the finest sanitorium in the country would have been beyond his means without a significant sacrifice. When the call for specialized experts came from Manchukuo, he brokered a deal—he would move out to foreign territory and dedicate himself to the success of its industry should the government pay for his family's healthcare.

As deputy director of the Industrial Department, Fukui-jichō was charged with organizing Manchukuo's industrial economy. He led projects in state infrastructure, facilitated the work of new conglomerates, and oversaw resource mining efforts. Manchukuo was at its foundation military-run, but as a civilian, he typically did not have to engage much with soldiers. This had been changing as of late, however. He was increasingly relying on Kantō-gun troops to secure their mines and infrastructure projects from guerilla sabotage. Food shortages and the currency crisis of the last few years were also pushing more of the rural poor into banditry. Quelling this rebellion and lawlessness would require coordinated military efforts.

The military officers Fukui-jichō dealt with were not as enlightened as his departmental colleagues, but they did at least present a certain degree of principled conduct. Lately, however, he was seeing alarming field reports of the Kantō-gun's delinquency. In an early report, he learned that not one but thirteen soldiers had fallen asleep midday at an important power-line construction site. Several key planning documents went missing on their watch. The government suspected opium to be the cause of this gross negligence. The soldiers were expelled from the army for falling prey to the abhorrent vice and sentenced to years of hard labor in a prison camp.

Another memo reported that soldiers had failed to defend a coal mine as Chinese outlaws set off explosives at its entrance. Fukui-jichō sent in laborers from Chōsen to dig out the debris from the caved-in mine, but coal shipments to Japan were still delayed for over a month. Some of the soldiers in a disciplinary hearing claimed they were struck with deep sorrow for the loss of their peers in battle and could not take decisive action in the moment. It was not uncommon to hear of such performance issues with externally recruited forces: Chinese, Koreans, Mongolians, and other foreign elements were known to resist being trained to a high standard of discipline. But the Kantō-gun were of a different caliber that should not have yielded any true dysfunction.

Military leadership was furious. They strove to keep rumors from spreading, but Fukui-jichō had already heard of soldiers fleeing in fear from routine village inspections before official reports of the incidents hit his desk. One low-ranking private caught disobeying orders was executed after his testimony that he burned with shame for his treatment of the Chinese. These problems of low morale and poor discipline seemed localized to a few areas in the province, but Fukui-jichō would have to cross-check with outposts near the borders with Chōsen and the Soviet Union to diagnose what plagued the military since they seemed incapable of managing the problem themselves. Whether it was a training issue to be fixed in Japan or some process deficiency in Manchukuo, these annoyances kept him and the rest of his colleagues working into the night. They were under immense pressure to prove that Manchukuo could generate revenue, but could not do so if the military kept failing to secure its assets.

As Fukui-jichō mulled over the soldiers' misconduct, his secretary brought in a tray stacked with letters and a cup of tea. Intrigued by the aroma, he inquired after it, as she had not served it before. A gift from some local businessman's wife, she explained, to express gratitude for their civil service in modernizing Manchukuo. Fukui-jichō had no doubt it was an offering to expedite the approval of some contract—these Chinese were no strangers to bribes—but something sweet was exactly what he needed to boost his flagging constitution in the late hour. He dismissed the secretary and started opening his letters, taking small sips of the tea as he read his evening round of messages. Fukui-jichō was surprised to find himself setting down his papers to pause and savor the tea's sweet pear essence. It was quite remarkable; he would have to ask the secretary for the name of it, though perhaps after he took a quick nap. The overtime was getting to him after all, and he would be able to think much more clearly after some sleep. He could not be productive in this state.

Fukui-jichō slouched over on his desk, not seeing that his secretary, too, had fallen at her post outside, the doors to their offices open for anyone to come in and access their statecraft secrets unseen.

Since Baek Yong-Woo's return, life at Fenghuang Teahouse had changed for Young-Ja. She was still expected to work her fingers raw, but she no longer faced any task unaided—the other women toiled alongside her. Although many still kept their distance, they at least did not shun her as they seemed to have been instructed in the first months of her arrival. No pile of laundry or dishes seemed quite so daunting when tackled in the company of others. Young-Ja was steadily regaining her vigor as she fell into the coordinated beats of the other working women's strong arms and no-nonsense efficiency.

While she produced hundreds of jars of cheong in her early months at the teahouse, Young-Ja had received her cheong-making punishments only a few times since, such occasions trickling to lower frequencies as she grew defter in her work. Her most recent turn had not even been due to her own error. She had instead stepped up when she saw the petrified face of the newest kitchen girl who had shattered a particularly fine plate. Young-Ja could still feel the gust of wind tickling her nostrils when Feng-nüshi's cane handle swung by her face and slammed into the wall in admonition. She trembled at the thought of losing her nose as she sat locked in the storage room, forced to peel and slice ginger to preserve in honey. Her foolish impulse to take the blame surprised her at first, but she did not resent extending a sympathy she had not received in kind from the others. If this was to be her home, she wished to act in ways that reminded her of the sister she had once been, the girl her parents had raised her to be.

Routine settled in as Young-Ja adapted to the rhythm of her working days, but no real comfort followed. A muted but ever-present anxiety made her fear that she could one day lose this nearly bearable life of servitude just as quickly as she had lost her previous lives. In a desperate bid to hold on to this stabilized footing, she kept a vigilant eye on the women around her. If someone walked with a limp, Young-Ja ran to help carry her load. If someone cut themselves on a knife while washing the dishes, Young-Ja took over the scrubbing without a word while the wound was dressed. She strove to ensure "burden" was never uttered in the same breath as her name and carried out her duties with unimpeachable excellence. This was in part to ward off Feng-nüshi's often punitive scrutiny. But it was also in part an urge to appease the women around her, to be accepted into the smiling, knowing glances they reserved for one another over Young-Ja's head.

Still, Young-Ja managed to find three sources of warmth in this modest life. Baek Yong-Woo was the first. He dropped by the teahouse periodically, seeking her out with a smile and his faint smell of pine needles. On such days, Feng-nüshi allowed Young-Ja breaks to greet her visitor. She would get to nibble on whatever new confection Yong-Woo brought with him from his travels and speak to someone who had known her in Joseon. She could not bear the thought of ever disappointing Yong-Woo—this she feared even more than Feng-nüshi herself. Her heart ached each time he left. She often wondered where he went, what he did, if she had just seen him for the last time. She did not want to give him a reason to avoid her and so did exactly as she was told without complaint, bottling up all unpleasant feelings for release only when she was alone.

Chinese classes were the second source of warmth for Young-Ja. Feng-nüshi required all teahouse women to master the languages of their customers. Even those who, like Young-Ja, never left the kitchens during the day. Older teahouse staff fluent in a given language tutored their fellow workers every day before Fenghuang opened for business. Young-Ja looked forward to each morning. Not only was it sanctioned time away from the drudgery of work but it also allowed her to tap into a pleasure she had always found in learning, soaking in these language lessons with as much eagerness as she once approached the lessons taught by her parents. As most teahouse staff focused on improving their Japanese, including the beautiful servers Young-Ja sometimes glimpsed at the edges of the kitchen, there were only three others in her Chinese class. All were Mongolian women who had come to Xinjing in search of opportunity. Young-Ja still could not communicate much with them, but the small group shared an eagerness in working through the right tones and words. The general rhythm of the local speech was pleasing to Young-Ja's ear, and she was gratified by the increasing pliability of her tongue. With every lesson the fog of incomprehension that had dogged her since her arrival began to lift. She could not help but claim a small pride at finally understanding what was happening around her in the kitchen.

Meiyu was the third and final source of warmth. The girl with the pigtail braids seemed impervious to whatever fear Feng-nüshi had lodged into the other kitchen women about interacting with Young-Ja and babbled away in her choppy Korean. Meiyu kept swapping her duties with others so that she could work with Young-Ja until people gave up on assigning them separate tasks. They took their meals together, slept next to each other in the dorms, and even developed the same red knuckles and blisters from laundry. Young-Ja found it easy to lean into the ebullient swings of Meiyu's chatter and rekindled her atrophied ability to laugh. When passing memories of her family threatened to knock her from the march of her daily labors, Young-Ja found solace in imagining that her parents, her siblings, and even Seiko Obaa-san would be happy she had taken refuge in Meiyu's vibrant nature.

Meiyu had also been brought to Fenghuang Teahouse by Baek Yong-Woo. She arrived only a few months before Young-Ja, when her father tried to sell her to a brothel to settle his gambling debts. Baek Yong-Woo—or Bailong, as he was known to the Chinese—purchased Meiyu's contract for a few yuan and placed her to be trained in the teahouse instead. She had not seen her father since.

"What's a brothel?" Young-Ja asked.

"It's a place where men pay to put their thing between women's legs," explained Meiyu.

"Why would they do that?"

"Men like it," Meiyu answered in a matter-of-fact tone.

Despite her best efforts, Young-Ja could not make herself forget the dread of feeling Masaharu Ojii-san's hardness against her back. She had no desire to behold a penis and scrunched her face at the thought.

Meiyu claimed never to want to see her father again. Her declaration had the practiced confidence of someone who had long since spent her tears. She confided in Young-Ja that her dream now was to grow into a beautiful woman and become Bailong's wife. She imagined running away to Mongolia with him, where they could ride horses all day and never wash another dish. As silly as Young-Ja thought this was, she envied Meiyu for having a dream at all. Other than the desire not to be thrown out of Fenghuang, Young-Ja did not know if she had any real aspiration toward which she could strive. The only thing she knew to yearn for was her family, and that was not something she could obtain through hard work.

CHAPTER FOURTEEN

Xinjing, Manchukuo, Empire of Japan, 1935

For all the changes in Young-Ja's life, Feng-nüshi's demeanor remained constant. The old woman asserted her stringent rule every day, inspiring a flinching but unconditional obedience with the bangs of her cane. It was said that Feng-nüshi could walk through walls, for her cane was heard in the wake of every broken dish or spilled cup of tea. The staff also suspected that the ceilings had eyes, for even an errant napkin could not be concealed from their mistress for long. While few dared open their mouths unbidden within Feng-nüshi's earshot, the women folded gossip into the margins of work, whispering wild stories about how their mistress had come to run this establishment.

Feng-nüshi, given name unknown, came to Changchun from afar. Some claimed from the mountains in the west; others claimed from the sea in the south. Everyone knew she had built Fenghuang Teahouse with her own wealth, but no one could recall when.

"I started working the kitchen when I was around your age," the grizzled old cook liked to tell the youngest Fenghuang girls. "If you think I'm an old crone, Feng-nüshi was just as gray the day I arrived as she is now. But while I've gone blind in one eye and deaf in one ear, she hasn't changed one bit in the past several decades."

The girls chided the old cook for teasing them, but no one else could recall a time when Feng-nüshi was not fearsome, elderly, and rich. The tempestuous turns of the world did not seem to faze her steady enterprise even as other businesses crumbled away. It did not matter who was emperor, what famines struck the region, what warlord threatened her supply chains. Fenghuang Teahouse always attracted gold.

No one questioned how a woman like Feng-nüshi had come to run her own lucrative establishment. It was not only her exacting business acumen that made her famous in Xinjing but also her penchant for violence. A local legend told of the time she used her cane handle to stab out the eye of a visiting Qing minister whose drunken gaze and hands had grown too bold with the teahouse women. Witnesses saw her whisper something to the howling minister that made him shut his mouth and flee the teahouse without retaliation.

"If you look closely, you can still see the stain where the minister's eyeball slid off her cane and splattered on the ground," said the cook. The girls dispersed into gasping titters but even the most skeptical among them would scan the teahouse floorboards for the rumored mark.

Such lore boosted Fenghuang Teahouse's profits. Some men were put off by tales of the brutal matron but many more were drawn to power in whatever form. Fenghuang attracted exactly the pan-Asian crowds the Japanese Empire alleged to promote in Manchukuo: wealthy Korean and Chinese businessmen, Japanese bureaucrats and officers, visiting diplomats from the Soviet Union, and the occasional traveling Mongol heavy with coin. The basis of the teahouse's interethnic tableau came not from its ability to inspire shared visions or political accord, however. It came from something to which all men of power were drawn regardless of credo or fealty: the suggestion of sex.

Beyond the kitchen, Fenghuang was staffed by graceful young women in red qipao who carried out the ceremony of tea service in silence. Men loved to watch these beauties tend to their every need without a word and melt away as business took place. Higher-paying clientele could reserve private rooms upstairs for meetings or performances—Fenghuang staff were also accomplished musicians and dancers of numerous Japanese, Chinese, and Korean traditions. As long as guests kept their hands to themselves, the women could serve a range of sophisticated experiences suited to every man's tastes for the right price. Fenghuang staved off the creep of ill repute by making its women untouchable—under threat of Feng-nüshi's interventions—giving the higher strata of society no reason to shy away from open patronage. Feng-nüshi knew exactly how to captivate a moneyed man's attention away from the shrinking bulk of his purse and made sure to train her staff accordingly.

Fenghuang's true success, however, hinged on men believing there were no real thoughts behind the pretty teeth of the women who entertained them. Unbeknownst to the clientele, the teahouse women understood most languages they came across and observed their guests' every action. The fan dancers made note of which ministers came in together and where they sat. The shamisen players counted how many times a businessman leaned into an official's ear. The tea servers picked up on the whispered missives of guests otherwise confident of their own discretion. Every night the red qipao–clad women ascended to Feng-nüshi's office to report on the intrigues of their guests. Feng-nüshi listened, jotting notes as she smoked her long silver tobacco pipe. Some she probed with curt questions, but for most, an audience with Feng-nüshi was more recitation than conversation. Each girl would eventually be dismissed with a flick of the hand as the next glided in to offer her own findings.

Feng-nüshi wove her many scribblings into gold. When she learned of a local construction company's desperation to secure a multiyear government contract, she promised its boss pivotal information in exchange for a new teahouse wing. As the company's men broke ground to Fenghuang's eastern section, Feng-nüshi advised the boss to send several bouquets of fresh lychee branches to the government office in charge of awarding the contract. Rage flooded the man at the seemingly random suggestion—had he been swindled out of such a large sum just to be advised that he send such a paltry gift?—but he kept mum while within reach of Feng-nüshi's famous cane. All was forgotten, however, when he was informed of his company's selection two days later, not having suspected anything about a certain bureaucrat's erotic predilection for lychees.

Of course, material gain was not information's only value for Feng-nüshi. When Fenghuang women reported on a

Kantō-gun captain's general indifference to them, Feng-nüshi sent a handsome Chinese boy for tea service at his post for a week until the captain came to demand it at a regular cadence. He sent for the young man even as he traveled out of Xinjing on assignment, giving the mistress of the teahouse—and by extension, Bailong—insight into his unit's numbers, missions, and location at all times. Feng-nüshi understood that all men, no matter how powerful, could be made to betray themselves through their appetites.

The teahouse servers did not always know what observations would rouse Feng-nüshi's interest and so reported everything they could recall: the names of their guests, the subtext of their discussions, the sentiments that danced naked on men's unwitting faces. The mistress rewarded girls with an extra coin if they delivered information she deemed particularly worthwhile. The women thus strove to tune their ears to Feng-nüshi's, hunting for salacious details that could stir open her ample purse. But the cleverest among them sniffed out information beyond the standard fare of rich men's sexual proclivities or political maneuvers. These women, who understood what was at stake, who had deduced that Bailong was no mere tea merchant, Feng-nüshi made rich.

Conversely, any woman Feng-nüshi found lacking in her duties was never heard from again. But this was rare; she did not have many lapses in judgment when selecting girls for the front of the teahouse. Despite Feng-nüshi's reputation, her women remained loyal and few left of their own accord. The teahouse staff would not deny that their mistress was terrifying, but they would also never accuse her of being unreasoned or unjust. By abiding by her rules, the staff could steer clear of trouble, make decent wages, and secure housing in a safe community of other women.

Nearly every woman employed at Fenghuang Teahouse was a rescue of some sort. Meiyu's story was not uncommon: there were girls whose families sold them off for opium or gambling debts, orphans who lost their families to Japanese violence, women who had the audacity to be born into poverty. Like Young-Ja and Meiyu, many of the recruits in the last five years had also been found and brought in by Baek Yong-Woo from across Asia. Fenghuang's women were thus all fond of the handsome merchant and looked forward to his visits bringing in tea shipments. Before he disappeared into the hazy tobacco smoke of Feng-nüshi's office to discuss secret matters, he greeted every girl he saw by name and passed out an assortment of gifts from his latest travels: face creams, medicine for womanly health, jewelry, and confections to share. That the men of Xinjing fell depressingly short of the bar set by Bailong was a favorite offhand refrain of the teahouse women.

Having risen from the depths of the world's cruel tides, Fenghuang staff did not waste the opportunity to rebuild their lives and found pride in developing their skills. For many, it was also the first time they had felt a sense of belonging. A few still sought love with their customers, venturing back into the world of men when wooed with the prospect of marriage and dominion of their own home. But many sought love with each other, stealing wet embraces in the dark of the shared dorms, exchanging knowing glances over the heads of their oblivious male guests. Petty jealousies and heartbreak could not be avoided with so many close-knit women at work and in love, though no amount of erotic angst could dim the glow of bonded industry Fenghuang women forged with one another.

Young-Ja and Meiyu spent most of their first year at the teahouse cleaning and taking language lessons. They did not interact much with their prettier older sisters who had graduated from gray kitchen tunics into the red service qipao. Meiyu was impatient to decorate herself and receive tributes from adoring customers—practice, she would say, for becoming Bailong's betrothed. The day both girls were tapped to train for the front of the teahouse, over a year since their arrival, Meiyu screamed and squeezed the breath out from a quiet Young-Ja. With Feng-nüshi's blessing, they would be allowed to wear red and greet customers at the door before ushering them to their seats. Meiyu jumped around the kitchen and sang incoherent little songs for the rest of the afternoon. Young-Ja, in turn, felt restless. A part of her was relieved by the endorsement. Feng-nüshi would not have selected her for this track if she did not value her in some way—her position in the teahouse seemed secure. A part of her worried, however, about leaving the circle of kitchen women in which she had allowed herself to find a guarded safety. She would have to steel herself to enter the world of men.

"Mei-chan!" a man sing-songed from the entrance.

Meiyu ran toward the soldier with a gleam in her puppy-dog eyes and embraced him.

"How pretty you look today, Mei-chan," he cooed. "Now, close those eyes and hold out your hands."

Meiyu obeyed and squealed with delight when he dropped a cheap jade hairpin into her palms. "I've never had such a nice pin before!" Meiyu cried in accented Japanese.

The soldier smirked. "Put it on," he ordered. Meiyu slid the gift into her hair with a coy smile before leading the man and his companions to a table for afternoon service.

Whenever Young-Ja saw the tan uniform of a Japanese soldier, she was brought back to the wretchedly sunny morning she last saw her family. Each time, she bit her tongue and lowered her head, using silent gestures to direct the soldiers to their seats. Young-Ja could not bring herself to mar Meiyu's happiness by telling her what horrors had been dealt to her family by men who donned that same uniform. Keeping quiet was not a problem. Soldier or not, the guests seemed to prefer Meiyu's unwavering smile—this was her third gift of the week from as many customers. They barely noticed Young-Ja shrinking into the wall at the door.

While Meiyu was busy entertaining the soldiers, a short man in a changshan and blue magua riding jacket strolled up to the teahouse. Freckles splashed across his high cheekbones above a wispy mustache. A well-dressed woman hung on each of his arms as he asked for a table in the pavilion in the courtyard outside. A flutter of sparrows landed on the awning of the pavilion as Young-Ja led the trio to their requested seats. Young-Ja viewed the chirping birds as an auspicious sign—it was not often they saw such songbirds in the center of the city. She bowed and left once the group was installed, though the man was too immersed in the laughter of his companions to acknowledge her gesture.

Young-Ja scanned the courtyard on her way back to the entrance. There were not many people seated outside in the brisk fall weather. An old Chinese couple occupied a corner, sipping their tea. Not too far from them was the third and last group seated outside: a pair of uniformed Japanese soldiers and a sheepish-looking woman in a Western-style dress. The woman stiffened as a soldier put his arm around her shoulders and tilted her chin toward him. The soldier across from them waved his hand over the woman's tea.

Young-Ja froze. Something had left the soldier's hand as it hovered over the cup. She swerved around to see if she could call for reinforcements, but no other red qipao flashed in the courtyard. Tables were strictly under the purview of the trained tea servers: greeters were ordered not to interact with guests once they were seated. The chirping sparrows grew louder as Young-Ja decided she could not walk past the scene without doing something. She resigned herself to accept whatever punishment Feng-nüshi would mete out once her transgression was discovered.

She approached the table with a big smile. "Would you like anything else? More hot water, a different tea, perhaps something to eat?"

The soldier holding the woman shot Young-Ja an annoyed look and shooed her away. She did not move. When the woman reached for the cup and raised it to her lips, Young-Ja yelped, not knowing what else to do. She then fell into a clatter of porcelain and wood across the table. The woman shrieked, hot tea darkening the lap of her dress.

"Stupid brat!" yelled the soldier.

Young-Ja lifted herself up and looked behind to see what had caused her fall. It was the short man in the blue magua riding jacket she had seated earlier. He had bumped into her as he passed, though there was plenty of space for him without having to come anywhere near her. She did not get to ponder him for long, however; the soldier grabbed her wrist and tugged her up, her feet nearly lifting from the ground in the violent jerk.

"What do you think you're doing—"

"The offense was mine," the man in blue said in Japanese. He stepped forward and stood next to Young-Ja. A flutter of sparrows chirped and circled the air above them. The man in blue puffed out his chest and looked the soldier in the eye. Young-Ja winced as the soldier tightened his grip on her wrist.

"Mind your own business, chankoro," said the soldier. Spit flew from his mouth as he emphasized the slur.

The man in blue stood unflinching. One of the sparrows landed on his shoulder and chirped at his ear. "Captain Tsuchiya won't be pleased to hear you're trying to bed a woman instead of monitoring the railway tracks."

The soldier released Young-Ja's arm. "How do you—"

"I'd think twice about causing a scene now if you don't wish the captain to know where you were." The man in blue smiled. He offered a cloth napkin to the woman in the wet dress without looking away from the soldier. The birds crooned loudly overhead in what sounded like laughter.

The soldier curled his lip as if to snarl, then backed off. He glanced at his comrade and tossed his head toward the exit. They left, throwing coins at their server who had come running toward the scene. The woman wiped herself down as the man in blue explained in Chinese what the soldiers had done. She stared at the fallen cup and hurried out of the teahouse clutching her elbows. The sparrows flew off and landed back on the pavilion to rest.

"You saw what he did, didn't you?" the man in blue asked in Chinese.

Young-Ja nodded, rubbing the wrist the soldier had crushed in his grip.

"You have a keen eye—that'll serve you well. What's your name?"

When Young-Ja introduced herself, he switched into lightly-accented Korean.

"A Joseon kkachi. Sorry I was a little rough back there, but it got sorted."

Young-Ja perked up at his language shift. Opportunities to speak her native tongue had grown scant, particularly when Yong-Woo was not around. Even Meiyu had stopped leaning into Korean once Young-Ja's Chinese became proficient enough to handle all their chatter. The freckled man smiled down at her look of surprise.

"When Feng-nüshi asks you about what happened, you can tell her Tayiji took care of it." He winked and returned to his beautiful companions as the courtyard slid back into its afternoon lull.

It did not take long for Young-Ja to discover that Tayiji was a teahouse regular. He directed his seating requests to Young-Ja when he could and always tipped a coin for her service. Everyone knew Tayiji preferred the pavilion and they rarely placed anyone else there, even during the rush of summer evenings. Sparrows gathered on the pavilion roof whenever he settled in with his female companions, announcing his arrival to the rest of the teahouse staff. Young-Ja suspected that he understood the sparrows' song, and they his, for only those chirruping birds could attract his eyes away from an ever-changing carousel of beguiling women. The servers sometimes bickered over who would get to attend to him; he was known to leave generous tips after his more recreational visits.

When Tayiji came in without women, it was often with lone uniformed men who did not speak much or touch their tea. These short visits followed the same beats. Tayiji would smile and lean in toward his guest as his sparrows flitted above them, keeping the man hooked on his every word. The sparrow calls would swell over the duration of their conversation and stop once Tayiji put his arm around the man to whisper in his ear. The birds dispersed when both men rose from their seats and walked out of the teahouse together. Young-Ja's heart fell when she witnessed Tayiji's smooth geniality toward Japanese soldiers, for she thought she had seen goodness in him. She was disappointed to be wrong in her first impression, though she was curious to know what he seemed to say with such zest to these men.

When Young-Ja asked one of the servers about Tayiji, the server looked over her shoulder to make sure no one was around to see her speaking.

"Tayiji runs a business not too far from here," she whispered. "The women he brings in work for him. The men he brings in go there next to relax and spend time."

"He has his own teahouse?" asked Young-Ja.

The server smiled. "You can think of it like that. But he doesn't really serve tea."

"What does he serve?"

"The chance to forget who you are," said the server.

"Why would you want to forget who you are?"

"Well, little sister—isn't there anything you wish you could forget?"

Young-Ja shivered, struck by the memory of Young-Ho's corpse falling to the ground, his hand still warm in hers.

CHAPTER FIFTEEN

Xinjing, Manchukuo, Empire of Japan, 1937

Guests brought to the teahouse a sense of anticipation. Anticipation of entertainment, of connection, of intrigue. Of aches being lifted from their shoulders by the delicate hands of their hostesses. While the teahouse staff lavished care on all without discrimination, they were most interested in guests weighed with the nerves of subterfuge, sniffing out the slightest of palpitations before long. As a greeter, Young-Ja learned to discern what occupied the minds of guests from initial physical impressions, an extension of the game Baek Yong-Woo had taught her three years ago. Hundreds of nights at the door helped her to follow the beat of certain patterns. Men with women who were not their wives carried smugness on their faces but hesitation in their gaits. Men in need of money were the quickest to laugh, oozing with desperation to charm their associates. Some façades were harder to crack than others, but rare were those the teahouse staff could not see through.

Young-Ja and Meiyu were now among the girls reporting to Feng-nüshi each night, but neither girl's findings in the last year had earned an extra coin. This was of grave concern to Meiyu.

"If she could just give us a hint of what she's looking for! You'd think it'd be the smart thing to do so we could just do as we're told instead of blindly guessing." Meiyu paced and waved her arms around until coming to a thoughtful halt. "Though I heard this morning that she'll give out coins if you can tell her the color of a man's nipple."

Young-Ja giggled. "You were clearly being teased. Why would she need to know that?"

"Don't you get it? It just means we have to get much, much closer to get valuable information! Something as intimate as the color of a nipple. The problem is, it's hard for us to do this just as greeters . . ."

In private, Young-Ja believed that her friend might be miserable in the more glamorous role of server, for Fenghuang servers were famously silent before their guests. Meiyu would have to go against the core of her nature, straining with all her might to hold her tongue.

As trainees, Young-Ja and Meiyu were not yet discharged from routine cleaning duties and so could not shelve their gray work tunics. Feng-nüshi expected a deep scrub of the kitchen every season; Young-Ja and Meiyu had been tasked with that winter's scrub of the back storage room and its array of massive earthenware jars. After a slow evening with little to report to Feng-nüshi, the girls worked into the late hours wiping away the dirt from the room's pockmarked stone tiles. With the other kitchen staff retired for the night, the girls welcomed the opportunity to shed their service smiles and speak freely without others milling about to tease them.

"It's not fair!" Meiyu said, stomping on a scurrying spider. "We're ready to be servers now; I don't know why Feng-nüshi's holding us back."

Young-Ja laughed. "We're still only fifteen—you know she won't make us servers until we're a little older. Qizhen's the youngest, and she's maybe twenty."

"Well, I'm better at Japanese and Korean than a lot of the others. Even Russian! And the guests like me best. They'll tell me anything I ask them, even things Feng-nüshi would pay to hear."

Young-Ja nodded in silent support as she cleared away the cobwebs. Meiyu was indeed the most popular greeter. Some guests had even taken to addressing her by name and lingering at the entrance to flirt with her. But Young-Ja did not share her friend's ambition. While she wanted Feng-nüshi to find no fault in her work, she would not be unhappy continuing her days as a greeter. Young-Ja liked seeing the varied flow of guests but not having to interact with them beyond an initial welcome. She dreaded the day she would have to force a smile and pour tea for a soldier. To have to obey their orders and follow their conversations. Since Japan had started to wage another war to invade China in the last few months, however, many soldiers in Xinjing had deployed to battlefields in the south. Young-Ja was relieved to note that fewer tan uniforms patronized Fenghuang these days. But this relief was quick to mutate into an uglier feeling: if soldiers were not occupied with leisure, they were likely out killing men. Out destroying families just like hers.

"Well, I think we're both quite pretty. Pretty enough to be servers," declared Meiyu, primping her hair and sliding her hand down her growing chest and hips. She slapped her wet rag against an earthenware jar to a hollow thunk. "We're definitely prettier than those duds that became servers last week!"

They continued cleaning as they switched to gossip about which teahouse girls had been found in another's embrace.

"I wonder if women really do make better lovers than men, like the older girls say," said Meiyu.

Young-Ja looked away. She did not know how a woman's touch would make her feel, but she knew that at least one man's touch had corroded a part of her. She shook her head to bury the memory and tried to maintain focus on her friend's chatter.

"Doesn't matter anyway, since I'm going to marry Bailong," said Meiyu. Two days ago she had given one of the older girls a coin to teach her how to kiss with her tongue. She wanted to be ready to catch Bailong in a private corner the next time he visited the teahouse.

"Want me to show you how?" Meiyu asked. The pair looked at each other in silence before collapsing into delirious giggles.

As the night progressed, their eyelids grew heavy. The girls hastened to finish their cleaning so they could rest before morning language classes. While they scanned for missed spots or stray cobwebs, Baek Yong-Woo barged in through the teahouse's back entrance, tracking dirty gray snow across the wet floor of the storage room.

"Go clear the large table in the kitchen. Now!"

Young-Ja and Meiyu jumped up and did as they were told. As the girls readied the table, four men lumbered in carrying what looked to be large crates of tea. The sour musk of unbathed workers filled the room, laced with the acrid notes of spent gunpowder. The odor instantly transported Young-Ja to the moment bandits had robbed all the passengers aboard her Xinjing-bound train three years prior. These men were dressed in similar changshan and fur vests, though less menacingly armed. Why Yong-Woo kept such company, Young-Ja did not have much time to ponder, for the men opened a large crate on the kitchen table to reveal inside a grimacing, pale man bleeding from his chest. His torso had been wrapped roughly in cloth, but blood had saturated through in a dark-red stain on the crate's wooden planks.

"Meiyu, get Feng-nüshi down here. Hurry!" Yong-Woo said, not looking up from the injured man.

The girl blushed at the sound of her name on Bailong's lips and dashed out in compliance. He then yelled at Young-Ja to bring clean linens and boiled water. She had never seen the self-possessed Yong-Woo look so manic—his normally well-coiffed hair was caked with dust and fell in messy strands across his sweat-soaked forehead. He hooked his arms under the injured man as the others helped to remove him from the crate and place him on the table. Yong-Woo threw off his jacket and rolled up his shirtsleeves before folding several linens into a bundle, laying the man's head down gently on the makeshift pillow. He stayed at the edge of the table to hold his injured comrade's head and whisper into his ear.

Waiting for the water to boil, Young-Ja held back the numerous questions she suspected Yong-Woo would not want to entertain at the moment. She instead glanced at the other men and noticed that one bled from his hand.

"Let me clean this," she said in Chinese, tugging at his sleeve. He tilted his head with uncertainty, as if he did not comprehend her words. Young-Ja nonetheless wiped the dirt from his upturned palm with a towel and wrapped a thin cloth around the gash.

"Thank you," he said in Japanese. A soft voice.

She had not expected this gruff-looking man dressed in a changshan to address her so meekly, let alone in Japanese. She released his hand and stepped back to ponder his appearance. In meeting his gaze Young-Ja noticed that his skin was unlined beneath the smears of dirt—he was still quite young. Certainly not like the grizzled old men the bandits were in her memory of the train. There was still a softness in his hands, none of the calluses that might be found hardened on the skin of laborers. She glanced at the others standing behind Yong-Woo and concluded with surprise that none of their dust-covered faces had seen many years past twenty. Who were these men? Why had they brought their smells of gunpowder and pain into this teahouse kitchen?

Young-Ja snapped out of her quiet reflections when one of the strangers cleared his throat and asked for some water in raspy Chinese. Admonishing herself for not having thought of it first, she rushed to draw what was requested. The men drank the offering and wiped their mouths across dirty sleeves.

Feng-nüshi's clacking cane approached the kitchen before the water had boiled, Meiyu trailing behind. The cane banged to a halt at the door. All looked up to a scorching glare darting between the man bleeding out on the table, the dirty horde gathered around, and their blood-covered ringleader.

"You fool—anyone could have seen you come through in such large numbers!" Feng-nüshi's admonition boomed against the walls. All but Baek Yong-Woo startled at the power in her voice.

"We brought him in one of the crates," said Yong-Woo. "If anyone happened to see us, it would've looked like a tea shipment, nothing suspicious."

Feng-nüshi hit her cane against the dark bloodstain on the crate. "Tea deliveries are not made in the middle of the night by tactless little boys with guns!"

Yong-Woo ignored the retort. He began removing the bloody clothes from the injured man when Young-Ja delivered the requested bowl of heated water. Yong-Woo dipped a clean linen into it and started washing away the sweat and dirt on his comrade's strained face.

"Your men cannot be seen here like this. You must leave. Now."

Yong-Woo did not look up. With a gentle hand, he cleansed his comrade and replaced the soaked cloth on his chest with fresh bandages. The pale man groaned as he was kneaded about on the table. Yong-Woo winced along as if in pain himself.

"We lost our safehouse and our doctor—we have nowhere else to hide but here," said Yong-Woo.

"You should've gone to Mukden—"

"He would've died!" Yong-Woo's eyes were wild, his teeth gritted into a snarl. "If we had to take him all the way to Mukden, he would've died."

Young-Ja and Meiyu froze. They had never heard anyone address Feng-nüshi in such a tone and were terrified of how she would respond. Even the other men stood still, shifting their eyes away from the conflict.

"Then let him die," Feng-nüshi said, voice low and tense. "He's just one man. He knew what he was getting into."

The man screamed as Yong-Woo increased pressure on the wound to stanch the bleeding. Yong-Woo put his forehead against his comrade's, apologizing to him for causing him further agony. Sweat gathered at Yong-Woo's brow as he clutched the ailing man's hand. His expression softened when their eyes met, blind to everyone else in the room. Young-Ja blushed and averted her eyes.

"Do not test me, Bailong—"

"Call for your physician," he said, half command, half plea.

Her eyes narrowed. Thick silence hung between them.

"Please," he added in a more subdued voice, though with the desperation of a caged animal in his eyes. The man writhed in Yong-Woo's arms, sweat dripping down his pallid face.

Feng-nüshi opened the door into the back storage room.

"I'll call for him if the rest of your men leave immediately and as discreetly as possible. I'll not have you put us all at risk to save one boy."

Yong-Woo snapped around at the men, who murmured to one another and nodded. They covered their faces and left through the back door one by one, melting away into the winter night. Satisfied with their departure, Feng-nüshi sent Meiyu to fetch the doctor. Young-Ja helped Yong-Woo coax the injured man to drink water and wipe the sweat from his clammy body.

"Well, which was it?" Feng-nüshi demanded. "The encampment or the arms factory? Or did you go somewhere else?"

Yong-Woo stroked his comrade's hair as he spoke. "The arms factory seemed like the better bet. The intel from your women said the factory would be thinned to a skeleton crew tonight since guards were being sent to the southern warfront. We confirmed separately that it'd been a while since the last major shipment, meaning the warehouse would be relatively full."

"Who went with you?" asked Feng-nüshi.

"The usual resistance fighters from Joseon and China, some of the communists from Tokyo—you've met most of them. We thought it'd be a good idea to make a dent in the Japanese arms supply chain."

"That was it? No outsiders?"

Yong-Woo looked away, hand in his injured companion's. "We were a little shorthanded, so I had some smugglers from the area join us. They wanted some new guns."

Feng-nüshi narrowed her eyes.

"I'd worked with every man before, that's not the problem. It's just that, when we got there, we were ambushed. There were dozens of soldiers waiting for us. We lost a lot of men, but some got away. I managed to convince a few to help me . . . to help us come back here."

Young-Ja stood in shocked silence. She had always wondered where Baek Yong-Woo went on his frequent business trips. Teahouse gossip on the subject often leaned fanciful—"all that handsomeness, he's probably in the movies!"—or dramatic—"he has ties to the Triad, it can't be just tea in all those crates!" Young-Ja, too, suspected that he was no mere tea merchant, but she had never imagined he would be outright defying the Japanese Imperial Army. Her mind raced through her memories, wondering what signs she had missed. In the many nights she was haunted by her family's final morning, she could not have fathomed anyone strong enough to confront the wielders of violence who had laid such waste to her life.

Feng-nüshi's face darkened at the mention of an ambush. Either Bailong's plans had been exposed, or they had deliberately been fed bad information. If the latter, these unwanted late-night visitors were not the only thing for Feng-nüshi to worry about. Fenghuang could now be under suspicion by powerful men whose very lack of misgivings she relied on for profit.

"Tonight's recklessness aside, you're not such a fool that you haven't figured out what this means," said Feng-nüshi. "You must lie unseen far from here while we figure out how those soldiers anticipated your plans."

Yong-Woo continued stroking his comrade's hair, refusing to meet Feng-nüshi's eyes.

When Meiyu returned with the old doctor, he extracted whatever iron he could from the chest wound and sewed up the torn skin. Agonized screaming was cut short when Feng-nüshi shoved a linen into the injured man's mouth and hissed at him to be quiet.

"Give him some morphine, he's in pain!" shouted a frantic Yong-Woo.

"Don't have any," said the doctor as he administered the final stitches. "I had to surrender most of my supplies to the military. For their invasion efforts."

Yong-Woo threw a look at Feng-nüshi, who remained impassive.

"You know very well that I don't keep tools for mindless vice under my roof," she said.

"Then go to Tayiji and get some from him," Yong-Woo said, voice breaking. "Please, he won't be able to handle this." He clutched the patient's hand.

Feng-nüshi looked down at the entwined men. She flattened her lips and said nothing.

"I can go," said Young-Ja. She had never stood so upright under the knife edge of Feng-nüshi's scowl, but the revelation of Yong-Woo's pursuits emboldened her. "Whatever it is you need, I can get it."

This rush of nerve enabled Young-Ja to lock eyes with her mistress, but it was not enough to keep her from shaking. The absence of speech crackled in the air as Feng-nüshi considered the scene before her.

"Tayiji does seem to favor you," the old woman conceded. "You may go tell him Fenghuang requests a vial of morphine."

Yong-Woo grabbed Young-Ja's arm and thanked her in Korean, asking her to run as fast as she could.

"No, do not run." Feng-nüshi's cane shot out against Young-Ja's chest. "You cannot behave like anything is wrong. You'll walk calmly and not draw attention to yourself. And don't tell Tayiji why we need the morphine."

Yong-Woo scowled but did not contradict her. He instead offered his crumpled jacket to Young-Ja as she left.

The rush of cold winter air swirled around Young-Ja with the exhilaration of what the evening had revealed. The thought of being able to help Yong-Woo lightened her hurried steps. Since her first days at Fenghuang, she had focused on obeying every order, terrified of being deemed a burden and thrown away. And unlike Meiyu, she had wished to burrow within the underbelly of the teahouse, avoiding any work within the orbit of Japanese soldiers. But this night had revealed that Fenghuang stood not merely for the amusement of powerful men. Young-Ja did not pretend to understand men's reasons for war or violence, but she saw that there was a greater purpose to the servers' duties, a reason Feng-nüshi rewarded certain observations, a drive that made men of all origins risk their lives. She was feverish with discovery. This was why Yong-Woo had brought her here. This was why he had taught her to read people. From the agitation of her mind rose an eagerness to don red and put her observation skills to the test. Even if it meant having to stomach the company of uniformed men.

Young-Ja had walked past Tayiji's before when running errands at the marketplace with the older girls. It was only a few streets down from the teahouse and thus not an unfamiliar walk, but in the late hour, the darkened windows along the street appeared menacing. Men slid out from the shadows, some obviously drunk and stumbling about. Others eyed her with alarming lucidity. Young-Ja kept her gaze locked ahead in her hasty walk, wrapping Yong-Woo's jacket tight around her body and trying not to appear as frightened as she felt. If she focused on her newfound determination, she could block out the chilling shapes flickering at the edges of her sight.

Tayiji's building was a large, three-story structure with blue roofing and ornate woodwork along the awning and windows. Young-Ja tugged on the creaking iron ring of the front gate, but the door would not budge. She knocked and called out for Tayiji in a whisper. No response. She called out again, her cry dissipating into the dark with the fog of her breath. Young-Ja refused to return to Fenghuang empty-handed. She could not bring herself to fail her first mission and disappoint Yong-Woo, not when he had been risking his life against the Japanese all this time. He was depending on her. She yelled louder for Tayiji, pounding on the door.

Behind her came a chirp. Young-Ja thought she had misheard, for birds did not sing in the night. As if a riposte to her doubt, another chirp rang out. Another joined in, and another, until the street lit up with the cries of sparrows. Young-Ja whirled around trying to tell the sparrows to be quiet, but iron creaked as the large door hinged open to reveal Tayiji in a fur-lined nightgown. He held up a small lantern to Young-Ja's surprised face. The sparrows went silent when he began to speak.

"The kkachi from Joseon. What brings you here at this strange hour?" he asked in Korean.

Young-Ja looked around to make sure no one was behind her and explained why she had come. Tayiji frowned but waved his free hand at her to enter the building in his wake.

Young-Ja followed Tayiji past the atrium into a large room thick with the smell of something ominously sweet. Dim lanterns hung high from the ceiling, though their light did little to illuminate the smoke-dusted space. The gentle swings of Tayiji's handheld lantern cast swaying shadows on the opulent surfaces of the room. The stairs wound along the wall, periodically opening up to little landings as they snaked around to the edges of higher floors blurred in the pungent haze. Plush mats and pillows were gathered in bunches, with what looked like corpses strewn about. Young-Ja gasped as the passing lantern light flashed on the exposed skin of fallen arms. Men dressed in Western suits and changshan were passed out in the middle of the room, against the railings of the stairs, buried in pillows on the ground. Tayiji glanced back at her.

"Don't worry, it's safe."

Young-Ja did not know whether he spoke for the two of them or for the men at their feet.

"What are they doing?" she could not help but ask.

"They're resting."

"Are they . . . hurt?" she whispered as they exited the main chamber into a long corridor.

Tayiji's gaze held steady ahead as he took them through the hallway with his lantern held high.

"No one lives without hurt, little kkachi, and many seek to forget their pain. We provide assistance with that here, much like Fenghuang helps to distract people from their woes."

Young-Ja kept pace with Tayiji while looking around the sumptuous hallway. Every door they passed was ornately carved and flanked by large jade statues of mythical beasts. Dimly lit red lanterns hung all down the path. Young-Ja was often in awe of Fenghuang's grandeur, but this was different. Fenghuang's elegance was understated, something that blended into the background of a generally serene ambiance. Here, the opulence felt overwhelming, as if designed to override the onlooker's senses and plunge them into another world. Young-Ja gawked at the adornments in the corridor while Tayiji paused to unlock a door with a key hung around his neck.

He flipped the light switch within to reveal a room that looked as if it belonged in a different building. Plain wooden paneling lined the walls. No decorative flair was carved into the molding or furniture. A modest shelf stacked with various sized bottles stood in the corner next to a table with a scattering of iron tools. Tayiji grabbed a small brown bottle and handed it to Young-Ja. She felt a jolt as his cold, smooth fingers touched her skin.

"I won't ask why your mistress needs this, but I trust you'll keep out of it."

Young-Ja was shocked at the implication she might take medicine that was meant for someone else. Tayiji chuckled at the look on her face.

"I'm just teasing, of course. I've always known you to do the right thing."

Tayiji led her back outside. Young-Ja clutched the bottle to her chest, wondering whether the men sprawled about needed the medicine she held, and if she were taking it away from them. She shuddered at the thought and walked through the main chamber, staring at the ground so as not to step on an arm or foot.

"Be careful on the way back, kkachi," Tayiji said at the entrance. "I'll know if you stray."

The door shut, extinguishing the light of Tayiji's lantern. Young-Ja turned toward Fenghuang. Within her first few steps, a sparrow landed on her shoulder. It chirped softly in her ear as she began her short journey back. Advancing in brisker strides, she heard a growing crest of other sparrows following above and behind, wings aflutter in their strange nighttime song. Young-Ja was glad for the company, for she feared the night less under the watch of her flying guardians. When she opened the back door to Fenghuang, the birds scattered back into the night sky, leaving no trace of their grand procession.

Young-Ja expected to walk into more screaming or groaning, but silence hung in the storage room. Upon entering the kitchen, her ears searched for Feng-nüshi's furious hissing. But the only noise came from Meiyu shuffling about gathering bloody linens into a basket. Feng-nüshi and the doctor were no longer there. Meiyu looked up briefly as Young-Ja entered before casting her red, swollen eyes back down, hurrying to tidy up.

Yong-Woo's face was buried in the shoulder of the injured man on the table. The man lay still, waxen and pale. Young-Ja was surprised to find that he was remarkably beautiful without the grimace of pain sullying his face. The skin on his high cheekbones was smooth, his lips a pleasing, full shape. As she stepped closer, she noticed that he, too, was quite young. Yong-Woo shook beside the man, head buried, shirt covered in his comrade's blood. Young-Ja felt as though she was intruding on a private moment and remained silent. She set the brown bottle of medicine by Yong-Woo's side. He did not stir.

Yong-Woo disappeared after they buried the dead man behind a shrub in the courtyard where the disturbed earth would not be seen by guests the following morning. His prolonged absence did not go unnoticed—other teahouse women wondered where Bailong had gone with all his gifts and easy smiles. Young-Ja and Meiyu did not need to be told the importance of keeping that night's events a secret. The girls even refrained from discussing the night with each other, for it might force them to acknowledge that the dashing Baek Yong-Woo was just as human as they were. That his protection, too, had its bounds in their ever-treacherous world.

CHAPTER SIXTEEN

Xinjing, Manchukuo, Empire of Japan, 1938

Spring Festival was quickly approaching. Despite the onset of war in China, the teahouse continued to attract high-paying guests seeking service and entertainment. The red-clad women of Fenghuang glided among the tables with their usual polish and smiles, crafting an atmosphere of leisurely interlude far from the rising fatalities of Japanese military campaigns. But Fenghuang behind the scenes did not boast a festive mood.

After learning about the ambush, the mistress of the teahouse rampaged. The server who first reported the factory's change of guards was brought into Feng-nüshi's office for questioning. She was made to recite the names and demeanors of every military officer from whom she had overheard the account. Every element of her interactions with the men was broken down many times over under the looming menace of Feng-nüshi's cane. The dancers who performed for the same officers were dragged into interrogations and squeezed for any divergence from the server's account. When none strayed from the emerging story, the server was permitted to walk out of Feng-nüshi's office two days later with her life, though the light had left her eyes. Feng-nüshi seemed satisfied that the ambush had not resulted from a traitor among her staff, but this was only the beginning. She would be a fool not to hunt for snakes elsewhere.

The terror of Feng-nüshi's scrutiny crept over every teahouse woman, though no one but Young-Ja and Meiyu understood why. The old woman was quicker to bang her cane in reprimand for any deviation from perfection. Fingers were threatened to be chopped off at any slips of the hand. When women came to report their observations, the mistress of the teahouse laid fiendish traps of lies. She would declare to have heard contradictions to servers' accounts, trying to catch women off guard or turn the weak-willed against their sisters. Feng-nüshi barked impossible follow-up questions at the quivering staff, asking for descriptions of even the slightest changes in guests' facial expressions. Faltering would be punished with toilet cleaning and docked wages for the week. Fenghuang's toilets had never been cleaner, its women never poorer.

The kitchen staff were not exempt from this tyranny. Since Feng-nüshi threw a scalding teapot at a girl's head—she had handed the wrong aged oolong to the server of an important guest—the women did not dare draw the attention of their mistress. Gone was the laughter floating above the clatter of the busy kitchen. No amorous glances were cast in passing. Voices now only dared to rise above a whisper when jockeying to accompany the cook to the market. Feng-nüshi's new era of control forbade excursions without explicit permission—it was only on these short trips to help the cook that the selected girl could breathe a little more freely. Even then, the cook alone was allowed to speak with vendors and the kitchen staff wondered if their tongues might wither from disuse.

When Young-Ja was summoned to see Feng-nüshi outside her usual office hours, she did not know whether to be afraid she had committed some offense or whether her mistress would finally deem her ready to be a server. Whatever the reason, Young-Ja knew she would have to do her best to demonstrate her perceptive guile. Every moment in Feng-nüshi's presence was a potential opportunity.

Since learning of Yong-Woo's endeavors, Young-Ja had thrown herself into greeting duties, trying to ascertain any details from guests that might aid his resistance efforts or alleviate Feng-nüshi's months-long rage. Militaries, occupation, war—all had been lofty yet inevitable features of a world she had never quite understood. These forces had destroyed her life with such unthinking ease; she had not imagined that someone like her would ever be able to contribute to their obstruction. But now, so close to the everyday men and women who somehow stood against this power, Young-Ja longed to do something—anything—to help. To make Yong-Woo proud. To honor the extinguished lives of her parents and siblings.

As her understanding of the stakes at Fenghuang grew, so, too, did her frustration. She was impatient to have her reports be deemed worthy of an extra coin and be deployed in important subterfuge, but Feng-nüshi remained unimpressed. Young-Ja worked harder to smile, bow, and charm the guests at the door so they might let down their guard and cede an indiscretion she could use. Meiyu, too, welcomed this development, happy that her friend finally shared in her aspirations to become a server.

"Remember to stand up straight and look Feng-nüshi in the eye," warned Meiyu as she brushed Young-Ja's hair to look presentable. "I heard that she'll suspect you if you're afraid to make eye contact." She squeezed her friend's shoulders and sent her to ascend the stairs. "Put in a good word for me too!"

Young-Ja tried not to cough when she stepped into Feng-nüshi's smoke-filled room. The old mistress looked more severe than ever, her cheeks hollowing to inhale through her long silver pipe. The beak of her cane glinted in her gnarled hand through the smoky plumes she blew from her nose. Feng-nüshi did not budge but her eyes followed Young-Ja as she approached the desk. She then tossed a folded note to the girl.

"Take this to Tayiji and return with his reply in time for the evening service. Speak to no one else." Young-Ja was dismissed with a flick of her mistress's wrist before she had a chance to convey the subtle observations she had made that day.

The streets of Xinjing appeared dreary in the cold winter's light, but Young-Ja was too submerged in thought to mind the passing scenery. What business did Feng-nüshi have with Tayiji? Did her mistress require more medicine? Had Yong-Woo stopped by again with his resistance fighters in the night—had she missed them? Young-Ja longed to see him, to tell him that she could do what he had brought her here to do. While she waited for him, she would prove to Feng-nüshi that she could rise to any occasion her work demanded. She quickened her pace to the blue-roofed mansion peeking above the row of buildings ahead.

Young-Ja pulled on the iron ring of the front door and knocked in haste. The door creaked open to a striking woman in a blue qipao with gray streaks in her tight black bun. She sat atop a stool as she welcomed Young-Ja into the atrium, asking what type of experience the young maiden sought.

"The eight-jiao room? One yuan? Or maybe the lady is seeking the sophisticated *two*-yuan experience . . ." The woman crossed her long legs and leaned forward, propping her elbows on her knees and resting her chin on her hand. She smiled with brightly painted lips as Young-Ja took a step back, stuttering that she was there with a message for Tayiji from Fenghuang.

"Just teasing, little kkachi. Come in," she said, getting up and opening the inner door for Young-Ja. The woman whistled lightly to beckon over another worker.

"Our cute little guest wants to see Tayiji," the older woman said with a wink. "Why don't you take her up?"

Young-Ja blushed and followed the other worker into the main chamber.

Recalling the last time she entered this space, Young-Ja steeled herself for what she was about to confront. The lanterns overhead burned somewhat brighter than in her memory, but an even thicker, sugary haze hung in the air, like clouds that dimmed the sun. Respectably dressed men were still sprawled about at her feet, though they moved now, somewhat quelling her suspicion that they were all corpses. They seemed to belong neither in the world of the living nor the dead as they took languid drags from their pipes, ignoring Young-Ja when she passed through their cloying trails of smoke. While she paid mind not to step on anyone as she walked, the daytime setting pulled her eyes toward something else: beautiful women lounging or drifting about attending to their guests. She recognized some as Tayiji's glamorous companions from the teahouse.

Young-Ja's guide led her up the winding stairs and into another corridor. She stopped to knock on an ornate carved door flanked by large calligraphy scrolls.

"Enter," said Tayiji.

The woman opened the door and ushered Young-Ja in before gliding away. Young-Ja stepped into a dim room filled with mounds of plush pillows and bedding. Her eyes landed on Tayiji splayed out in the middle of the room. He lay with his head thrown back on a pile of silken material, a loose shirt tossed over his torso and naked women lazing around him. Without opening his eyes he gestured to a low table at the side of the room.

"Just place the tea there—" Tayiji stopped as he raised his head to see a blushing Young-Ja averting her eyes. He smiled and rose from the tangle of long legs.

"I thought you were someone else," he said, switching into Korean. "I'm sorry for having been indecent before you." He grabbed a crumpled changshan from the floor and pulled it onto his small body. Young-Ja stared at her feet and flushed red.

"It's okay," she mumbled. "I'm sorry for barging in unannounced."

Tayiji smiled, stroking his thin mustache with his thumb. "It's always my pleasure to see you. Now, what brings you here? Sick of the old woman and want to come work for me instead?"

She handed him the note from Feng-nüshi and waited as he read.

"So, the Phoenix needs my sparrows." Tayiji folded up the message and placed its corner in the small flame of a nearby candle. The fire crept across the edge of the paper to devour it into glowing ash. Young-Ja stared at Tayiji's impassive freckled face, struggling to discern his mood.

"You can run back and let your mistress know I accept her price."

Tayiji of the Sparrows made it his business to know. In his forty years on Earth, forty generations of sparrows had served him, bringing him information that he used to protect himself and transform into riches.

Born Ilha—Manchu for "flower"—Tayiji entered the world with a crown of fragrant hair. Noses gravitated to his head's pleasant scent, which grew famous in his village for clearing sinuses. Women made their husbands smell his head to silence their deafening snoring. The elderly sought good-luck whiffs to breathe in a new day. His sweetness was so inviting it drew sparrows and bees to circle him as they would a true flower. Tayiji learned early on he did not much like bees after one stung him and caused his fat baby hand to swell to twice its usual size. When none of the villagers' usual remedies for insect stings worked, the sparrows rose to his cries. They plunged into a nearby mountain spring rumored to be the home of a great healing spirit and shook the water drops from their feathers onto his hand to rid it of poison. The sparrows then swatted the bees away until only songbirds remained to tend to their plump little flower.

Tayiji's sparrows were a garrulous bunch. Day and night they chirped to him, eager to share with him what they and their brood had seen. They told him tales from thousands of miles away should he be curious, traveling on the songs of millions of sparrows scattered across the world. They sang of an iceberg that felled the world's largest ship. They sang of the Giriama rebellion in Kenya, of holy bathers in the Yamuna River, of Zapatista fighters in Mexico, all to keep young Tayiji engrossed. As the boy grew older, however, his focus turned away from his birds and toward the concealment of his changing body under heavy layers of clothing. As Tayiji's attention shifted, so, too, did the sparrows'. The birds stopped chirping stories from afar and instead warned of much nearer perils at home, of the glint of ill intent in his father's gaze. But sweet Tayiji was too concerned with suppressing his growing bosom and hips to listen.

The sparrows tended to their flower despite his disregard. They stayed by his side when his father tried to enter Tayiji's bed one night, screeching in large bursts to alert him of the danger. Waking to the call of his sparrows, he scratched and bit his father until his teeth drew blood. When his father cried out in pain, Tayiji dealt a swift kick to his testicles to keep him from retaliation. He then fled his home and shed the name given to him by his wretched father, living nameless on the streets of a city far from his village. He cut his long hair, bound his breasts, and learned to pick pockets to stay alive. His birds were content to flit around spotting targets for him to rob, warning him of any approaching police. And so he became the most elusive thief in all of Changchun, until a roaming street gang noticed his encroachment on their turf. The older boys followed the sparrows and beat a sleeping Tayiji until he could not see through the puffing of bruised flesh around his eyes.

Unable to rely on sleight of hand in such an injured state, the temporarily blinded Tayiji listened to the sounds of his sparrows to scrounge for food. In attempts to keep their brother alive, the birds told him about a rich old poppy farmer who lived in a blue-roofed mansion and paid any swift young boy from the street to run errands. They led the boy to the old man, who shut him out for his pitiful physical state, saying that he was in the business of making money, not helping any passing beggar. Eager to prove the old man wrong, Tayiji lifted a package off another boy, made his delivery, and returned to the blue-roofed mansion with the account of the successful run. As he healed, the old man put him to work shuttling small packages of refined opium to households across Changchun. Young Tayiji did not understand the implications of his work at first, but the old man provided him with hot meals and gentle pats on the head, making the boy want to please him. The old man noticed that the short, freckled youth with the birds was skilled at evading the police and returned quicker than any other delivery boy. He thus favored the child, lavishing him with greater rewards and more consequential tasks. In a nod to the singing sparrows that trailed him like a procession of royal attendants, the old man took to calling him tàizǐ, "crown prince," and treated him as his son.

Tayiji gave himself the same name in Manchu and was known as such ever since.

When the Japanese invaded northeast China, they seized the region's poppy fields and poisoned its people with opium habits, draining the addicted populace of their money to fund their occupation. All across Manchukuo, government licenses were required to produce, sell, or purchase opium, shutting out local peddlers who did not conduct business within the state's laws. Opium revenue started to flow in from across the land, but officials seemed unable to take hold of the market in Xinjing, the center of their own operations. The Kantō-gun raided several opium dens in the city, believing withheld profits to be the reason for Xinjing's low revenue. There was no shortage of opium users in the city, but none seemed to frequent government-sanctioned parlors.

The old poppy farmer managed to hide his production and refinement labs from the Japanese in hard-to-reach mountain passages outside Xinjing. But his grip on the city came from his massive underground network of opium delivery, upheld by Tayiji and his sparrows. People had no need to go to state-run opium dens when the sparrows could anticipate their urges and call on Tayiji to deliver their fix. The Japanese, in turn, targeted Chinese warlords and opium-den owners until one clever bureaucrat among them noticed the flight patterns of the sparrows. Orders to kill and trap the brown songbirds spread throughout the city until the police were brought to the flutter above the blue-roofed mansion. When they realized that the old man was their only means to access his profitable local network, their enthusiasm for slaying him waned. Instead, they gave him an ultimatum: pay a hefty tithe to the empire or burn with his house. The poppy farmer, grown too old and complacent to fight, agreed to pay. Tayiji resented the shift, but saw wisdom in keeping his enemies close.

With his dying breath, the old man left his adopted son full run of his blue-roofed opium empire. Tayiji continued to supply most of Xinjing but also turned his attention to the moneyed elite of Manchukuo—the wealthy Chinese and Japanese from whom there were more funds to be gleaned. Rich men were perfect targets: they sought indulgence but were arrogant enough to believe their bodies would not cede control to their vices. Business boomed as he transformed his home into a luxury opium den staffed by beautiful yanhua that attracted wealthy clientele. For some time he fell into his own traps of decadence, discovering that he had quite the appetite for consuming the feminine beauty he had not wanted for his own body. For years he lived in his castle of women, smoke, and silk, keeping tabs on the Japanese with his sparrows to maintain this stasis of opulence.

While their brother fell to vice, his sparrows remained industrious, fluttering about watching China transform under occupation. The sparrows sang to Tayiji of Japan's ruthless labor practices as they plundered the land. The occupiers built factories where young men and women lost limbs to machines. They pushed underfed workers into caves to mine iron and coal. They shipped the crop yield to Japan, shrinking Chinese stomachs. But such birdsong did not rouse the wet-lipped Tayiji from his euphoric daze.

One frost-bitten morning in 1934, the birds brought Tayiji news of his birth father, a man he had tried not to think of over the decades since he had left his people. The sparrows told him of a large fortress northeast from Xinjing where Japanese soldiers held men and women captive. The prisoners were sometimes petty criminals, but for many, their only sin was being visibly poor. His father, dirty and passed out from drink on the streets of Harbin, had been taken into this prison. The birds told Tayiji of horrible things done there in the name of science. People were bled empty to see how organs changed in the moment of death. They were injected with the plague to test new vaccines. They were sliced open alive, feeling the drag of blades carve across their bones. The birds admitted they could not tell which mutilated corpse was his father's but that he had been buried somewhere on the fortress grounds.

This image haunted Tayiji for days. He had no love for his birth father, but the ghastly accounts of these Japanese experiments shook him out of his daily indulgences. He had never been one to think much about whether the choices he made were virtuous so long as they made him feel good. But he had observed throughout his life that a consistently good man was almost always an exception, that given the chance to flourish, the evil or weakness lurking within could override any man's humanity. He did not think there was much he alone could do, but he began to use his birds to identify soldiers who might be susceptible to the enticements of opium. Soldiers who may have seen or done things in the name of the emperor they might prefer to forget. One by one, he lured these men to his orbit with his knowledge of their secrets and neutralized them with the scourge of addiction until they wasted away into the void, leaving nothing but their coin for him to take. Tayiji had since made it a sport to hunt for these weak-link soldiers, finding perverse pleasure in inviting them to tea, inviting them to his home, and inviting them to their downfall passed to them in a pipe.

Now Feng-nüshi requested the help of his sparrows to protect her own empire against Japanese sanction. His sparrows served no master but he, though he would instruct them to keep watch on Fenghuang for any threats. Feng-nüshi allowed him into her teahouse but made a show of keeping her distance to protect the irreproachable moral reputation of her establishment. His money was good at Fenghuang, but not much else. Nonetheless, Tayiji's love of the teahouse and its offerings was genuine. He did not wish to see it felled by its own fumbled jabs at powerful men who could retaliate. Feng-nüshi had great disdain for being beholden to anyone, let alone any man; she would pay him handsomely for his troubles. What he had not expected was for her to offer Young-Ja, or any other Fenghuang girl of his choosing, as part of that payment. Feng-nüshi must have been truly spooked to risk sacrificing something so dear for his help. His sparrows had kept him informed of Feng-nüshi's and Bailong's little poison bandit brigade, though in a time of war, small raids would get them nowhere. The cheong-induced shame or guilt of low-level Manchukuoan bureaucrats could not stop marching armies from decimating China.

Tayiji had been intrigued by the round-faced Joseon girl since he had first seen her in Fenghuang. She did not have particularly striking features; perhaps it was her plainness that made her stand out to him from among the beauties of the teahouse. He had at first thought her naïve for putting herself at risk for a woman she did not know, though he appreciated the clumsy valor. But over time, it was her lack of obsequiousness, her reluctance to curry favor with the guests that made Tayiji want to crack her secrets for himself. Even now he did not want to let little Young-Ja leave his den so soon; he enjoyed watching the unguarded reactions to his teasing blossom on her little round face. He eventually sent her on her way, for with Feng-nüshi's blessing, he would wait to claim her into his house—should she so wish it.

Baek Yong-Woo could not bear to return to Fenghuang. He lay in the dark staring at the ceiling of a small hut for days, hiding in a village northwest of Xinjing. He knew it was imperative to get his house in order and root out whatever had led to the ambush. Every hour that passed without action was an hour lost to failure. But the doubt that had plagued him for months had become so heavy, he felt he could no longer lift his body to feed himself, let alone continue his pursuits. The small missions he had supported for the last decade against Japan had barely made a dent in the occupation of Joseon and China. He had sweated and bled until he lost everything—his home, his love, his hope. Even his appetite and sleep now eluded him. How much more would he have to sacrifice for freedom? In the past, Yong-Woo had been able to persist for the sheer numbers of people who relied on him. But his group was dwindling to death and desertion. New recruits were harder to come by and were often young and inexperienced.

A part of Yong-Woo wished to go south to aid the efforts of his comrades closer to the battlefield. But he could not leave the capital unmonitored with so few men. He continued his subtle espionage and worked to establish a new safehouse for his associates in this remote village. When he got word that his fellow Joseon comrade Go Nam-Choon was alive after fleeing the battlefront of Japan's war against China, he welcomed him with open arms, eager to learn of his cell's activities in the south.

When Nam-Choon arrived at Yong-Woo's hideout, he did not speak for two days and lost himself in drink and sleep. As he came to, he informed Yong-Woo that he had lost most of his men as Japanese aggression continued to rage. Nam-Choon confessed, however, that the horror of losing his men was nothing compared to what he had seen in Nanjing.

There the Japanese had massacred the city, razing it to the ground until nothing remained of its humanity. Thousands of women and children lay slaughtered, having been unable to evacuate before the Japanese arrived. Nam-Choon had been caught in a rush of people fleeing a spray of bullets, losing his footing and consciousness under the stomping of the terrified masses. When he opened his eyes again, he was in a tangle of corpses, awakened by the sounds of soldiers laughing and bayoneting any signs of movement among the dead. Feeling someone squirm beneath him, Nam-Choon willed them to stop moving until he found his fingers had wrapped around the person's throat to still them. Anything to ward off the attention of the soldiers. Night fell hours later as he lay above a man he had slain to save himself. In the cover of the dark, he crawled out of the mound of rotting bodies and into a nearby cluster of trees where he could continue to hide. Nam-Choon ran past thousands of desecrated women's bodies littering the ground, with missing limbs and stalks of bamboo shoved into their perforated wombs. Spilled blood congealed on the streets of Nanjing, slowing his tread as if in a cursed marsh risen from hell. A row of severed heads had been placed along the side of the road, lining the path of destruction. All sound ended. There were no birds, no insects, no life—the stream of running water could not be heard. He could not fathom what evil had curated the stage before him. He no longer thought he could fight it. He did not know what extant being on Earth could defeat this malevolence he would not have imagined in a thousand years.

Yong-Woo's ears rang. Nam-Choon had drunk himself back into a daze. Bouts of incoherent shouting punctuated his snoring, keeping Yong-Woo from succumbing to his own night terrors. They were mere men. What did they know? What could they do?

He pulled out the brown bottle Young-Ja had brought him on his last night in Fenghuang. It had sat heavy in his pack for weeks and he wondered if a small taste might help him rest. With his mind in disarray and bereft of sleep, he would be of no help to anyone. With some aided slumber he would be able to reset his troubled thoughts and shoulder his duties in the light of the new day. He pulled a syringe from his medicine pack and extracted what felt like a negligible dose of liquid from the bottle. The needle slid into taut skin. Coolness surged through his veins, muting the heartbeat and screaming throbbing in his ears.

CHAPTER SEVENTEEN

Xinjing, Manchukuo, Empire of Japan, 1939

Feng-nüshi's enduring snake hunt had yet to locate a nest, but it was not without consequence. Her claws hooked into every corner she saw, drawing blood from even those who committed no sin. Despite the chaos of the ongoing war in China, more girls than ever had left the teahouse within the last year seeking their fortunes where fingers might be less at risk of detachment. It was in this shortfall of women that Young-Ja and Meiyu, at seventeen years of age, became the youngest yet to be tapped for the role of server. Meiyu was ecstatic; Young-Ja, determined.

The older servers taught Young-Ja to mute her walk so that she might approach tables before men had the chance to lower their voices. They taught her to smile and keep her eyes downcast so men never saw in them traces of comprehension. Young-Ja absorbed every correction to her bearing in preparation for the main tearoom. But with each table she served, each group of men she infiltrated, she could not deny the swell of disappointment in her chest. She found that even the meanest-looking soldiers largely engaged in vapid conversation, guffawing over crude jokes or complaining about military rations. Officials did not pick apart their superiors' strategic decisions but instead grumbled about their horrible breath and haughty demeanors. Her most recent table had discussed at length one officer's long-suffering issues with constipation, his fellow officers each chiming in with their preferred remedies. Was this what she had feared for so long? To think that they were just ordinary men whose laughter came so cheaply. Utterly unremarkable men with stained shirts and food in their teeth. Realizing that such small men had murdered her parents and siblings, Young-Ja stoked a new vigor in pursuit of their downfall. She may not be able to bring her family back from death, but she would not join them without taking a few soldiers with her.

As disheartening as she found her interactions with guests, Young-Ja still committed to memory each detail she witnessed to report back to her mistress. Feng-nüshi would know best what could be used, and Young-Ja was eager to learn how to hone the same discernment. When she climbed the stairs to Feng-nüshi's office after her shift that night, she encountered a huddle of servers whispering conspiratorially outside the closed door.

"What's going on?" Young-Ja asked.

"Bailong is here."

Young-Ja straightened her back and slid past her older sisters to reach the door. She put her ear to the wood. "That can't be him. There's shouting."

"It's him. We saw him walk in not long ago," said one of the servers.

"He didn't even say hello to any of us," said another, crossing her arms.

"Has anyone shouted at Feng-nüshi before? Isn't he frightened of what she'll do?" Whispers swelled in the corridor as the women speculated on the nature of their quarrel.

Young-Ja waved her hand at the others to be quiet and pressed her ear harder against the office door. She closed her eyes to decipher the wood-dampened sounds on the other side.

"*No, Bailong. You've lost men three times in the last month. We have to wait.*"

"*We're wasting time! You cannot deny me these leads. We're barely making a dent as it is.*"

"*It's too risky now. One wrong move and you'll bring this house down with you. Know your place.*"

"*You think the Imperial Army won't bring you down just as well? We have to go bigger—nothing we've done has been enough!*"

"*No. You'll continue to get nothing from me if you keep showing poor judgment. And don't think I don't know about your new little habit.*"

The thumping of footsteps drew nearer and Young-Ja backed away from the door. Bailong barged out of the office. The gathered servers yelped and cleared a path for his angry strides. Young-Ja chased after him to the staircase.

"Mr. Baek, a moment, please."

Yong-Woo did not turn, continuing down the steps.

"Mr. Baek!"

"What do you want?" He whipped around and stared up at her.

Young-Ja startled at his sharp tone, at the dark circles under his eyes. She grabbed the banister for support. "I want to help you."

"Help me with what?" He glared, unblinking.

"Your . . . well, I—" Young-Ja stuttered. She had not presumed to know exactly how Yong-Woo would react, but hostility was surprising—he had never taken such ire with her before. "I'm a server now. I can help you get information on the Kantō-gun."

"What information could you possibly have for me?"

"I thought . . . you see, I—"

Yong-Woo narrowed his eyes. "We are at war. You are just a girl who pours tea for men. Nothing you do will make a difference. Know your place."

A chill displaced the color from Young-Ja's face.

"But . . . you brought me here for a reason. To do something," she said, her voice small.

Yong-Woo let out an exasperated sigh. "Your mistress would think you a fool for looking to me like this. If you can't find your own reasons for being here, then you really are nothing but a silly teahouse girl."

When he saw that she had no reply, he disappeared down the stairs.

Young-Ja stood numb for some time, clutching the banister so hard her knuckles blanched. The darkness that marred Baek Yong-Woo's face made him a stranger to her, no longer the man she had always looked to as a beacon of protection. She told herself that the stresses of his missions must have come to a head—he could not have meant what he said. When other girls walked by with concern on their brows, Young-Ja assured them she was fine and hurried downstairs, away from Feng-nüshi's office. All the observations she had been so eager to report now seemed immaterial. Not worth her mistress's time. She ran out into the night and toward the alley by the teahouse. Halting at a dark corner of the building free from prying eyes, Young-Ja crouched down and set her forehead on her knees, Yong-Woo's words echoing in her head.

Did he still see her as the frightened little girl he'd brought to the teahouse five years ago? A naïve child who had lost everything and knew nothing of the world? Tears welled in Young-Ja's eyes. She did not like thinking back to those miserable early days trapped in the storage room with all that rotted cheong. Perhaps Yong-Woo was right. She was just a silly teahouse girl. It had taken her so long to gain her footing at Fenghuang, to learn Chinese, to win the favor of the other women. It had taken her even longer to grasp what he and Feng-nüshi strove to do. And while she now toiled hard every day in that same pursuit, driven by thoughts of her lost family, she had accomplished nothing.

Teardrops darkened the fabric of her qipao. Yong-Woo may think she had little to show for her time in the teahouse. But Young-Ja pictured the men sitting inside, laughing with shoulders unweighted by fear, lounging without remorse. Determination still burned inside her and she would not give up on finding their weaknesses. Yong-Woo underestimated her. She knew in her absolute core that she could help, if only he knew how she felt.

If only.

Young-Ja raised her head from her knees.

She knew exactly how to show him what she felt.

How to show him her usefulness.

How had she not thought of it before?

"Joseon kkachi, is that you?"

Tayiji approached her, arm hooked around a tall woman with gray streaks in her bun. Young-Ja recognized her as the beautiful yanhua who had greeted her the day she delivered Feng-nüshi's message to Tayiji. They appeared to be heading home from their evening in the teahouse pavilion.

"What are you doing out here in the dark?" he asked. "Are you all right?"

Young-Ja swiped her palms across her eyes and stood up to straighten out her qipao. "Yes, I'm fine."

"What's upset you? Anything we can do?"

"No, no, I'll be all right. Please don't trouble yourselves on my account." Young-Ja tried to force a polite smile but could not suppress a sniffle to keep her nose from running.

"Hmm." Tayiji cocked his head and grinned. "What is it they say in Joseon again? 'If you laugh while you're crying, you'll grow hair on your ass'?"

Young-Ja laughed and wiped away the tears pooled at her chin. "Who taught you that?"

"Someone with a hairy ass, probably," he said, winking. He leaned closer. "Just say the word and you can come with me. Leave here whenever you want. I certainly would never wish to make you cry."

Young-Ja met Tayiji's warm gaze. He had always been kind to her. She briefly wondered what it would be like to enjoy the finery of the blue-roofed mansion and hide away in its hazy rooms. To walk into Fenghuang on Tayiji's arm as a customer to be served. But she did not entertain the thought for long.

"Thank you, but my place is here. There's work for me to do."

"As you wish. Cheer up, little kkachi—it pains me to see you so."

The yanhua by Tayiji's side leaned in and kissed Young-Ja's cheek. The scent of jasmine enveloped her as if with a gentle caress. "Good night, little one," the woman said.

The color returned to Young-Ja's face and she watched the two guests depart, laughing softly with each other as they strolled down the street. She dusted herself off, wiped her face with the skirt of her qipao, and walked back into the teahouse. There was work to do.

Young-Ja resumed her duties the following day as usual. She was no less diligent in monitoring her guests while still finding time to laugh with Meiyu and the other girls in passing. But she quietly slipped coins to the greeters and a few of the kitchen girls, requesting they alert her as soon as they next saw Bailong. Young-Ja did not expect he would come back to Fenghuang for a while yet but privately steeled herself for his return every day. Her wait lasted one month.

When Young-Ja entered the kitchen to retrieve an order one spring evening, two girls in gray tunics scurried up to whisper that Bailong had arrived through the back kitchen entrance. Young-Ja smiled and promised to give the girls an extra tip later that evening. She flagged Meiyu to take over her tables—all questions to be answered later—and ran into the storage room, where she had set aside a large jar, a knife, salt, honey, and a pile of kumquats she had paid the cook to retrieve for her at the market.

Young-Ja laid out the materials on the low table. Countless times she had shed her lonely tears in this room, fearing the day someone might discover that her cheong was tainted and cast her out. As a child she could not see beyond her own woes and had not understood why Feng-nüshi tormented her so with honeyed fruits. Even now, Young-Ja could only imagine where her cheong would have been taken, who might have consumed those many hundreds of jars. But the manipulations of the past did not matter now. She was resolved only to see the current moment through.

Young-Ja made quick work of paring the kumquats in half. She raced against the urgency of her task, not knowing how long Baek Yong-Woo would linger at the teahouse this time. When the storage room filled with the scent of freshly cut citrus, she took a deep breath, laid her left hand on a linen on the table, and plunged her knife in between the tendons of her hand until its point lodged firmly into the wood below.

Young-Ja cried out at the fierce pain radiating through her left hand and up her arm. She gritted her teeth through the agony and scooped the kumquat halves into the jar with her free hand, taking care not to let her blood or tears touch the fruits. When the pain started to dull, she clawed at the salt in a bowl and packed it into the slit of cut flesh where the knife remained embedded. Searing heat burst through the left side of her body as she poured honey over the kumquat slices. Dizzy and panting, Young-Ja worked nimbly despite having use of only a single hand. By the time her blood slid down the table and splattered on the stone floor, Young-Ja had removed the knife, wrapped her hand in a fresh cloth, and exited the storage room with a jar of honeyed kumquats clutched at her side.

Young-Ja ignored the other servers' concerned questions at her appearance as she hastened up the stairs to Feng-nüshi's office. She strode past the usual line of women in red waiting for their audience with their mistress and pushed open the door to the smoky room. Feng-nüshi and Baek Yong-Woo snapped up at the intrusion as Young-Ja marched up to them and set the jar of kumquats on Feng-nüshi's desk. The room stilled when she raised her arm to display her bleeding hand. Feng-nüshi recovered first.

"What is this—did you put her up to this?" she said, glaring at Yong-Woo. "We agreed to stop with the cheong—"

"No one told me to make this," said Young-Ja. "It was my idea. I want to help."

Feng-nüshi's eyes jumped from the bloody cloth around Young-Ja's hand to the golden jar on her desk. She set down her long silver tobacco pipe and stood. "What have you done, child?"

She dipped a pinky into the honey and dabbed the sticky residue on her tongue. The old woman crumpled onto her forearms against her desk and groaned. Yong-Woo rushed to her side and tried to catch her from collapsing on the floor. Feng-nüshi looked up at Young-Ja, shock twisted into her pained grimace.

"I want to help," said Young-Ja.

"We stopped using your cheong years ago," said Feng-nüshi, breath heavy. "It's too troublesome to transport and not always quite so precise in its effects. Difficult to find access points to use it too."

"I'm sure Bailong will find a way," replied Young-Ja, locking eyes with the man. Blood trickled down her wrist from the saturated bandage.

Feng-nüshi exhaled sharply as she pushed up from the desk and steadied herself back on her feet. "Go see to your wound. What you've done is reckless—you won't be able to work the tearoom until you've recovered."

Yong-Woo sealed the jar and pulled it to his side.

"Bailong," said the old woman, voice stern, "we agreed no more cheong. It's not sustainable."

"But this batch shouldn't be discarded, I'm sure you'll agree," he said. Yong-Woo and Feng-nüshi stared at each other in silence until she reached down for her silver pipe and put it to her lips.

"If you have ideas, I won't stop you. But she is not to make any more. I forbid it." She blew out a long plume of smoke.

Yong-Woo nodded and walked toward the exit with the jar in hand. He stopped by Young-Ja's side and put a hand on her shoulder.

"Let it ferment for a month before you use it," Young-Ja instructed in Korean. "It'll be easier to slip into food, water, whatever is best."

He replied, also in Korean, "Your contribution won't go to waste." Yong-Woo turned, offered a slight nod to Feng-nüshi, and hurried out the door.

Feng-nüshi ordered the women pretending not to eavesdrop outside her office to take Young-Ja down to the dorms. By the time Young-Ja was seated at her bed, word had spread among all the teahouse staff about what had transpired.

It was not long before Meiyu came running up to her friend in panicked tears and shooed the others away.

"You idiot, are you crazy? Oh, it must hurt so much! What has gotten into you? You poor thing!"

Young-Ja reminded Meiyu to breathe. She watched with calm as her teary friend hurried to gather the necessary medical supplies from the cabinet in their dorm.

"Ooh, if I have to work shifts with that snooty Qizhen because you're out, I'm going to kill you!" Meiyu plopped down by Young-Ja to clean the angry wound in her hand. Once seated, she seemed to pick up that Young-Ja was in no mood to talk and so held her tongue while she worked. But quiet was not Meiyu's natural inclination; she began to hum softly as she layered the healing balm of honey on the gash and wrapped her friend's hand tight with a clean cloth bandage. Young-Ja closed her eyes, letting her breath fall in time with the melody.

"My sister, Young-Sook, used to sing to me when I got hurt," she said in Korean. "She'd fix me up just like this if our Uhmuhni wasn't around to do it."

Meiyu stopped humming and looked up from her task. Young-Ja had never mentioned a sister or mother before. She kept silent as Young-Ja continued to speak about her crooked-nosed father's comforting hugs, the clever mother to whom she could never lie, the sister and brother for whom she loved to cook. When she had finished recounting their lives and what became of them, speaking aloud for the first time of that sunny morning in the yard, they wept. Meiyu moved her friend's bandaged hand aside so that the tears they shed would not ruin its fresh cloth, hugging Young-Ja to her chest as they lay down to sleep.

Young-Ja lay awake in the dark, soothed by the gentle rhythm of Meiyu's breathing. Even if she accomplished nothing at the teahouse, even if her family was now a collection of fading memories, she knew she could always find comfort in Meiyu's arms.

From that night on, Meiyu asked greeters not to seat Japanese soldiers in her section. She ran upstairs every hour during her shifts to look after Young-Ja in the dorms, refreshing bandages as needed and checking that the stitches Feng-nüshi's physician had eventually sewn in did not lead to infection. Young-Ja was not permitted on the Fenghuang floor again until the tendons in her hand had healed enough to carry a filled teapot unaided, though her left hand never regained the dexterity of the right. Feng-nüshi threatened to kick her out if she harmed herself again, claiming that the fantasy of server perfection would be ruined if she had visible blemishes. Young-Ja accepted whatever sliver of protective concern was veiled in the threat and took to wearing delicate silk gloves to hide her scar. Although it was not her intent, her gloves possessed such stylish flair that other servers also opted to don them to improve their allure.

The next time she saw Baek Yong-Woo heading up to clash with Feng-nüshi, he greeted Young-Ja with a slight bow of the head. Unease persisted in his increasingly sunken eyes, but never again did she see herself reflected there as a silly teahouse girl.

CHAPTER EIGHTEEN

Xinjing, Manchukuo, Empire of Japan, 1941

I've bedded him. I'm a woman now."

Meiyu's downturned eyes crinkled in excitement. The girl was often skirting the Fenghuang server rule of silence; she could not help but wink at guests who enjoyed her playful disposition. Even Feng-nüshi reserved tacit leniency for this behavior, as it drew in guests and opened their pockets, though no other server tried her luck in the same vein. Many guests favored the lively Meiyu, but one well-to-do Japanese merchant had taken particular notice. He had thick eyebrows and a strong jaw he would stroke as he watched Meiyu sway her hips around the main tearoom. At first he threw her long stares over appreciative smiles. Then came expensive gifts. A jade necklace. A pair of fine red slippers, bright-pink flowers embroidered across the silk. When she bent over to pour him chrysanthemum tea, he pushed her hair back behind her ears and promised her the world. He described his childhood home in the port city of Kobe, where he would take her to eat delicious fish. He spoke of his favorite street lined with magnolia trees, where they could observe the spring blossoms. Meiyu shivered with delight at each whisper, falling with abandon into the vision he wove with every word.

"He wants to take me to Japan. Me, in Japan . . . I've never even seen the ocean before!" Meiyu squealed as she examined the tight needlework on her new red slippers.

Young-Ja clutched her friend's hand. "It wouldn't hurt to be a little more cautious. Your trust should be harder won—you barely know him."

Meiyu laughed her usual disarming laugh. "I'll never find love if I keep shying away from men like you do. And he's not just any man after my body. He actually listens and asks me questions. He cares what I think, I know it."

Meiyu launched into details of their intimate encounter, sighing over her lover's caresses. Young-Ja listened, curious. She recognized handsomeness when she beheld it, though it did not induce tittering as it did in Meiyu and the others. It warmed her to see her older sisters in love with one another, though she herself did not yearn to be touched. After watching Meiyu lose herself in the snare of romance, however, Young-Ja was relieved never to have felt its disorienting tug. But she also worried about what might come next. She did not want to imagine what her life would be should Meiyu run off to be someone's wife, and longed for the days when her friend dreamed of marrying Bailong. Simpler days when he was the handsome man who could do no wrong. But they had not spoken of him for years. Meiyu's attention had since turned from Bailong to the merits of other men whose shine had not been dulled by misery.

Baek Yong-Woo no longer commanded the same presence in the teahouse. Many of the new kitchen girls did not know who he was, while the older servers had stopped thinking of him. His visits were rare—now once every several months, and in the company of churlish, unshaven men who threw vulgar looks at the staff. On the occasions he did have business at Fenghuang, he did not turn heads with his once-gleaming smile. People preferred instead to turn away from his sunken cheeks, his sallow skin, the fraying edges of his dirty suit sleeves. Yong-Woo did not spare any winks of flirtatious recognition for the women in red, hurrying to Feng-nüshi's office and avoiding all eye contact. There were no gifts, no shipments of tea, no faint smell of pine needles. He had thinned away into an unkempt revenant Young-Ja no longer recognized. Even his voice had lost its strong tenor, now heard only as discordant shouts through the closed door to Feng-nüshi's office.

Young-Ja wondered if she could still catch glimpses of the self-assured man who had bought her yeot candies back in Cheonan, of the passionate resistance fighter who infiltrated government arms factories. As she mourned the dimming light of Baek Yong-Woo's valor, she wished she could calm whatever disquiet had rotted his being. This was in part out of concern—she had, after all, grown to care for him—but also out of frustration that he no longer seemed up to the task of resistance. No matter how many coins Feng-nüshi awarded Young-Ja, watching Yong-Woo's degeneration eroded her faith that a valuable observation would be put to effective use against the Japanese. But her growing vexation with the man was shunted aside, however, as a crisis unfurled in Meiyu's world.

Meiyu's handsome Japanese merchant had not been seen at Fenghuang for a week. Not since he had finally tasted Meiyu's flesh and made her cry out under his touch. This at first had no effect on Meiyu's luster. Convinced that he was away on pressing business, she, too, threw herself into her work. But with each day that passed with no word, she fell further into despair. The downturned eyes that were so pleasing when she smiled transformed in misery, drooping as if the slope of her eyelids had been pulled low by the weight of her tears.

Young-Ja cared for her grieving friend. She bathed her and brushed her hair in silence, listening to Meiyu's choked theories about where the merchant had gone: perhaps he had gotten stuck somewhere with a major shipment, perhaps he was unable to cross the lines of war to make it back to Xinjing, perhaps he was dead in a ditch somewhere. When her sisterly touch failed to ease Meiyu's distress, Young-Ja brewed the calming root tea she had learned to make from her father. After drinking the concern Young-Ja could not help but infuse into the tea, Meiyu lost her words, weeping for the man to whom she had given her body, her heart, her mind.

Young-Ja did not know what to say to restore Meiyu's spirits. So she tried painting her friend's nails and braiding flowers into her hair. She tried getting the cook to make her an extra mung bean cake. She tried ceding Tayiji's table to Meiyu, though even Tayiji's charm and generous tips had little effect. Young-Ja suspected that the merchant had simply done what her older sisters at Fenghuang told her men do—abscond after taking his prize. But battles raged on as Japan clawed at control of China; few went untouched by its destruction. It was not implausible that the merchant was an otherwise honorable victim to circumstance, trapped behind some wartime barrier longing for Meiyu as she did him.

The strains of war were beginning to show even among wealthier Fenghuang clients. With ongoing conflict suppressing commerce and drying up wages, few had the coin or the time to spare on lazy afternoons with teahouse women. Japanese ministers were occupied trying to manipulate the surrender of the Chinese from their desks in Manchukuo. Xinjing's leisure class had fled for calmer environs overseas. Tayiji had also been showing his face less frequently, though when he did turn up, it was typically to whisper into the ears of shifty-eyed men rather than to lounge with his beautiful yanhua.

Despite the troubles of their usual clientele, Fenghuang was no less busy, no less famous for its promise of an elegant experience. The teahouse was instead beginning to attract a different class of men to fill its tables, ones who came in with unshaven faces covered with the dust of horseback raids, baijiu lingering on their clammy breath. The bluster of these more uncouth guests chased away what little remained of Fenghuang's old crowd.

One such group of rough-looking men had been seated at a table for Young-Ja to tend to in the courtyard. She suspected she had seen some of the men in this group before, accompanying Baek Yong-Woo during one of his late-night visits to Feng-nüshi. She felt her tension release somewhat at the thought that they were Bailong's associates; perhaps she could pick up hints on his whereabouts or latest ventures from this table. As she approached, the red-faced man nearest her ran his eyes down her body and placed his hand on the small of her back when she stopped at the table.

"Fetch us your best tea. We're in a generous mood tonight," he said in Korean.

Young-Ja held back a flinch at his touch. She bowed and hurried away to retrieve their order.

When she returned to set the cups down and placed the teapot on the table, the man who had touched her before grabbed her wrist and jerked her toward him.

"Why don't you join us? Maybe we'll pour *you* some tea," said the man, smiling to reveal rot across his yellow teeth. She shook her wrist free from his grip and poured the tea as intended, acting as if nothing were amiss.

"I like virtuous women. I have to work a little harder for my reward." He seized her waist and pulled her toward his lap. The other men laughed.

"Let go!" Young-Ja cried out. The reek of alcohol exuded from the man's pores as she tried to push him away. He held strong.

"Not thinking of saving yourself for a particular man, are you? Who is it? Baek Yong-Woo? We all know he wouldn't bed you . . . you're not his type. Not enough hair on the lip."

The others laughed. Young-Ja burned red and twisted around to loosen his hold.

"Baek Yong-Woo wouldn't be able to get it up anyway now, from what I hear," the man continued. "Not with those needles in his veins—"

Young-Ja lifted her arm and elbowed his jaw. The strike caused him to clench down on his tongue and cry out in pain, blood trickling out with his saliva down from the corners of his lips. Young-Ja wrenched herself free but stilled when

Feng-nüshi descended on the table, sparrows fluttering behind her. She would surely be punished for her defiance of protocol.

The old woman pushed Young-Ja out of the way and swung down her cane. Its beak handle cracked into the wood of the seat between the man's spread legs.

"This is not a brothel. Go satisfy your lust elsewhere," she said in Korean.

"You old bitch—"

Feng-nüshi yanked her cane free from the seat, then thrust the flat top of its handle into his throat. The man choked and fell out of his chair, gasping for breath. The other men jumped up and drew their weapons. Feng-nüshi did not pay them mind as a sparrow landed on her shoulder.

"And you are Hwang, a gun for hire that few will hire because your aim is so piss poor. I would think twice before you start trouble here, or I'll make sure no one can hire you at all."

The man narrowed his eyes at the sound of his name on her tongue.

"Wen. Im. Liu," Feng-nüshi said, looking every man in the eye as she listed their names. "Don't think I don't know every man who sets foot in my house. I know how much coin you have in your pockets, which whores you favor, whom you call master. Leave before I show everyone here what else I know of you."

The men exchanged looks before deciding to leave, kicking down chairs as they exited. The other guests settled back into their own teas, but few eyes left the tall, gaunt mistress of the teahouse.

"Hurry up and clean this. Get back to serving your tables." Feng-nüshi clacked away with her cane as sparrows lifted up into the sky. Meiyu rushed over to Young-Ja and helped her clear the mess.

But Feng-nüshi could not always be present to quash the growing aggression of the new clientele. So the teahouse women taught one another how to free their wrists from an unwelcome grip and made sure to pair off so no one would be left in the tearoom alone to be devoured by the wolves that had found a new den.

"Ichikawa-sama!"

Young-Ja and the party she was serving turned their heads to Meiyu's squeals. The girl slammed her tea tray down and ran toward a man in a dark-gray suit striding into the main tearoom. Her handsome Japanese lover, returned to her at last. Her red silk slippers pattered to a halt when several police walked in behind him, fanning out to block the entrance.

"You're back—" Meiyu began to speak when she was interrupted by the man's booming announcement.

"Manchukuo summons the mistress of Fenghuang. She is to show herself now." The man ignored Meiyu and scanned the room. It had been a quiet afternoon with only a few tables seated, but all chatter stopped as guests turned to examine the disruption.

"Ichikawa-sama, what—" Meiyu ventured.

"Go tell your mistress that she has important guests to answer to. Now!" he commanded, with no trace of his former tenderness.

Meiyu searched his eyes with a pleading look, but he simply barked at her to hurry. She flinched and ran upstairs. Some guests left their money at their tables and hurried to the door, wanting to distance themselves from what looked to be ominous police business. A few curious onlookers remained seated. Young-Ja rushed to gather with the other servers near the hallway to the kitchen to observe the clamor.

The steady beat of the brass cane tip echoing on the floorboards announced Feng-nüshi's approach. She descended the staircase, Meiyu shrinking behind her, pausing on the last few stairs to maintain vantage over the men before her. She looked down at the crowd but did not say anything, her wordless gaze demanding they announce their intentions. The man in the suit met her defiance with a stony expression. "You are to answer to the government of Manchukuo for your many crimes. Step down and bow before the authorities," he commanded.

Feng-nüshi did not budge. "This is the first I'm hearing of wrongdoing in our simple teahouse," said the old woman. "The gentleman will have to inform me of my alleged offenses."

The man continued in a harsh baritone. "Your first offense: assaulting an innocent citizen of the Empire of Japan."

The man gestured at the police behind him. Hwang strutted in, the Joseon rogue with rotted teeth who had attacked Young-Ja a few days prior. He walked over and stood next to the man who was very likely not a merchant named Ichikawa. Hwang held his sneering head high and glared at Feng-nüshi, who in turn looked only at the man in the dark-gray suit.

"To my knowledge, it is not a crime to discipline a dog for its feckless barking," she declared.

Hwang growled and reached for a weapon tucked in his belt, but the man in the suit held his arm up to keep him back. He continued listing off Feng-nüshi's transgressions.

"Your second offense: trading in flesh and operating a brothel without the proper license. Your third and most severe offense: countless thought crimes amounting to treason and conspiracy against the emperor."

Feng-nüshi was not fazed. "You have no proof," she said, her voice low and unwavering.

"We have several witnesses of these crimes," the man said. "The very man you assaulted reported on your extensive web of spies and their work to bring harm against the empire. He also disclosed that he was made to pay a steep price to bed one of your prostitutes."

"I did not think this government valued so highly the false word of a drunk buffoon." Feng-nüshi stroked her beak cane handle with her thumb. Hwang gritted his teeth, seething, his breath heavy through his nostrils.

The man in the suit shifted his glare from Feng-nüshi to Meiyu, who had been staring wide-eyed at her lover's incomprehensible transformation.

"I also have direct testimony from the very women you have hired to carry out your whoring and conniving espionage," he said.

"Ichikawa-sama—" Meiyu started shaking her head.

"Silence," the man barked. "You, whore, are also under arrest for abetting the traitor Feng, along with every other prostitute working in this nest of vipers," he said, looking around at the other servers gathered by the hallway to the kitchen. "Bow down before the authority of the emperor!"

Meiyu released an anguished wail and fled up the stairs.

Feng-nüshi narrowed her eyes. She glanced at the five police posted by the door before stepping down from the last few stairs. She took slow strides and drew closer to her accuser.

"I bow for no man."

Feng-nüshi swung her cane at Meiyu's duplicitous seducer. He jumped back in surprise but the point of the beak pierced his throat with a dull thud. He gurgled out a command to kill and burn as blood spilled from his neck and soaked into the expensive fabric of his suit.

What few guests had remained to watch now fled, screaming in fear. The police let them pass and converged toward Feng-nüshi. The mistress of the teahouse jerked her cane free from the man's neck and landed her second strike on the temple of the nearest policeman. He fell to the floor and did not rise again.

This agility stunned the men who had not assumed it would require much effort to detain an old woman and some teahouse girls. But one man reminded himself that Feng-nüshi was a mere woman with a lame leg, no fearsome warrior. He drew his pistol, aimed, and shot her in the chest.

The servers shrieked as Feng-nüshi crumpled to the ground. All was still except for the writhing of the man in the suit, choking as he clutched the fountain of blood at his throat.

"You know the orders," said the policeman who had fired the shot.

The police began to pour kerosene over the tables and chairs in the tearoom. Young-Ja and the other servers ran back into the kitchen to alert the women who were gripped by the rhythm of their tasks, unaware of the madness transpiring in the next room.

The servers shouted into the kitchen. "Get up, all of you! We have to leave, now!"

Most of the kitchen staff jumped up and followed the stream of women toward the back exit, while others who did not react so quickly were dragged away from their work. Satisfied that the women in the kitchen were finding egress, Young-Ja pivoted back to the tearoom—she needed to run upstairs for Meiyu and any others.

As Young-Ja left, the women poured into the back storage room and tugged at the door. It did not move. They did not realize that the police had already boarded up the back exit to trap the workers inside. The women banged at the door, hitting at it with whatever items were within reach, but it would not budge. Some kept chipping away at the exit, while others debated turning back toward the main entrance, facing whatever awaited them in the tearoom. By the time the women gave up on the door and spilled back into the kitchen, a curtain of flames blocked their path. They ran to fill whatever vessels they could with water to throw on the fire, but it was not enough. The flames ate into the kitchen and pushed the women out onto the laundry patio, where they clawed at the towering wall and shouted at one another to grab anything to help them scale the smooth stone. But the wall was too high, their reach only so long.

When Young-Ja left her sisters in the kitchen, she ran back into the tearoom, where the police had set torches to the kerosene as they left the building. Flames spread on the tables, the delicate screens, and the beautiful woodwork of the windows.

Panic shooting through her body, Young-Ja sprinted upstairs in a frantic search for Meiyu and any other remaining women. She cried out her sister's name, looking for that puppy-eyed face in the rooms of the second floor. Her shouts directed the few women she saw to escape their burning house.

Young-Ja ran to her shared dorm and found it empty. Upon seeing the clear blue sky through the window, she briefly wondered where Tayiji's sparrows were. Did he already know of this chaos? Young-Ja did not realize that the bodies of Tayiji's fallen sparrows littered the streets of Xinjing. She did not know that in the dark of the previous night, police had scattered poisoned grains across the city for the sparrows to consume. She did not know that one by one, the birds dropped from the sky, unable to warn Feng-nüshi or Tayiji of the approaching danger.

Young-Ja climbed farther up into the building's third floor, screaming for Meiyu to no response. There were no signs of other women either, but the smell of smoke was floating up from the stairs below. Young-Ja knew she did not have much time and so hastened to check each room. All empty.

Only Feng-nüshi's office remained. Her mistress's papers were scattered on the desk of the otherwise unoccupied room, fluttering in the breeze from an open window that was usually kept shut. When Young-Ja turned to the open window, she blanched.

There, beneath the windowsill, sat a single red silk slipper with pink flowers delicately embroidered across its side, its mate or owner nowhere to be seen.

Young-Ja wailed and ran out of the room, away from what she would have to confront if she looked down from the window. Possessed with the urgency of running outside to hold Meiyu once again, she could not, in that moment, allow herself to believe that she would be too late. That she had been too late.

Flames licked at Fenghuang's columns, ornate ceilings, and walls. The loud crackles of burning wood rang like thunderous death knells. Young-Ja screamed at the tears prickling her vision as she sprinted downstairs, inhaling thick clouds of smoke. She doused herself with a pitcher of water that sat on a table before falling to her knees to crawl. She could barely see as the embers bit at the flesh around her eyes. Hovering cinders flew into her mouth. She crawled toward the daylight, convulsing in a fit of coughs as she felt around for a path to her fallen sister outside. But the smoke in her eyes blinded her to the soldier who dropped his rifle butt against her skull.

The soldier picked up Young-Ja's limp body. He carried her away from the flames behind them, away from her home. He carried her like yet another piece of cargo and tossed her into a truck headed out of the city limits, away from Xinjing.

Fenghuang burned as a message to anyone who dared challenge the Japanese Empire. Observers surrounded the building in shock and stared at the dark columns of smoke surging into the clear sky. The screams of the women within faded as the crackling blaze devoured Fenghuang's daughters, stealing their final breaths with its glittering veil of flying embers. Ash fell for miles around, leading villages far away to think that winter's first snow had come early.

Many years after Fenghuang Teahouse burned to the ground, people still spoke of its legend. The grace and allure of its women were unmatched. The tea, the purest and smoothest anyone had ever tasted. Many believed that such a significant beacon of culture could never be established again to welcome guests. Among the fond memories were whispers of its final day. Those who claimed they were present to witness the fire swore they spotted a bleeding Feng-nüshi in the window of her third-story office, looking down at the people below with a terrifying serenity as the flames engulfed her.

CHAPTER NINETEEN

Unknown, Manchukuo, Empire of Japan, 1941

Young-Ja's head pounded. Her vision blurred in darkness and she could not glean her whereabouts. Her finger brushed over the tangle of hair on her head to inspect a wet scab, the epicenter of a throbbing pain. Bodies jostled around her. They were moving in some sort of vehicle, the roar of its engine nearly drowning out the chorus of moans and sobs. A fog of confusion and pain slowed her thoughts, but her vision came into focus on the fading sunset seeping through the slots in the wall near the ceiling. Young-Ja discerned that she was packed in the vehicle with other people, some crying, some asleep, many staring off in silence. Panicking, she turned to the girl sitting to her right and asked where they were.

"I don't speak Chinese," said the girl in Korean. Even in the dim light, head throbbing in pain, Young-Ja noted that this girl was remarkably beautiful. Her skin was unblemished and her eyes hooded in sultry flair. Young-Ja repeated her question in her native tongue.

"Oh, you're from Joseon. I didn't think you were because of your clothes," the girl said, eyeing Young-Ja's soiled qipao. "I don't know where we're going. Someone told me I could get a job at a factory if I got in the truck, but some of these girls were forced on along the way. You were knocked out."

Young-Ja swiveled her head and took a closer look at the people around her. There were at least fifteen others, if not more. All girls. At nearly twenty years of age, Young-Ja appeared to be one of the oldest in the group. Many looked a few years younger. No one seemed to want to meet her eyes or answer her questions. These were not the girls Young-Ja was desperate to see. She needed to hold Meiyu, she needed to behold the smiles of her other Fenghuang sisters, she needed to know that those sputtering flames had been a misplaced nightmare. Young-Ja propped herself up from the floor on her forearms and tried to rise, ignoring the pain in her head. She examined the space for an exit and found none. There were no doors or windows, only narrow slots to let in air and light near the ceiling that her hands could not reach even if she could stand. An incoherent wail erupted from her hoarse throat, animal-like, dripping with gruesome suspicions that she could not choke down in the dark.

"Stay calm. They already beat that girl over there for screaming earlier," explained the beauty, pointing at another girl nearby whose left eye was swollen shut. She patted Young-Ja on the shoulder and gently pushed her down to rest. She introduced herself as Bok-Hee and asked Young-Ja for her name. Young-Ja did not have much to say after the introduction. Her thoughts were malformed and reeling, grieving Meiyu, trying to divine how she had gone from the blinding flames in the teahouse to imprisonment with strangers in this dark vehicle. The girls jerked around to the lurches of the truck until it finally came to a halt.

Men's voices rumbled outside before the door to the compartment opened. A rush of cold air blew in.

"Shit, they stink of piss," said a tan-uniformed soldier. "Out, all of you. And stand over there."

The girls climbed out of the truck and trudged into a fenced area outside of a wooden building. They stood shivering, in part from the cold, in part from fear. There was a large trough of water with several buckets scattered about. When the captives were told to take off their clothes and bathe, no one moved.

"Are you deaf? Hurry up and wash."

"But it's cold and we're outside. It's not decent," said one of the girls in accented Japanese.

A soldier walked up to the speaker and slapped her across the face. He raised his bayoneted gun at her. Gasps rippled through the line of girls.

"Clean yourselves now. Or we will do it for you."

The girls stepped out of their clothes in silent terror, clumsy but quick in their movements under the threat of violence. Muted squeals followed the splashes of cold water they dumped on their heads. Young-Ja shuddered as she washed off the filth and smells of the trip from her body. They were not given soap, and no one dared ask for it. Even in the darkening dusk, Young-Ja could see that the pale bodies around her donned bruising or red gashes across the skin. The beaten girl whom Bok-Hee had pointed out earlier wiped away the crusted blood on her face, appearing younger and shorter than when she was crouched in the truck. The soldiers leered at the solemn young bathers from behind their rifles. Some lit up cigarettes and laughed. The cold water stripped the heat from the girls' hot tears as it ran down their faces, flowing into gray streams that sank into the soil between their pallid toes.

The girls shivered against the wooden building as the guards passed out cotton gowns that could cover up their nakedness. Once dressed, they were brought inside to a corridor lined with closed doors. Each was to wait her turn to enter the door at the end of the hall. Guns in the arms of the soldiers enforced silence during the wait. When it was Young-Ja's turn, she walked into a small room with a cot, a table, and a scale. A middle-aged man in glasses with a trim haircut sat at the table writing notes in Japanese.

"Please, sir, I need to go back to Xinjing," said Young-Ja. "I don't know how I got here, but there's been a mistake—"

"Shh, calm yourself," the man in glasses said, standing up. "In due time. But since you're here, let's do your medical checkup first." He motioned at her to stand on the scale.

"Please, you don't understand," pleaded Young-Ja.

"We'll get to that. Just step up here first," he said gently.

Young-Ja stepped onto the scale with hesitation and watched him note down her weight. He then instructed her to sit on the cot.

"What year were you born?" the man asked.

Young-Ja did not answer. The man looked at her over the top of his glasses.

"It's okay, little one, no need to be afraid of me. I'm just here to help you and check on your health. I won't hurt you." The doctor smiled. "Now, how old are you?"

"Nineteen," Young-Ja whispered. He seemed different from the soldiers outside. Calmer. Softer.

"Good, good. Any injuries I should know about?"

Young-Ja reached for the back of her head where she had been struck outside Fenghuang. Pain lingered, but she could not help but feel a sliver of hope that this doctor with the soft voice might be able to heal her, tell her how to get back home. The doctor turned her head to part her wet hair with his delicate hands. He examined the wound through his glasses.

"Just a minor bump. A scab is already forming nicely and you should be fine with a little rest. Now, lie down on the cot," he said.

Young-Ja hesitated, not wanting to put the weight of her head down on her wound. The smiling doctor patted her hand.

"I only need to check a few things. Don't worry, I'll be quick and it won't hurt. Then we'll get you on your way."

Young-Ja lowered her back onto the cot, taking a sharp breath as her tender head met the fabric. She stared up at the wooden ceiling. The doctor took her pulse and jotted further notes.

"When was the last time you had a health inspection?"

"I haven't—"

Young-Ja gasped. The man had thrust his dry fingers into the slit between her legs. The pain from the sudden intrusion caused her eyes to water.

"Shh, just relax," the man said, staring at her. "This is routine."

His fingers moved inside her. Young-Ja tried to push away from him.

"Keep still, I'm checking for disease." He pushed his free hand on top of her abdomen to hold her down. "If you move, I'll have to start the examination process all over again."

The man peered down at her through his glasses, his fingers sliding in and out, his breath quickening. Tears gathered at the corners of Young-Ja's eyes and she let out a meek cry, asking him to stop. The man moved his hand from her stomach and pressed down over her mouth. The other hand shoved its fingers into her until the man apparently felt satisfied she was not diseased.

"You may get up and exit out the other door."

Young-Ja stood up, void of thought, and walked out as ordered. Another soldier then led her into her final stop of the night.

The girls who had undergone their health checkups before Young-Ja lay huddled on mats strewn about the new room. Some cried into their knees, others sat in silence. Young-Ja put her back against the wall and slid down to the floor. She wanted to scream but could not find her voice. Shame and regret surged through her as she wondered why she had not kicked the man off. Why she had not shouted for help. The dull soreness between her legs was a testament to her weakness, and she buried her head into her knees, shaking her head and willing these sensations to leave her.

Someone next to her started to bawl loudly, gasping for breath in between her wails. When the soldier returned to deposit the next girl into the room, he walked over to the source of the racket and kicked her until she fell to her side. She yelped as his boot dug into the soft flesh of her stomach and knocked the breath from her body.

"Shut up and go to sleep, all of you!"

Everyone stilled. He looked around, daring them to defy him before slamming the door.

Young-Ja crawled over to the fallen crier, who was now coughing up blood. She looked up at Young-Ja through the slit of her puffed-up eye, a token of her earlier punishment for screaming in the truck. Young-Ja sat her up, wiping away the blood on her chin with her sleeve. She whispered assurances and tucked away the strands of hair that had fallen out of the younger girl's braid. As Young-Ja inspected the girl's swollen face, she brushed against a certain familiarity. The high cheekbones, the oval face, the long black braid. In the girl's pained expression flickered a mild resemblance to Young-Sook, her older sister whom she had believed dead since the soldier abducted her ten years ago in Cheongju. Confronting the memory of Young-Sook in this stranger's tear-soaked eyes, Young-Ja, too, felt her vision blur with wet heat. She took the girl into her arms and held her, wondering if this was what those soldiers had done to her child sister so many years ago. She tightened her hold around the girl at this thought, embracing her as she would the sibling she could not save.

"Where are we?" the young girl whispered in Korean. "What's going to happen to us?"

"I'm not sure. But it's late. Get some sleep and we can figure things out together in the morning," Young-Ja said, trying to soothe the shaking girl. She stroked her hair and whispered kind words until the girl's sniffling slowed into steady breaths. Young-Ja closed her eyes to sleep, trying to ignore the moans from the others in the room. The girl curled in her arms radiated a trembling warmth that helped lull Young-Ja to rest.

Young-Ja did not know how long she had been out when she woke again, though darkness still blanketed the sky outside the window. Soft snores suggested that everyone was asleep. Young-Ja closed her eyes, but the room was cold and her shivering kept her from holding on to her fading slumber. The girl she went to sleep holding was still nestled in her chest. Some time passed before Young-Ja realized that she could not hear or feel the girl's soft breaths. Her bruised body lay stiff and cold. Young-Ja rolled away in panic, gasping as she convulsed into dry heaves. She coughed up what little liquid remained in her empty stomach: a clear, bilious mucus that burned her throat. She collapsed back onto the floor, void of thought. The coolness of the mat against her cheek remained the only sign she could feel something, anything, and she stayed there, unmoving, as the light of sunrise filtered in through the window.

In the morning, the girls were taken by armed men to a long shanty structure in the fenced yard outside. It looked like a stable for farm animals: a wood panel wall split the structure lengthwise down the middle, creating two long rows of stalls under the roof. In each stall of the stable lay a mat hiding behind a flimsy curtain. A total of sixteen mats in sixteen stalls. Fifteen girls were told to step into the space and lie down on a mat inside. One mat would be left empty that day.

Young-Ja sat on her mat awaiting further instructions when a soldier approached, climbed on top of her, and pinned her arms down. Her shrieks were lost in a chorus of splitting howls as the others confronted their own horrors. Young-Ja flailed and hit the soldier, who in turn had no compunctions about striking her across the face. He pressed his knee into her stomach until she lost her breath. When the soldier felt her go limp, he wriggled out of his pants, pushed up her dress and shoved himself inside her. Hot pain shot up her spine. Young-Ja screamed. She had never prayed to the heavens before that moment, but she prayed for it to end. She prayed for lightning to strike her dead. She prayed for the earth to open beneath her and swallow her up. It was not long before the soldier shuddered and pushed hot, vile breath in her ear. He slumped his body weight on top of her for a moment before pushing himself up to his knees, his limp penis slick with her blood.

"My lucky day," he said, wiping the blood off on Young-Ja's dress. "Since you're clean I won't have to regret not wearing a condom." He rose and pulled up his pants.

Young-Ja could hear distant screams from the others even though her eardrums burst with a horrible ringing. Her own voice seemed to catch in her constricted throat as she fell into panicked spasms gasping for breath. She did not register when the soldier left and the next came in. This one, too, climbed on top and held down her wrists. He emptied his seed into her mechanically. A third one came in and Young-Ja felt she had gone blind, unable to see what was happening to her as reality. She floated in and out of consciousness, her head bumping into the central wall of the stable in a steady beat as soldiers thrust into her slack body. She did not know how many soldiers she received that day, but she recalled the last one of the night. He spat on her once he finished.

"Chōsen pi," he called her. Joseon cunt.

Young-Ja's vision blurred in and out of focus as a scratching sound came from somewhere beyond her stall. The girl in the space next to her carved a notch into the wall with her jagged fingernail, adding to numerous coarse lines that had been grooved into the wooden paneling. When the guards came by and told the girls to get up, the one next to Young-Ja spoke up.

"I tallied the number of men I saw today. How much will I be paid for them?"

The guards laughed. "Paid? I think plenty of deposits have been made to the Bank of Chōsen today."

The armed guards barked at the girls to follow them to the trough of lukewarm water outside, the same one they had used when they arrived the previous night. They were told to clean themselves out so they did not bring their disease to the soldiers the next day. As Young-Ja washed her groin she noticed the angry red patches that were appearing elsewhere on her body: her arms, her hips, her legs. New bruises in the shapes of fingerprints darkened on the other girls, some with blood on their faces and lips. Their flesh had already been mottled blue from the voyage into this ruinous place. Now they had been beaten red by the brutish hands that kept them there. No part of their bodies would be left unsullied by their captors.

Bowls of millet gruel and fermented soy paste were laid out in the room where the girls had slept. Young-Ja stared at the small bowl with no urge to reach for it. Fog settled in her mind and all sensation was lost to its haze. Hunger and thirst could not exist if her body did not. Pain could not exist if her body did not. Shame could not exist if her body did not.

When Young-Ja came to, her bowl was empty. Someone else had eaten what she had been too slow to touch. She sat frozen, unfeeling. Young-Ja did not flinch when one of the others smashed a bowl against the wall and pressed the broken ceramic shard to her own neck. The girl held it tight against her throat until a bead of blood pooled at the divot in her skin. She was punished for her hesitation to move, however, for the guards came in and dragged her out before she could glide the sharp edge across her skin. Only wooden bowls were used thereafter and a guard was posted to stand watch during meals.

The girls prayed to the heavens to let them breathe their final breath in their sleep. Most gods were deaf to these pleas. The girls opened their eyes to the same living nightmare the next morning, their organs rotting with bile and agony. But as they rose from their mats, they looked with fear and envy at one blue-lipped girl whose god did seem to take pity on her cries. The comfort station doctor could not surmise the cause of death in the autopsy, unable to find anything but abrasions and bruising that he believed to be insufficient to kill. Her cause of death was thus recorded as unknown and she was lost to nourish the soil of a foreign land where none knew her name.

Another soldier rolled off Young-Ja as she lay flat, lip busted into a trickle of blood. He had slapped her when she turned her head away from his demand to face him. But he had gotten satisfaction and departed without another thought. Young-Ja braced herself for the next soldier, but no one else crawled into her stall. Yelling erupted in the yard. She sat up to see what trouble unfurled.

"She's mine, I was here first."

"Well, I've got her now so wait your turn, idiot!"

"No, you're taking the best-looking one for yourself and you only just got here! We've been waiting for hours!"

"Well, I have to leave in thirty minutes!"

Two soldiers were yelling at each other, swiping at the pale arms of one of the girls. Young-Ja looked closer and saw that it was the beautiful girl with unblemished skin, the one she had spoken to on the truck. Bok-Hee.

"Both of you, shut up!"

A sneering officer stepped out into the fray as the spectating soldiers in queue stood at attention. The officer sported a red-and-gold gochō collar tab with a single star. He pulled apart the fighting men and scolded them for losing their discipline. The soldiers tried to defend themselves in another shouting match when the officer shot his pistol into the sky. He glared at the men, then examined the girl between them for a moment before lunging to punch her in the stomach. When Bok-Hee folded over with the wind knocked out of her lungs, he kicked her in the face so hard that a few teeth flew out of her mouth as she fell to the ground. Bok-Hee, startled, had not had a chance to scream when he squatted down and pulled her dirt-covered head up by her hair. He unsheathed a large knife from his belt and ran its blade slowly down her left cheek from her eye to her chin, cleaving the fatty flesh and releasing a stream of blood like red teardrops from a single eye. The yard was silent except for Bok-Hee's cries for mercy. The officer threw her to the ground and stood up.

"There, not such a beautiful prize after all, so stop your bickering," the officer commanded. "You are proud soldiers of the Empire of Japan. You will not behave like animals over a Chōsen pi. Don't disturb me again unless you wish to be treated like animals."

He spat on the ground and grabbed another girl he had chosen for the afternoon. They disappeared into the main building—officers were entertained in the comforts of a private room indoors, not in the overrun stable. The soldier who had been waiting in line picked up the crying, disfigured girl and dragged her to the stall next to Young-Ja's.

When night fell and the last of the soldiers left, Young-Ja lifted the curtain that hung over Bok-Hee's stall.

"Are you there?"

Bok-Hee sat up on her mat, face swollen and bruised at the lip. A thin bandage saturated red wrapped the left side of her face. Young-Ja crawled beside her and shared some of her water, stroking the girl's back. Bok-Hee was slow to swallow the liquid.

"My mother told me that beauty could be a curse," she said, running her fingers against her wet bandage. "I wonder if this was what she meant."

"Ok-Ju, come here and eat—" said Bok-Hee.

"Don't," Ok-Ju replied in Japanese. "Do not speak her name. Do not speak that language. That girl is not here. These things are being done to Hanako now."

Unable to pronounce or remember the girls' native names, the soldiers forced a new Japanese name on each. Young-Ja was called Fujiko. Bok-Hee was Sachiko. There was a Hanako. A Mariko. A Yukiko. A "ko"—child—for every soldier's tastes. The guards forbade the girls from speaking around them in their native tongues, not wanting to give them the opportunity to conspire openly in their secret language. It was not enough for soldiers to take their bodies—names and tongues, too, were necessary consolation prizes. With each girl gutted, pretty shells would be left for the men to fill with what they wished to see.

During the day, the soldiers lined up outside the stable, yelling at men who took longer than their allotted half hour. Hayaku, hayaku, hayaku! They compared these Chōsen pi to ones they had used at other comfort stations, trading notes on which had the prettiest girls, the most submissive stock. The girls learned not to fight back too much, for soldiers were quick to wield their fists and knives to force compliance. Some kept screaming until the sound was choked out of their throats. Others gave up entirely, lying limp as struggle would only worsen the pain.

When the girls were not receiving soldiers, they laundered uniforms and kept the comfort station clean. They were also made to darn socks and mend clothing, but after Yukiko used a needle to stab at an artery in her neck, the girls were forbidden to sew. During the first week in their cramped prison, very few girls spoke, most drifting about in a fugue state. But as the days passed without change, as the weeks accumulated into months, they clung to one another for whatever could pass for comfort. Older prisoners like Young-Ja taught the others how to tend to minor wounds and helped those who had just arrived from Joseon with their Japanese. All swapped ways to dissociate when receiving soldiers, resigned to the unyielding march of time.

The girls were fed twice a day, in the morning and evening, with just enough food to keep their hearts beating. To ward off syphilis and other diseases, they were forced to receive periodic sarubarusan injections filled with arsenic. The military liked to ensure that the dirty Chōsen pi would not disable their valiant troops with disease. If the doctor was feeling generous that day, the girls would get medical attention beyond the cursory weekly checkup in the infirmary. Some girls had grown so swollen between their legs it hurt to walk. Others were brought in to drain the pustules on their labia. Those who merely bled from abrasions were told to stop complaining, for the doctor was busy taking care of real ailments that could threaten the health of the soldiers.

Armed guards were ever-present. At any one girl's disobedience, the men would shout and strike, threatening to maim all those present until they could work no more. Some girls wondered if that was really a threat and not an improvement in their lot. But the risk of undiscriminating group punishments kept casual acts of individual defiance at bay, for no one wished to be responsible for inflicting further pain on their fellow prisoners. Many attempted to take their own lives over the course of the year. Those who failed to perish tried to run away without success. Each time, all girls were punished for even a single one's insolence by whip or withheld meals. Those who were inevitably recaptured were also stabbed in both calves, forcing them on their backs and submitting to their duties as their legs healed. Not all legs healed.

There was little other natural life at the comfort station. It was as if birds and insects knew not to linger. Young-Ja broke each time an errant sparrow landed on the fence opposite the stable.

"Have you come to mock me?" she would ask hoarsely before the bird flew away in a blur. Envying its freedom was too painful to bear, and she desperately hoped that it would not sing to anyone of her disgrace in this accursed place. Young-Ja tried to quash whatever reminiscence of Xinjing those brown wings stirred. If there was something in her left to die, it shriveled at the thought of presenting her broken face to Feng-nüshi. To Tayiji. To Baek Yong-Woo. To have them know what she had done for countless days and nights, whom she had been made to serve. What she had become. To any departing sparrow, Young-Ja would cry, "Don't show yourself here again!" for thoughts of loves past served only as torture. In this madness she would eventually find solace in having lost her family, for they would never have to live knowing her shame.

At daybreak when the girls were released into the yard for their chores, Young-Ja had taken to looking at the well in the yard and wondering how easy it would be to throw herself inside and drown. When no one was looking, she could tie a large rock to her waist and jump, disappearing before the guards noticed she was gone. She approached the edge of the well and peered down at the murky water. Young-Ja saw in her expressionless reflection the swollen, bruised eye she received from a soldier two days ago. Impulse compelled her to reach out and join that girl in the water. To reunite with her family. With Meiyu. As she thought about climbing over the stone edge of the well, her reflection distorted. Teardrops had fallen below, rippling the placid black surface of the water.

"Fujiko-san."

Young-Ja jerked back. Hanako approached, clutching her arms across her chest.

"Sachiko-san needs your help with the laundry." Hanako maintained a flat tone as she spoke in Japanese, despite a wincing avoidance of Young-Ja's eyes. "I know it's not your turn today, but she wanted me to ask you."

It did not take long for Young-Ja to note that Hanako's right wrist had swollen out to a lumpy protrusion mottled blue. Neither girl felt the need to remark on the cause of the injury or acknowledge that Hanako was usually paired with Sachiko—Bok-Hee—for their laundry shifts during the week.

"Yes," said Young-Ja, wiping away the remaining moisture at the corners of her eyes. "I can help with the laundry. But let's go to the infirmary first—"

"The doctor's not in today. He wasn't yesterday either."

"Hm. Wait here."

Young-Ja hurried to the lone mulberry tree in the yard. Hoping that the guards were not paying attention, she tore off the slim ends of a few branches to the length of her forearm and stripped them of any leaves or errant twigs. Within moments, she had sunk her canines into the hem of her dress, torn off a few strips of cloth, and bound the branches tight. She laid the makeshift splint against Hanako's wrist, the scar on her own once-nursed hand bobbing up and down as she wrapped the last few cloth strips around the girl's arm. Hanako drew sharp breaths but otherwise complied with Young-Ja's ministrations without a word.

As the girls walked toward the laundry, hand in hand, Young-Ja knew she could not allow herself to return to the murky reflection in the well. Not so long as girl hands grasped hers, squeezing her for whatever warmth she could provide. And for all the hands she could no longer hold, she would squeeze back to say, *Don't worry, I'm still here.*

CHAPTER TWENTY

Unknown, Manchukuo, Empire of Japan, 1942

Anytime she was allowed outside, Mariko searched for rocks and swallowed them when she thought no one was looking. The rocks kept her low to the ground, her soft organs heavy with the clatter of stone. Clack. Clack. Clack. The girls could always hear her approaching. Young-Ja took pity on the rock swallower and offered to share her meager dinner, thinking this proclivity an attempt to stave off the hunger pangs clawing at the stomach of every girl. Mariko refused each time, preferring to slide a dusty stone over her little pink tongue.

Mariko spent most of her day lying in her stall of the outdoor stable. From over the shoulder of whichever soldier she was receiving, she could see the lone mulberry tree that grew in the yard through the crack of the curtain. With no other trees to be seen, its stark branches always caught the eye. At first, she resisted and screamed like all the others. This provoked beatings from the soldiers, which she learned could be abated by lying still. So she taught herself to focus on the branches of the mulberry tree when her back was on the mat, to forget she had a body to move at all.

Mariko noticed that when her defiled body was weighed down, its pains could not follow her soul to rest in the mulberry tree. The more rocks she devoured, the longer her soul could evacuate from her body when soldiers barged in from the queue at the foot of her mat. In the mulberry tree, she did not have to think about the soldiers. She could cry, laugh, seethe, desire. Exist without shame. She could think about her grandparents' Mokpo seaside home where she played with her sisters. She could think about the clams she collected to eat, feeling the burst of their briny flesh on her tongue. She could recall the warmth of the sun drying the ocean water in her hair, leaving salt crystals to refract the light as she moved. Lost in her recollections, Mariko consumed so many rocks that her belly swelled and invited suspicions that she was with child. This did not stop the soldiers from using her as they had come to use her.

While crouching over the laundry one morning, Mariko howled in pain and fell over holding her distended, wriggling stomach. Young-Ja rushed to help her up, but the guards dragged Mariko to the infirmary to have the child removed. When a man's shout erupted from the operation room, the guards rushed in to inspect its cause. The doctor lay unconscious on the ground next to a smooth boulder smeared in blood. Mariko was sprawled on the examination cot with her belly sliced open, a beatific smile on her glassy-eyed face. The doctor's assistant stood lamely in the center of the room, stuttering that the boulder flew from her open belly and hit the doctor in the head when he reached inside to extract the baby. The guards ignored the assistant's protests and dragged him off to be detained and tried. Assaulting a medical officer of the Imperial Army was a serious offense.

Young-Ja and the others were ordered to clean the infirmary and bury Mariko's body. As their shovels broke the earth, each girl wondered whether and when she would encounter the same fate. Without needing to exchange a single word, they chose to lay her to rest under the mulberry tree. While Mariko's buried flesh nourished her beloved tree, her mat was filled by "Setsuko," a poor girl from Pyongyang who had followed a soldier's promise to give her new shoes. Setsuko, too, noticed that she could see the branches of the mulberry tree from her mat. She did not know that it would soon be her turn to dig a grave for a girl under the mulberry tree and watch her mat be filled by another.

Hanako was one of the first girls at the comfort station to lose a child and survive—most had perished or been sent away for being unable to perform their duties. She carried her child for half a year working just the same as all the rest. When the hunger within her stopped one morning, she did not raise an alarm. There had been no pain, no struggle. For weeks Hanako said nothing, believing herself well though her belly had stopped growing. She could no longer be deceived by her own bluff when an abrupt sharpness in her gut made her drop her bowl of evening gruel. Clutching Young-Ja's hand and leaning against the other girls around her, she wailed and pushed an inert, purple lump out from between her legs. The guards forced the girls to clean up and dispose of the lump in the yard.

After that night, strange, garbled noises no one else seemed to hear followed in Hanako's wake. Each day the noises came more into focus, their slow but persistent echo boring into her ears. One night, lying awake amid the gentle breaths of slumber in their prison, Hanako confronted what she had been dreading.

"*Ma. Ma.*" A strained gurgling came from outside the boarded window.

Hanako had never heard this voice before but had no doubts about to whom it belonged. She knew then she had finally lost her mind to this torment and released a loud, high-pitched scream. Bok-Hee and Young-Ja, lying on either side of her, sought to calm the girl, trying to determine what new pain had triggered the wail. Ignoring the others, Hanako sustained her unbroken scream. Guards ran into the room and jerked the possessed girl from Young-Ja's arms. They struck her across her face so hard it dislocated her jaw.

The next girl to hear strange noises had not forgotten what happened to Hanako. She strove to ignore the sound, hoping not to feed its volume with her reaction. On the mat, in the laundry, in her sleeping cell, the noise slithered around her trying to coax a response. The night she gave in and acknowledged the voice as her daughter-son—the blood that had leached out from her one morning in the stable—the ghosts of the comfort station's spawn unleashed their wails. They wailed into the sky, they wailed into the ground. They wailed unseen from every corner their mothers turned.

"Hold me!"

"I'm cold . . ."

"Hungry!"

Each girl-mother knew which voice belonged to her.

Some put their hands over their ears, rejecting these sounds as kin. Nothing they were forced to carry would they ever accept as their own. Whatever blood they shared, whatever tissue was wrenched from their bodies, these girls would not give them life, what little left they had to give. They would see it all buried deep in the dirt beneath the comfort station so the world could never discover what dirty fates had befallen them.

And yet, some could not help but reach out to soothe the cries as they imagined their own mothers would. But they swiped at only air in the inky dark.

The creatures first emerged as mere sounds, though as loud and close as if cradled in arms. Within days they began to leave traces of presence only their girl-mothers could perceive. Thin trails of blood streaked on the walls. Infant handprints peppered across stable mats. Bloody stains on hands and legs that would not wash away.

During the day, ghosts could be heard pattering about the stable roof above their mothers, casting shadows that undulated across the lines of soldiers in the yard. The girls scolded their howling creations, telling them to close their eyes, to go away. They may be phantoms of their lunacy, but they were not to witness such vile acts.

"Don't look! Don't look!"

The soldiers were blind to the shadows of their young and believed these imperatives were addressed to them. Most ignored any sound that came from the Chōsen pi. Some retaliated, forcing their girls to look them in the eye as they emptied into their bodies. No matter the scene, the ghosts wailed for their mothers' attention, dripping blood from the roof's edge onto the ground outside the stable.

Drip.

"*Kaa-san.*"

Drip.

"*Mama.*"

Drip.

"*Hold me.*"

If ignored, they screeched so loudly that sleep could not come. If acknowledged, they left the whisper of a tug on the girls' dresses, little red handprints blooming across frayed hems. Some asked their girl-mothers why they swallowed toxic weeds to prevent their growth. Some warned that this was their final chance to rear children, that their wombs were now contaminated by blight and poison. That they could never again be mothers with bodies so worn and spoiled.

Young-Ja's began as a spasm. It gnawed at her stomach as she trudged toward her place in the stable, exiting from her in a blood flow she had not seen for two moons. The queue of soldiers trampled the drops into the dirt beneath their boots while a weak-kneed Young-Ja was carried to her mat. At night it rose from the ground to find the carrier of its womb. It was vocal, oozing as blood down her scalp and into the conch of her ear to whisper in Japanese sing-song.

"*Hungry, Kaa-san. Feed me.*"

Young-Ja grew increasingly numb to these cries. She was no mother. This hell took life, it did not give it. And so she would nestle closer to the other girls, to Bok-Hee and Hanako, sinking into their still-warm breaths and living heartbeats to escape death's call.

For Bok-Hee, there were two. The scar on her face twinged with pain every time the voices emerged, trickling blood down her cheek and crying out for a pink scar just like their beautiful mother. Although she could not see them, they begged her to slice their ugly faces until they matched hers. These dreadful pleas echoed in Bok-Hee's every waking moment until she learned she could subdue their cries by hiding the scar from view. She took to sleeping on her maimed face, exposing only her beautiful right cheek to the night. If the pitiable ghosts could not see it, they would not envy it.

Madness seized the girls. They burned with loathing for themselves and the monsters who created these wretched beings. They went mad with love and shame for their malformed flesh and heard their cries as proof someone in the world still needed them. While the echoes of ghostly cries corroded their senses, they found refuge in knowing that these forlorn apparitions were not true children. True children who could suffer the abuses they shouldered.

The girl-mothers would receive it all in their stead, for it was the mother's duty to keep her children from harm.

CHAPTER TWENTY-ONE

Unknown, Manchukuo, Empire of Japan, 1943

A tiger visits Young-Ja's slumber in the third year of her bondage. It climbs down from the sky on a large rope and lands before her. The beast approaches with a soft growl but Young-Ja senses no hostility. It considers her for a moment through the yellow of its eyes before nudging her stomach with its broad head.

Young-Ja woke submerged in the dread that she had beheld a taemong—a conception dream. She could still summon her mother's descriptions of the taemong she had for her children.

"I saw all three of you coming to me," said Jung-Soon, a gentle smile pulling at her cheeks. "Young-Sook came to me as a persimmon. I was so hungry in my dream. I saw a tree in the distance and ran to it, but its branches were bare. I squinted my eyes and looked up: there was one perfect persimmon at the top of the tree. So I climbed all the way up to pick it from the branch. When I bit into it, I knew right away it was the most delicious fruit I had ever tasted.

"Young-Ho came to me as a bear cub. I had been walking in the mountains for a long time and sat down to rest. This small, furry bear cub crawled up to me and nestled into my lap. He was so warm and cozy, he fell asleep right there. I played with his fluffy ears and felt so happy and protected.

"Young-Ja was tricky. I thought she would be a boy. I saw a big tiger approaching me, so I got scared and ran. It caught up to me and tackled me to the ground. I thought that I would perish, but it dropped a mugunghwa blossom in my hands and left. The flower stayed with me and grew in my palms."

Young-Ja recalled looking up at her mother as she told her these stories. She had difficulty picturing the exact contours of her mother's face, but she knew that she liked to run her fingers over the raised web of flesh on Jung-Soon's burn scar. The bumpy, slightly discolored skin brought her comfort, a tactile sensation only her mother could provide. In this cursed place, Young-Ja provided comfort to no one. Only phantoms claimed her as a mother. But this taemong did not foretell an early expulsion from her womb. It pulsed with life and she wished to extinguish it.

The next morning, Young-Ja ran outside near the latrines and searched for poison weeds. She would rather smother the life inside of her by her own hand than allow it to be smothered by the hands of her captors. She grabbed a clump of jagged leaves and gnashed the plants into a bitter, gritty paste with her teeth. She swallowed before the guards had a chance to grasp what she was doing.

Young-Ja had barely wiped the soil from her lips when a man walked out into the yard. He had a balding, gray hairline and wore a familiar smile. He had hung around the stable before, sometimes stopping to chat with the soldiers in line. He never interacted with the girls directly, always abstaining from speaking to or touching them. But now, with his hands clasped behind his back, he informed the girls that they would not receive any soldiers that day. General Akagawa was to stop by the comfort station for an inspection—they would clean the building in preparation for his visit. It had been under the general's orders that this station was established as soldiers' demand for comfort rose. It was imperative that they present their best front to the highest-ranking officer stationed in Manchukuo.

"You will show your gratitude to the man who has given you your jobs, this opportunity to serve the empire," he announced. "You're well acquainted with what these guards will do if this place does not look impeccable by this afternoon."

The man scanned the grounds and examined the shuffle of girls before him. Several walked with scarred limps—mementos of failed escape attempts. Many otherwise sported unseemly bruises on their faces and necks, cigarette burns on their arms. The man's smile fell as he considered the limited options, then pointed at Young-Ja near the latrines. She was not the comeliest of the bunch but she at least had an unblemished face.

"You, Fujiko. Go help the cook clean and prepare in the kitchen. You will serve the delegation when they arrive."

In all one thousand days she had been a prisoner, Young-Ja had never been inside the kitchen—the girls were not permitted inside the building anywhere except the infirmary and their sleeping cell. Occasionally they would be forced into the rooms upstairs if a passing officer had selected them for more private consumption in the evenings. Like livestock, they were kept mostly outdoors. They received soldiers outdoors, they washed the reeking undergarments of laboring men outdoors, they bathed and relieved themselves outdoors. Even in the cold of winter the girls were forced on their backs in the outdoor stable, meager fires burning at their frost-nipped feet.

The kitchen was a modest nook down the corridor from the infirmary: a small expansion in the limits of Young-Ja's life in bondage. She tried to recall when she had last prepared anything in a kitchen and looked at the scar on her left palm. Its gnarled, discolored line was a vestige of a resolve so bygone that Young-Ja could hardly recognize the hand as her own. Had she once truly believed that she could do something against all this, a force that was capable of devising the loathsome prison around her? As she passed the pots on an iron stove, she wondered if she would even be able to wield her old tools to any effect. She had been drained so empty of feeling that whatever food she touched would also likely taste empty, void of all flavor.

The guard handed Young-Ja off to the cook, a young Japanese man who leaned against a crutch in lieu of a missing left leg. Despite the eye patch over his right eye, he managed an intense glare as he ordered her to clean. When not tending to breakfast on the stove, the cook sat and watched Young-Ja scrub down the grimy pots lined with stale halos of an undetermined crust. He had already collected the kitchen knives and kept them in a pouch hung around his shoulder; the guards had long since learned not to allow these girls anything sharp. But Young-Ja kept her eyes downcast as she had been taught, betraying no signs of subversive intent; she quietly cleaned the large pots and gave the cook little to monitor. When he grew bored of her, he limped over to the pot of millet gruel and declared it ready to be portioned out. Young-Ja complied as he turned to prepare the guards' rice, pickled vegetables, and canned meat. She salivated at the smell—an involuntary reaction from a tongue that had not tasted meat in years.

Young-Ja sank a spoon into her own bowl of millet gruel in silence. She peered at the cook between bites, wondering if he would admonish her for taking too long to finish her meal, or if he meant to harm her in any way. There was no relaxing in the presence of men.

The cook met Young-Ja's probing eyes. He searched for any hints of pity or mockery of his body. Satisfied that what lingered in her gaze was fear, he ventured a few words.

"If you're worried I'm going to hurt you, I don't beat women," he said. "Save your energy for cleaning. Those guards are the ones who will hurt you if this place isn't spotless."

Young-Ja knew he did not need to strike her to do harm but did not disagree with his assessment of the guards. She cast off this thought before getting up to rinse her bowl and scrub more grime from the kitchen floor. The cook rose to clear his dish when he dropped his spoon. On instinct, Young-Ja turned to the clatter and reached down to retrieve the fallen utensil.

"I can get it myself! I lost my leg, not my hands."

Young-Ja retracted her hand at the rebuke. To think that this man worried about her pitying him. Laughter was a years-forgotten impulse, yet she suppressed its bitter tickle as she went back on her knees to scrub the floor. She had learned in her years of watching men that only fragile egos jumped to see assistance as pity. It would be best not to provoke.

The cook spent some time assessing the kitchen's inventory but otherwise sat observing Young-Ja work. The guards had clearly thought that watching one girl clean the kitchen was not a worthy task for them; they had brought in the cook from his usual rotation in the nearby barracks to supervise in their stead. This seemed to bother the cook, as if he needed reassurance that his station was not so far beneath the guards.

"You know, I was a soldier, too, once," he mused. "Lost the leg and eye in Mongolia in a skirmish against the Russians a few years back."

Young-Ja glanced at him but kept working in silence. Encouraged by the flash of attention, the cook continued his monologue.

"Going back to Japan like this was out of the question. At least the others don't cringe at my appearance here. They understand the sacrifice I've made."

Young-Ja wiped at the floor without looking up.

"I can make a living and do my duty with some semblance of dignity," he said, eyes somewhere far. "But what would a whore know of dignity?"

Young-Ja grimaced but held her tongue; again, it was not worth reacting. The cook mumbled that a stupid Chōsen girl probably would not understand Japanese anyway and did not say much more as Young-Ja crawled about to clean.

In the afternoon, a guard came into the kitchen with a box of tea that had been specially ordered for the general. He commanded Young-Ja to undress and wash herself, tossing over a clean gown for her to wear. The general would be arriving soon and everyone had to look presentable. Young-Ja hesitated. She did not wish to be presented to the man to whom she and the other girls owed their shackles. Neither did she wish to bare herself alone in front of the guard and the cook. But as the guard glared on, hands on his rifle, she pulled her dirty dress over her head and began washing up at the basin. With the eyes of the two men gliding down her body, no amount of water could help her feel clean.

Once she was dressed, the guard ordered her to brew the tea and the cook to prepare the guards' lunches. The cook threw him a dirty look for barking demands but hopped over to the storage bins to take out the materials. Young-Ja set about to boil the water and place the special tea leaves into the pot. It was a fine, woody pu'erh, long-aged, something that would have been reserved only for the most important clientele at Fenghuang. Young-Ja's hands shook with angry mortification at the thought of serving anything to the architect of this place. But with the armed guard watching for any misconduct so closely she could smell his fetid breath, she could do nothing but hope that the drinker at least choked on the distress she steeped into the tea. She was then forced to take the pot on a tray and march toward another room.

Inside sat the general, the comfort station's doctor, and the balding man who had given the girls their instructions that morning. The men did not acknowledge Young-Ja while she entered and poured the tea, instead discussing the number of soldiers served every day at the comfort station.

"Fifty to a hundred a day on average, over two hundred at our busiest," the balding man reported. "With officers getting precedence, of course."

Nausea gripped Young-Ja's throat but she held steady in an elegant pour. The guard nudged her with his rifle to bow once the tea was served. Dizzy with wretchedness, she lowered her head and bared her neck to her captors, nearly losing her footing as the guard ushered her out to rejoin the other girls.

The doctor and the balding man raised their cups to their lips. General Akagawa ignored his, having avoided contact with most things since his arrival.

"We've made relatively high profits for very low operating costs, which we've funneled back into the military budget for the region as per your guidance," said the balding business manager, taking a sip from his tea.

The doctor, also eager to preen, jumped in. "This station also has some of the lowest incidence of venereal disease in the region, largely thanks to your premium selections, General."

General Akagawa was not so quick to bend to this flattery, inured to sycophants who flocked to his power. As he listened, however, the two men before him were becoming increasingly taciturn in their answers, clutching their teacups like women trying to warm their hands in the cold.

"And what of the soldiers, are they in high spirits?" the general asked.

The manager averted his eyes. "They seem . . . fine," he replied, squirming in his seat, knuckles white against the teacup.

The general narrowed his eyes and turned to the doctor. "And the health of the stock here? Low incidence of disease is good, but how are their general constitutions?"

The doctor, too, lowered his gaze and his voice, staring into his cup. "Some sort of summer cold is going around . . .

rest assured I'll try to keep the girls here from becoming vectors of disease." The doctor hesitated before adding, "In fact, I may not be feeling too well myself, and if you'll excuse me, I wouldn't wish to get you ill, General." He stood up and bowed.

The manager also stood up to bow, muttering some sort of half apology about feeling a bit dizzy.

The general ended the meeting early. He would rather inspect the goods directly than deplete his patience with soft-bellied managers.

General Akagawa understood what men needed to succeed in battle. He issued the directive for more comfort stations not only for troop morale but also as an important component of military strategy. If the state did not provide their soldiers with women to bed, they would turn to rape in the battlefield and occupied lands, spreading anti-Japanese sentiment among the Chinese they sought to rule. The general also wished to minimize relations between Japanese men and Chinese women, for the tongue of a besotted man knew no discipline. Military secrets could not be leaked if soldiers only lay with women under complete control of the Imperial Army. And as with any other important supply, quality assurance was necessary. It was by design that these comfort stations were often filled with Chōsen girls, whose conservative, agrarian society conveniently prized female purity. The girls they shipped in from the peninsula were more likely to be virgins and could limit the spread of venereal disease among soldiers. With these considerations in mind, General Akagawa had expedited the creation of ten more stations in Jilin in the last three years. This outpost he was visiting now was one of the smaller operations, with fewer than twenty girls. Although it was shabby, it was at least efficiently run, with fewer deaths or expulsions than some of the larger comfort stations. His inspection would not last long and he could soon leave for dinner in more sophisticated company elsewhere.

General Akagawa sent his aides outside to prepare the girls in advance. When he walked out into the yard, they were lined up in a row as he had specified. If this was what his men needed to give them the strength to take on China, so be it. He would gladly provide.

The girls at this comfort station did seem rougher than he had seen elsewhere. They were underfed and bony, their skin baked from laboring in the sun. Dullness lurked in their eyes. The general would have to order an increase in the girls' rations if they wanted to keep their stock viable for the long term. The site medical officer had claimed these girls had low rates of disease, but there were plenty of rashes across the bare limbs in front of him. He would have to have a word with the doctor, for he did not wish to have his troops fall prey to blight when China was proving to be tricky to overcome.

The general paused to examine a girl whose skin was beginning to grow syphilitic spots. She shook under his gaze.

"Step forward," he ordered.

The girl shuffled out to where he pointed. The general took a turn to examine her from behind.

"Lie down."

The girl continued to shake, tears streaking down her cheeks as her breathing turned into erratic pants.

"Don't make me wait."

As the girl lowered her body to the ground as directed, the general unsheathed the curved steel blade of his shin guntō. A wretched sob erupted from the girl's throat as he dragged the sword's point from her chest to her knees, cutting open her dress. Contemplation settled into his brow as he examined her exposed body. His gaze did not linger long before he pushed the sharp metal of his blade into her skin, carving lines in the flesh under her breasts to connect the spots of her syphilitic rash. The girl screamed and tried to squirm away. The general stomped on her shoulder and pushed down his weight to keep her pinned. With a few more slashes, the characters for "vermin" bled on the broken skin of her stomach. The girl cried out as the others stood trembling.

The general took a step back to examine his work. He then plunged the shin guntō into her chest and watched her bleed out until she moved no more.

"Disposing of your defective stock," the general declared, addressing the guards as he withdrew his blade. He turned to the remaining girls, tense in their waxen stares. "But it seems my strokes are not fine enough yet. My writing requires more practice."

His eyes grazed over the yard until they settled on a particular girl. Even the general caught himself admitting that her face could be elegant if not for the long scar that stretched from her eye down to her chin. He grasped the hair at this new target's scalp and pulled her to him. She screamed in protest as he threw her on the dirt and pressed his bootheel into her shoulder.

"Stop it."

General Akagawa looked up.

"Who said that?" He scanned the girls. No one was shaking anymore.

"Don't be shy. You have something to say. I'm giving you permission to speak."

No one stepped forward.

"No one? Fine."

The general drew his pistol with his free hand, pointed it at a girl in line near him and shot her between her eyes. Her corpse crumpled to the ground as shrieks burst out in the yard, the loudest from the girl pinned under his boot. The hot scent of urine rose from streams pooling in a froth by squirming bare feet.

"Now that I think about it, it couldn't have been her," the general said. "The voice came from farther down the line."

He pointed his pistol at another girl who screamed and cowered behind her hands.

"Stop." A girl stepped forward. "It was me."

General Akagawa strolled up to the source of this impudence and recognized the spindly girl who had served him tea. He thrust the barrel of his pistol under her chin. Her black gaze met him up the length of the gun he had pointed at her jaw. He ordered her to lie down on the ground.

"You've given me an idea for my next character. But mind your tongue this time. If your voice breaks my focus, I will not be so gentle with you or the others."

The general cut open her dress and dragged his sword down her narrow belly. Blood leaked down her sides in tiny streams as she lay unmoving, no sound escaping from her mouth. Eleven smooth strokes of red: uji.

Maggot.

"The stroke work here is a bit better," said the general to no one in particular. He turned to face the others. "Never forget that you breathe only because I allow it. Never forget that your sole duty is to prepare our soldiers for battle. Those who forget," he said, pointing the blade at the girl on the ground, "will be branded for what they are."

He removed a cloth from his pocket and wiped the blade of his shin guntō before sliding it back into its scabbard. He threw the stained cloth on the ground and left the station with his aides.

CHAPTER TWENTY-TWO

Unknown, Manchukuo, Empire of Japan, 1943

Bok-Hee pressed a linen to the angry gashes on Young-Ja's belly. She kept her tears from falling on the cuts so as not to worsen the sting, willing the drops down the path of her long, pink scar and neck where they could be swallowed by the skin of her chest. She tore the hem of her dress into long strips to bandage up the maimed torso lying before her.

"It should've been me," Bok-Hee murmured.

Despair soaked into the marrow of Young-Ja's bones. It worked its grip into her lungs and caught in her throat, stealing her breath as she had stolen Hanako's. She did not understand exactly what had possessed her when Bok-Hee was pushed under the general's foot; the words burst out of her from a visceral, unknowable place. Her hesitation after the initial disruption, however, had as good as shot that bullet into Hanako's face. Young-Ja's mind curled into a spiraling chorus of self-reproach until all voices converged into a single refrain: that she should have died in Hanako's stead.

While Young-Ja lay crushed by the weight of her thoughts, the others, too, sat in the dazed aftermath of their brush with the general. They had been locked up early in their sleeping cell without dinner. The skipped meal did not register as much of a loss. Appetites shriveled when their vision was stained with blood. Few could bring themselves to look at the paralyzed Young-Ja. Many were relieved it had been her speaking up and not them, her mutilation and not theirs. Others were shamed knowing they could never have done the same. Some even thought her a fool.

"It should've been me." The soft undertone of Bok-Hee's mantra was the only sound in the room. "Not you. Me."

Young-Ja stared up at the ceiling, unmoving. The others squirmed in silence. That morning they had welcomed the respite from the queues of soldiers, feeling fortunate to dedicate themselves to cleaning. But they now knew that an audience with the general was merely a different chamber in the same hell.

Gripped in their quiet torment, they jumped when the guards threw open the door and seized Young-Ja. Bok-Hee held on to her injured friend's hand in protest but was kicked off. The others looked away.

Young-Ja allowed herself to be hauled away by the guards, accepting whatever form her death would take. She feared pain no longer. But there were no guns or swords in the kitchen where she was taken. Merely the cook.

"The general's provided this station's staff with extra rations as a reward for our work. You'll help me ready the guards' dinner and clean up after them." The cook pointed his knife at the stove. "Prepare the rice."

She was not being marched to her death but to more servitude. The cook slid a knife down the length of an eel, making quick swipes to gut and debone the fish. Young-Ja stared, half wanting to wrest the blade from his hands and slit her throat to atone for what she had done. The cook issued an order that Young-Ja did not hear as she fell in the reverie of her own imagined death. He cleared his throat and knocked the handle of the knife against the cutting board to command her attention.

Young-Ja's ears rang. All the food on the counter appeared to her rotted. Putrid heaps of decay she could not fathom anyone would wish to consume. Nothing could move her toward the stove. Not the cook's glare, not his pointed demand. When her stony gaze met his, he huffed with irritation.

"If you don't hurry, they'll keep withholding meals from the others and blame you for it. Your resistance helps no one. Just do as you're told."

These words of caution had come too late to save Hanako, but they moved Young-Ja to give in and fill a pot with rice to wash away the impurities. Her fingers had not sifted through such precious grains in over a decade. Now she reunited with the sensation only to gratify her enslavers. Her fingers swirled around the rice water, submerging the grains in her spite, her torment, her wish for death. She was sick with a desperate hope that the guards would all choke on their food and know her anguish. She squeezed the clumps of rice until her knuckles turned white with grief, pouring her despair into the pot.

With the rice simmering on the fire, Young-Ja was made to sit near the cook as he cut the eel into filets and prepared the sauce. She forced her eyes to lose focus. She would not be a willing audience to her tormentors being rewarded. The sizzling of fat on fire, the sweet scent of grilling eel flesh—nothing could mask the taste of bile raked across Young-Ja's tongue. She could not say how much time passed as she sat imagining her final breath, but the cook eventually barked at her to deliver the completed dishes to the guards.

Young-Ja held the heavy tray of food and limped to where four comfort station guards sat waiting, one door down the hallway from the kitchen. A red stain began a slow spread across the fibers of her cotton gown. Blood saturated through the bandages Bok-Hee had placed on her wound and was now soiling the dress and dripping down her belly, legs, and feet. The rivulets of blood smeared under her toes, left as shiny splotches on the wooden floor in her wake.

The men paid little mind to her bleeding when she entered the room with their dinner, eyes locked on their reward. It was not particularly hard work to keep sixteen frail, underfed girls subdued. But the general knew that small gifts for grunt workers could pay long-lasting dividends in loyalty and productivity that far exceeded their initial cost. Indeed, these men grabbed their meals from Young-Ja with the intent to speak highly of the general for years to come.

The first guard raised the whole eel filet into his mouth and chewed, something he had not been able to do in months. The rest took generous portions of fish and savored its sweet, rich flesh; this was a luxury reminiscent of home. As the guards paired the eel with hefty bites of the rice Young-Ja had prepared, one by one they fell into silence. Their eager molars gnashed into the plump white rice grains, releasing despair onto their tongues. The four guards sat chewing her wretched desire for death and swallowed it down with the fatty flesh of eel.

One guard dropped his chopsticks and stared at his dinner, tugging at the collar of his uniform. He then reached for the pistol in his holster and, without another word, fired a bullet into his temple. Young-Ja shrieked. She looked around frantically at the other men to react, but they did not flinch at the blood spray creeping down the wall. They had fallen too engrossed in the private storms of their own tense bodies.

Young-Ja jumped back when another guard began to cough violently, sending masticated bits of eel and rice grains flying across the bowls of the other men. She watched in disbelief as he reached for the dagger he had set on the table before dinner. He unsheathed its blade and dragged it red across his choked throat to cough no more.

The remaining two guards knocked over their bowls as they collapsed, clutching at their bulging purple throats, curling into the sharp stabs in their stomachs. Young-Ja yelped as one guard grabbed her ankle and tried to pull her down with him, but she kicked free from the weak grip. She watched, frozen, her captors reaching for their own knives to plunge into their stomachs. As the men twitched, she saw a glint of brass fall from the breast pocket of a guard curled on his side—the keys to the building. The keys to the girls' sleeping cell.

The keys rattled against her shaking hand as she retraced her bloody steps in the hallway. When she opened the door, the girls inside gasped at the sweating Young-Ja covered in blood, heaving for breath.

"The guards, they're . . . they're gone."

Bok-Hee ran to hold Young-Ja and keep her from collapsing. A few others rose and looked out into the hallway. Seeing no one, they spilled out into the dark, not allowing doubt to cloud their bid for escape. Many remained still, trying to grasp the situation.

"Follow them, go see," said Young-Ja.

When the throng of girls arrived in the room where the guards lay, Bok-Hee grabbed a discarded knife and stabbed one of their corpses in the chest.

"Here, you dropped your knife." Bok-Hee stuck her angry blade into his soft flesh anew, clenching its handle with both hands to pour as much of her strength as she could into the plunge.

The others followed suit, their small fists thudding fury into the lifeless bodies that had once held dominion over them.

Dozens of feet stampeded bloody footprints down the corridor as the girls hastened to leave the guards behind. They poured out of the station and into the yard, grabbing chairs and tables from inside the building to stack so they could climb over the fence into the dark of night. Once they touched down on that long-unfelt soil of the other side, they flung themselves in different directions. Patrolling soldiers saw flashes of white streaking past the barracks and turned to the source of the apparitions. By the time the soldiers entered the building, their stock of Chōsen pi was long gone, leaving behind the butchered remains of four guards and a cook who seemed to have disemboweled himself with a boning knife, alone in the kitchen.

Bok-Hee helped Young-Ja over the fence and landed like a cat beside her. She grabbed her hand and together they bolted into the darkness. With thick clouds burying the moon from view they could not see far. They knew only to run, to flee from any source of light. Where there was no light, there would be no men. They tripped and fell countless times, tumbling over rocks and other protrusions in the ground they could not see in the starless night. Other girls tumbled around them, muting their cries of pain as much as they could for fear of being discovered. Each time she stumbled, Young-Ja picked herself up and reached for Bok-Hee's hand. They continued to run, hoping for as much distance as possible. But there came a fall in the dark when Young-Ja was not able to feel the searching grasp of her friend's hand. There came a stretch of field when all she could hear was her own breath, her own tread, and nothing, no one else. She slowed to a walk but lurched ever forward, hoping that the others would not stop in their pursuit of liberation.

As sunlight diffused over the horizon, Young-Ja approached a river's edge. She had lost sight of the others hours ago in the unforgiving black of night. She could not say where she was, but yet again she found herself there alone.

No parents, no siblings.

No Yong-Woo, no Tayiji.

No Meiyu.

No Bok-Hee. Her last remaining friend, the only person who cared that she bled, who helped her scale that fence out of their prison, who reached for her hand in the dark.

She was alone. With nothing but the unwanted grain of life within her.

Young-Ja crawled into the river and submerged her body, willing the current to take her. She drank in the water and let it fill her lungs, for she was done breathing in this godforsaken life.

CHAPTER TWENTY-THREE

Jilin, China, 1945

Xiuying was never blessed with children of her own, though she was no stranger to care. Both her parents had fallen prey to disease of the liver—as an only child, she had no choice but to devote her life to nursing their health. While her friends wed and left their riverside village for better prospects in the city, Xiuying stayed behind to tend to her parents, scrounging for whatever work she could find as a washerwoman, a farmhand, a seamstress. A true paragon of filial piety. But for the poor, filial piety was more necessity than vaunted choice. They could not afford the luxury of care provided by hands they had not created.

Life only got harder as Japan invaded China. Food prices rose. Medicine supply fell. The weight of her daily labors bent Xiuying's spine into a gnarled hump. She did not know how much longer she could tolerate her ailing back for such meager income, but she was fortunate to have bartered for medical services from the doctors hiding in her village.

A few years back, two large Westerners with light hair and ruddy skin arrived in Xiuying's village. They spoke in distorted, cloggy words that frightened people into keeping their distance. One of the village children, too young to have cultivated a fear of the unknown, approached them and realized they were repeating the word yīshēng—doctor—with the most inane pronunciation the villagers had ever heard. The discovery triggered a wave of laughter that dissolved any initial fear or bafflement. The lone child who could decipher the visitors' thick-tongued speech further explained that they were from a country called Sūgélán, and had come to help the sick in the countryside of China. Baoluo and Agenisi. Brother and sister. Both doctors. The villagers wondered how good these doctors could be when they themselves were covered in red splotches, but Xiuying was desperate for help. She brought the Westerners to see her parents and they provided medicine to subdue the jaundiced swelling of their joints.

Having benefited from the Westerners' remedies, the village banded together to hide them in their grain storage when Japanese soldiers drove in looking for foreigners. The Empire of Japan was at war with the West and looked to imprison any whites left in Manchukuo, including any foreign doctors and proselytizers trying to spread their creed among the peasantry. The villagers replied that Europeans had indeed come through but left weeks ago for Mukden. The soldiers did not think Westerners could survive for long in the manure piles of Manchukuo's minor villages and moved their search elsewhere.

Since then, Baoluo and Agenisi wore wide-brim straw hats to conceal their light hair as they helped the farmers of the region. They slinked from village to village, removing parasites, resetting bones, and treating all manner of ailing organs. They even sought to learn and work with the traditional Chinese medicine of the old village doctor. In exchange for her parents' treatments, Xiuying washed the foreigners' clothing and taught them to pronounce their words properly. They improved under Xiuying's tutelage; soon, it was not only the pliable minds of children that could understand their heavy words.

Xiuying found Jian when she was washing a pile of Baoluo's and Agenisi's bedding in her usual spot at the Liao River. When she settled into a crouch and began her work, the unusually loud trill of sparrows made her turn her head and glimpse a hand sticking out of the marshy reeds along the river shore. Alarmed, Xiuying ran over to inspect, swatting away the noisy flutter of sparrows and hoping that the hand might still be attached to a body with a pulse. It was not unheard of for body parts to wash up on the river shore in those days, but the hand did not seem to be in too terrifying a state of decay.

Xiuying parted the reeds to discover a woman with black hair streaked across her ashen face. A wet, blood-stained dress clung to her bony body. Xiuying reached out and put her finger to the corpse's nose. As soon as a feathery exhale brushed her knuckles, she pulled the woman out of the reeds and called for help as the sparrows scattered into the sky.

With Baoluo and Agenisi tending to the sick in another village, her neighbors helped Xiuying bring the unknown woman to the traditional medicine doctor. He shooed everyone out except Xiuying before removing the patient's wet, filthy clothing. The doctor's jaw slacked at the word butchered into her stomach. Xiuying moved first to dry the woman off with a warm cloth as the doctor cleaned the cuts so angry with infection.

When the woman came to, she let out an earth-shattering wail. Xiuying discovered later that nearby villages mistook this screaming for ghosts and burned bamboo in hopes the explosive crackling would ward off the evil spirits. The traditional medicine doctor tried to pacify the woman with a tonic. Her flailing toppled the first cup but the second was eventually drunk with Xiuying helping to hold her down. The stranger slept, being fed small portions of the tonic each time she woke until she eased into consciousness a day later without erupting into panicked shrieks.

The strange woman would not speak but did seem to hear and understand, making it easier to direct her recovery. When Baoluo and Agenisi returned to the village, they took immediate pity on her, explaining that their god wanted them to tend to this mute despite the difficulty of having one more mouth to feed. They named the woman with the torn belly Jian and took her in. But as Jian healed, she proved to be useful—she assisted the farmers in the fields, helped Xiuying with the washing, and even foraged medicinal plants for the village doctor.

When it became clear Jian was pregnant, envy struck Xiuying. She had always wanted a family of her own, but at nearly forty years of age, she was not an appealing bride to any man. When Jian went into labor, Agenisi had Xiuying assist in the delivery, noticing that Jian stiffened around Baoluo. It transpired as smoothly as any birth could, but Jian did not seem pleased with her newborn. It was only with great reluctance that she took him into her arms, as if she had been handed a pile of heavy logs and ordered to carry it a long distance. She looked away from the squirming bundle, but Xiuying could not stop staring: he was the most perfect child she had ever seen. And while Jian's breasts produced little milk, Xiuying's swelled at the sight of the child until the front of her tunic ran wet. With no other food source for the hungry infant, Xiuying took him, eager to hold and nourish him.

Xiuying's body transformed. She radiated a warmth that eased her aches. Her skin softened to a comforting plush. She spoke to the baby with deep affection while he fed on her, looking into her eyes with the unflinching smile of absolute innocence. Xiuying took to calling him Jun—"handsome"— pleased by the symmetry of his tiny face. Jian seemed unconcerned as everyone adopted the name for the lack of an alternative. But the first night Xiuying heard the woman speak to Jun in Korean, she knew that he was not meant to stay there with her, that he was meant to tread on lands far from China.

As she finished nursing Jun for the final time, she looked at the folds of skin at his wrists, his ankles, his filled-out fingers. Xiuying's milk had given life to this child and she wondered how long he could survive without her. How long she would survive without him.

As Young-Ja opened her eyes, she wondered why. Why, when so many others before her could succumb to an enduring darkness, was she cursed to wake into a light she had so toiled to snuff? Young-Ja was sluggish with disappointment, her vision coming into focus in a small, enclosed room. The skin on her stomach burned and her legs ached. When she took a reluctant breath, a pressure within distended her organs. This tension expanding across her every fiber surged until she released its force in a scream. When strangers ran into the room, Young-Ja flung herself into a corner, unable to stop the sound pouring through her dry, taut throat. She cried, not knowing what else to do, chest heaving into her bellow. The strangers forced a bitter liquid into the mouth she could not close and she saw black once more.

When Young-Ja woke again, she could not find her voice. It had fled with the scream she sent rippling across the surrounding villages. She did not care enough to discover whether she could lure it back. When the strangers probed who she was, where she had come from, how she had sustained her injuries, Young-Ja willed her voice to stay hidden. She would never utter what she had borne to a single living soul. By burying the comfort station in her mind, she could erase its shameful truth. That which was not known—that which was not spoken—could not have happened. If fate was forcing Young-Ja to live, she would at least kill the knowledge that made her want to seek death.

Young-Ja did not understand why the villagers showed her kindness. Xiuying gave her clothing and set her up to work with the two white foreigners from a faraway country. The foreigners spoke Chinese with a halting, heavy accent that took some time to understand, but they mostly meant well. They liked to speak of their god a little longer than was polite but they had helped many people in the village, including by dulling the pain of her torn stomach. Young-Ja gave in to her persistent life, doing as she was told, working where she was asked to work. Her daily labors could at least help her tamp down the cascade of comfort station memories that jailed her anew in the confines of her mind.

Whenever Young-Ja could peel away from her work, she went to see the old village doctor. He had not only noticed she was with child before anyone else, but he seemed to be the only person to recognize her true desire. He prepared for her a bitter tonic made of the yuán huā lilac she foraged by the river. Many times over, Young-Ja swallowed the medicine hoping it would render her womb inhospitable. But her belly continued to grow. She could not tell whether the tonic that the doctor brewed was ineffective or whether he had deceived her from the start. With every failed attempt, she distanced herself from the doctor, eventually keeping away from him as she did all other men in the village.

As Young-Ja's stomach rounded into an undeniable announcement of her condition, she questioned whether her motherhood would be an atrocity. Was she at fault for forcing life into a world that held such grief, such evil? She had tried to save this child numerous times, but its tenacity prevailed over her efforts to spare it the curse of existence. Young-Ja then found herself hoping that it would stop growing of its own accord and die within her, that it might be a stillbirth like so many buried beneath the comfort station. It would then never have to know pain outside the womb. She wept, haunted by the monstrous thoughts she could not accept were her own. Ones a mother should not have. Young-Ja feared the impending birth, dreading what poisonous thoughts of harm might grip her should traces of the father be glimpsed in its newborn face.

Agenisi and Xiuying helped to deliver the baby, keeping Baoluo or any other man away from the room. Young-Ja ruptured into sobs when she saw that the infant took a breath, that it screamed with the air it consumed from outside of her. It was alive. She could not bear to look at his little eyes, nose, mouth. He would be faceless, nameless for days. The doctors urged her to breastfeed but Young-Ja stared into the distance, tears streaming from her eyes until her body dried up, leaving little moisture for her or for the child. The baby wailed every time he was forced to her teat, her breast milk sparse and bitter with lost hope. Young-Ja did not resist when Xiuying welcomed the child into her arms and began calling him Joon.

Young-Ja learned from Baoluo and Agenisi one morning that the war was over. Japan had been made to bow its head to a power that eclipsed the sun and extinguished cities. Young-Ja did not understand what terrible force could defeat an empire that had so choked life from Joseon and China, but she accepted this new state of the world with little fanfare. What little conviction was left in her numbed body was not enough to inquire after further detail, though she wondered how many of the soldiers she encountered perished in battle. She wondered if she would see one, or live in fear of one, ever again. Should fate so insist on stripping her of her loves, she implored it to strip her, too, of her tormentors. To mete out her sentence of solitude in its truest form.

Young-Ja's voice returned to her on Joon's dol—his first birthday. When he would not stop crying, an exasperated Young-Ja found herself starting to scold him.

"Be quiet, be strong. Big boys don't cry."

When Agenisi heard her speak to the infant in Korean, she asked if Young-Ja had interest in accompanying the siblings on a mission for their god in Joseon. The Allies had seized control of Joseon as Japan retreated. They could continue their charity work in the capital under the protection of Western soldiers. If she came with them to translate, they could help the poor of Joseon together.

Young-Ja had long stopped dreaming of her motherland. She had been so far for so long. There was nothing left there for her. No family, no home. No one to recognize her with a kind word on the street. But it made no difference to her whether she stayed in China or went to Joseon under its new Western occupation. Baoluo and Agenisi had been kind enough to shelter her and provide a livelihood she did not think she had the resolve to seek elsewhere. So she agreed.

Joon cried when peeled from Xiuying's warmth. Young-Ja wondered if he might fare better left behind here, loved by Xiuying. Did he not deserve to be cradled by arms that had never once thought to stifle his breath? To be fed on the milk of an untainted body? But she could not abandon what she had brought into this world. She could not bring herself to curse this child with the same loss that had shattered her since her family fell breathless to the earth. Since Seiko Obaa-san retreated from her wails. Since Meiyu dove out into the sky. Since Bok-Hee slipped from her grasp. If being left behind was to be Young-Ja's fate, she would accept her duty to stay for this child.

Young-Ja boarded a train with her crying son to Dalian, a port city where they would find a ship bound for her native country. Facing the unbounded horizon of the open sea for the first time in her life, Young-Ja did not look back on the land that had buried her last remaining loves. All she had left to her in the world was asleep in her arms. She could not describe what she felt for him, but she knew she would have to protect him in her own way, no matter how corroded a husk she had become.

CHAPTER TWENTY-FOUR

Seoul, Korea, 1974

Of all the things that could have followed Young-Ja across the sea, it was the vicious specter of war that tailed her to her native land. Not long after she taught a growing Joon to write his name in Hangeul, a Soviet-backed army from the north crossed the line Westerners had cleaved across the peninsula. Millions of lives were extinguished. Every city was leveled to rubble. The glaring absence of trees, burned or cut to stumps, laid bare the nation's war-torn horizon.

Young-Ja floated through the all-too-familiar turmoil of bloodshed. It was her duty to shield her son from the world she had failed to keep him out of. So long as he was not hurt, she did not pay mind to the students laying down their lives against an American-educated authoritarian. So long as he did not know of his origin, she did not balk at the country's descent into military dictatorship. With her ambitions focused so narrowly, decades passed without fate awarding

Young-Ja much more than what she asked: Joon lived without knowledge of his mother's sordid past.

One autumn morning in 1974, Young-Ja slipped out from the church basement where she resided, treading lightly on her creaky joints, hoping not to attract notice. She rose early that day to grind rice grains into flour and pound the resulting dough into rice cakes. She kneaded out her frustrations and welcomed the slight ache of her muscles. Although she had run low on funds, she could not bear to ask her grown son for money, nor could she allow herself to go to the kindly pastor for help. So she made rice cakes to sell despite knowing they would attract few buyers. When Young-Ja did manage a sale, customers returned only to complain of her food's bitterness.

"Look here, Ahjumma, these are rotten! You can't sell this—give me my money back or I'm reporting you to the city!"

It did not take long for these complaints to reach the other market vendors. They banded together to ask Young-Ja to leave; the parade of unhappy customers was not good for business. She left the market and sold her rice cakes at different busy street corners where people would not find her again to fault her goods. Once she was rid of a batch, she would come back to the church at the foot of Namsan and set about her afternoon cleaning chores. The church had sheltered her for decades when no one else would, with only the gentlest of nudges to be grateful to their god. She did not think she could give them her belief, but she would never shirk her duties to earn her keep and pay her modest rent.

"Joon-Uhmuhni, you have a call from your son," said one of the church volunteers as Young-Ja walked by with her broom.

Joon rarely called. Nor did Young-Ja know how to dial his number. Even if she did, she would not call, so as not to tie up the church's telephone line. She did not want to ask any more of them than she already had over the years. But she was always glad to hear from her son. A new energy jolted into her shuffle toward the receiver.

"Hello?"

"Okaa-san," said Joon.

"I'm not your *Okaa-san*, I'm your Uhmuhni," said Young-Ja in Korean, more bite in her voice than intended. The call was a special occasion but she could not abide by his choice to address her in this other tongue. "Joon-ah, are you well?" she pushed ahead in Korean.

"Please, it's Shun now," Joon said, continuing in Japanese. "I'm calling to confirm that I've sent you some money. Check with the bank and make sure it's come through."

Young-Ja whispered her thanks. Despite her gratitude that Joon had thought to send her funds without prompt, her heart dropped, weighed down by the distance and time in which she had become a burden to her child. She shook her head of this gloom and asked after his baby.

"I don't really have time to talk—I'm busy at the office. International calls are expensive too."

"Ah, all right. Well, I'm sure the bank has the money—"

"Take care of your health, Okaa-san."

Joon hung up.

Young-Ja had last spoken with him in the summer. Joon informed her then that she was a grandmother, though the child had been born several months prior, in the spring. Young-Ja could still recall the cold strain in her chest as she processed this news. She had not known that Joon and his wife had been expecting. She was briefly curious to know what the baby girl looked like and if she might ever get to see her, though she perhaps did not deserve to. No granddaughter would be proud of a poor, aging grandmother who spent her days making rotten rice cakes and cleaning toilets in an old church.

Young-Ja walked out to the wooden pews and sat to rest her feet. She glanced at the large wooden crucifix at the head of the remodeled nave, the one that had hung there since before she and Joon first arrived in Seoul with Paul and Agnes. The young pastor of the church had let the doctor siblings set up shop to treat the poor in their congregation. In exchange for a basement room and meals, Young-Ja took up odd cleaning jobs and taught Korean to passing foreign missionaries. Sitting in the pews now, she recalled a growing Joon running through the aisles with stray children while yet another war erupted around her. As with most of her past, she tried not to think about cowering in the church basement and leaving only to acquire rations for the others sheltering in place. The early days of the civil war echoed with Joon's cries of hunger—her son would not eat whatever passed through Young-Ja's distressed hands and instead turned to Paul and Agnes for sustenance. She began to avoid handling food altogether to keep from sullying the church's limited supply.

When the fighting threatened the edges of the city, Young-Ja and Joon followed the doctor siblings down to Busan with millions of others fleeing for their lives. Paul and Agnes continued their work as medical missionaries among the throngs of the wounded and afraid on the southern coast. But their god put an end to Paul's service with sudden illness before he put an end to the war. After the ceasefire, Agnes alone returned with Young-Ja and Joon to rebuild their demolished home church in Seoul. There the doctor continued tending to the poor who struggled to regain footing in the country's wreckage, but she eventually retreated to Scotland to stave off homesickness.

Once Agnes departed, Young-Ja had no one left who could speak of her life in China or the scars on her stomach. No witness to her ever having left Joseon, no witness to her return. She was surprised to find herself missing the foreign doctor in her absence, though it was easier to bury the darkest parts of her with no one around to care for anything but their own postwar woes.

Without Paul and Agnes to keep him busy with structured tasks around the church, Joon started to grow curious about his origin. For the first several years of his life, Joon had not broached the topic of his father. Young-Ja wondered if his interest had never emerged because war had left so many of his peers fatherless. Children that age did not often talk to one another of what they lacked. But when Joon asked the first dreaded question, Young-Ja wielded her reticence as a shield, hoping to outlast his curiosity with equivocation. This she did to protect him as much as to protect herself.

"Umma, where is my appa?"

"Your father passed away in the war."

"Oh. Here?"

"No."

"Where?"

"China."

"Did he fight in the war?"

"Mmm."

"What about your parents? Where are they?"

"Joon-ah, Umma is tired. Let's go to sleep."

Questions poured from Joon for months, spilling into lingering pools around Young-Ja as she cleaned, as she cooked, as she relieved herself. Each time Joon pressed her, eager to know more of himself, of his inscrutable mother, she answered in monosyllabic disinterest until he learned to stop asking about his family. When Joon had uncovered every possible dead end in his interrogations, recognizing it sapped what little energy could be coaxed from his mother, he pivoted to asking how Young-Ja had met Paul and Agnes. Why he had been born in China.

"Paul and Agnes said I was born in China."

"Mmm."

"Umma, what were you doing in China?"

"Working."

"What kind of work?"

"Joon-ah, Umma is tired. Please wash the dishes now."

Young-Ja cocooned herself in her secrecy, weaving a barrier that kept her son unmarred by her truth. He did not need to know how and why he did not have the gift of kin. He did not need to know he harbored the face of a monster whose name she would never learn. His entry into the world was no fault of his own. He was owed a clean start. And while she would never be able to give him the childhood she could not believe she had once had, he would live unhindered by her soiled fate.

Engrossed in her efforts to subdue, Young-Ja did not see how Joon's hungry eyes dimmed each time their conversations tapered, how his small child frame shrank when he relented to her unspoken wishes. Her silence was teaching her son to seek the comfort of answers elsewhere, to drift away from her with a distance she mistook for protection. As Joon began school, he redirected his unsated curiosity to teachers who welcomed his inquisitive nature. In their praise he discovered a certain aptitude for language—both in Korean and in Japanese—falling into his texts with boundless hunger for the histories of his world he could not get at home. In the early days, he would become so enthralled with his schoolwork he would forget having given up on asking his mother questions.

"Umma, did you learn Japanese in school?"

"Mmm."

"How long did it take you to learn?"

"Mmm."

"Can you help me with this homework?"

"Joon-ah, Umma is tired. You should ask your teacher."

Joon had watched his mother recoil in the basement over time, evading the church staff and neighborhood ladies who would ask after her. For years he prayed for his mother to change, to shed the heaviness lodged in her eyes and tongue. When these prayers went unanswered, he sometimes wished he could switch mothers entirely, to those of his school friends. Ones who could spare him a kind word or give him coins to buy candies after class. An acceptable mother that the neighborhood had not started whispering unkind things about.

"See that? She ignored me."

"Don't mind her, she's like that."

"I heard she was in China during the occupation. And well, women who went overseas then . . ."

"Uhmuhna . . . and her son doesn't have a father. You know what that means."

"That poor child. So skinny too."

A thousand pins prickled at Joon's neck when neighbors did not lower their voices as he ran errands with his mother. But what disturbed him most was not that she appeared unbothered by such comments. It was that she did not seem to hear them at all, her pupils cloudy as she appraised the meager produce selection at the market.

Joon feared the unknowable darkness tailing his mother and endeavored to ward himself against it. He lingered in the light of school after hours, keeping himself fed on the praise of teachers happy to instruct a bright student. Under their attentive tutelage, he achieved top marks: a stepping-stone to his teachers' affection far from the pitying eyes in his neighborhood.

Seeing Joon's potential, his mentors set his sights on an ambitious education. While Korea was split and left to build up from the ruins of war, the star of Japan was rising on the global stage. Its economy was in boom and there were jobs to be had. It was not a difficult choice for Joon to hone his Japanese and seek his fortune abroad, for his curiosity had not been able to take root in the brokenness of his home country. Joon's efforts gained him a scholarship at Waseda University in Tokyo, where he excelled in the study of business and economics.

Young-Ja did not express her disappointment when she learned that Joon would leave for Tokyo, and later, that he would remain. After dropping his Korean name for a Japanese one, he was one of a few international students in his class to secure a position in a respectable company. The day he called to announce his intentions to marry a Japanese woman, Young-Ja crumpled into a nearby chair. She knew she could not stop him. It was neither her place nor her right to tell him how to live his life. To tell him the truth—to weigh him down with what she was—would be to tar his impossible success. In what she understood as an act of love, Young-Ja let him walk the paths he had chosen for himself. And while he enjoyed his hard-won prosperity, she would live out the remainder of her days quietly, causing him no additional worry or burden as a good parent should.

PART III
MATSUMOTO RINAKO
마쓰모토 리나코
松本 凛那子

CHAPTER TWENTY-FIVE

Tokyo, Japan, 1989

Matsumoto Rinako was an unusual child. Although she was born in Tokyo, her father was Korean. Before he met her mother, he had changed his name to Matsumoto to facilitate assimilation into Japanese society. Despite his efforts to mask his origin, he sometimes misplaced the high and low pitch accents of his syllables when he spoke. Such slips revealed that Japanese was not his mother tongue, making it apparent that Rinako was of mixed blood. While Rinako felt that she could be nothing but Japanese, her classmates' parents would quietly tell their children to play with anyone else but her.

Her heritage, however, was not the only thing that made Rinako unusual among her peers. She also seemed to know things that were not her business to know. She knew her classmates' siblings' names. She knew where they had gone on vacation. She knew what their pet cats liked to eat at home. Although her classmates had never once conversed with her, she knew which ones feared thunder, which ones feared sharks, which ones feared the night. Even as six-year-olds, her classmates sensed that this was not right and kept their distance from the strange girl.

Once, during playtime, Rinako captured a spider in the fleshy cup of her hands. Wishing to make friends, she sought to teach her classmate not to fear the harmless creature. The boy leapt back with a scream at the twitch of hairy legs in Rinako's palms. He tripped and fell, crashing his soft child skull on the corner of a table. The resulting gush of blood plunged the whole classroom into teary screams.

"Monster!" the children yelled, pointing at the stunned girl whose spider had long fled from her grasp.

Through snot and tears, Rinako swore that it was an accident, that she only wanted to help her friend. She had not meant to hurt anyone. The injured boy was taken to the hospital and the head teacher had no choice but to suspend Rinako for a few days to forestall parental outcry. Isolated from her classmates, she waited for her parents to pick her up from school under the supervision of her rattled teacher. She was eager to demonstrate to the school that she was not a monster, that she was a nice girl who liked nice things and wanted to get along with her class. She thought hard about what would best appeal to her teacher.

"Sensei, can we please watch *Ohayō* when I'm back? You like it, right? Your mama too?"

The woman froze. The Ozu film was indeed a favorite of her late mother's, but she had never discussed her personal life at work, let alone with her young students. There was no explanation for how Rinako could know this, and the teacher backed away, pulse quickening.

After enough complaints from parents and faculty, the Matsumotos moved away and enrolled their daughter at a new school. This marked a new era in Rinako's life. She was kept inside where she could only watch from the window as the neighborhood children ran by in the street. Her parents shouted at each other behind their bedroom door every night. There was neither laughing nor playing. When her parents did speak to her, she was told to hold her tongue and not cause any more trouble. People liked girls who were obedient and quiet.

"This is what's best for you," they said. "You'll understand when you're older."

Rinako adhered to her parents' commands, desperate to follow the rules if it could make them happy again. While she longed to make friends at her new school, she hid behind her books and growing bangs, anxious not to scare anyone off. Most teachers forgot they had a Matsumoto among their students; those who did not forget mistook her reticence for dullness. When the unfamiliar Matsumoto turned up at the tops of exam score lists, the faculty suspected foul play and made her sit through new tests under increased observation. After Rinako sufficiently proved her aptitude, they left her alone once more to fade away in the back of the classroom. Some version of this scenario played out each year as she progressed to new crops of incredulous teachers, chipping away at her belief that adults knew what was best.

Rinako's classmates had no trouble accepting her invisibility. Sometimes they sat in a chair she was already in, standing up only when they felt something uncomfortable beneath them without acknowledging what they had done. In the cafeteria she waited until she was last in line, not wanting to be bumped into lest she end up with lunch dribbling down her clothing. Throughout it all, she bit her tongue, learning not to share what she had come to know of the people around her. Their hopes, their fantasies, their fears. From a young age, Rinako internalized the lesson that disclosure led to ruin. Secrecy preserved comfort and safety.

Things changed when Rinako dropped her pencil in her junior high school math class. It rolled loudly over to the foot of her classmate Kōsuke, who sat at the desk next to hers. When the pencil tapped against his shoe, Kōsuke picked it up and handed it back to her with a smile. Rinako was so taken aback by his acknowledgment that she broke her silence.

"Thank you, Koko," she said.

She was near inaudible, but Kōsuke blanched as if she had screamed.

"What did you call me?" he asked.

Rinako turned back to her algebra equations, surprised by her own voice. She did not realize that she had called him a name that only his mother used. The name his mother would use to soothe him when Kōsuke wet the bed occasionally, even as a teen. He was terrified that his shameful secret had been discovered.

Kōsuke was a smart, athletic student whose bright smile made him popular with boys and girls alike. When he started calling Rinako a creep and a stalker, no one had reason to doubt him. Her classmates shunned her. Rumors started to float that she was dangerous.

"She's absolutely obsessed with him."

"Isn't it a crime to follow people around like that? They should throw her in the loony bin!"

"Someone in Class 3 saw her eyes glow yellow like a demon. Soooo creepy."

"I heard she's not even Japanese . . ."

Invisible no longer, Rinako sat in silence as her classmates hurled open cartons of milk at her in the cafeteria, afraid speaking up might worsen the situation. But when the boy sitting behind her cut off her braid and left her hair in a jagged bob that pricked at her neck, she turned around and stabbed his hand on the desk with her pencil. The lead point punctured through the spongy flesh between his thumb and pointer finger and left a bloody pockmark in the soft wood of the desk. She walked out of the classroom without a word and did not return.

Rinako had vivid dreams. Some were ungraspable and forgotten, but some played so clearly behind her closed eyes she could not always recall if she had been asleep. Her dreams rarely centered her, however. Some were a pastiche of absurd situations featuring people she did not know. If her dreams presented more familiar faces, she would see her neighbors' pleasures, her teachers' hobbies, her classmates' nightmares.

As a child, she could not always discern what she learned in her dreams from what she learned in waking life. Rinako was often left confused when attempts to talk to people about what she knew made them happy were rebuffed; people would grow suspicious when she knew harmless things about them if they had no recollection of divulging such information. If anything, these dreams made her like the people around her more. To watch the smell of a dog's paw trigger joy, to feel the regret of breaking a grandfather's prized ceramic—such small yet distinct scenes of vulnerability rendered each person Rinako saw decidedly sympathetic. But people never carried themselves as openly in reality as they did in her dreams. While these dreams stoked her sense of kinship toward others, no one returned the sentiment. She did not understand why connecting with people was so difficult for her when it came so easily to everyone else, in dreams or otherwise.

Rinako also dreamed of her parents. Her dream mother frequently tended to an old sanka house in the mountains. Gardening, cleaning, watching the foliage turn colors. Her dream father often stood at arm's length from an older woman. The old woman's round face housed cold, downcast eyes that refused to look at her dream father as he spoke to her in a language Rinako did not know. But these dreams of her mother and father gave her no greater familiarity, no greater insight into her parents. When not lecturing her about the importance of school, her waking mother and father tiptoed around Rinako, afraid of saying anything that might worsen her descent into whatever uncanny realm had possessed her.

The months after Rinako stabbed her classmate whirled by in chaos for the Matsumotos. Rinako's parents were forced to bow in apology to the boy's family, cover his medical bills, and take their daughter to be evaluated by a gallingly expensive child psychiatrist. The doctor was unable to pry many words from his patient, who, in his opinion, presented as a maladapted youth suffering lapses of self-control. Such violent outbursts were not uncommon for children of mixed blood, he noted, before authorizing a rare medical leave to finish off her final months of junior high from home. This sparked a new series of arguments between the couple about what to do, both horrified by the shame of having to pull their daughter out of school. They eventually conceded, however, that it might be best to rehabilitate the girl of her issues in private and set her up to begin high school with a clean slate. University was what mattered; these adolescent transgressions could be buried.

As Rinako spent more time at home, she noticed that her father was changing. Overtime kept him office-bound until ten o'clock, eleven o'clock, even past midnight, leaving Rinako and her mother to eat more modest dinners as a pair. He explained that a significant promotion was imminent; he needed to work on the weekends to lock it in. A promotion would enable them to move to a nicer neighborhood and pay for Rinako to attend a private high school with a strong record of placing its students into the most prestigious universities. Rinako clenched her jaw every time he said this, her teeth aching with indignity that he believed her a problem to be fixed with money.

You don't need to do all this for me, I'll be fine, she wanted to say, outgrowing the need to please her hand-wringing parents as quickly as she outgrew her retired junior high uniform. *And if you're doing this for yourself, stop using me as an excuse.*

But speaking her mind had never been to her advantage. Rinako already knew what her parents would say to end further discussion anytime she challenged their decisions.

"This is what's best for you. You'll understand when you're older."

Rinako was dubious of such a refrain from two adults who increasingly did not seem to understand her or each other. Still, she kept quiet, no longer out of a desire to make her parents happy but to deter the nuisance of their lecturing. She pretended not to hear them bickering about her. She pretended not to notice her father emerging sleepy-eyed from his study instead of the bedroom in the mornings. Some nights he did not come home at all.

It was not by choice that Rinako stayed with her father after her parents' divorce, though she was unsure which parent she would have chosen if anyone had thought to consult her. Her mother's family had always disapproved of her marriage to a foreigner with no connections—a Korean, no less—and had kept their distance from Rinako. After the divorce, they resolved to forget Rinako's troublesome existence altogether and whisked her mother back to Sendai. She had departed in the night, leaving nothing but a thin, banknote-sized envelope on Rinako's nightstand. The unopened envelope lay in a desk drawer, sitting heavy with an apology Rinako did not wish to indulge. Her father never spoke of her mother's absence, choosing instead to burrow further into his work.

Rinako had no love for the maternal family that had abandoned her at the first opportunity, but she could at least picture the faces to resent. Her paternal family she did not know at all. Her father liked to maintain that he, Matsumoto Shun, was Japanese, that he had not once come from Korea with the name Song Joon.

"This is what's best for you," he said. "You'll understand when you're older."

Rinako came to accept that she had no other family, no past deeper than what her father was willing to acknowledge. Yet, for a country she had never visited and did not know much about, Korea cast an inescapable shadow over her life. She was Japanese. A child of Tokyo. She had not chosen to be born to a Korean, though this distinction clung to her like a faint odor that made people keep their distance. Rinako thus often scavenged for more flattering details about the country to balance out so much of what was not. South Korea had hosted the last Olympics, for example. Despite its poor, rural nature, it had come remarkably far in developing its economy. Still, she tensed anytime someone mentioned the country, ears vigilant for those common aspersions about its paupers and criminals. The details of how her father came to so loathe his origin remained a mystery, but she too found herself not wanting to be seen through such a filter.

Although her father stayed out late most nights, he left Rinako plenty of cash to feed herself and keep groceries stocked in the fridge. But there were only so many hours she could spend studying by herself in the stuffy apartment. Wishing for an excuse not to be alone, Rinako secretly took a part-time job at the neighborhood konbini as soon as she turned fifteen. She smiled and attempted small talk with the customers who came in, but quickly learned from the muted replies that people did not want to be perceived when running errands at the corner store. So Rinako shrank into herself yet again, blending into the wall until a customer needed to pay. From her invisible perch she watched the cast of her neighborhood rotating through for milk, errant toiletries, cigarettes. When these neighbors later emerged in her dreams, she felt that familiar pang: the more she learned about them in her sleep, the greater the chance she might inadvertently distress them in waking life and sever a potential bond.

While Rinako longed for conversation, she was not indiscriminate. She knew right away that she disliked speaking with her konbini supervisor, a middle-aged man who had a penchant for monologuing his utterly average thoughts: which brand of chocolate he liked best, replays of the latest Yomiuri Giants games, whether winter would be harsh that year. Taking Rinako's silence as consent, he began to close the space between them, letting his hand linger on the small of her back. Rinako stared at the dandruff dusting his shoulders and debated whether to kick him between his scrawny legs.

When Rinako woke one morning having witnessed her dream supervisor grunting into her over the konbini counter, she ran to the bathroom and splattered watery vomit into the toilet bowl. She never went back to the konbini again, looking forward instead to the start of high school in a few weeks. Maybe this academic year would be different.

An old man watches the television from his hospital bed. He floats in a half-awake daze as the young anchor reports the news. He thinks about his children who have not visited him in years, claiming that Hamamatsu was too inconvenient, that they could not step away from their work in Tokyo.

An elderly nurse enters the room, perhaps only a few years younger than him. She shuffles toward him and eyes the few personal belongings on his nightstand—some worn books, a khaki military-issue cap, and a red-and-gold gochō collar tab with a single star at its center. She picks up the cap from the nightstand and places it on his head. She meets his eyes and smiles, revealing a few missing teeth. She has a long, thin pink scar on the left side of her liver spot–covered face, falling from her eye to her chin.

He demands to know what she is doing, as he has already had his evening checkup with his usual nurse, but only a small rasp escapes from his throat. The smiling nurse takes out a clear syringe and places it into the injection port of his morphine drip. She pushes *the plunger slowly down the barrel, releasing a new liquid into his veins. He tries to grab her wrist but cannot find the strength to lift his arm. His vision fades as he tries to grip the starchy sheets of his hospital bed. His fingers do not listen. The nurse walks out without glancing back.*

CHAPTER TWENTY-SIX

Tokyo, Japan, 1991

Rinako ran down into the subway station, dodging the churn of commuters. The July humidity drew sweat from her pores, enveloping her in an amphibious slick she could not wait to wash off at home. She searched her pocket for a train ticket, her shoulders aching from the weight of the university entrance exam prep books she had come to this district to purchase. A swarm of mostly men jostled past her on both sides, brushing her arms with their haste. She did not notice immediately that the line she had shuffled into had slowed. Ahead was an elderly woman hunched over a large canvas bag rooting around for her subway ticket. She stood on swollen ankles and focused on her bag, not registering the annoyed station worker or the line of men shoving behind her to another gate.

"Granny, move if you don't have your ticket ready," said a red-faced man as he swung her to the side and rushed through the gate. With one person already having committed the discourtesy, the crowd streamed past without sparing the woman another glance. The old lady stumbled from the surge, tripping and falling onto her hands and knees. Rinako ran to her as the commuters barged ahead. She helped the woman to her feet and ushered her to the side, where they would not be swept under the feet of salarymen. Rinako quelled the urge to throw her heavy books at their retreating heads.

"Are you all right?" Rinako asked.

A long pink scar ran from the woman's left eye down to her chin. Her rheumy eyes darted around before locking onto Rinako's. She grabbed Rinako's wrists and launched into rapid Korean, large, gummy gaps in her mouth announcing her missing teeth. Rinako stiffened at the foreign sounds of the language, hoping that passersby did not associate it with her. She regretted engaging with the stranger whose yellowed nails were pressing into her arms.

"*Wenji naega aneun saram dalmatne. Chahm biseuthage saenggyutsuh, fujikorang. Jigeum mwo haneunji . . . Ahjik sarait-neunji . . .*"

"I'm sorry, I don't understand," she said, trying to pull her arm free from the old woman. All the surrounding noises—train brakes screeching, hundreds of shoes marching against the tiles, indistinct overhead announcements—seemed to swallow her words. She could not tell if the old lady heard her. Rinako felt short of breath, as if the mugginess of the station were constricting her throat. Having confirmed the woman was not hurt, she was eager to leave.

"*I neulgeunireul dowajwoseo gomapda. Ahgassido joshimhaera.*"

Rinako let out a nervous laugh and kept trying to pull away.

"Thank you, young lady," the woman said in accented Japanese. She tapped Rinako's hand and let go of her arm, producing a ticket from her pocket and hobbling through the gate toward her platform. The commuter rush engulfed her until she disappeared from sight.

It was nearing ten p.m. and her father was still not home. Rinako flipped through her exam prep books. The sentāshiken was next year and her father was insistent she aim for Waseda, his alma mater. If she did not make significant progress in the workbook tonight, she would have to suffer his usual refrain about the singular importance of academic achievement for guaranteeing her future. *A future of what?* she wanted to ask. A future like his? If success meant working eighty hours a week, she did not want to be successful.

Still, Rinako felt the tug of university and let herself fantasize about how it could improve her life. For the first time ever, her introduction to her teachers would not be heavily mediated by her parents or her behavioral record. She could live on campus away from home. She could pursue any path of study, present herself in any way she wished, maybe even make some friends. It certainly would be easier blending in at a large university than her small private high school. Having learned to stifle comments about her invasive dreams, she had not attracted unwanted notice over the past two years at her new school. She had even contemplated trying to make light banter with her classmates, ones who did not look at her with fear. But she hesitated to risk the peace that her current anonymity had afforded her.

Rinako turned on the TV, requiring its noise in the background as she studied so as not to have to stew in the familiar emptiness of the apartment. As the rainbow glow of a detergent commercial jingled across the screen, the phone rang. She muted the TV before picking up the receiver.

"Hello?"

"*Annyeonghaseyo, seouleh itneun youngwonhan huimang gyohweindeyo, hoksi songjoonssi gyesingayo?*"

"I'm sorry, but I'm Japanese. I don't speak Korean," said Rinako, surprised to encounter the language yet again that day.

"Ah, sorry." The speaker let out nervous laughter as she switched into Japanese. "Ah— Song Joon-san?"

"No, he's not here," said Rinako.

"Ah . . . uh. Song-san mother. Hospital. Seoul. Hospital in Seoul."

Rinako snapped still. "May I ask who's calling?" She spoke slowly, hoping the voice on the other end would understand.

"Mmm. Church. Uh . . . friend."

"Do you have a number you can leave? I can ask him to call you back."

"Mmm sorry, don't understand."

"Phone number?" Rinako enunciated each syllable.

"Ah, ah. Wait, please."

The speaker set down the receiver for a minute and returned, reading out a phone number in stilted Japanese. Rinako transcribed the figures on a notepad and scribbled *Grandmother in hospital. Seoul. Return call.*

After hanging up, she stood by the phone, exam books forgotten. Rinako's whirring mind would not take in any information unrelated to the revelation of a grandmother. Her grandmother. She paced around the living room late into the night, anxious for her father to come home and answer questions, only to succumb to an exhausted sleep before he returned.

That night, Rinako dreamt of the old woman with the pink scar from the station. The dream woman appeared to be a nurse attending to a bedridden old man wearing a military cap, administering drugs into his IV drip. There was nothing exceptionally odd about the scene—Rinako had certainly witnessed many stranger things—but she woke in a feverish sweat as if having watched something gruesome unfold. It was still dark outside; she settled her burning body back into her sheets until her heart stopped pounding in her ears. The fuzzy outline of her room faded again to nothingness.

"Rinako. Wake up."

Her father hovered at the foot of her bed, dressed for work with his briefcase in hand. His shoulders hunched as he rubbed at his left eye. "I'm flying to Seoul tomorrow," he said. "I have work today but I'll take the first flight on Saturday morning."

"To see your mother?"

Her father paused for a moment before confirming. "Yes. She's fallen ill."

"I didn't know you had a mother."

"We all have mothers."

She shot him a look of annoyance. "Can I come?"

"No. I'm coming back on Sunday, so you'll only have to take care of yourself over the weekend. It'll be quick."

"Why can't I go? It's summer break and I wanna meet my grandmother."

"Stay home and focus on your studies." He walked out of her room.

Rinako heard the front door close and looked at the time. It was only 7:05 a.m., but the July heat had already made her nightshirt stick to her back. She sat up from her bed and scanned the room. On her desk was the pile of exam prep books she had purchased at her father's insistence. The drawer below hummed with the unopened envelope from her mother. Next to her desk was a full trash bin she needed to empty and a pile of clothes she needed to launder. As her burdens encircled her she was overcome with the urge to flee.

Rinako ran to the living room and strained to slide open its largest window. She stuck her head out of their sixth-floor apartment and waited for her father to emerge from the building's main entrance below.

"I want to meet my grandmother!" Rinako yelled into the parking lot.

Her father whipped his head up at the noise. He hated when she made a scene, when she brought attention to herself in any way. Rinako knew the expression skulking over his face all too well. It was the same blend of panic and disappointment that soured his eyes every time he was asked to pick her up from school because she had disturbed the people around her.

"I WANT TO GO WITH YOU!" Rinako screamed louder than she had ever screamed before, startling a host of sparrows to flee from a nearby maple tree.

Her father inhaled as if to shout something in reply but instead turned back to his commute. He walked briskly and disappeared around the corner. As if distance could make the aberration of his daughter go away.

Matsumoto Shun had attained top marks in every class, enabling him to land a well-paying job at a prestigious company. He had also managed a respectable marriage and was blessed with a daughter for whom he hoped to provide a better life than his own. At his peak, he was confident of his own success, having achieved everything his humble upbringing might have otherwise precluded. But he could not pinpoint the exact start of his descent, at what moment his loud internal assurances that he should be satisfied with his life were overcome by signs to the contrary. His wife had left him a few years back, likely at the insistence of her family. They never liked him much, and fanned her suspicions that he had been unfaithful. As difficult as it was for him to accept the stigma of divorce, he found it laughable that anyone thought him capable of an affair when he was averaging fourteen hours a day in the office. In the end, he understood. Shun and his wife spoke almost exclusively in arguments and had long stopped having sex when Rinako was in junior high school. This suspension was as much his preference as his wife's.

Rinako was always a cause for concern. To his great relief, his unusually perceptive daughter received excellent marks in school, just as he had. But unlike him, Rinako had neither a love for school nor the affection of her teachers. Instead, her failure to keep her observations to herself troubled everyone around her. Shun and his wife had desperately tried to teach her to hew to the norm, to be like the other children, though the girl seemed too lost in her own rhythms to understand the importance of social convention. He was proud to have bestowed on her this privileged upbringing: wealth, stability, an attentive family invested in her education. But now, sweating and packed into the subway car, Shun dreaded the next time he might run into a neighbor in case they complained about Rinako's shouting that morning or any other behaviors they wished to dissect as parental incompetence. He grasped one of the car's hanging rings to catch his balance when something zoomed above him near the lights. A sparrow had gotten into the compartment and was flitting about over the passengers. Some eyed the creature with mild interest while others ducked under their briefcases or newspapers as if afraid the bird might land an attack.

Shun ignored the winged disruption, hoping his daughter would be calm again when he returned home that evening. He had tried his hardest to give Rinako a normal Japanese childhood, knowing that any hint of foreignness might worsen her alienation in school. It was best if she—or those who might judge her—did not know that Shun was Korean, that he had grown up poor and fatherless in the shadow of war, raised by a woman who did not seem to care for much in the world. The last time he had seen his mother, over seven years ago on a brief business trip to Seoul, he had taken her out to eat at the upscale French restaurant in his five-star hotel, hoping in part to impress her with his success, but also to treat her to something special she could not and would not have accessed on her own. She had barely touched her expensive canard à l'orange and only maintained stilted conversation. Shun's ears turned hot when she drew judgmental looks from the other patrons by requesting kimchi and rice with her meal.

Shun pushed down thoughts of his family with practiced ease as he entered the office. The clock read 7:37 a.m., long before his team would file into their cubicles. He had just placed his briefcase on his desk when a drawling voice interrupted his introspection.

"Matsumoto-san, you're a little later than usual. I was about to page you. When you're settled, come see me. I want you to go over the Yonamine numbers again. Your calculations don't seem quite right."

"Good morning. I was told Accounting had already approved it."

"Still." The team lead tapped on his cubicle wall. "Promotion season is coming up and we don't want to make it harder for your case, right? Make sure everything is perfect."

Shun tensed. His well-connected superior was five years his junior, having been promoted twice since Shun's last tepid pay raise three years ago. The rest of the team liked to comment on how grateful they were to be working for such a charming team lead, but Shun's ears often caught on a certain tone in the man's voice. He would need caffeine for this meeting. The breakroom's instant coffee would have to do.

As the oldest in his department, Shun kept his head down and worked hard, trying not to give anyone an excuse to reproach him for his age. While the other employees were civil, they did not offer him the same brightness they offered to one another, and would put out their cigarettes to return to work when they saw him approaching with his own pack. Shun never declined the rare, trickling invite for after-work drinks in order to preserve the image of sociability, but he preferred not to advance himself through ingratiation. His exemplary work quality could carry him through. Just as it always had.

When he turned the corner, shouts erupted from the breakroom. One of his colleagues backed out into the corridor in a jittery clack of heels. Behind the door came the screech of furniture legs dragged across the floor. When Shun peered inside, two men were swatting at something at the ceiling. A small brown bird chirped about, evading capture and refusing to go toward the open window. Another sparrow. He wondered if the city needed to do something about the out-of-control sparrow population and helped his coworkers shoo the bird away before making his cup of coffee.

Shun did not leave the office until past ten p.m.—the discussion with his team leader had avalanched into rehashings of several closed accounts, none of which had the errors he had been accused of making. Infuriating as it was, the undertaking had at least kept his mind off his mother for most of the day. On his walk home from the station, he recalled what the chatty church office assistant had told him when he returned her call that morning. His mother had collapsed last evening and was rushed to the hospital. The assistant had not been told the exact cause of the ailment, but she urged him to visit, foisting on him the hospital's address and the promise to convey to his mother that Shun would visit on Saturday. He wondered how much older his mother would appear tomorrow, frail and disengaged in a hospital bed. Something coiled inside him.

Even as the hour approached midnight, the July air was pregnant with humidity. Shun opened his bedroom window in the hopes of catching a breeze while he unzipped a small duffel bag and stacked some clothes inside. As he reached for his sock drawer, something grazed the top of his head. He looked up, saw nothing, and slid his hand across the solid tracks of his gelled hair. He continued to pack until he heard a chirp coming from somewhere in the room. He swiveled his head around for the source of the offending noise. A sparrow was perched on his nightstand next to his pager and a pile of coins, staring at him.

He rolled up a newspaper and waved it around to usher the bird back outside when another brown blur flew in. Then another. And another. Soon, a stream of sparrows poured inside his bedroom, swirling around in a frenetic, piercing chorus of chirps, knocking things over in loud crashes as they bounced off the walls.

"Otō-san?" His daughter knocked on his door, no doubt startled by the sudden cacophony. She opened the door before he could yell at her to stop.

The sparrows flew into the rest of the apartment as Rinako jumped back with a yelp. The birds flew onto the counter, into cups, under the kitchen table. They hopped about on the TV and dove into the water in the toilet bowl. Bird shit streaked down all their furniture.

"Otō-san!" Rinako yelled from the ground, having fallen in shock. Her eyes widened as she looked to him for an answer.

Shun ran around opening the front door and all the windows, trying to give the sparrows as many exits as he could. This only caused more to flap in and join the whirlwind intent on ignoring the way out. He reached for the phone in a panic to call his landlady and the exterminator, but he could not leave Rinako in the midst of this freak infestation. Shun would just have to take his daughter to Seoul with him while the pests were dealt with.

CHAPTER TWENTY-SEVEN

Seoul, Republic of Korea, 1991

Foreboding trickled down Rinako's back as she followed her father out of the hospital elevator. She had not felt like herself since learning about her grandmother, and the morning's flight to Seoul had worsened the tightness in her lungs. As dizziness swirled behind her eyes, she took a deep breath and blinked slowly to refocus her vision. This granted no relief. The harsh hospital lights only unsettled her further, bringing to mind the scarred subway woman and the dream in which she had appeared as a nurse.

It was surreal to watch her father speak with the medical staff so casually in Korean, as if it were not something he had kept from her for her entire life. Rinako observed these unfamiliar shifts in his mouth with some curiosity at first, but when the inscrutable discussion stretched on, she slipped away from the floor's reception desk hoping to find a washroom and splash some water on her overheated face. Down the hallway, she noted with surprise that the Korean hospital she had pictured to be somewhat shabby was in reality well equipped and modern. Her roaming gaze continued to search for a bathroom sign until it stopped at an open door that drew her attention.

Through it was a room that housed six occupied beds, in two rows of three. Rinako shuffled forward until her eyes locked with those of an old woman at the corner bed by the window. She had a round face, one Rinako felt she had seen somewhere before. Familiar cold eyes, tight lips that conserved their words.

They stood regarding each other in silence when her father hurried in from behind her toward the woman's bed, speaking in rapid Korean. He gestured at Rinako to come closer.

The old woman did not reply to what sounded like a scolding from her son and instead stared at his daughter.

"*Geurae, ne ddaliji,*" she said. "*Nae ahbuhji dalmatda, nuh. Teukhi nooni dalmatsuh.*"

Rinako bowed and introduced herself, apologizing for not knowing Korean. The old woman furrowed her brows at her son and turned back to her granddaughter.

"It's okay," she said, switching to Japanese. "I said you look just like my father. You have his eyes. Come here."

Her grandmother's fluent Japanese surprised Rinako. She had not imagined they would be able to communicate and threw her father an accusing look for his usual failure to disclose. She approached the bedside and let the woman cup her cheek in her wrinkled hand, noting a long brown scar slashed across her palm. The touch was much cooler than Rinako expected, a pleasant sensation against her flushed skin. Her grandmother frowned.

"You feel warm. Are you unwell?" The old woman turned to her son and launched into Korean. Alarmed, he placed his hand on Rinako's forehead and ushered her toward a chair.

"I'm fine," said Rinako as she took a seat. "We didn't sleep much last night. Or maybe I'm just tired from the flight."

A nurse walked in to interrupt the family reunion with an update: after two nights of observation, the doctors had finally cleared the patient for discharge, provided she took her medication, got some bedrest, and moderated her salt intake. She was beginning to show signs of kidney disease, and her hypertension would worsen without appropriate precautions.

No one spoke much on the taxi ride leaving the hospital. The old woman clutched Rinako's hand, searching her face for something she had lost long ago.

"Watch your step." Shun propped his mother up at the elbow as he helped her down the stairs to her room in the church basement.

She shooed his hands away. "I can do it myself."

Shun watched his mother lumber down the stairs on her own. He had been steeling himself for the worst, but she seemed well enough now that he could leave the next day as planned. He could not believe she still lived in this dingy basement. Shun's childhood memories trailed him down the stairs: wearing the same dirty shirt and pants to school every day, pretending to eat his mother's terrible cooking and feeding it to stray cats when she was not looking. His grievances still prickled his skin but he could not bring himself to resent her, knowing how it was for everyone in those days after the war. Not that he could judge—his own faults as a parent chastened him to acknowledge that his mother had likely tried her best. No matter how much he had been left wanting.

As they reached the foot of the stairs, a loud greeting rang out above them.

"Halmuhni, you're back—we were so worried. And you look well!"

Shun recognized the voice of the office assistant with whom he had spoken on the phone. He bowed and thanked the middle-aged woman.

"How lovely to meet your family! I hate to interrupt, but Halmuhni, the professor from last month was calling again about her research. Remember? To talk to you about your time in China."

"I'm busy, I have guests."

"She told me she's been able to help some others, too, those who had the same experience as you, you know, working in China back in the day . . ." She trailed off, darting her eyes between Shun, his daughter, and his mother.

"I'm busy. My granddaughter is sick and I have to take care of her."

"Oh, yes, of course, I'll leave you to it. Please let me know if there's anything else you need." The office assistant bowed and left in a hurry.

Shun itched to know what a researcher wanted with his mother, but an old instinct dammed his questions under his tongue.

"Lay out the blankets for your daughter so she can rest. She's still burning up," his mother said.

Shun hastened to roll out the futon. Rinako looked dazed and he wanted her to sleep off whatever seemed to be ailing her—he needed her to be well enough to fly back tomorrow. The final year of high school was a critical hurdle and Rinako could not afford to be distracted from her studies. She had seemed so much better lately too—there had been no reported incidents at her new school. It had been the right choice to keep her busy with exam prep. There would be time to spend with family later.

The basement room where his daughter was now lying down to rest looked shamefully unchanged from the room he remembered from his youth. It held the same wardrobe, the same worn coat rack, the same mismatched cups and large comforter that his mother had used since Shun left for university nearly three decades ago. A half-empty bundle of Shin Ramyun packs and a crumpled box of instant coffee sticks sat in the corner beside an old antennaed TV. He had sent her money all this time, yet it was unclear whether she had spent any of it on herself.

"Let me put on some tea for you," said his mother as Rinako shut her eyes.

"No, I'm fine," Shun said, declining out of habit. "I'm going to run out for some medicine and see to a few errands. May I leave her here with you?"

While he was out, he planned to buy replacements for his mother's worn, threadbare things. At least with new items there would be less visual evidence of his negligence, of the distance he had allowed to widen between them.

His mother nodded. "Yes, leave her here to rest. You go."

Shun ran out, unable to look any longer at the room and all that it conjured.

Young-Ja was relieved to be home, away from the hospital's bothersome probing. When the doctor explained the treatment of kidney disease—the potential need to visit a clinic regularly for something called hemodialysis—Young-Ja tuned out most of the details and instead sat marveling at her poise and command. All women born after the war appeared youthful to her, and this smooth-faced doctor with the neatly coiffed bun and fancy words was no exception. Young-Ja felt old and squat in comparison. She nodded along to everything the doctor said, hoping acquiescence would be the fastest path to discharge.

"There was one other thing I wanted to discuss," said the doctor. "It's a bit difficult to say, but I believe it's medically relevant. The staff and I noticed the keloid formations on your abdomen . . ."

Young-Ja looked down at her lap. This was exactly why she avoided going to the doctor.

"It's an old wound, not infected or dangerous to you now. But it didn't look self-inflicted, and if someone else has done this to you, with that character, I think—"

"Young lady, if it's not going to affect my health now, I don't want to talk about it. It happened a long time ago and there's no point discussing it now."

"Ah, but . . ."

"Are we done here?"

Young-Ja hoped the doctor had not mentioned anything to Joon, neither about the scars nor about the clinic treatments. She pressed a cold towel to her sleeping granddaughter's forehead. The resemblance to Geum-Jin—that glimmer of yellow she had seen in Rinako's eyes at the hospital—made Young-Ja's breath catch. It felt odd to see traces of her strong father's features so vulnerable and weak, lying on the futon in feverish sleep. Such reminders of her bygone youth would normally have been unwelcome, but Young-Ja's instinct in that moment was not to dispel those memories. While she wished a quick recovery for her granddaughter, she found herself happy to tend to the young woman whose face evoked the mountains. It had been so long since she had taken care of someone so intimately. Since she had felt needed and useful. Something she did not get from Joon.

Everything about Joon seemed more faded. His body, his hairline, his spirit. Young-Ja saw the way his face fell when he had stepped back into this room. It was the same look he had worn when he took her to that overpriced restaurant the last time she had seen him: he was ashamed of her. Heat splashed across Young-Ja's face, and she turned to the small gas range and kettle. She would make some tea for herself and banish such thoughts.

"*Young-Ja-ya.*"

Had Rinako's mouth moved? She bent over the girl and set another cold towel on her forehead. Young-Ja believed it a blessing to see the granddaughter she thought would be lost to her, but wondered how long it would be before Joon's look of shame appeared on Rinako's face.

"*Fujiko-san.*"

Frost crept into Young-Ja's chest. That voice. Calling a name she had not heard in decades. The only one among them who insisted on those labels. But she was imagining things.

"*Why do you ignore us?*" The sleeping Rinako spoke in unaccented Korean. In a voice that had once insisted on speaking only in Japanese.

Young-Ja fell back. "Child, what did you say?"

"*We know you hear us.*" Rinako's eyes remained closed as her mouth moved to vocalize the words. Young-Ja blinked. Her granddaughter's breath otherwise remained deep and steady in the way only sleep could regulate.

"*It's good the young one finally found you,*" said Rinako. "*Much harder for you to ignore us now.*"

"*You should talk to that woman who calls. The educated one. She wants to help.*" A different intonation came from Rinako's mouth, this time a little higher in pitch.

Young-Ja knew these voices. She could never forget these voices. She took a deep breath before venturing to speak.

"I have no right to tell you what to do," she said, "but you should be at rest. This world can't hurt you anymore."

"*Listen to this, the restless telling us to rest.*" Rinako's head jerked from side to side.

"Leave me be."

"*Please, they can't hear us. But they can hear you.*"

"Oh, what I'd do if they could hear me. I'd curse them to hell and back."

"*You have such a foul mouth for someone who barely lived sixteen years.*"

"What makes you think they'll listen to me? I'm nobody." Young-Ja eyed her kettle, waiting for the water to boil.

"That professor wants to listen to you. Go tell her."

"Yes!"

"Tell her what? You know what the officials say. That we went on our own volition to make money. That there's no proof those soldiers did anything wrong . . ."

"And you're gonna let them get away with those lies?"

"They'll deny until no one's left to remember our kind. There are thousands of us. Tens of thousands. Hundreds of thousands." Beads of sweat glittered on Rinako's temple, growing fat until they slid down her fever-warm skin into her short bob.

"Go make more people see. It's been decades, we're running out of time."

"Exactly, it's been decades. No one cares. And if they did, they'd say we're tainted."

"You can't let them win your silence."

"I'm old and tired. There's sickness in my bones," said Young-Ja, wiping the sweat from her granddaughter's face.

"My bones are dust, but my spite lives on."

"I'd give anything to be a body again, even an old, sick one like yours. I want to eat beef. Some naengmyeon!"

"I'd take a hot bath!"

"Who will remember us when you're gone?"

"Who remembers now?"

The sleeping Rinako gasped and let out a soft cry. "Uhmuhna, listen to this. I know you remember every day you spent in that hell. Every last thing they did to you. What makes you think others don't? What makes you think they won't do it all over again?" Sweat pooled in the curve of Rinako's ears.

"What's done is done. Don't make me relive that pain."

"You know, this child witnesses dreams. She's even seen dreams from other survivors. What angry hearts project in the night. She'll understand. She'll listen."

"Leave her alone." Young-Ja wiped away the child's sweat once more and fanned a magazine at her burning face.

"She'll keep seeing. You can't hide from her."

"She can help us."

"Yeah, help us bury those sons of bitches!"

"Oooh, what I'd do if I saw one of them again. I'd cut off his testicles."

"Chop 'em up and feed 'em to my family's pigs!"

Rinako, eyes closed, cackled in a chorus of overlapping voices. A shiver rattled down Young-Ja's spine.

"How horrid. I don't want to think like that. Like them."

"How else do we get even?"

"We don't have to stoop to their level."

"There's a little darkness in all of us."

"But not like in those soldiers."

Rinako's sleeping head nodded as she hummed her assent.

"Be at rest. Don't drag me back there . . ."

"Our souls died in that prison. But that wasn't enough. They're killing us again by burying our memories, burying their sins. They wish on us a second death."

"They win if you wallow here in your self-pity."

"You always looked after us younger girls. Why can't you look after us now?"

"That girl died long ago. I'm just an old woman."

"You and the others who still walk the earth, you don't know how it feels to watch them spit on our graves."

"*I didn't even get a grave. My bones are at the bottom of a lake with all the fish shit and garbage. No one knows I'm there.*"

"*Help us. Please.*"

"I can't. Now, leave. My granddaughter is burning up and she can't handle all of you swarming around her. She's just a child." Young-Ja swatted at the air above Rinako's nose.

"*We were just children too.*"

The kettle behind her screamed. Young-Ja reached to turn off the gas range and looked back down at Rinako. Tears welled through the lashes of her granddaughter's closed eyes and trickled into her hair. When the kettle fell silent, she opened her eyes, brimming with understanding.

"Harumoni."

Her unaided tongue could not help but split the first syllable of the Korean address and slip on its vowels, no longer able to mimic native pronunciation. In that plaintive accent Young-Ja sensed that her granddaughter had heard all, felt all. Rinako sat up—skin free of her ghostly fever—and embraced her. They held each other tight, two solitary bodies offering and receiving a warmth to which they were both unaccustomed.

"Song Joon-ssi! Rinako-ssi!"

Shun and Rinako turned to the office assistant scurrying out of the church to catch them on their way to the airport. She regretted they could not stay for Sunday service, but assured them they were welcome again any time. Once she had cycled through adequate pleasantries, she turned to Shun.

"Song Joon-ssi, it may not be my place to bring up your mother's business, but I think it's important."

Shun laughed nervously but nodded for her to continue. She explained that an academic who had called the day prior had stopped in just now and asked if he might persuade his mother to meet with her. Shun recalled how his mother's face tightened in that distressingly familiar way when she declined the previous request. How she withdrew from him that very morning with the same look, insisting that he stop fussing over her and leave for Tokyo at once.

"She's free to do as she wishes," he said. "I don't want to force her hand. Especially now, given her health."

"I know, it's just, I think this professor is trying to do important research. I wouldn't insist otherwise, but our late Pastor Kim—you remember him, right? I heard you also lived here as a child? Our Pastor Kim was very passionate about helping people who had a hard time during the war, especially those who were forced to leave the country. He thought that Halmuhni would benefit from talking to this woman."

Not understanding the rapid words, Rinako looked to her father for clues. He was tapping his feet in the way he did whenever he was annoyed. Rinako wished that the office assistant would convince him to stay longer, just as she had desperately tried to do that morning. She did not wish to leave her grandmother in this state and could not believe that her father would, no matter what the old woman insisted. This was his mother. Did family mean nothing to him? Did he care about anything other than work? But accusations of heartlessness would not provoke those who were, she thought bitterly.

When Rinako woke the day prior saturated with the ghostly rages of forgotten girls, she was moved to spill tears that were not quite hers into her grandmother's shoulder. Those voices still echoed into the roots of her teeth. Wisps of anguish lingered on her skin. Having peered into the black of that cavernous grief without fully grasping its origins, Rinako desperately wished to know her grandmother better, and in turn, be known by her. To offer what solace she could, even as a mere girl. But her grandmother was not ready to offer explanations, and Rinako did not wish to scare away another person with the knowledge she had gleaned in slumber.

Yet there was hope. Before her father had returned in the evening with giant bags of newly purchased home goods, her grandmother had made two requests. The first was a request for time. The time to prepare, to summon the right words. The second was a request for discretion. Rinako was to tell no one of those ghostly voices, especially not her father. It would be their little secret. She learned for the first time that her father's penchant for concealment was perhaps an inherited trait, not some unique failing of his character.

And so she promised to honor these requests, though she fidgeted in agitation as the three of them ate delivery jjajangmyeon for dinner in silence, sitting between piles of new blankets, kitchen goods, and clothes that her grandmother had scolded her father for wasting money on. Rinako's eyes darted between mother and son slurping black bean noodles, willing their leaden tongues to move beyond maddening courtesies. *Pass the napkins? More water? Let me clean up.* Why was it so difficult for adults to speak simply and directly to one another? This wooden scene hardly appeared to be the reunion of a parent and child sharing a meal for the first time in years.

That morning, as the family trio said their muted goodbyes, Rinako asked her grandmother if she could call her on occasion.

"You don't want to waste your time talking to an old woman like me."

"Don't say that. It's not a waste of time."

"*Geurae, sigani dwehmyeon.*" Her grandmother nodded. "Now, go on," she said in Japanese. "You'll miss your flight." She waved and retreated back into her room.

Rinako was imagining what she would say on that first call when an older woman in glasses and a well-tailored dress interrupted the conversation between her father and the office assistant. The woman was not much younger than her grandmother but held herself with an assured elegance that shed a decade from her appearance. She introduced herself in Korean as a professor at a nearby university in Seoul.

Shun and Rinako bowed as she scribbled her name and number on a piece of yellow paper and handed it to Shun.

"My colleagues and I are working to get testimonies from people forced to work abroad under Japanese rule," the professor explained. "I understand this is a difficult topic and could potentially put some strain on your mother, but her testimony would be of great importance in the pursuit of justice. Not only for her, but for many people. For the country." She smiled softly and looked at Rinako.

"History is often what we as a society deem worth remembering," the professor said to a surprised Rinako in Japanese, handing her a sheet of yellow paper that stuck to her fingers. "And your family is worth remembering."

A young woman stands before the stable of the comfort station. There are no guards or soldiers to be seen. Only her fellow captives stand scattered about the yard, dressed in white hanbok. Some are pale little girls with color in their cheeks, some have the creased, sunbaked faces of a life reluctantly survived. When the others notice the woman, they converge on her, clamoring to speak, each louder than the next. The woman shakes her head and backs away. This is not her life anymore. She does not want to hear what she knows they will say. She has spent a lifetime forgetting.

Be at rest, she tells them, you're lucky not to be in this world anymore.

The women in white hanbok surround her, swiping at her arms and body with translucent grasps. They fall into her, through her, the agitation of their tangled, melting limbs managing only the slight bristling of her body hair.

Please don't let them bury us.

They've already buried me, she says. *There is nothing I can do.*

The writhing mass of white erupts in a wail and scatters as soldiers file into the yard, bellowing at them to get in line. They bash in the women's heads with their rifles, they drag the girls by their hair to the stable, they tear at the jeogori of the elderly. The soldiers trample the collective into the earth, grinding their ghostly bones to dust amid the pleas to remember.

Please.

Please.

What can I do?

CHAPTER TWENTY-EIGHT

Tokyo, Japan; Seoul, Republic of Korea, 1991

Rinako cajoled her father to translate his conversation with the professor and the office assistant for the entirety of the drive to the airport, but had not managed to get much beyond his usual evasions. She held her frustrations in silence as they made their way through passport control and boarded the plane, but once they had taken off, she renewed her demands for an explanation with such vigor that other passengers began turning their heads. Her father hissed at her to be quiet, ceding a brief, whispered summary to placate her.

"We should absolutely talk to the professor," Rinako whispered back.

"It's not our place." Her father sighed and looked out the window.

"Aren't you curious to know what your mother was doing in China? How she got there? If she speaks Chinese like she speaks Japanese?"

"I told you, it's none of our business."

Rinako was indignant. "She's your mother. We're family."

"You don't understand what your Obaa-san is like." Her father closed his eyes and leaned back into his seat for the remainder of the flight.

Rinako called her grandmother every evening after returning to Tokyo, taking advantage of the time before her father came home from work. Those slow-passing, lonely hours in the apartment she now filled with stories, recounting memories of childhood to quiet hums of understanding from the other end of the line. Rinako hoped that her disclosures might inspire her grandmother to reciprocate with tales of her own, yet to no avail. She kept her verbal meandering from where she wished to go the most, muzzling her curiosity about the professor or the scenes in her dreams to respect her grandmother's wishes. But these daily conversations came to a halt when her father saw the astronomical phone bill for July.

Shun called the phone company in a huff about the egregiously inflated charges, only to walk back his accusations with embarrassment when his daughter admitted guilt. On impulse he forbade Rinako from calling her grandmother outside his supervision. He did not try very hard to enforce this restriction once his initial shock waned, however, as Rinako was changing for the better.

Shun was mystified by this transformation. These taciturn women lost in their own worlds had somehow cracked the hardened resin of each other's shells. Rinako emanated a brightness that lifted her voice, her general stature. She thrummed with new determination. Shun was pleased that his daughter was shedding the quiet gloom that left her ambling without purpose for so long, though he hoped she might direct this energy into her university admissions rather than into the stubborn reticence of an old woman. What would it take for Rinako to understand that life would not be handed to her, that she would have to strive to prove herself—as he once had and continued to do? Perhaps it was because he had ensured she lacked for nothing that she took so much for granted. But his strange daughter's wishes had rarely been legible to him. Not when Shun cradled her as an infant, promising to give her everything he did not have in his own youth, and not now as she plunged into the terrifying opacity of near-adulthood. Rinako was just as inscrutable to him as his mother had been. She, too, was so little like him.

What was it about his daughter that made his mother so solicitous, in ways she never had been for him? Shun was too proud to name what pricked at his ears as envy, but he could not pretend to be unbothered. Further agitation dragged across his skin when he received yet another message from the professor asking after his mother. He did not wish to be rude, but if his mother had not wanted to tell her own son about her life—if he was not owed knowledge of his own origin—what made this stranger think she would disclose anything of importance to her? He was done scratching at those old scabs. Shun fell deeper into his work and, with what energy remained, more closely monitored his daughter's exam prep. He would not let her bungle this pivotal moment.

Rinako hovered over books every day, but her focus lay beyond exams. She had become possessed with the need to understand the contexts in which her grandmother would have encountered soldiers in her youth, scouring texts at home and the public library for accounts of the Japanese in Korea and China. Something concrete. A record of real events with which she could pin down those elusive dream images or grasp the professor's search for Korean women who had worked abroad.

Everyone knew that Japan had annexed Korea in 1910 until the end of the Pacific War. Every nation understandably sought independence from foreign incursions, and many Koreans had lost their lives in resisting Japanese authority, though Rinako had always been taught that her country had also done some good. It had brought modernizing technology and education to an agrarian society, building infrastructure and many industrial capacities from which Korea benefited even now. There was still friction to this day between the two countries, of course, but Japan had paid a terrible price for war, more terrible perhaps than what any single nation had ever suffered. However, beyond the passages devoted to the victims of American atomic bombs, her textbooks did not dwell much on the lives of civilians, focusing instead on battles, national policies, and the ideologies of men in power. The perspective of Koreans—and that of women in particular—rated no mention at all. The more Rinako combed through the same history she had learned for years in school, the more dismayed she became at how shallow her understanding had been all along.

Eventually, books and phone calls became insufficient. Rinako demanded a return to Korea for the remainder of summer break.

"Absolutely not. Stop pestering your Obaa-san."

"Harumoni wants me to visit her."

"No. And certainly not until you pass the sentāshiken."

"That's not till January. No one studies in August. Everyone's on holiday!"

"All the better to give yourself an advantage over them."

"I'll pay for the trip." Rinako tossed the thin envelope of 10,000 yen notes from her mother on the table.

Shun grimaced at the unexpected sight of his ex-wife's still-familiar cramped script. Was that all she had left her daughter?

"Go to your room and study." He pushed the envelope away. Rinako threw him a flinty look he could not parse. She said nothing more and retreated into her room.

When Shun grabbed his briefcase to leave for work the next morning, he found that he could not. The leather oxfords he kept lined up by the entrance had disappeared, as had every other pair of shoes he owned. Even the grimy plastic sandals he wore for late-night cigarette runs to the konbini were nowhere to be seen. Shun could only imagine where his daughter had hidden them, but he did not have time for such nonsense. He squeezed his feet into the largest shoes he could locate—his ex's abandoned rubber gardening slippers—and walked to the local market, where he bought cheap sneakers to wear before descending into the subway.

Rinako's bedroom door was still closed when Shun returned home from work. He took the new leather oxfords he purchased during his lunch break into his bedroom for safekeeping. As he undressed to ready himself for the bath, he discovered that all his suits had gone missing from his wardrobe, including the winter suits he had stored away in bags to ward off moths. He hurried out to Rinako's room and pounded on her door, his unbuttoned dress shirt half-tucked into his pants.

"Return my things at once."

"Let me go see Harumoni," came the voice behind the door.

"If you focused half the energy on your studies as you do on your Obaa-san, you'd already be a star pupil at Waseda."

"If you focused half the energy on Harumoni as you do on your dumb work, you wouldn't die alone with no family!"

Shun jiggled the doorknob knowing it would not turn. He beat on the door again and declared he would break it down, deeply aware of just how unthreatening he sounded. He leaned against the door with one last thud of his fist. Silence was his daughter's only reply.

Shun was determined not to reward such obstinance. After changing into a T-shirt and shorts, he ran out to get the summer suit he had worn that day dry-cleaned overnight. His coworkers might not notice the repeat wear the following day if he at least swapped in a different shirt.

When Shun emerged from his bedroom the next morning, Rinako stood waiting by the living room window she had slid gaping wide. The shadows of passing birds danced across the sunlit floor of the apartment. Shun ran to close the window in panicked remembrance of the last cleaning bill but his daughter blocked him, a glare boring into his sleep-dusted face.

"If you don't let me go see Harumoni, I'll scream into the neighborhood that you're abandoning your family."

Blood rushed to Shun's head in a dizzy swell. He lowered his slim arms from the window and sank into the newly replaced sofa behind him. He did not understand where he had gone so wrong. When he had lost all control.

"Fine. Go. But you might be disappointed by what your Obaa-san is willing to offer."

Rinako descended from the airport bus to meet her grandmother and the smiling office assistant. She gifted pretty boxes of senbei crackers to the church staff for their hospitality, along with a modest sum from her mother's envelope as a general offering. The office assistant declared she was welcome at any time and saw to it that Rinako was installed comfortably, though she was not so guileless as to bombard the visitor with undue attention. This freed Rinako to set about helping with anything she could. Her grandmother resisted her attempts to take on church cleaning duties on the first day—"guests shouldn't dirty their hands"—but yielded to a more balanced distribution of responsibilities after Rinako rose early the next morning to mop around the pews while she slept.

There were no such objections, however, when Rinako bought groceries and cooked their meals. She quietly disposed of the empty instant ramen packets lying around the basement and made a fresh pot of rice every morning, happy to chatter away as she served unsalted grilled mackerel and lightly pickled radish—foods she had heard might be good for kidney health. After meals Rinako sought to unburden her grandmother with helpful little tasks in the margins—laundry, trash removal, general tidying—waving away her admonitions for working on vacation.

"I don't consider spending time with my grandmother to be work," she retorted.

The visit, of course, was not all chores. The pair took to hiking the nearby Namsan Mountain every morning before the August heat peaked in the afternoon. Rinako liked to amble forward and admire the Seoul skyline through the sun-drenched trees, the crunch of her steps on fallen twigs engulfed by screaming cicadas. She would eventually run back to link her arm into her grandmother's as sparrows trilled in the canopy. Her grandmother was less reticent when asked about the different types of plants that comprised the undergrowth, and so Rinako questioned her about the wild herbs they crouched down to examine, plucking a few sprigs for later use. When their sweat-soaked blouses clung to their backs, they returned to the basement room to sit by a small rotating fan and eat slices of cold makuwa uri in front of the TV.

"We call it chamoe here," Young-Ja explained, watching her granddaughter scoop out the slimy seeds from the yellow melon. The laugh track from the variety show crackled through the old TV speakers.

"Cha-mu-eh." Rinako sounded out the word, adding an extra syllable. "Korean pronunciation is hard," she said, biting into a fruit slice.

"Chamoe. It'll come to you."

Young-Ja, too, popped a slice of fruit into her mouth. Its sweet cold flooded her teeth as she watched the flickering TV.

Within a few days, the two fell into these domestic rhythms as if life had never been any other way, quietly avoiding the reason for Rinako's visit lest they break this spell.

"Why did you come?"

Young-Ja whispered into the cup of barley tea she had just drawn, eyeing her sleeping guest who had been subdued into a late-afternoon nap by the weight of August humidity. Everything about her Japanese granddaughter exuded *new*. New skin. New sounds. New life. The basement room had never felt more cramped, her worn things never more drab in the presence of such indisputable newness. How the vibrance of Rinako had come to appear at her door earlier that week, she still did not understand, but Young-Ja felt she should not chase it away with too many questions. Although she had nothing to offer, she permitted herself to lean into this new voice, nodding along to the cadence of the language she had avoided for decades. But something had dislodged within her since she met the ferrous glint of her granddaughter's eyes in the hospital. It shifted in her joints when she moved. It rattled about the loose change of her thoughts when at rest.

Young-Ja set her teacup by the futon before resting her hand on Rinako's forehead. Apart from the constellation of faint acne at the temple, the girl's face bore no marks of stress, no signs that troublesome fever would continue to haunt her. She stood nervous vigil each time her granddaughter yielded to sleep. Watching. Listening. Neither those voices nor dreams had returned, and Rinako—true to her word—had not pressed. But the girl's unspoken anticipation lingered, expanding to fill any silence, probing the empty space between them.

A part of Young-Ja wished to take back the promise she had made Rinako in that heady moment weeks ago—she did not know if she could summon the words those ghosts had urged. And was it not unconscionable to expose an innocent child to such sordid things? To taint the success of her son, the peace of her granddaughter for the world to judge? But something still tugged at her to oblige the girl who had not fled at what she had seen. Each time Young-Ja thought she had mustered the resolve, however, her thoughts crumbled into powder as glimpses of her father emerged from the contours in Rinako's face, in the way her eyes crinkled into cheeky smiles, in the expectant nostril flare of a question. The old woman found herself unable to grasp the frayed threads of her explanations, shy around the vestiges of a face she had lost so long ago.

"Thirsty."

Rinako stirred, trying to lift eyelids swollen with sleep. Young-Ja rose to fill a glass with water but froze when her granddaughter instead rolled over to grab the half-drunk teacup by her head.

"Don't—"

Young-Ja moved to snatch away the barley tea she had made. Rinako was faster; the girl downed the remaining liquid in a single swig. She paused to examine the bottom of the cup before meeting the look of a cornered animal in her grandmother's eyes.

"This is tea?" Rinako's voice was soft, lacking its usual verve.

"Barley tea," Young-Ja said slowly, waiting for the girl to flinch. Retch.

"You made it?"

She bobbed her head.

"Can you make some more? It tastes familiar."

Young-Ja took back the cup, disbelief at her fingertips. "Don't they drink barley tea in Japan too?" she asked, for a lack of anything better to say.

"That's not what I meant." Rinako blinked. "I just . . . like it. Makes me think about being here with you."

Young-Ja wrote off Rinako's tolerance of her tea to the incoherence of half-sleep. Her steps lightened toward the kettle, however, as she obliged the request for more. A request she could not remember having last fulfilled.

Rinako's father called every other night to scrutinize her progress in exam prep. He did not inquire after the time she spent with his mother, nor did she bring it up. But when he insisted she recite basic math formulae out loud for him to check, she threw her head back and tugged at her left cheek.

"Ugh, I know this stuff already. You don't have to quiz me."

"Never hurts to practice. You're lucky to have a parent who cares so much about your education."

Rinako rolled her eyes. "Since when do you have time to revisit old math textbooks? Shouldn't you be going to sleep?"

A pause. "I'm not home yet."

"It's after ten."

"So it is."

Rinako nestled the receiver on her shoulder while twirling the phone cord in her fingers. Her father was in a snare of his own making—he did this to himself, for no one else but himself. Nonetheless, she felt a twinge of pity at the smallness in his voice. She grasped for words to break the tension, eyes scanning the office until recognizing the yellow note on a board near the phone.

"Otō-san."

"Hm?"

"Did you ever talk with that professor who wanted to meet with Harumoni?" Rinako took the yellow note into her hand, examining the woman's neat, blocky writing.

"No, and don't go bothering your Obaa-san with that nonsense. Just . . . look after her and keep up with your reading."

"You keep saying I'm bothering her. I'm not."

"Well, let's keep it that way. Do as she says."

Rinako sighed. "Do you want to talk with her?"

Another pause. "No, it's all right. It's late. We'll talk again soon."

With the yellow note stuck between her fingers, Rinako flopped down the receiver to silence the dial tone.

The negotiated two weeks in Korea were drawing to an end. She had loved indulging in the small discoveries of companionship for the first time in her life. Her heart had grown full on recognizing which lines in her grandmother's face could be coaxed into a smile, on knowing how hot she took her tea, on noticing that she favored her left foot when climbing down the stairs. Even the menial household tasks Rinako loathed doing back in Tokyo prompted enjoyment in Seoul, bringing her the satisfaction that came only from helping someone so unassuming. As if a person's lack of material demands made her more deserving of them. But after so many hours of largely one-sided chatter, Rinako was no closer to catching another glimpse beyond the wall of her grandmother's reserve. How the old woman walked through the world, where she had hidden the soft inner fruit of her person, Rinako could not say. She was awash in the loneliness of waiting before a locked door. Listening for stirring on the other side, wondering if anyone would heed her knocking.

Rinako left the office and descended into the basement room where her grandmother was hunched over laying out the futon and light summer blankets on the ground. She rushed to help, but her grandmother had already smoothed out the bedding and gestured at her to settle in.

"Harumoni? How did you get that scar on your hand?" Rinako ventured casually as they both sat on the covers.

Young-Ja withdrew her left hand and held it to her chest. "This? It's nothing."

Rinako's lips fell into a frown but her gaze stayed lifted. After a beat threatened to slip into another impasse, Young-Ja cleared her throat and tried again.

"It happened so long ago, it's hard to remember the details."

"Here?" Rinako leaned forward.

"No, not here."

That now-familiar swell of expectation crept into the girl's brow. Young-Ja inhaled slowly and let herself continue, subduing the instinct to turn away from that urgent look.

"It happened in a kitchen when I was around your age. I was trying to help someone."

"And were you able to help them?"

"I don't know. I hope so."

A pause. "It must've hurt a lot."

Young-Ja shrugged. She stared down at the covers, hands still clutched to her chest. "It's all healed now. It's just . . . not nice to look at."

"You're brave."

Young-Ja whipped her head up toward her granddaughter, taken aback. She could not accept this word. Such a word did not belong in a room where she spent her days hiding from so many things. But Rinako spoke again, pushing past the knotted silence.

"I mean, I can't imagine getting hurt like that to help someone. You must've been really brave to do it."

Tension leaked from Young-Ja's shoulders. She lowered her hands onto the bedding and let those declarations settle.

"No, I just . . . wanted to help. That's all. I think you understand what that's like."

The acknowledgment lured a smile from Rinako as she slipped under the covers. The pair lay still, waiting for the other to say more, each nervous to spoil the soft new ground they had tread. But the hour had grown late. They let that silence preserve the tenderness they held for each other to be uncovered in the light of a new day.

After Rinako had fallen asleep at Young-Ja's back, girl arm slung around her thickened old waist, she searched herself for the truth in her granddaughter's words, wondering what else she might be ready to tell her.

Young-Ja woke to the heat of Rinako's face burrowed into her shoulder blades. She turned her body and stroked her granddaughter's hair—lightly sweat-damp in the August morning. A new fluidity coursed in her movements when she peeled away from the sleeping girl, the usual aches in her joints somehow quieter than usual. She strode over to put water in the kettle and prepare tea for the pair to drink.

As Young-Ja busied herself, Rinako stirred in the covers. She stretched out her arms and rolled onto her back with a raspy "good morning." The kettle whistled steam and Young-Ja turned off the gas range.

Rinako sat up, hair askew. "I wonder if it'll rain today," she said, turning on the TV and flipping through the channels for the weather forecast.

"Maybe," Young-Ja said absentmindedly, waiting for the water to cool slightly from its boiling point. The snippets of each channel bled from tinny advertisement music to laugh tracks to serious male narration.

"—yor of Seoul announced tod—"

"—grab and don't let you go, those Japa—"

"—latest model only availa—"

"—of rain. It'll be 32 degrees with swelt—"

"Go back." Cold shot through Young-Ja. Had she heard that right?

"Huh?"

"Go back to that other channel." Young-Ja turned away from her tea and scrambled over to the futon near the TV.

Rinako flipped to the previous channel, a peppy advertisement for the latest Goldstar refrigerator.

"Go back one more."

Rinako obeyed. Young-Ja's every sense snagged on the resulting broadcast. She saw and heard nothing else except the old woman weeping on the screen, speaking of how soldiers had taken her forcibly, not letting her go no matter how hard she struggled. How no one in Korea or Japan acknowledged what people like her had been subject to.

Young-Ja was stunned. She did not know how many others like her there were, but she could not fathom what would possess a woman to expose this shame so openly. Did this woman have no family who might be hurt by this knowledge, who might shun her as polluted? Was she not afraid of public judgment, the millions of eyes on stains she would not be able to scrub clean? Who was this lone, impossible beacon, shining light on the dirty fate Young-Ja had long sought to conceal?

"Who is that? Someone you know?" Rinako leaned in and squinted. "Wait. Is that . . . the professor? The one who wants to talk to you?"

Young-Ja had been too focused on the elderly speaker to notice the other men and women on the program writing on their notepads as they listened. Among them was an elegantly dressed, bespectacled old woman seated in quiet attention.

"What are they saying?"

Although Young-Ja knew that Rinako's ears were closed to Korean, she was mortified to have this damning testimony occupy the same space as her grandchild. Dread knifed through her veins. She dared not face her kin, as meeting Rinako's eyes in that moment would expose her every thought before she could dress them in the right light. She had endured this shame for so long, borne her losses in silence for decades, afraid it would ruin her, ruin her son.

The TV continued its din even as its images blurred through the tears pooling at Young-Ja's lashes. But when those tears spilled into a steady path down her cheeks, something within her burst: a continuous roar from the void she had carried since she was a young girl of nine, one fatal, sunny morning in the mountains of Cheongju. She did not know how long she wailed, a vessel for grief that blotted out all vision and deafened her to any voices.

When Young-Ja regained awareness of her body kneeling on the ground of that basement room, her hands were clasped in Rinako's. The TV screen a powerless black, only the gentle cadence of their breathing stirred the air.

She lifted her watery gaze to her granddaughter's eyes. In their steady, concerned luster, Young-Ja found not the shame and revulsion she had feared but the overwhelming, undeniable warmth of compassion. There, the echoes of a face she had once loved looked back to tell her it was all right.

"You know, you remind me a lot of my father. He'd teach me about wild plants and tell me stories at night before we'd fall asleep."

Young-Ja continued to offer pieces of her heart, beginning with hazy but warm memories of her crooked-nosed father, her lively mother, her beloved siblings. Rinako sat witness to it all. She wept when the tiger roared over the bones of her lost kin. She laughed along to tales of girlish mischief at a Manchurian teahouse and choked at its fiery end. She fell silent before the account of captivity in a Japanese military outpost. For days and nights neither woman moved. One spoke, flush with the terrifying elation of being known. The other listened, moored by the weight of granted trust. Together they relived a life once forgotten and gave in to the sorrow that bound them in love.

Once the time had come for Rinako to leave, she felt she no longer knew the girl whose life she was to resume in Tokyo.

Those stagnant days yearning for someone to talk to, burying herself in textbooks that now raised more questions than they answered—it all seemed like scenes from a distant past, the anemic desires of a stranger. Now, in the present, every atom in her body pulsed, oriented toward her connection to her grandmother. Toward these revelations that made her doubt so much of what she had assumed about herself, her family, her country.

"Are you sure you don't want me to stay? Because I will."

Her grandmother smiled. "We'll see each other again soon."

"But we're just getting started. I want to be here for you."

"The best thing you can do for me is to live your own life. You're young. You don't know how much solace it brings me to know you can live in the ways you choose. Now, go. There will be time for another trip later."

Rinako leashed the instinct to argue and embraced her grandmother. "I think I understand why that professor wanted to talk to you."

"Hmm."

Young-Ja pondered these words as Rinako waved from the departing airport bus. She stood in place for a while even after city traffic swallowed the vehicle into its curtain of smog. Walking back alone toward the church and descending the basement stairs, she was struck with just how vast an emptiness her granddaughter's absence had carved into her small room.

When Young-Ja sat to rest her swelling ankles, her hands brushed against two small pieces of paper that had been left for her to find. One was a lightly crumpled yellow note with the professor's phone number. The other was a short message in Rinako's hand.

We can't be the only ones to know your story.

Young-Ja considered the note, studying the slants in her granddaughter's script and the numbers on the yellow paper. When Rinako called to say she had arrived at home safely, she made no mention of what she had left behind. She instead inquired after what Young-Ja had eaten that day, if she had gotten enough sleep, what time she had scheduled her next checkup with the doctor. In the girl's voice Young-Ja detected nothing but warmth, a genuine concern for her well-being unmuddled by obligation. Her granddaughter would not pressure her. It would be Young-Ja's choice, and Rinako would accept it with all the tenderness in her heart.

Only a few days passed before Young-Ja phoned the number on the yellow paper and asked to speak with the professor.

"Song Young-Ja-nim. I was hoping to hear from you." The voice on the other end was gentle, yet confident.

Young-Ja stalled. How did a conversation like this begin?

"We're around the same age, I think," the other woman volunteered into the silence. "Pardon my asking, but you were born in the early 1920s, no?"

"Yes," Young-Ja managed.

"I can't help but think that it could've just as well been me in your place at that time. I'd hope, if that were the case, that someone would believe me. That someone would fight for me."

Young-Ja gripped the phone cord with her scarred hand. It took her a moment to gather her words. "And what is it you want to do, exactly?"

"I'm here to listen," said the professor. "And to make sure that others do too."

A man tends to the garden outside his home as his son scatters seeds for the chickens in the yard. A woman nearby hums softly and braids her daughter's long black hair tight. Sunlight glimmers through the canopy's dancing leaves and casts a glow on the sleepy house.

An old woman cuts into the clearing from a mountain path she finds strangely familiar. Her knees ache. Her wilted flesh struggles in the ascent, but she walks with help, clutching the hand of a young woman. The girl's short bob brushes against her shoulders from another land, another time.

The family in the yard stands, turning to the two women emerging from the tree line. They wave and call out. But the visitors' legs yield to sudden heaviness. They cannot approach the faces in the yard whose features are distant blurs. The old woman calls back names she has not uttered aloud in years. The family's feet root into the earth and neither can they approach her, forever affixed to that sun-drenched yard, washed out in the blinding light.

Somewhere beyond the mountain clearing a tiger roars. The echoes rumble down through the roots of trees, the roots of the family in the clearing, shaking their legs free from the soil. Timid steps approach timid steps until those feet, once nations apart, arrive reunited at home.

CHAPTER TWENTY-NINE

Tokyo, Japan, 1991

People often remarked on the irony of Andō Makoto's name. Andō, "peaceful east." Makoto, "truth." As a columnist for one of the largest newspapers in the country, he was called many things amid typical accusations of pandering or biased lies. But Makoto was endowed with a temerity that made him convinced of his own integrity, allowing him to brush off any complaints with the facile laugh of a tall, handsome man.

"Andō-san, I just came from your desk. There's a visitor to see you," said one of his coworkers as she walked by.

"Oh? Is it that city hall staffer—"

"No, it's your niece. She seems nice," she said as she hurried around the corner.

Makoto paused. He did not have a niece. As he waited for the elevator to take him back to his floor, he ran into more reporters mid-discussion.

"You hear the latest thing those old nationalists said about that comfort woman? It's one thing to say it's exaggeration, but to say such rude things about a defenseless granny..."

"Typical Jimintō. But you know the Koreans did that deliberately. Find an old lady to tell some sob story to garner sympathy. People eat it up."

"They can eat it up all they want, but it's hearsay until they find sufficient documentation."

"Even with proof, what can they do about it now? It's not like this is brand-new information, and everyone from that time is so old."

On August 14 that year, the morning before Korea celebrated its National Liberation Day, a sixty-seven-year-old woman named Kim Hak-Soon testified about her imprisonment as a "comfort woman" sex slave for the Japanese Imperial Army. The revelations of the military's alleged depravity brought Korea to a standstill. Cameras flashed in blinding spurts, the audience rapt with the violent torments of the granny who had suffered in silence for decades. News outlets spoke of her han—the deep collective sorrows of a Korean people wronged—and demanded redress from the Japanese government that had denied any formal state involvement in such sordid matters. Officials further claimed that the San Francisco Peace Treaty of 1951 and the reestablishment of Japan–Korea diplomatic relations had already resolved all postwar liabilities. Japan had definitively paid for its wartime and colonial acts even though they themselves were victims of atomic bombings; it was now a closed chapter not to be used to smear the contemporary government.

Makoto knew that the government was not as guiltless as it claimed; there had been many criticisms of the Japanese military from foreigners over the years. But this particular subject held no interest for him. He did not shy away from controversy, but women's issues simply did not appeal, especially when couched in decades-old allegations from foreigners. His preference was to write on more hard-hitting, prestigious topics, like the prime minister's costly support of the American war in the Middle East. Or the role of technology in Japan's global economic dominance. Topics that were ripe to showcase the quality of his intellectual arguments. Not ones that relied on emotional theatrics.

Once off the elevator, Makoto turned the corner toward his desk. A short-haired girl in a navy-blue high school sailor fuku sat in front of his workstation. She looked up as he strode toward her with his hands on his hips.

"You have a minute to speak. A girl who somehow conned her way to my desk deserves that, at least."

"Andō-sensei, I have an exclusive source for you." The girl placed a small piece of yellow paper on top of the files stacked on his desk. A phone number with a Korean country code was written in neat script. Below the number was a name in Hangeul, which Makoto did not understand. The kanji below he read as "Matsu Eiko," though the katakana underneath said "Son Yon Ja."

송영자
松永子
ソン・ヨンジャ

"What is this?" Makoto asked, annoyed at the girl's presumptuousness.

"This is my grandmother's name and phone number. She was one of the Korean comfort women imprisoned in Manchuria by the Japanese military."

He raised a thick eyebrow at her school uniform. "Your grandmother's Korean?"

The girl ignored his question. "You should talk to her and write about it."

"Let me guess, condemning the Japanese government? Demanding they get on their knees and beg for forgiveness?"

"I'm not here to tell you what to say. Just hear her story. You could be the first journalist to report it."

"I'm not really in the habit of letting children dictate my pieces," he said shortly.

"People take your column seriously. They'll listen to you."

"I won't deny that, but they'd rather listen to me talk about other things. Your minute is up. Why don't you go back to school."

The girl tapped her knuckles on the yellow paper atop his files.

"Just one phone call. It's a story you can't afford to ignore."

"Get out. I don't want to have to call security on a schoolgirl." He flicked his hand toward the door.

Makoto did not watch the girl walk away. When he rose later to refill his water cup, the yellow paper she had left behind caught his eye. He reached out and crumpled it up before tossing it in the waste bin at his feet. He would have to speak with the slackers at reception if they were letting just anybody walk in. He imagined if one of the nutcases who railed against his column could so easily make their way to his desk. They might light it on fire, or attack his colleagues. But Makoto enjoyed the idea that his words could incite such passion. Someone had even called in a bomb threat to the building because he had excoriated Emperor Shōwa's wartime legacy on the day of his state funeral. Although the call turned out to be a false alarm, the incident shot up his profile at the paper. This was just as well; he did not wish to court any true danger, just reap the benefits of having overcome its perceived threat.

Later that afternoon, Makoto was called into a meeting with a few editors. On the way to the conference room, he walked past the staff bulletin board hanging in the corridor. Yellow popped in the corner of his eye. He whipped his head back, searching the numerous missives tacked onto the board. There, amid the building maintenance announcements and staff notices, was a yellow paper with that phone number and name: Son Yon Ja.

Makoto ripped the paper off the board. It was marred with the same crumple marks from when he had balled it up and thrown it into the trash earlier. He looked around to see if anyone was watching. Someone was clearly pulling a prank on him. Makoto scrunched up the note in his palms once again and threw it away.

Concentration eluded him for most of the meeting. He stole a surreptitious glance at his watch wondering when he could go outside for some fresh air. He had smoked his last cigarette earlier and was feeling the tug to buy more.

No one else was outside when Makoto made his way to the corner of the roof where other men liked to loiter for breaks. He tapped the newly purchased pack of cigarettes against his palm in automatic habit before tearing into it. He nearly dropped the pack when he saw what lay within.

Inside was the customary deep gold of cigarette filters, though an incomplete set of nineteen. The twentieth slot was occupied by a roll of yellow paper waiting to be pulled out.

Makoto pinched the paper between his thumb and pointer finger. He pulled the yellow cylinder from the pack and unfurled it to reveal what he knew would be scribbled inside. That same number and that same name. Son Yon Ja.

Makoto ripped up the paper and threw the scraps into the waste bin underneath the ashtray. He lit a cigarette and inhaled a deep first drag. He was not amused by whatever trickery this was. He faced the door, hoping for someone else to join and engage him in conversation. When no one came, Makoto put out his barely smoked cigarette and returned inside. He needed to make some progress on his next piece. That would take his mind off things.

Hiding behind the papers at his desk, he wrote in furious scribbles, pressing his pen with a heavy hand into his notepad.

"Andō-san."

Makoto jumped. One of the recent junior reporter hires stood before him. He cleared his throat and asked what she needed. Makoto only half listened to whatever the woman was saying, wishing she would leave him alone.

". . . and so I corroborated the account with Son Yon Ja in Archives, and she said that—"

"What did you say?" His question came out in a loud, shrill interjection. This startled the junior reporter into silence and turned nearby heads. He smiled nervously and nodded at the others to signal that all was fine.

"Excuse me," he said, forcing a smile at the junior reporter. "I meant, what was that name you said? In Archives?"

The woman shrank back. ". . . ah, Hayashi-san? I corroborated the account with Hayashi-san?"

Makoto shook his head and told the reporter to excuse him, for he was not feeling well. She gave a slight bow as he swept past her toward the corridor. The room began whispering about Andō-san's outburst.

He rushed to the sink in the men's bathroom. A splash of cold water on his face calmed him, though his reflection appeared grotesque and haggard in the harsh overhead lighting. He threw more water on his face and turned the faucet off before reaching into his pocket. His fingertips brushed something that was not the cotton handkerchief he sought. He did not have to see what he touched to know what it was. The water on his face dripped down his neck and wet the collar of his shirt. Makoto pulled out of his pocket the yellow paper with that same number and name. Son Yon Ja.

Nausea struck his throat. Saliva pooled at his teeth. He was unwell—he would excuse himself on sick leave for the first time in his decade at the paper.

Back at his apartment building, Makoto decided not to check his mailbox, wishing to avoid contact with any paper for the remainder of the day. He was eager to get back into his apartment and sleep off the whole affair. Start anew. His hands shook as he pulled out his key and tried to put it into the lock of his front door. His pulse pounded in his ears as he wondered if that same yellow could await him inside. He turned the handle, shut his eyes, and pulled open the door.

The space was as he had left it that morning, including the half-drunk cup of coffee on the kitchen table he had forgotten to dump out into the sink. He kicked off his shoes and admonished himself for getting so worked up. Thinking back, he wondered if he had just eaten something funny and overreacted. He downed a glass of water and took a hot bath to settle his frayed nerves.

Falling facedown onto his bed, Makoto finally felt calm enough to laugh at the absurdity of his day. He must have been overworked. Things would be fine. He rolled over from his stomach to his back, letting out a loud sigh of relief as he splayed across the bed. But his body seized in cold shock when he looked up: dozens of yellow papers were plastered across the ceiling, their corners rustling from a nonexistent breeze in his still room.

One of the papers dislodged from the array and floated down, swerving in a zigzag path to land on Makoto's disbelieving face. He grabbed it to inspect the number and name written in that same neat script. Son Yon Ja.

It was paper. It could not hurt him. But Makoto could not shake the suspicion that he was being hunted. That the girl's message would follow him until he relented. He recalled her request for one phone call and sighed. Simple enough. If he did as she asked, perhaps he would never have to act a fool for a sheet of paper again. He stretched out his arm toward the telephone near his bed and dialed the number that had followed him all day.

"Son Yon Ja-san? I hear you have a story I can't afford to ignore."

A blanket of yellow butterflies undulates down from the sky and perches to rest in a grove. A girl with a long black braid laughs and spins, waving her arms to mimic the movement of the wings.

A man approaches. He pinches the wing of a nearby butterfly between his forefinger and thumb and drops it into the girl's hands. The creature flutters meekly before perishing motionless, dusting her palms with its residue. The others fly away in alarm, surging past in a mad flurry. The man pursues the butterflies, snatching them midflight and crushing them to powder in his grip. The girl yells for the man to stop. He does not heed her words and disappears into the distance.

The girl is now an old woman. Her wrinkled hands remain smeared with butterfly dust. She rubs her hands hot, but no amount of skin-tearing friction rids her of the stains. She cries out, hands raw to the touch. She cries but does not know who will hear her.

CHAPTER THIRTY

Seoul, Republic of Korea, 1992

Rinako slipped gloves onto her grandmother's shaking hands and patted them gently. A chill rippled in the January air, but anticipation dulled the cold. Hand in hand, the pair walked toward the bus stop.

On the bus, Rinako stared at the passing buildings of Seoul. She was able to read some of the signs now—pharmacy, bookstore, dentist—having purchased a few Korean language workbooks to go over in the evenings when her father believed she was doing her homework. While his admonishing displeasure with her behavior had been a constant in her life, she suspected she might finally witness the full extent of his fury when she returned to Tokyo. Rinako had lifted money from his pockets every day over the last few months that winter until she had accrued enough to purchase another flight to Seoul. It was unfortunate this trip had to fall the week before her exams—it would only make whatever punishment he had waiting for her that much more severe. But she would not miss the opportunity to be with her grandmother on this day.

Once the bus dropped them at their destination, Rinako and Young-Ja walked over to the sizable group of mostly women gathering outside the Japanese embassy. Smiles greeted them as they entered the crowd's embrace. Although many were meeting for the first time, these women were known to one another. They bore scars of bondage across their connected bodies. Their hands were gripped with shared purpose. All donned white vests over their coats and raised banners against the Japanese government that continued to deny that its colonial apparatus had systematized and profited from the sexual slavery of young girls all across Asia.

The bespectacled professor Rinako had worked with since the fall was handing yellow papers to passersby who had slowed with curiosity about the growing mob. The professor had identified journalists, scholars, civil servants, and other figures of influence in Japan who could join them in investigating the history their government had buried. Rinako had taken to helping where she could over the last several months, sneaking into these men's offices to gain their audience and pique their interest in the truths she was learning from her grandmother and the professor. She was improving at the deception required to gain access to her targets: claiming to be their family, making unrequested flower deliveries, acting as a lost errand girl. After all, few people saw young girls as threats to fend off.

Maintaining the ruse had been harder. Rinako had been kicked out of more buildings than she could count and did not feel that she had been capable of persuading anyone. But the professor had expressed such gratitude for Rinako's help, assuring her that progress was being made. It had been difficult to grasp at any sense of headway the past few months, but more people continued to assemble for the demonstration that cold January day. Whatever private disappointments Rinako endured while acting alone melted away in the light of so many others. All those gathered drew their breath with resolve.

The crowd began to chant, their calls for justice steaming out on their breath into the winter air. They demanded acknowledgment; they demanded apology. The muscles in their mouths—taut from years of unyielding silence—stretched and tensed.

These demands emerged in halting puffs until the women grasped the rhythm of unison. They roared. They raised their fists above their heads. They shattered the quiet shame that had dictated their lives for decades. From the dais of their united bellows rose their sorrow, their resentment, their han, louder and louder as their chants merged into harmony. But the doors and windows of the Japanese embassy remained opaque. There was no movement, no reaction, as if this assembly and its message did not warrant one.

The white-clad women marched on nonetheless. Their collective anger roused the land beneath their stomping feet. The ground began to agitate, lurching in heed of wills so forceful in concert, of spirits united for the first time. The earth shifted, recalling the agonies of a mother who had lost her loves. It swayed as if to the forlorn night song that once turned girls into tigresses. It pulsed, summoning the voice that could compel the truth. And now the earth bowed, yielding to hands that could pass on pain, yielding to eyes that witnessed truths revealed in slumber.

Tremors rippled under the marchers' feet, intensifying as their voices grew. The women did not falter but instead drew from the earthly surge. They chanted louder to be heard over the booming cracking of concrete. They linked their arms and stood tall as the ground raised broken slabs of pavement that could not restrain the swelling of angry soil below.

The steel frame of the Japanese embassy shivered in resistance. The closed doors flung open as employees streamed out of the shaking building crying for help.

Panicked phone calls flooded the Seoul Metropolitan Police. People shouted about an attack on the embassy. Some believed a bomb had gone off. Some believed a gas main had exploded. Amid the pandemonium, dozens of officers arrived on the scene to find women in white marching through the steam rising from newly split fissures in the ground.

"Bear witness," they cried. "Atone for your wrongs!"

"Japan must acknowledge us!"

The demonstration was quashed when the police took the old ladies into custody for their alleged act of terrorism. Each woman had her hands pinned to her back as the police locked handcuffs over knitted gloves. Scarves and hats littered the broken ground as the women were shuffled into cars and taken to the station. Police tape wrapped the embassy perimeter. Traffic rerouted to calmer streets.

Although the police had never arrested so many elderly women, they did not expect it to require much exertion on their end. The women swiftly disabused them of this view.

They banged their fists on the officers' desks and continued their demands for apology, scolding the young men of the police force with barking rebukes.

"You should be ashamed of yourselves! You call yourselves Korean?"

"Is this how you treat your grandmother?"

"This is a democracy! We've done nothing wrong!"

"At least give me a hot tea, it was cold out there! Young men these days have no manners."

Hours of circular questioning and examining recorded footage did not produce a crime. The police had no choice but to release the detained grannies after no trace of explosives was found on their hands, their floral-print clothes, their graying hair.

The women emerged from the station in the winter night tired but cautiously triumphant. Under the smile of the crescent moon, they promised to congregate at the Japanese embassy the following Wednesday, and the Wednesday after that, and so on indefinitely until their demands for acknowledgment and apology were met.

The following day, the front page of every major newspaper in Korea was splashed with giant photographs of young police officers pushing hunched elderly women into handcuffs. The country exploded in outrage.

"Who do they think they are, arresting helpless old ladies? Is that what you need to do to feel like a man?"

"What a joke, they thought that a bunch of grannies did this?"

"Since when was protesting a crime? Young people these days have already forgotten their country's history."

"Do you really think those old ladies bombed the embassy? I mean, it's crazy but no one would suspect an elderly woman, right?"

Across the sea in Tokyo, several columnists with yellow papers sticking to their desks opined on the powerful voices of women and the importance of heeding their message, but few people paid them mind. That week, the Japanese public was transfixed on the folly of the visiting American president who had vomited on the prime minster at a banquet reception. The incident at their embassy in Seoul was relegated to a mere afterthought in the international politics sections of newspapers, where it was dwarfed by larger pieces on conflict brewing in the Balkans.

Shun nearly spit out his morning coffee when he saw the picture of his mother and daughter being led away in handcuffs. Both of their mouths were dropped open mid-shout, the conviction in their eyes glinting even through the blurred gray of the tiny inked photo.

Shun called in sick from work for the first time in his life and spent hours trying to get in touch with the church and the police in Seoul. Without any answers, he resolved to fly to Korea when Rinako finally called home, voice sheepish in anticipation of his anger. But he merely expressed his relief that she was all right and announced he would be joining her in Seoul that evening.

When Shun approached his daughter and mother, he bowed his head awkwardly before presenting them each with a block of tofu—a customary gesture in Korea for those released from jail. He slumped into silence as the women bit into the soft white of their new beginning, not knowing what to say to the mother whose sorrow he had not been able to see, to the daughter whose drive he had not been able to understand. Shun did not feel he could look his mother in the eye, ashamed by his inability to muster the right words in that moment.

Boundless questions had ricocheted in his jumbled skull the entire Seoul-bound flight as he reexamined his mother through the filter of this terrible history. Her distance, her refusal to meet his eyes, her reticence toward his questions. He strove to quell the anger that had been simmering somewhere deep. Anger at the implication that had been thrust onto him about when and where he had been born. What these circumstances meant about him.

But now was not the time to find a target for his anger. Whatever darkness may have been roiling within him, the situation demanded that he be present and acknowledge his aging mother before him.

"Joon-ah. I'm so sorry. Please forgive me."

Young-Ja brushed her scarred hand on her son's face. These unexpected first words—offered before he could relay his own contrition—demolished whatever poise Shun had wrested in his face. He collapsed into his mother's shoulder and sobbed.

Young-Ja held her wretched, shaking child. She would no longer look away. She would no longer say she was too tired to provide answers, even as fatigue creaked into her weary bones. There was still so much to tell, so much to impart, and she had lost so much time to a fear of ruin that had not materialized. Young-Ja had finally uncovered a voice that could move the earth and she would not let it lie dormant any longer.

A boy falls into a pit.

He tumbles headfirst, careening past the wall of soil and rock into the shadows. The thump of impact does not kill him, but he can no longer see from his left eye, and moving proves difficult. His bones rattle, his flesh has split.

He squints up with his one good eye. The pit's dirt walls frame the sky in a circular window. A silhouette appears at its edge and blots out the fading red of the sunset. The boy cries out for help. He cries out for his mother. He cries out for his father.

The shadowed man hovers above, unmoved by the childish echoes of Okaa-san. Otō-san. Okaa-san. Otō-san.

But something else stirs to these cries. The soil darkens with a ferrous, wet smell. Viscous drips slide from the walls of the pit, shifting the pebbles and insects and roots and remnants of decay lodged in the earth. Okaa-san. Otō-san. Detritus tumbles out of the pit walls. From those holes new voices also call for Okaa-san. Otō-san.

The boy is not alone. The chorus of cries layer and distend until the drone of Okaa-san Otō-san Okaa-san Otō-san drives away the unknown watching from the top of the pit.

CHAPTER THIRTY-ONE

Tokyo, Japan, 1992

Shun's week in Seoul was filled with purpose. He was possessed with drive to anticipate his mother's every need. He nudged her to extra health checkups. He treated her to a carousel of hearty Korean restaurant meals while paying mind to her sodium intake. He walked everywhere by her side, letting her lean into him when her joints struggled to hold her weight. In this whirlwind of concern he would have relocated her into a new apartment had she not convinced him it was perhaps not best to remove an old woman from her support system or the work that kept her moving and occupied. It was only on his mother's tired yet resolute insistence that she needed a break from all the attention, that she would otherwise be in the care of her newfound community of women, that he and Rinako flew back to Tokyo.

But Shun's last-minute trip had cost him. His desk was buried under files to compensate for the burdens his absence had put on the team. Even months after his return he was the last person to leave the office, while his boss had long stopped paying lip service to the possibility of advancement in the company. Shun inhaled cigarettes and caffeine pills to chase away fatigue after everyone had left. Regular stress dreams now kept his eyes ringed with a dark yoke and people seemed even more inclined to keep their distance. None of this deterred him from putting forth his best effort. He would endure anything to safeguard what he had built, to maintain normalcy and provide for his family. His greatest struggle arose, however, in the bull-headedness of his daughter.

Despite her detour to a jail cell in Seoul, Rinako managed to achieve top marks on her university entrance exams back in Tokyo. But the girl declined to finish her school applications, announcing instead her decision to work full-time with the professor. Shun was dyspeptic.

"Have you lost your mind? You're throwing everything away!"

"This is the only thing that matters."

"I'm ensuring your Obaa-san has a comfortable and supported life, what else do you think you can achieve? You are a child."

"Why can't you see that that's not enough? Don't you hear what the government is saying? How they're denying it all? How can you not be angry?"

"It's just political chatter, don't be so naïve. What's done is done, it was decades ago. They're not going to change their stance now because one girl decides not to go to school."

"Of course they're not, because people like you think this way."

"Well, what can you do about it? Those people will take you even less seriously without a university degree. You're ruining your future for nothing!"

"I have the rest of my life to go to school. This is happening now. Harumoni needs us."

"People will look down on you. And that'll hold you back."

"People already look down on us. Who cares? We're holding ourselves back if we do nothing!"

The Matsumoto shouting match halted only when the neighbors came by to request that they respect the building's quiet hours. With the deadline for university applications approaching, Shun hid his daughter's passport to keep her from fleeing to Korea. Neither felt they had much to say to the other since.

Shun continued to devote his waking life to the office, half to chip away at the target on his back, half to mute the screaming thought that nothing in his life was what he had hoped or believed it to be. He still found time to call his mother every few days, as if maintaining his show of concern were a sort of penance that could keep the fragile old woman from breaking apart.

Have you eaten?

Did you go to the clinic today?

Please let me know if you need anything else.

With every hum of confirmation from his mother Shun felt the day's tide of anxiety ebb. He was at least doing what was needed of him. He settled into this new frantic routine—working, calling, working. The unpredictable swings of his daughter's whims he would corral later. Perhaps after Rinako had time to stew in the shame of falling behind her peers, he could try to direct his wayward child toward a more secure path.

However strained interactions had become at home, early mornings preserved a softness in Rinako before the day's frost had a chance to set in. On days Shun startled awake from his recurring stress dreams, she would sometimes draw a fresh pot of coffee and leave it for him without a word. He wondered how miserably tired he must look to warrant such a gesture of pity.

One morning in March, Rinako offered the olive branch of conversation when Shun emerged from his bedroom.

"Are you okay?"

"Hm?"

"Your eye. It's red."

Shun glanced at the mirror by the apartment entrance. His hollow reflection stared back, a burst blood vessel violently staining the white of his left eye. He was too sluggish still to have his muscles enact his surprise.

"Looks worse than it feels," he said, voice hoarse.

"Hm. Well, we're all gathering at Yasukuni Jinja today while the professor's in Tokyo," said Rinako, skepticism in her brow as she handed him a cup of coffee.

"What? The shrine?"

"Yes, the one where they've enshrined war criminals. You know it. It's not that far from your office."

"Huh."

"We're protesting a Jimintō rep who's taking some foreigners there and the professor wanted me to ask you to come. She said it'd be good to have more men at the demonstration."

Shun sipped his coffee without responding.

"I know it's during business hours but you could walk over during your lunch break? It's important."

Shun would not meet his daughter's eyes. "You know it's hard for me to step away."

"I knew you wouldn't. But I said I would ask." Rinako retreated into her room and closed the door. Shun did not see her again before he left for work.

After much contemplation on his commute, Shun decided that his burst blood vessel would draw less attention than an eye patch. He popped another aspirin for the intensifying pain and hurried to the breakroom for more caffeine. In his rush, he knocked over the box of instant coffee and launched dozens of shiny packets spilling across the floor. Shun groaned and crouched down to tidy the mess. His knees ached against the cold tile as he crawled about, eye throbbing.

"Grown man can't take a hint. Guess even Waseda grads can be pretty dense." A man's voice rang in the hallway.

"Oh, you're so terrible!" A woman laughed.

"If he had any dignity, he'd resign. He clearly doesn't belong here. Though it's not so bad having all that grunt work taken care of—"

Shun stood up, instant coffee packets poking out between his fingers. His colleagues stopped as they turned into the breakroom doorway, swallowing their laughter.

"Ah. Matsumoto-san."

"Are you all right?" the woman asked at the sight of his twitching red eye.

Shun's pager rang at his belt before he could reply. His boss was asking to see him.

"Excuse me." Shun set the coffee packets on the counter and walked out, ignoring the whispers behind him.

The team lead did not react to the eye. He launched into a critique of Shun's work, pointing out the errors in the models he was supposed to have finalized yesterday. Shun did not protest that the errors were not his, that these faulty versions were the result of others changing his initial calculations. He knew it would be best if he just swapped out the numbers with his original figures and resubmitted the project without a word. It was never worth the trouble to be defensive or contrarian. He should accept what his superiors said and not risk further attention. He only wished for this conversation to end as quickly as possible so he could swallow another aspirin and press something cold against his head.

"With the economy the way it is, we're all lucky to have jobs. I fight to protect you from the higher-ups every day, and you're not making it easy for me, Matsumoto-san. I suspect you'll have to work through lunch to fix this."

But Shun did not work through lunch to fix it. After excusing himself from the team lead's office, he tossed his pager on his desk and walked out of the building. Pressure drained out of his aching eye with each step he took.

Shun was delirious with relief. The eye pain receded to a light, manageable twinge after some time roaming the neighborhood. He had not paid much mind to where he walked so long as he was not wandering into traffic, but he was starting to note with alarm the number of police cars and officers congregating in the stretch of road his feet had followed of their own volition.

That morning, the Tokyo Metropolitan Police had been briefed that problematic elements would gather near Yasukuni Jinja to protest a senior representative of the Diet. The representative would be guiding a European trade delegation around the shrine for photo opportunities to showcase foreign reverence of Japanese traditions and history, both for domestic and international audiences. Emperor Meiji had founded the shrine in 1869 to commemorate the brave men who had perished while serving their nation. Japan—like any other country—had every right to mourn its dead. It was unclear, however, whether the visiting dignitaries knew of the criticisms that had brought the protesters to the shrine that day. That so many condemned the inclusion of war criminals among those Japan lauded as national heroes. Regardless, police stood at every entry point and erected road barriers to keep the trade delegation far from the agitators' propaganda.

"Otō-san!"

Shun turned, surprised by the familiar voice. His daughter stretched her arm out and jumped into a tall wave, flashing a grin so rare and brilliant that its beacon allowed Shun to navigate toward her through the milling crowd.

"You came. I didn't think you would." Rinako patted his arm and started to shout with the group before he could tell her that he had failed her. That he had walked out on his responsibilities.

Shun watched his daughter chant with the other protesters. He then turned to regard the green copper roof of the Yasukuni Jinja haiden. *Otō-san.* When was the last time she had said that word without admonition? He could not remember. Of course, he himself had never had the opportunity to use Otō-san as a direct form of address, neither with reproach nor with respect. Otō-san. He thought about who that man could be. He wondered whether his name could be listed somewhere within the shrine before him. Otō-san. Was he a powerful man who sent others to their deaths, or was he mere fodder for the front lines of battle, immortalized only in the aggregate? Once death had claimed them, was there really a difference?

Otō-san. Strange, the feel of its pop on his tongue. *I am here.*

Otō-san. Strange, the angry rumble in his throat. *You made me into this.*

Otō-san. Echoes joined him. *We are here.*

Otō-san. Otō-san. Otō-san. The wailing chorus swelled. *You made us into this.*

Closer to the shrine, the representative addressed his guests.

"We are here to pay respects to the heroes who have made noble sacrifices for Japan," he said, pausing to allow the interpreters to convey his words' meaning to the white men before him. He raised his voice as the protesters yelled and pushed against the police in the distance. The Europeans had yet to turn their heads at the commotion.

"On this sacred ground we have enshrined the men whose valor—"

The representative stumbled as something dripped from his temple. It was not a warm day and he was not sweating. He brought his fingers to the slip of wetness on his head, gasping when his hand came away smeared with what appeared to be blood. His bodyguard lunged to cover him even as the representative insisted that he felt no pain, when a shriek erupted from the shrine behind them. The crowd looked up to streaks of dark liquid cascading from the green copper roof of the shrine, dripping viscera on its wooden beams and splashing onto the stone path below.

Drip.

Drip.

Drip.

The ground shimmered red.

The crowd froze, not sure whether the scene before them was real or a collective hallucination. But when thick crimson strokes of kanji began to bloom across the white walls of Yasukuni Jinja, all those in attendance, shrine staff included, screamed and fled. No one was left to recognize the strokes on the wall as those that had once been carved across the bellies of girls. No one was left to hear the howls of the unborn whose blood smeared down the copper roof. Yasukuni Jinja stood empty, glistening red in the bright light of the day as ghosts of a bygone past cried out for the fathers whose bones had long turned to dust. *Otō-san. Otō-san. Otō-san.*

When the guests ran out from the shrine grounds, they passed a large wall where hundreds of yellow papers hung rustling in the wind. In all their terror, they did not notice when the papers detached from the wall and floated about in their wake. The papers stuck to their backs, their shoes, their bags. The papers followed them to their homes, their hotels, their homeward-bound planes. Persistent yellow papers that urged them not to forget, to seek truth in history.

The man whose questions summoned his ghostly brethren eventually departed Yasukuni Jinja with the other protesters. The crowd steeled themselves for a long fight to come. Powerful men could be sent running from the sight of blood they had spilled but were not marked by it for long. Any stain could be erased just as summarily as it had appeared. While the group retreated for the time being, they knew that they had more to show, that they would not be so easily erased.

This old woman is tired.

    She tidies up her modest room, stacking away the pile of cards she has received from all over the world. Some are in the languages she speaks, many more are in ones she does not. Some are from other countries whose girls were taken. China, the Philippines, Indonesia, Taiwan, Burma, among others. So many countries.

    Lying down to rest, the old woman thinks about what she has promised for tomorrow. She has much to do in preparation for her visit to the National Assembly next week. She and her new friends have been invited to speak about their time in Manchuria. But she will start her next morning with a call to her granddaughter and her son, for there are still many words she reserves for her family alone. Her heart flutters in anticipation of their voices, grateful to have recovered those sounds in an otherwise muted life.

    The old woman closes her eyes, feeling a warmth trickling down from her head to her feet. She has flirted with the darkness behind her eyelids before: desired it, chased it, tasted its wispy ghost on her parched tongue. But it has never before offered its embrace. She hesitates now, not knowing whether to accept it when she leaves so many things undone, so many things unresolved. While the call of this darkness is welcoming, it gives her no choice but to discard her worries and drift to sleep.

The old woman slips into a calm, her muscles free of tension, her mind free of ghosts, her hands free of abandoned duties. But leaving no venture unfinished is a luxury afforded to no one. She passes into the darkness, stepping over the unmet wishes of all before her. She leaves the echoes of her own wants in a flickering trail at her heels for the next traveler to find.

CHAPTER THIRTY-TWO

Tokyo, Japan, 1992

Rinako stirred from a stolen afternoon nap. Her face was crusted with the dried residue of tears shed in her devastating dream, though the memory of it was as hazy as her vision in the dimming light of dusk.

Mugginess hung in the still apartment, as if the air also felt too sluggish to move. The echoes of her dream pressed on Rinako's lungs; breathing required some effort. She gathered enough faculty to leave her bed and open a window, but there was no breeze, only the deafening drone of cicadas bursting in from outside. She walked to the kitchen to pour herself some water. Something cool would release the tension in her body.

When Rinako had called her grandmother the day before, she was told to keep an eye on the mail for a gift she could enjoy with her father. The package had shipped a few weeks ago and it was due to arrive soon. Rinako was struck with the sudden urge to call her grandmother again and check that everything was all right, but they had already promised to speak that weekend. She could wait. They would all be together in Seoul next week anyway to attend her grandmother's testimony at the Korean National Assembly. And while Rinako was eager to watch her address these officials, she was most looking forward to hiking together in the lush green of Namsan as they had last summer. Perhaps her father would want to join this time.

Rinako descended to the mailboxes in the building's lobby in search of her grandmother's package. A single brown box sat on the dull tiles for her to snatch up and take back upstairs.

The package contained a sealed box of cookies and a short letter written in Korean. Rinako's language studies still had a long way to go. Frustration jolted through her as she recognized some of the words—her name in Hangeul, the word *grandmother*, the phrase *I miss you*—but could not string the rest together into coherent sentences. She wished she could read her grandmother's note unaided, speak to her in her native tongue, but her father would just have to translate when he returned later that night.

Things had been improving between them at home. Her father was starting to come around to her work with the professor, especially after Rinako hinted that it was the older woman who had convinced her to enroll in university after all. She did not admit to him that her previous threats to defer her education had largely been empty, hurled as the only bit of leverage she had to make him comprehend the stakes of her work. His obsession with convention had dictated her life for so long, it felt strange to push with such force against the grain of his comfort.

And it was true that the professor supported Rinako's entry into higher learning. While she continued to give Rinako the names of men to track down and meet, she also encouraged her to think about the opportunities education could offer.

"I think university life will suit you."

"I hope so. Though I've probably learned more from you and my grandmother than I ever have in school."

The professor laughed. "Your education is what you make of it. If you go into it thinking it'll be useless, it will be. But if you go in with the intent to learn and to unlearn, to be critical of the world around you, you'll start to pick up on how institutions work. See how beliefs are made and taught."

Since meeting the professor, Rinako had watched so many in power continue to deny the past, to belittle these elderly women as a nuisance. She had been arrested three more times since the first protest in Seoul: twice for trespassing in offices in Tokyo, once for elbowing a police officer in the stomach when he tried to take away her protest sign. Each time, her father paid the penalty fees and scolded her into the late hours of the night, desperate for her to balance her devotion to her cause with the education that he swore would spare her struggles later in life. He did not seem to understand that the list of men to target grew longer each day. Every minute that slipped by diminished the urgency of the past.

Fury had thus grown to be a constant in Rinako's life. Each morning, anger roused her from sleep to recall the long arc of brutality eclipsing the light in her grandmother's life, to recall just how much of her own life she had been made to live in ignorance. This anger propelled her into the world, fueling her search for repentance from men who believed such an act beneath them. Like a diver stabbing into the ink of the night sea, determined to prise a lost pearl from its depths. While rage took from Rinako her peace, it left her the satisfaction of clarity. She had no doubt that fighting for her grandmother was the right path. She hungered to do more. Have more impact. Sharpen her fangs.

Despite his annoyance, her father at least seemed resigned not to limit Rinako's access to her grandmother. In fact, he had taken to calling his mother nearly every day as well, urging her to consider moving to Tokyo so that he could look after her in her flagging health. He insisted that she could be with her family and receive more advanced medical care in a Japanese hospital. She refused. Rinako did not take her father's consternation at this rejection seriously. Even now, his job search in Tokyo took precedence, regardless of the amends he claimed to want to make to his mother. Her father meant well, but Rinako sensed that he did not quite have the intuition to speak to his mother about anything beyond arranging for her material comfort. He was trying, in his own way, and his mother, in hers. It would take time for both to shed certain instincts that had calcified in all those years apart. For them all to learn how to exist as a family.

Rinako examined the rows of honeyed cookies in the opened package. Yakgwa, they were called. She remembered trying some with her grandmother in a local market the last time she visited Seoul. The old woman held her hand tight and walked her through the colorful stalls, explaining what each vendor sold with a sort of pride in their work. Rinako would not forget the brightness of her grandmother's face when introducing the tastes of her childhood's few happy memories.

She bent down to give the yakgwa a closer inspection and could see that the sweets before her had not been purchased from the market. They bore the imperfections of her grandmother's hand, small inconsistencies pockmarking the cookies that Rinako treasured as a labor of her grandmother's love.

The yakgwa's oily, sweet scent hit her before she took a large bite and began to chew. An unexpected bitterness washed over her tongue. Rinako nearly spit out the half-chewed mouthful as she was possessed with thoughts of the people who wished her grandmother ill. She gritted her teeth in the next involuntary chew, the accusations of attention-seeking slander hurled about in the enraging echoes of her memory. Her eyes prickled with the heat of new tears as she tore through these thoughts. Before she could take possession of herself, Rinako found her hand reaching out for her cup and flinging it at the kitchen wall. An explosion of water and glass sprayed down its surface, falling into crevices between the counter and gas range.

She stared at the jagged points of wet, broken glass. The notes of bitterness faded in her mouth as she clenched her jaw, releasing a deep, flavorful grief from the yakgwa. Tears soaked Rinako's cheeks as she was consumed with thoughts of those who had not come forward, those who had already perished, those for whom now was too late. The honeyed sadness bore through her as she struggled to swallow the yakgwa's remains. With the ghost of her first bite on her lips, she fell into a sob and crushed the half-eaten cookie in her hand.

Rinako gasped for breath as traces of yakgwa lingered as a sweetness on her tongue. This soft aftertaste imparted a gratitude that she had known her grandmother well enough to receive these gifts, that she had seen her as she wanted to be seen. And while she sniffled alone in her apartment, she took another bite of the debilitating yakgwa, each mouthful cycling her through waves of complex flavors she felt ill-equipped to name and confront.

After Rinako finished devouring the mashed-up cookie from her sticky palms, she swept up the glass shards from the kitchen floor. Her father would be home soon, and she did not wish to cut his unsuspecting feet with the remnants of an outburst meant for someone else.

Rinako wondered if her father might like to sample his mother's confections. Would he be able to appreciate its swirl of flavors? If he would not eat them, she would share them with anyone who could also carry this burden. Should there be no one else, she would gladly finish off the lot. She would devour all the yakgwa her grandmother had sent and savor each glazed, bitter bite to the end. She would taste her sorrows, she would mourn her losses. She would see her and have her seen, her life alight on her tongue.

At seven o'clock, an attendant carries tea and the day's *Yomiuri Shimbun* to the main study where General Akagawa begins his mornings. She balances the lacquer tray on a forearm and taps at the door with her free hand to announce her presence. She bows and enters a pristine room lined with books blanketed by the morning sun. A white-haired man is slumped over his desk. The woman—a long-practiced stoic—does not betray her surprise at witnessing her employer's sleeping form for the first time in her two decades of service.

She sets the tray down and calls out a morning greeting in a soft voice. He does not respond. She allows herself to approach closer and notices that he has soiled himself. She gasps and runs out for help before she can see the glazed brown cookie lying half-eaten on the desk.

As the medics arrive, the household staff hurry about in cool efficiency. The general had been in acceptable health, but his passing is not a shock given his years. He is fortunate to have lived a full life. There is nonetheless much to do to prepare the manor after the general's family is notified. In this commotion, no one thinks of the young woman who had delivered a flower arrangement from some unfamiliar sender the day before.

By the time the body is moved to the morgue and the study cleared of any mess, the young woman is long gone. No one may remember her, but that does not matter. She has seen to it that he tasted their sorrows. She has seen to it that he did not forget, that his final breath was taken in the remembered torments of his own creation, no honey in the wound to soothe what lay festering in that darkness.

Now she walks on, the bitterness of the past lingering on her tongue. Her path ahead is yet unknown, but she vows not to forget, to see to it that others do not forget. As long as she keeps walking, death will not follow them a second time.

No, death would not be permitted to return here and claim the knowledge they paid for with their bones. From death she takes the power to end: she lives and tells. She tells and lives.

ACKNOWLEDGMENTS

This book would not exist without many dedicated, hard-working people, each whose contributions I hold in the highest regard. I can't thank you all enough, but I'll still try:

Heather Carr, my stellar agent. Your mighty advocacy and exacting eye for narrative clarity powered our journey. Thank you for taking a chance on me, for always pushing me to be better on the page. For fielding my rookie hand-wringing with tact and wisdom. The tremendous Marin Takikawa—I'm grateful for your discerning reads and efforts to introduce this novel to the wider world. Caspian Dennis—thank you for being our lighthouse across the pond and ensuring smooth sailing to port. Lucy Carson and Molly Friedrich—I owe everyone at the Friedrich Agency so much.

In the UK I have Zoe Yang, the most marvelous editor. I will forever be buoyed by your vision for this story, your immediate understanding of its emotional core and dedication to its themes. I could not have asked for a better partner to bring this novel to new readers abroad. Infinite thanks to everyone at Manilla Press and Bonnier Books—the wonderful Sophie Orme and Helen Reith for their amplifying support; Nick Stearn and Jung Suk Hyun for the UK edition's stunning design; Flora Willis, Jodie Lewis and Clare Kelly for their engagement of readers everywhere; Kevin Hawkins, Kelly Samler, and Vincent Kelleher for their business savvy; Alex May for ensuring the final package is just as beautiful within.

In the US I have Carolyn Kelly, the most phenomenal editor. Thank you for truly seeing this story at its core and for championing it so valiantly even through the most harrowing of times. Your perceptiveness, empathy, and knife-sharp instincts drew out impact from these pages that I could not have achieved on my own. My deepest thanks to everyone at Avid Reader Press and Simon & Schuster—the boundlessly generous Lauren Wein and Meredith Vilarello for their pathmaking guidance; Alison Forner, Clay Smith, Sydney Newman, Lexy East, and Ruth Lee-Mui for all their iterations to hone the US edition's exquisite design; Allison Green, Hana Handzija, Rachael DeShano, Alicia Brancato, Jessica Chin, and Rachelle Mandik, Megha Jain, and Rebecca Munro for their eagle-eyed, polymathic execution; Kayla Dee, Katya Wiegmann, Alex Primiani, Rhina Garcia, and Eva Kerins for the brightness of their beacon so tirelessly guiding this book to its readers; Wendy Sheanin and Kim Shannon for making shelf space across the country with such acumen and care. Your partnership and support are a dream.

I would not be here without my cherished friends and first readers helping me persist from the earliest days: Kim

Johnson, Marina Gafni, Helena Li, Laura Van Gerpen, Katie Harger, Jon Hayes, Josh Shin, Óscar González Díaz, Phil Underwood, Kyelee Fitts, Kanyinsola Aibana, Colin Eide, Eric Chan, Stephen Cha-Kim, Colby Silver, Joshua Burcham, Jo Beckett-King, Lisset Pino, Karen Gu, Nina Rodenko, Abi Ramanan, Rachel Berkowitz, Rachel Zarrell, Bourree Lam, Olga Zilberbourg, Erin Shaw. Your candor, understanding, and healthy bouts of roasting keep me afloat. Special thanks as well to the San Francisco Writers Workshop for gifting me with community as I was initiated into the singular madness of novel writing.

I am forever indebted to the scholars, journalists, artists, and writers that captured the testimonies of those who encountered tragedy in 20th century Asia. Thank you for building these windows to our history that enable many future generations to peer through and remember. There is still much to learn and I aim to be a lifelong student of your work.

Of course, to our honored grandmothers, 할머니들에게, sa ating mga lola, 致祖母们, untuk nenek kita, kepada nenek kita, おばあさんに: thank you for your resilience, strength, and dedication to peace. It is now our responsibility to ensure your willingness to shed light on darkness does not go to waste.

I owe all the many privileges I have had in life to the efforts of my family, especially my mother, Chae Seung Yeon. Your hard-won histories are an inspiration.